SOMEONE ELSE'S
FAIRYTALE

SOMEONE ELSE'S FAIRYTALE

For JoAnn, Thanks so much for being on my listserv, and all your support! All best, Emily

E.M. TIPPETTS

E. M. Tippetts

Copyright © 2011 by Emily Mah Tippetts

Someone Else's Fairytale is a work of fiction. Names, characters, places, and incidents are either the product of the author's imagination or are used fictitiously. Any resemblance to actual persons, living or dead, events, business establishments or locales is entirely coincidental.

No part of this book may be reproduced, scanned, or distributed in any printed or electronic form without permission. All rights reserved.

ISBN-13: 978-1467940153
ISBN-10: 1467940151

Cover design © 2013 Sarah Hansen, Okay Creations

for Char

It is said that a writer has to write 10,000 pages of crap before they produce anything worth reading. I think I had more, but you'd have to ask Char.

She's read them all.

1

THAT DAY

I STEPPED out our front door into the frigid, Albuquerque night. The crisp air, tinged with the scent of woodsmoke, flushed through my lungs, and the stars winked distantly in the deep cobalt sky. It was three thirty a.m., way too early to be awake.

A truck turned the corner and rumbled its way over to our house. I watched it parallel park, then go silent as the lights switched off. The driver's side door opened, and my best friend, Matthew, stepped down. His cowboy boots thudded against the asphalt, then crunched across the gravel that covered our front yard. "Howdy," he said.

I stifled a laugh. He was the walking stereotype of a Texan, with his muscular build, tight jeans, and flannel shirt. His hazel eyes were smiling, though. Like me, he was a senior at UNM, and he was a source of sanity, something I needed to counterbalance my housemate, Lori, who just then skipped out the front door, jumped down onto the gravel, and struck an action pose, both hands up, ready to karate chop whatever imaginary adversary might be lurking under the giant cottonwood that dominated our front yard. She wasn't wearing any nylons with her skirt.

"Aren't you cold?" Matthew asked.

"Yep, but I don't think this is a cold weather scene we're in."

"We're extras," I said, for what felt like the millionth time. "Nobody's going to notice what we're wearing."

"How did she talk you into this?" Matthew asked me. The three of us started towards campus, on foot. We'd been told not to drive because there was limited parking.

"I don't know," I said.

"Come on, just picture it." Lori waved a hand, setting the scene "-we're on the set, and Jason Vanderholt walks by."

I rolled my eyes.

"I tell him how hot he was in the *New Light* movies-"

"Because I'm sure he never hears that," I said. The *New Light* franchise was a trilogy of gladiator movies that I'd managed to avoid seeing, despite the fact that Jason Vanderholt's long haired, shirtless figure had been plastered on every vertical surface for three years straight while they came out.

"Sarcasm," chided Matthew.

"You should ask him why his character was named 'sword,'" I said.

"Gladius," Lori corrected me.

"Right. That's Latin for, 'sword.'"

"It was his *nick*name. But you're ruining my narrative here."

We stepped off the curb to cross the street. Given the hour, there was no traffic, though in the still night air, we could hear voices of other groups who, like us, were headed towards campus on foot.

"He stops to talk to us," said Lori.

"Then what?" said Matthew.

"That's it. He stops to talk to us."

"That's it?"

"A girl can dream."

"Apparently not. That the best you can do?"

"Shut up okay?" Lori stuck her tongue out at him. "I'm a math major."

"At least come up with something to talk to him about."

"Ooooh! You know what? I should totally ask him if he remembers Vicki Baca! Remember, she said she had a locker next to him in high school?"

Aside from being the star of the multi-bazillion dollar *New Light* franchise, Vanderholt was also a local, or he had been before he'd hit it big with a show on the Disney Channel back in his teens. I cleared my throat. "I know about thirty people who claim to have had the locker next to him in high school, which makes me wonder how they do the lockers at La Cueva."

"I so hope we get to meeeeeet him." Lori turned a pirouette.

Matthew shook his head. "You're gonna catch a cold."

I sneaked in a smile the next time he glanced my way. He chuckled, his shoulders moving silently.

The film set was barely controlled chaos. "Just line up here!" a woman was shouting when we walked up. "We're still getting the catering area set up for you. Line up here!" She gestured at the walkway that led up to the UNM anthropology building, a wide strip of concrete that bisected the lawn. The pre-dawn light washed the color out of everything, making the world look like a faded photograph. The rounded, stucco walls of the building seemed old and historic.

Matthew, Lori and I found a place in line and stood with our paper cups of hot chocolate that we'd bought from The Frontier on the way. I sidled up to Matthew. "Okay," I said, "I get why Lori's doing this. Why are you?" I noticed that he'd combed his light brown curls with water, and a couple of them had frozen.

He smiled. "It's once in a lifetime, you know?"

"Don't tell me you're a closet Jason Vanderholt fan?"

"Sarcasm?"

"Oh, and you were being serious just now?"

"Ohmi*gosh!*" Lori shrieked so loud that I had to cover my ears. Not easy with a cup of hot chocolate in one hand.

"Lor-" I said.

But I was cut off by more shrieking up and down the line. I turned and saw that the girls on the other side of us had collapsed. One of them sobbed. The other just shook. "I love you!" someone shouted.

Lori dropped to her knees.

"Uh," said Matthew. He knelt down next to her. "You all right?"

Tears streamed down her cheeks and she shook like a leaf in a windstorm.

"Yes, hi," said a deep, male voice behind me. "Hello. Yep, sure. How do you spell that?"

"Ohmi*gosh!*" shrieked Lori again.

"You really gotta stop that," said Matthew.

I turned around, and found myself face to face with Jason Vanderholt. He was just like his publicity shots, blue eyes, tanned skin, toned physique.

He looked at me, one eyebrow slightly raised. Around him were several guys with cellphones out. An entourage.

"Yeah, hi," I said.

"Hey. How are you?" He was wearing a t-shirt and holding a paper cup in one hand, which he raised to his lips. I watched him shake something into his mouth, which he then crunched between his teeth. "It's ice," he said, with his mouth full.

The sun wasn't up yet and it felt like we were standing in a giant refrigerator. This guy was crazier than Lori.

He gave me a wry smile. "You want some?"

"Aren't you cold?"

"Freezing. Gotta do this between scenes so my breath doesn't steam when I say lines. See?" He was right. His breath did not steam as he spoke.

"Fascinating," I said.

He chuckled. "You look really familiar."

"Never met you in my life."

"What's your name?"

"Chloe."

"Chloe what?"

"Winters."

His eyes popped wide with recognition. "Like Chris and Beth! Okay, okay, now I know why I recognize you. You're... what? Their cousin? You gotta be related."

My pulse edged up a notch and I wrapped my jacket more tightly around myself, as if its insulated fabric were an invisibility cloak. "You know Chris Winters?"

"Heck yeah. He was in my class in high school. His dad was my dentist."

"He was?" My pulse edged up another notch. I felt stupid. I'd gotten after so many other people for making up tenuous connections to this guy that I'd overlooked the fact that he really was from town. Had grown up here and known people.

"Yeah. When I was a kid... Something wrong?"

"No." I said it too fast. "No, it's just, I don't really know him, his family. I'm not a close relative."

"Really? But you look so much like Beth."

I shrugged. "I'll take your word for it."

"But-"

One of his team of guys put a hand on his arm and said something into his ear. "Okay," he replied. "Chloe, right?"

I nodded.

He held out a hand. "Jason. Vanderholt."

"Yeah, I know."

He grinned as if that was a clever, witty reply. We shook. His hand was like ice, his skin dry. I let go and he moved on down the line.

As soon as he turned his back, I sank down to the ground and gulped the rest of my hot chocolate, which was now almost cold. Lori stared at me with wide eyes. "He knows you?"

"No."

"Who's Chris Winters?" said Matthew.

I looked at him, then at Lori, then at him again. "I don't want to talk about it. I'm sorry. My family's a little messed up and-"

"Say no more," said Matthew.

"Thanks."

"Just, tell me you didn't fall for that Mr. Charming act he pulled?" He nodded in the direction of the actor's retreating figure.

"Was he charming? I guess he knows how to work a crowd."

Lori cursed. "I didn't get his autograph! Ohmigosh! I can't believe it."

"What do you want his autograph for?" said Matthew. "What would you get him to sign anyway?"

"He coulda signed this." She held up her cup. "And what do you mean? It'd be a souvenir."

"It'd be a dirty cup with writing on it."

I loved how literal Matthew was.

"What?" Lori snapped.

But by now the line was moving. The woman who'd yelled at us to line up, was now yelling at us to move into the anthropology building. "We've got food set out for you in the first room on the left," she announced.

Lori pulled out her compact and checked her makeup.

I drained the last dregs of my hot chocolate and tossed the cup into the nearest trash can.

This is what I did for my big film debut. I stood around in short sleeves at five in the morning with a bunch of other people next to the anthropology building. And I did that for over an hour. Every little while someone would shout, "Quiet on the set!" and several minutes later, "Cut!"

We could start talking after every "Cut!" and at least they didn't make us chew ice. Goosebumps stood out all along my arms and I wished I hadn't had my hair cut the week before. I could've used more warmth on the back of my neck.

The camera and crew were a good thirty yards away, as were the actors in the scene. I wasn't near the front of the crowd, so I couldn't really see what the actors were doing, or who they even were. Besides Jason Vanderholt, the film starred Corey Cassidy, a blond, former model turned actress. Supposedly the two were a hot couple, involved in real life. Lori had told me this. I didn't read tabloids.

"I really feel like I'm growing, artistically," I said to Matthew.

He smirked at me. "Working on your irony?"

"How do you know I'm not serious?"

"This is so cool," said Lori.

"If you say so," I said.

"Quiet on the set!"

I looked over at Matthew again, who was smiling down at me. He didn't look cold. He'd had the foresight to wear long sleeves.

"Cut. That's a wrap!" someone shouted.

"Okay, okay, okay!" yelled the woman who'd been herding us all morning. "Everyone I've asked to stay, please stay. The rest of you are free to go."

I tromped with the rest of the crowd back inside. "That was really glamorous," I said. I glanced at my watch. It wasn't even seven yet.

Standing at the doorway of the catering area was a guy with spiky blond hair and all dark clothing. At the sight of me he said, "Chloe Winters?"

"Yeah."

"Come with me."

I glanced around. The yelling woman had made it crystal clear that we weren't allowed to wander.

"It's okay," the guy said. "Just come with me."

Lori and Matthew and I exchanged glances. Matthew frowned at the guy, but didn't say anything.

I stepped away from the crowd and followed Mr. Spiky Blond Hair back out of the building. "I'm Dave," he said.

"Hi."

"So did you have fun this morning?"

"Sure."

"You been an extra before?"

"Nope."

"Dave!" Someone called out.

We both turned, to see a guy standing at the far corner of the building, but Dave pointed at me and the guy put up both hands and turned away, as if amused. "He need you?" I asked.

"No, it's fine. Come on."

We cut across the lawn in the direction of the parking lot, where row upon row of trailers were parked. The sun was just over the horizon, washing the campus in pale, gold light. The stucco walls of all the surrounding buildings glowed as if lit from inside.

"It is a pretty town," Dave agreed. He'd seen my wistful gaze.

Another woman in a headset stepped out from between the trailers, saw me and Dave, and smirked, as if to herself. When she caught me looking at her, she shook her head and kept walking.

Dave and I stepped into the shadow of the trailers and walked around the first one to the door. "Go on in," he said.

I looked askance at him.

"It's fine." He pulled it open.

I stepped up the stairs and inside, seated on a couch with his feet up, was Jason Vanderholt, reading a magazine. "Hey," he said. "Come on in."

I looked around again. He'd just summoned me here? Alone? Dave hadn't come in with me and I had the feeling he'd shut the door behind me once I took another step forward. The amused looks from the other crew now took on a new context.

"No thanks," I said. I turned to leave.

But a crowd of men cut off my path and boxed me in by the stairs. It was Vanderholt's entourage from this morning. They made a wall of black t-shirts and muscle that stood between me and freedom. "Let me go, please," I said. I tried to elbow through, but one of them grabbed my arm in a grip like a vise.

2

"**M**iss?" said one of the men to me. "You can't just walk around-"

"I'm not trying to wander around the set," I snapped. "I'm supposed to be back with the extras. Do you mind?" I tried to push past again and the grip on my arm tightened. "Let me go!" I shouted.

"Guys, guys!" That was Jason Vanderholt, stumbling down the steps behind me. "Back off."

"Look," I rounded on him. "I don't know you. I don't know why you summoned me like this, and this-" I gestured at his goons "-is not okay. Let me leave."

"Right, sorry." He spread his hands. "Guys, back off. Come on. Don't block her in like that. Give her space."

"Is there a problem, Mr. Vanderholt?" Another woman in a headset appeared in the crowd that had gathered. "Is this woman-"

"No," he said. "No, and call me Jason, will you?"

My outburst had caused a flurry of commotion. More people were pouring into this lane between the trailers. The sky was pale blue overhead and the sound of traffic on the main road had picked up.

"Is this woman causing problems?" another man asked.

"No," said Jason. "This is Chloe. She's a friend and I was just going to walk her back to... wherever she needs to go." He looked at me, one eyebrow raised.

"I just need to get my things from where the extras were, and then leave," I said.

"Okay, let me walk you. It's okay, everyone, move along." He came over to put a hand on my arm, turned me back in the direction of the anthropology building, and we started on our way.

The crowd stayed behind. I could feel their gazes boring into the back of my skull. Now that all the excitement was over, the embarrassment set in. "I'm sorry," I said. "I hope I didn't just get you in trouble." My face burned hot. I'd just behaved as if he'd propositioned me, when he hadn't even said two words. He probably thought I was the most presumptuous, ridiculous girl he'd ever met.

"No, I'm sorry." We rounded the trailer. "I didn't mean to give the wrong impression. I just wanted to talk to you."

"Oh." We reached the open parking lot.

He paused and turned me around to face him. "You okay?" he asked.

"Yeah, I'm fine. Just... guess I got up too early this morning. My head's not clear." I looked down at the asphalt.

"You can look at me, you know?"

I lifted my gaze to that face I'd seen on countless movie posters and tugged my arm out of his grasp. "Sorry."

He dropped his hand and smiled. "No, don't apologize. I just... I don't know what kind of instructions people gave you. Sometimes they tell the extras not to look at the actors and with me, it's fine. You can... Okay... no one told you that, did they?"

I shook my head.

"I must sound like the most arrogant person ever." He ran his fingers through his hair, and I noticed it stayed perfectly styled. Weird.

"Well, if everyone behaves the way they did in line-"

"Right, yeah. It's to prevent stuff like that, but... anyway. Listen, I didn't get a chance to really talk to you. Since I know your family-"

"No, you don't."

"Well, some of them at least. I've spent some time over at Dr. Winters's house, hanging out with Chris."

"Were you friends with the Winters?"

"Yeah, I guess you could say that."

"So, yeah. I should go-"

"Whoa, wait a minute." He put his hand on my wrist again. His skin really was dry, even the palm was a little scratchy. If he was Chris's classmate, he was twenty-eight or so, but his skin was older. "Who are you, then?" he asked. "A cousin?"

"Something like that." I pulled out of his grasp once more. I'm not a touchy-feely person, especially not with men I've only just met.

"*Something* like that? You can't be any more distantly related. Come on." His gaze scanned my face. I'd always assumed that his blue eyes were airbrushed, but no, they really were that shade of dreamboat blue lined with thick, dark lashes. Just then, they looked puzzled. "Am I asking something... wrong?"

"No... it's just..."

"Just... what?"

"You don't really want to know who I am."

"I am totally and completely confused right now. Please. Enlighten me."

I pushed a stray strand of hair back from my face. I didn't see a graceful way out of this conversation, other than to say I didn't want to talk about it and leave, and I wasn't entirely sure he would leave me alone if I did. He was genuinely curious. Which, I figured, was his prerogative. If he really wanted to know, I'd tell him. The sun was up now, and it was getting hot. I didn't want to stand around all morning.

"I'm Chris's half sister."

"His... he's got a half sister?"

"Yeah."

"Wait, how old are you?"

"Twenty-one."

I watched while he did the math. "So, your mother..."

"Had me out of wedlock with Dr. Winters, who was married with kids at the time. More than you want to know about their family, I'm sure."

His eyes widened with surprise and he shifted his weight. "The Winters still married?"

"As far as I know. I don't keep track of them. Just living my own life, here. Anyway." I made as if to leave.

"Okay. I'm really sorry." He put his hand on my arm, only to let go when I flinched. "I shouldn't have pried."

"You just didn't think you'd turn up something like that? It's okay. I'm not ashamed of it. It's just that most of the Winters's friends don't want to know about me and their other issues."

"I'm not a friend of theirs anymore. I haven't talked to them in over ten years."

I shrugged. "I should go."

"Can I get your phone number?"

At that I just smiled and held out my hand. "It was nice to meet you."

"Yeah, you too." We shook.

"Hope the rest of the filming goes well." This time I really did leave, and he let me. When I glanced back over my shoulder, he still stood there, watching after me.

The following morning, I woke up to the sound of the doorbell. I glanced at the clock. It was seven a.m., and I was nowhere near ready to wake up. The early morning yesterday coupled with a late night at work had taken its toll.

The doorbell chimed again.

I pawed my sheets away from my face and dragged myself out of bed. The thin carpet was rough under my bare feet as I stumbled out my door and down the hall to the front room. "Lor?" I croaked.

"Who is that?" was the irritated reply from her room.

"No idea." I reached the front door, put my hand on the cool metal knob, and waited. Maybe the person had gone away.

"It better not be the Mormons," said Lori. "Or the Jehovah's Witnesses. It's seven freaking o'clock." She emerged from her room, looking rumpled and disheveled. Her hair was still up in a messy bun.

Whoever it was outside, knocked.

I sighed and opened the door. Harsh sunlight streamed in, and I blinked while my eyes adjusted.

"Honey?" said a voice from the blinding brilliance.

It was my mother, holding a newspaper. She wore a skin tight mini skirt and a tank top under a denim jacket. Her leopard print bra stuck out from under her shirt and her hair was done up in a French twist. She smelled like lavender body wash. "Hi," I said to her.

"Let me in, honey."

I stepped back from the door and she bustled past, her high heels clicking against the concrete, then going silent on the carpet inside. "Oh, hello," she said to Lori. "I'm Karen."

"This is my mother," I explained to Lori. "Mom, Lori. My housemate."

"Nice to meet you," said Mom. She plonked herself down on the couch and dragged the coffee table up to her knees. "So have you seen this yet?" She spread out the paper.

I rubbed my eyes and went to look, only Lori beat me to it. She snatched it up. "Ohmigosh, Chlo. When did this happen?"

"When did what happen?"

She turned it around with a rustle of paper crumpling. It was a large picture of Jason Vanderholt talking to me in the parking lot. I'd turned my head, so they'd gotten a clear shot of my face. "Vanderholt and a female companion," read the caption.

"Oh," I said, "that."

"When did this happen?" repeated Lori.

"I'm sorry I didn't get his autograph for you. I forgot." The kitchen tiles were cool under my bare feet as I retreated to the sink.

"Chloe?" said Mom.

I filled the coffeemaker with water and grinds. "It was yesterday, after we did our extras thing," I said to Lori.

"When that guy came and got you?" she asked.

"Yeah."

"Wait, explain," said Mom.

"We were extras on the set of his movie yesterday, Mom. I ran into him. We said, like, twenty words to each other. It's nothing."

Lori shook her head. "But-"

I shot her a silencing look. I did not want to have to explain to anyone, least of all my mother, what yesterday's conversation had been about.

"So are you going to see him again?" Mom asked.

"What?" I said. "No. Gimme a break. Lots of people met him yesterday. All of the extras did. I don't know why they used that picture."

Mom sat back, deflated. "Oh."

I rolled my eyes as the coffeemaker hissed and spewed steam.

"Well, this is a nice place." She looked over our sitting room. "How long have you lived here?"

"Since I gave you the address. Last year."

"I didn't know you lived in town, Ms. Winters," said Lori.

I winced, but Mom only giggled. "Just call me Karen. I'm not a Winters."

"Oh, right. Sorry, dumb of me to assume," said Lori.

"It's fine. You known Chloe long?"

"Since freshman year," I said.

Lori, sensing that I was about to lose my temper, put the newspaper down and said something about needing to use the bathroom. She beat a hasty retreat.

Which told me I needed to calm down. I pinched the bridge of my nose between my thumb and forefinger and took a couple of deep breaths.

"What is it, honey?" said Mom.

"Nothing. Just that... I've lived here almost a year. I've been going to UNM with Lori and all my other friends you've never met for three years, and the first time you come visit me is when I get my picture in the paper with some random famous guy?"

"Well, I just wanted to know what the story was," she said.

"I know, but there are much more interesting things going on in my life."

"Really? Have you got a boyfriend?"

"No, but I have a 4.0 with a double major. That mean anything to you?"

"Well of course you do. Well done."

"No," I said. "Not of course. I work hard on that-"

"I didn't mean to imply that you don't." She picked up the newspaper and folded it carefully. "But you were always very smart. You've got those Winters genes."

"Of course, it's *genetic*."

She frowned at me, as if I'd been the one to say something offensive. "Well, fine. I can see I'm not wanted-"

"No, come on. You want some coffee or something?"

"I've got to get to work." She got to her feet.

"You want-"

"I don't want anything," she snapped. "You have a nice day."

"Come on, Mom."

But she'd already crossed over to the door and was letting herself out. "Bye now."

I watched her leave, then grabbed a mug down from the shelf. I desperately needed coffee just then.

My shift at Flying Star started at ten, and I spent an hour pouring coffee and ringing up orders before someone came in and slid a copy of the newspaper, with my picture exposed, across the counter next to the register.

I groaned and looked up. It was Matthew, a questioning smile on his lips.

"We had an affair. Really short one," I said. "It was torrid."

"What?"

"I'm joking."

"When did this happen?"

"Put that away, all right? I don't want anyone to see it."

He folded the paper and tucked it under his arm.

"You want coffee? Cupcake?"

He shrugged and started to dig in his pocket.

"No, I've got this," I said. "What do you want?"

"Just coffee, black."

I looked over at Abby, the strawberry blond who shared the shift with me. "Okay if I go on break?" I asked her.

"Yeah, sure."

"Okay, you find us a seat," I told Matthew. "I'll be right there."

"He's cute," said Abby.

"Yeah," I agreed. Matthew had a slight swagger in his walk, due to the fact that he wore his cowboy boots everywhere.

"Too bad he's married," said Abby.

"No, not married."

"Engaged?"

"Huh? No." I set out two cups on a tray and poured the coffee.

"He's got a ring."

"No it's a... what do you call them? A purity ring."

"Oh, religious and Texan."

"You say those like they're bad things."

"Great butt."

"Yeah, I'll tell him you said that." I headed over to the table he'd staked out, Abby's giggles fading behind me. Flying Star was a restaurant and coffee lounge. The décor was bright, primary colors. A large, glass case of pastries dominated the serving counter, and one whole wall was magazine racks. The place had power outlets and wifi, so a lot of students hung out here to study during the school year. Otherwise, it was a very popular lunch and dinner spot. The traffic was already picking up, and two other employees had just shown up to help.

"So when did this happen?" Matthew held up the paper as I sat down.

I slid into my chair, set his coffee in front of him, and dismissed the newspaper with a wave. "Ran into him after we finished yesterday. How exciting was yesterday? Two whole hours of the Hollywood experience."

He gave me an odd look as he sipped his coffee. "You never did say what happened after that guy came and got you."

"It's kind of embarrassing."

"Embarrassing how? Did Vanderholt proposition you or something?"

"*No.* Of course not."

But Matthew just sipped more coffee and said, "I saw the way he looked at you in line."

"What's that supposed to mean?"

"He noticed you. Take it from another guy. I saw."

"He did not proposition me and we didn't really have a torrid affair. It was a different kind of embarrassing."

"Okay."

I dumped two sachets of sugar into my coffee and stirred. "Can you keep a secret?"

"You know I can."

"My mother, when she was sixteen, had an affair with her married boss. She had me when she was seventeen, and carried on with this affair for over a decade. The guy was Dr. Winters, the dentist. Jason was friends with Chris Winters, Dr. Winters's son, and so when he asked me if I was related..."

Matthew blinked once, twice.

I sipped my coffee, which was still a little bitter, despite all the sugar. "Ye-ah."

"I had no idea." He leaned closer.

"Yeah, well. It doesn't matter anymore. Not to me. I don't live at home and-"

"Chloe, you're on track to be valedictorian."

"Whatever."

"I never knew you came from a background like that."

"You knew I went to Rio Grande High School and had a single mother. You got the gist."

"I don't know high schools around here."

"Rio Grande's in one of the poorer areas. I mean, it's not a bad high school... well, some would say it is. It's not La Cueva, okay? That's where Jason Vanderholt and my half siblings went. That's up in the Northeast Heights where the property values are higher. It's got this weird, eighties look to it, kind of built like a shopping mall or something, but anyway. It's one of the nicer schools and about as opposite as you can get from Rio Grande."

"Okay. Well, dang, that musta been an awkward conversation."

"Yeah. The Winters are well known. I mean, you can hear ads for Dr. Winters's dental practice-"

"On the radio. I never thought about you having the same name, though I guess I should. This whole state's like a small town."

"Doesn't mean we're all related."

Matthew took a big gulp of coffee. His purity ring glinted in the sunlight. "Well," he said, "I knew you were cool. Just didn't know how cool." He winked at me.

The winking thing was new. I shrugged in reply.

3
COFFEE AND VANDALISM

THAT Friday was slow at Flying Star, which was odd for a Friday, but business was like that. Some event at some other restaurant was probably funneling customers away. I had time to stand and page through a magazine behind the counter. I always liked pictures of next season's fashions, not that I could afford any of them.

A small knot of customers whooshed in the glass doors and I put the magazine aside and moved to the cash register. Rather than pause to look at the pastries and read the menu, like most people did, this group came straight up to me. They were all men, and the guy in front wore a baseball cap and sunglasses. I hated when people did that indoors.

"Can I help you?" I asked.

The guy right in front of me took off his sunglasses to reveal sky blue eyes. "Hi."

I blinked. It was Jason Vanderholt. "Oh, hi."

"You ever get to take a break?"

"Um..." I looked over at Abby who stared, open mouthed.

"Go," she said to me.

"Sounds like a yes?" said Jason.

I looked around at the other guys surrounding the cash register. They prevented anyone in the dining room or outside from seeing Jason, but Jason glanced around at them and said, "They don't have to sit with us. You sure you don't want coffee or something?" He looked unsure of himself, like he was afraid he'd crossed a line. But the restaurant was open to the public. He was as welcome here as anyone.

"Sure," I relented. "That what you want? Coffee?"

"Yeah, and a biscotti." He tugged one loose from the jar on top of the pastry display with a crackle of cellophane. I rang up his order, but he shook his head. "You're not having anything?"

"I can get-"

"Put it on." He nodded at the cash register.

I paused. He was just being nice, but I didn't really want to be taken out for coffee by this guy. I didn't want to create an awkward moment either, so, reluctantly, I added a second coffee and let him pay. His people fanned out across the dining room and staked out a table. "Shall we?" said Jason.

"Gimme a sec. I'll bring the coffees."

"Okay." He headed across the room with his biscotti and I poured a cup of regular for him and decaf for me. His visit had given me the jitters.

"Oh. My. Gosh," said Abby.

"Not you too."

"You *know* him?"

"He knows my family. It's nothing." I crossed over to the table in the far corner where Jason's people had seated him, his back to the dining room and windows. Several members of the entourage got coffees and pastries and sat at nearby tables. It was all very over the top, as if they feared a group of ninjas would break into the restaurant and take Jason away. Which I'd seen happen, in the theaters.

But, I had to admit, if his fans usually behaved the way the extras had in line, this wasn't over the top. I slid into my seat and passed Jason his coffee. Jason broke the biscotti in two and put one half in front of me. The other he dunked in his drink.

"So how've you been?" he asked.

"Fine. How's the film?"

"Wrapped. Yesterday."

"Oh. So you're leaving town soon?"

"Yeah, in a few hours. I just wanted to track you down and say sorry. I was way too nosy about you and your family and all that."

"It's fine. How did you find me?"

He tugged his phone from his pocket and held it out to me. It was sleek and hi tech and displayed a web page with a picture of me grinning. That, I knew, was on the Flying Star website. I'd been employee of the month last month.

"Oh," I said.

"I love this place," he said. "It's the old Rainbow Cafe, right? Started over on Juan Tabo?"

"I don't know."

"I'm pretty sure it is. Used to go there when I was a kid."

"Did you Google my name?" I asked.

"Yeah."

I frowned. "Anything else come up?"

"I didn't look, why?"

"Um... never mind..."

"I'm really sorry if I dug into your privacy again-"

"If it's on the internet, it's not private."

"Yeah, but sometimes it should be. Believe me, I know."

I shrugged. "Um, okay. Things with the Winters got ugly sometimes, so... yeah. Kind of embarrassing what might be still around in old news stories."

"Gotcha. Okay." He put his phone back in his pocket. "So tell me about you?"

"What do you want to know?"

"Where'd you grow up?"

"Near the South Valley."

"And now? You at UNM?"

I nodded. "Yeah, I'll be a senior."

"What do you study?"

"Archeology and biology."

"Nice. UNM's a top archeology school, right? Got a really good department?"

"Yeah, that's why I majored in it. Figured it'd give me the best shot at a good graduate school."

He nodded, munched some more biscotti, and washed it down with coffee. "You going to be an archeologist?"

"No, forensic science. Which I learned last year requires a hard science bachelors, and not everyone considers archeology a hard science, so that's why I took on the second major."

"Oh, so you'll be like *Bones*– did you ever watch that TV show?"

"No – yes, I have seen it – but no, she's a forensic anthropologist and I just want to be a forensic scientist. She deals with dead bodies, and I just want to do stuff like fingerprinting, munitions testing, DNA evidence. Stuff like that."

"Like *CSI*?"

"Right. Without as much funding."

"You probably think it's stupid that I'm citing television shows to understand what you do."

"I dunno. It'd be a little more disturbing if you had real life experience."

"Okay, true." His blue eyes twinkled. I could see why millions of women found him dreamy. I just found him odd. He was too perfect looking. His teeth were pure white and even. His tan was bronze and fake. At least with the baseball cap on, his hair stuck out around the edge like a normal person's. His hands and nails were manicured and flawless.

As if sensing my scrutiny, he went quiet, as if it mattered to him what I thought.

I tried to fill the silence. "I guess I don't know much about you. Other than that you went to La Cueva."

"I did, for two years. I mean, I graduated from there too, but I had to transfer credits back to do it. Loved that school."

"And my housemate heard in an interview that you do martial arts?"

He gave a wry smile. "Maybe I said that. I don't know. I don't bother to tell the truth in interviews."

"You just lie?"

With a shrug, he drained his coffee. "People don't watch interviews to get to know me. They don't want to know the real me. They just want to be entertained, and I don't want to share my personal information with a bunch of strangers, so I just make up stories and stuff. I don't think I ever said I knew martial arts, though. I try not to claim to have skills that I don't. I might've made up some story about a karate fight or- yeah. Yeah, I did. Karate fight on set where I broke my little finger and cried over it while all the stunt guys laughed at me. Didn't happen, though I probably would cry like a baby if it did."

This guy had a seriously strange life.

He looked up at me again, as if unsure what to say next. "Look, can I get your phone number?"

"Not to be rude, but why?"

"You seem really cool. Real down to earth. Talking like this? It's been nice."

"And you seem very nice." I looked past him at his security guys–that's what I assumed they were –all trying to look like they weren't with us. A group of girls headed in our direction and one of the men got up to block them. "You also have one of the weirdest jobs on the planet. Sorry, that's-"

He laughed. "The truth? Like I said, you seem really cool. I'm in town sometimes to see my family. We should hang out." He pulled out his phone.

It seemed rude to say no, so I gave him my number, and keyed his into my beat up little flip phone. More women and girls were streaming into the restaurant.

Jason turned and surveyed the scene. "Maybe this'll be good for business for you?"

"I can disarm the alarm so you can go out the back door?"

"That'd be great, but in a few. I can sign some autographs and stuff. Get them to buy food, I hope." He got to his feet.

"You don't have to-"

"It's cool." He and his guys all rallied together and turned to face the growing crowd.

I stole away. It was cowardly, but I had the feeling that if these women noticed me sitting at his table, they might lynch me. Besides, it was past time for me to get back to work. I ducked behind the counter and tied my apron on. Abby was wrestling with the Red Stuff machine, which dispensed a mix of cranberry juice and red tea that was very popular in the summer.

"Here," I said. I grasped the handle and twisted it back so that the machine would work again.

"Okay, so spill. How do you know him?"

Everyone behind the counter looked at me. "Shh," I said. "I don't want to get beaten up by a bunch of fans."

"Are you involved with him?" Abby asked.

"Um. No. He's dating Corey Cassidy, right? I barely know him. Like I said, he kind of knows my family and recognized me when I was an extra in his movie. He grew up in town."

"Yeah, I know," said Abby. "I have a friend of a friend who had a locker next to him at La Cueva. Junior year."

"Oh," I said. "Cool." He'd just told me that he hadn't been there for his junior year, but whatever. I felt a little sorry for anyone who felt the need to make up a claim like that. Surely they'd done something more interesting in their life than have a locker next to a guy who now pretended to be other people for a living?

The crowd surged as people mobbed Jason for autographs, and we sold four hundred to-go orders for coffee in an hour. It was insane. What was also insane was the number of girls who were crying and shaking as they paid, as if they were in the presence of divinity. Jason was "sooo sexy" and "sooo nice". I let him and his crew out the back door when he texted me to explain he needed to catch his plane to LA.

"I'll see you, Chloe," he said as he put his sunglasses on and stepped out into the brightness.

Usually I walked to and from work, but that day I'd driven. Big mistake. I walked around to the parking lot at the end of my shift and found the tires on one side of my car had been slashed. It listed to one side, like a sinking ship. I called my insurance company, then the police – their non-emergency number. "I need to file a report," I told the woman who picked up. "Someone vandalized my car."

"Do you know whom?"

"No."

"Have you got any enemies or-"

"You know, this is really stupid, but I vaguely know Jason Vanderholt. We had coffee this morning and, maybe I'm paranoid but-"

"One of his fans vandalized your car?"

"Dumb theory?"

"No. There's a cruiser that should be there any minute."

"Thanks."

"You really know Jason Vanderholt?"

"Not well."

"What's he like?"

I shut my eyes and turned my face skyward. The sun still shone down, scorching hot. I got a detailed view of the blood vessels in my eyelids. "He's nice. When did you say the cruiser would get here?"

"Should be there any second."

Much to my relief, a shiny silver police car rounded the corner right then. "Okay, here it is. Thanks!" I hung up.

"So you've got celebrity connections?" the cop said as he stepped out.

I just pointed at my car. "Need to file a report. I didn't see it happen. Don't know about any witnesses."

"Name?"

"Chloe Winters."

"Chloe Winters?"

"Yeah."

He took off his sunglasses and looked at me. He was middle aged, graying black hair, wrinkled skin. Kind, brown eyes. "I'm Officer Baca. You probably don't remember me."

I shook my head.

"I was a rookie way back when. Helped them airlift you."

"Oh. Hi."

"How are you?"

"I'm good."

He looked down at my leg. I was wearing a skirt, so he could clearly see the little silver scar on my calf. "I'm glad to hear it. Have a daughter your age."

"Oh, uh-huh."

"How long did he get put away? The guy who did that to you?"

"Twenty five years maximum or something? It was a few consecutive sentences, but I don't know how all that works with parole or whatever."

"Not long enough." He started scribbling away on his notepad. "Okay, this is your car?"

I nodded.

"You got insurance?"

"Yeah. Tow truck is coming."

"Just gimme a sec to write this up." He looked up at me again. "It really is good to see you. Had nightmares about that incident for years, but you look great."

4
DANGER FIELDS

"They slashed your *tires?*" Matthew was over for the evening, his last evening in Albuquerque before he went home for a couple of weeks. I'd just taken enchiladas out of the oven, so the whole kitchen smelled like warm corn tortilla, melted cheese, and green chile.

"I know, it's so stupid," I said.

"So, wait, Jason Vanderholt-"

"Just stopped by to apologize for digging up family dirt. It's nothing. And I told my coworkers what happened with my car, so they all know not to tell anyone he came by to see me."

"Maybe he should pay for your tires."

"No. Come on. I was able to repair them for twelve bucks. They weren't even slashed, really. The person used nails or screws or something like that."

"If the person had keyed your car-"

"I wouldn't pay to fix that."

"But... you drive a sports car."

"Which is kind of a long story. Dr. Winters bought that for my mom to buy her off, I guess, right before they broke up. She doesn't want the thing anymore, but it still runs, so she gave it to me. I would never get one like that for myself. And it's old. It's ten years old."

Matthew was perched on the kitchen's one barstool. The house was small and badly designed, and there wasn't really anywhere to eat, just one square of counter space with that barstool. Lori and I had talked about getting a table off Craig's List or Freecycle, but in order to make room for it, we'd have to move the couch out, and that would leave us no place to lounge and watch television.

"So, rumor has it that Jon wanted to take you to Tia Anita's tonight," said Matthew.

Dang, I thought. Caught. "How did you know?"

"From Lori. Things definitely over with him?"

"Yeah, they've been over for a month."

"But he's not getting the clue, huh?"

"Nope."

"At least he remembers your favorite restaurant. You sure you wouldn't rather go? They're getting a new chef soon. The food might not be the same."

"I'm positive. And yes, I'm totally using you tonight as my excuse. Sorry."

"I don't mind. Not if you cook."

I got out a spatula and pried apart the rolls of tortilla. Gouts of steam spurted up where I parted the melted cheese. Matthew came around and got plates down from the cupboard and I put two enchiladas on his and one on mine. Strings of cheese reached after each serving that I had to cut with the blunt spatula edge.

"You want water?" I asked. "Or I think we have juice."

"Water's fine." He carried the plates into the living room and put them on the coffee table. He was too polite to eat on the couch, even though it wasn't a very nice couch. Instead he parked himself on the floor.

I filled two water glasses and went to join him.

"Dare I ask why you're so abruptly and completely over Jon?" he asked.

"We had the Talk."

"What's the Talk?"

"It's when I explain to a guy that I'm not going to sleep with him."

"Oh."

"More info than you want, I'm sure."

"You've never spent the night with any of your boyfriends?"

"No."

"Really?"

"Yes, I'm twenty-one and therefore a societal freak-"

"You're not a freak. Or we're both freaks." He held up his left hand with his purity ring. "So you want to wait until marriage?"

"For now. In a few years I'll re-evaluate, but while I'm getting my degrees and working my way towards a career, it's just a stress I don't want to deal with. I can't think about out-of-wedlock sex without thinking about the potential consequences, given my childhood was one big long consequence, you know? And Jon's not interested in marriage right now. He's ruled it out while he's still in school." He was a med student.

"Well, and most people nowadays don't marry people they haven't slept with."

"I know... but things were falling apart anyway. We just weren't on the same page about it all. He went on and on about how long we'd been together, like there's a time limit, and you know? Maybe there is. Maybe it was time to go our separate ways, if it wasn't what he wanted. Now you know why I never have a relationship that lasts longer than six months."

"Well, given the type of guy you date..."

"What type is that?"

Matthew took a bite of enchilada and chewed, slowly. I could tell he was stalling. Putting his thoughts together. "I don't wanna sound mean."

"We're friends. Shoot."

"Okaaay, first of all, you aren't religious. Most of us chastity types are. And you don't date religious people."

"I'm a Christian."

"When's the last time you went to church?"

"I go on Christmas sometimes. Easter."

"Yeah, well, I go every week. But besides that, you date... guys who are... um..."

"Just spit it out."

"Older. Probably experienced, sexually. Probably feel like they're past the age of just holding hands and goodnight kisses. And just look at the world nowadays. The way it works for people is they date, become intimate, live together, and then maybe marry. You get off before the second stop, people assume you don't want any of that."

"This is probably not what you wanted to talk about."

He reached over and patted my knee. "I respect you, Chloe. The stuff I've found out about you in the past week just makes me respect you more."

"Sorry to use you tonight."

"I really don't mind. You gonna be okay the next coupla weeks?"

"Yeah, tonight was definitely Jon's last ditch effort."

"You going anywhere before school starts?"

"I want to."

"You should."

"I don't have any plans."

"Then make some. You work too much. Take a break."

"Well, I'll think about it. Maybe Lori and I can go to the Grand Canyon for a weekend or something."

"Lori's not the camping type, and I'm betting you that you don't get out of town. You'll put it off and I'll come back and you'll still be here."

Lori walked in then, followed by Charles, a guy she'd been dating for about a month. I sort of knew him. He was tall and gangly and played basketball. The two of them said polite hellos as they passed through the living room and went back to Lori's room.

Matthew gave me a knowing look, which I ignored. But after we finished our food and washed the dishes, he gave me a hug, which wasn't like him. He was just the right height for me to put my head on his shoulder. Apparently tonight had been a bonding experience. "You take care, okay?" he whispered to me. "I'll see you in a coupla weeks."

A WEEK later, I was out for my morning run when my phone rang. I glanced at it. Jason.

I slowed down and answered it. "Hello?"

"Hey, how are you?"

"Not bad." I turned toward home. It was only a block away. The walk was a good way to cool down. "You in LA?"

"I am. Doing the press junket for *Danger Fields*."

"That a movie?"

"The new one I have coming out this weekend. It's based on a World War II novel."

"Oh, okay."

"Soooo... I've been calling around. I have two extra tickets to the premiere. You want them? You could bring someone."

"Where is it? In LA?"

"Yeah. Day's drive from Al-b-q."

"When?"

"Thursday. Kind of an awkward day for normal people. You probably have work."

"How much are the tickets?"

"Oh, eh. I didn't pay for them. I got them for my sister, but she can't come, so they'll go to waste if someone doesn't use them."

One day's drive, a short hotel stay, and a chance to see a movie. I was at my house and Lori stood in the doorway, fiddling with her cellphone. "Hang on," I said. I put the phone to my chest. "Hey, Lor?"

"Hmmm?"

"You want to go to LA for a couple of days?"

"Heck yeah! Why?"

"See a movie premiere?"

"Yes! That would be cool. It in your budget?"

"If we get a cheap hotel, yeah."

"Yes! Yay! Cool."

I put the phone back to my ear. "Um, sure, okay."

"Yeah?"

"Yeah, why not?"

"Okay, cool. Can I get your email address to send you the times and stuff?"

I gave it to him.

"So I'll see you next Thursday," he said. "I'll make sure to say hello. You just need to come find me. It gets really crowded at these events, so I'm sorry I won't really get to talk to you."

"Yeah, that's fine. Thank you."

"Eh, free tickets. I'm not gonna use em. Gimme a minute and I'll email you stuff."

"Okay."

"Talk to you later."

"Later."

Lori glared at her phone as if it had said something rude to her, then tossed it back inside the house. "What movie we see- wait a minute. Who was that on the phone?"

"Jason." I rubbed a kink in my shoulder as I pushed past her into the house.

"Jason who?"

"How many Jasons have tickets to the premiere of *Danger Fields?*"

"Vanderholt?! You called him?"

"He called."

She followed me into the kitchen while I got a glass of water. "He called *you?*"

I shrugged. "Yeah."

"He *called* you?"

"You feeling okay?"

"Why is he calling you?"

"He had tickets he wanted to give away."

"Just happened to think of you, huh?"

I drained my glass and put it in the dishwasher. "Didn't you tell me he's dating Corey Cassidy?"

"Yeah."

"So yeah, he's just being friendly. Or he wants to have a torrid affair, in which case he's really subtle about it."

"C'mon, there's gotta be something there. This have to do with you maybe being related to those people he knows?"

"Lor..."

"Please? Tell me?"

"He was talking about my half siblings. He went to school with my brother."

"Ohmigosh!"

But the admission left a bitter taste in my mouth. I headed for the shower.

"Can I meet your brother?" Lori called after me.

"No," I said. "You can't. Pretty sure he doesn't want to see me." I shut the bathroom door.

"Hey, how close are you to town?" Jason asked via cellphone as Lori drove us on the 110 into Los Angeles. The sky had gone from blue to pale blue to rather gray, and there was no sign of those mountains we'd just driven through. They were hidden in the haze. My air conditioning was finally turned down, though. The Mojave had strained it to its limit.

"I think we're in downtown now," I said. "I guess? Bunch of tall buildings."

"Move to the right lane," Lori's GPS intoned. We'd mounted it on my dashboard.

"And where are you staying?" asked Jason.

"Um, up the 405 a ways."

"What, the Valley?"

"I don't know."

"Well, so a bunch of us are having dinner at my house tonight, you should come."

"Oh, I don't know if we'll get there in time."

"It's four. You'll make it here by six, no problem, even with rush hour."

"Is that what time dinner is?"

"Dinner?" said Lori.

"Around then. It's just me, some friends, and my brother and his family. Really casual. Everyone else is here, hanging out, so it's just whenever you show up. Come on over."

"We're going to dinner?" squeaked Lori.

"Um..."

"That a GPS I heard a second ago?" said Jason.

"Yeah."

"Okay, put in my address. It's... you got a pen?"

I looked sidelong at Lori, then at the ceiling of the car, then grasped the GPS with one hand. "Go on." I hit the button to change the destination.

"Where are we going to dinner?" Lori asked.

I didn't answer, just punched in the address that Jason gave me.

"What restaurant is that?" she wanted to know.

"It isn't," I whispered.

"Cool. We'll see you when you get here," he said.

I smelled my shirt and pulled a face. "Okay. See you."

"So where is that?" Lori asked.

"It's... just..."

"Ohmigosh! Is that *his house?*"

"Yeah."

"Are you serious?"

"Look, calm down. No selling the address on Ebay."

"No way. We are going to *his house?*"

"Not if you drive us off the road we aren't."

She jerked us back into the middle of our lane. "I can't believe we're going to his house! I bet he has a pool."

"Mmmm."

"Do you think he has, like, an indoor movie theater?"

"You can ask."

"And one of those big marble staircases?"

"Just drive, okay?"

She let out another squeal.

It took nearly an hour and a half to get to his house, thanks to gridlock traffic. GPS was a lifesaver once we left the freeway. It took us through a labyrinth of narrow roads that wound their way up into the hills. These seemed to go on forever, but we finally turned in at the base of a long driveway, blocked by ornate wrought iron gates.

Lori gave me an excited smile as she rolled down her window. "Hello?" she said into the intercom.

"Hello, Ms. Winters?" replied a male voice.

"Yes."

"Come on in." The gates shuddered and swung open.

"This is so cool," Lori said as we drove in.

I got out my hairbrush and wished I could put my hair in a ponytail as she drove up the long, uphill driveway. The house was ahead, all white stucco, and it stair-stepped its way up the hillside. We were approaching it from the side; the "front" looked like it faced out across the nearest ravine.

"It looks Mediterranean," said Lori as she pulled in behind the other cars parked in the driveway. There were a couple of Mercedes, but the car we were behind was a minivan with two children's carseats in the back. It had California plates and a rental company sticker on the back.

"Okay." Lori turned to me. "How do I look?"

"Fine."

"You look good."

"Thanks." I opened my door and stepped out.

"Ohmigosh!" Lori got out of the car. "We're about-"

"Lor, please." This was a mistake, I just knew it.

But rather than bounce around or skip, Lori straightened her posture and squared her shoulders. "Okay, okay. I'll be you. Don't worry."

I wasn't sure what she meant by that, but since it seemed to involve no more screeching, I didn't pry. The house door stood open and Lori and I approached it.

5
DINNER AND A MOVIE

I wasn't sure if we should just walk in or what, but once we got close to the door, Jason stepped out and waved us in. He was wearing a t-shirt and cargo shorts and sandals. "Hey!" he called out. "How was your drive?"

"Good," I said. "This is my roommate, Lori."

"Yeah, hi. Come on in."

The entryway to his house did not have a giant, marble staircase. In fact, it was pretty normal looking, even a little narrow. There was a staircase that led up to an expansive kitchen and living area, where several other people were milling around. The smell of grilled meat and vegetables was in the air. One wall was open and beyond it was a pool deck. The pool was built like ones I'd seen in Las Vegas, with water spilling over the far end so that it looked like it went on forever, and the view was spectacular. Tree covered hills as far as the eye could see, dotted with mansions and not too much grungy haze in the air.

Lori seized my arm and clamped down tight. "It's Donovan Reilly," she whispered. "Ohmi*gosh*. Okay, sorry, sorry." She took a deep breath.

Jason, who'd followed us on the stairs, slipped past and said, "Okay, so let's see. Don, this is Chloe and Lori."

Donovan Reilly stood over by the counter, all bleached blond hair and surfer tan. He turned and looked me up and down. I knew who he was, of course. He'd been in the *New Light* movies with Jason. I'd seen plenty of promo posters of the two of them in gladiator gear. He was at least ten years older than Jason.

"And I am the younger, better looking brother," said a guy approaching from the pool.

"That's Steve," said Jason.

Steve was much stockier than his brother, but he had a nice smile and a hand extended, which I shook. His eyes were blue, but not as blue, and his skin was pale. I suspected Jason's was the same color under that spray on tan.

His other hand, which grasped a glass of lemonade, sported a wedding ring.

"Nice to meet you," I said.

"So you're from the Q?" he said.

"The Q?" said Donovan.

"Albuquerque," said Jason. I could tell from the angle of his voice that he was going outside.

I nodded.

"You're at UNM?" Steve asked.

"Yeah."

"Me too. The law school. It's the family trade to sell our souls for money."

"He's always been so supportive of my career," hollered Jason.

"And I didn't want to come to Hollywood and overshadow my big bro. You know, he's so enthusiastic about his acting, and that's great and all."

A few more people had filed in from the pool deck and one was a woman who patted Steve's shoulder on the way past. She had a baby balanced on her hip.

"Did you see that? My own wife patronizing me. What?" He held out his hands and followed her.

Someone tugged at my shorts and I looked down to see a little girl, wearing a sun dress, who stared up at me with wide, blue, Vanderholt eyes.

"That's Maddy," said Steve. "Honey, come over here."

Jason strolled back in. "Shan," he said to Steve's wife. "We can cover the pool if you want."

"Actually, I was thinking of putting their swimsuits back on and letting them play some more. Is that all right?"

"Yeah, sure." Jason went into the kitchen and came to lean on the counter. "You thirsty?" he asked me. "We've got lemonade, soda."

"Lemonade would be great."

"Howabout you, Lori?"

"Yeah, sure."

He poured two glasses and set them out on the counter for us.

"Sooo," I heard Donovan Reilly say, "you're from Albuquerque?"

Lori giggled in reply. "Yeah."

"First time in LA?"

"Uh-huh."

"First time in a house like this?"

"Yeah."

"Jason's keeping it real tonight. No caterer. No chef."

"You have a chef?"

A couple more people wandered out from the back and Jason introduced me to them. None of them were famous enough for me to recognize, and from the look of them, I wondered if they were all even actors. What surprised me was that they were all male. I'd expected Corey Cassidy to be around somewhere, but maybe she had another movie to make or something.

"How's it look?" Jason said. He was back out on the pool deck. "Rice is almost done."

"I think it's okay," came Steve's voice. There was a puff of smoke and the scent of roast vegetables and meat came even stronger. I realized they were grilling out there. "I dunno if Jen would approve."

"You tell her you cooked it, she would. You mention I touched it, no way."

Steve cracked up at that. "It's true."

"Seriously, she thinks you're her twin and I'm the dorky little brother."

"It's because you're not married. No kids to make you respectable."

Jason wandered back in, a resigned smile on his face.

"Jen your sister?" I asked.

"My mean sister, yes."

"Older?"

"By three minutes. Not that she'll ever let me forget it."

"Hey." Steve followed him in. "Don't complain. You took off in high school and left me alone with her."

"She mean to you too?" I asked.

"Worse." He patted his stomach. "She's a chef. Ruined me. It's the real reason I'm not an actor." He gave a dramatic sigh.

"Right, that's the reason," said Jason.

"Now who's being mean?" Steve grinned. "I think we're ready."

"'Kay." Jason went outside and around the corner. His kitchen, now that I got a good look at it, was something else. All industrial grade appliances in stainless steel. It was like the Flying Star kitchen, almost. The countertops were granite and the cabinets were a trendy, medium tone wood with abstract artsy handles.

"Here we go!" Jason announced. He and his brother put platters piled high with veggies and meat, on the counter. Steve dumped a handful of kebab skewers into the sink. Jason put out plates and dished brown rice from a rice cooker into a bowl, and the buffet was ready. "Here," he said to me. He spooned me up some rice and asked, "You eat meat?"

I nodded.

He put both veggies and meat on my rice and handed me the plate.

"Thanks," I said.

He handed me a fork and grabbed my lemonade glass. I watched him refill it while everyone else helped themselves to the food.

"Thanks," I repeated, as I received my glass back.

"We just eating out on the deck?" Donovan Reilly asked.

"Can if you want. Or there's a table in the other room," said Jason.

"Nah, the weather's nice," said Bill, one of the other guests I'd met. He went out to sit in one of the metal pool chairs and everyone else followed suit.

I found a spot on a chaise lounge and put my glass down on the ground. The view from the deck really was spectacular. Steve's wife emerged from a doorway across the deck, wearing a swimsuit and sarong. Their two kids were in suits and floaties and made straight for the pool, despite her protests that they not run.

I realized the part of the house she'd come from wasn't attached to the rest of the building. It wasn't part of the house. It was a guesthouse, and it was bigger than my house. Unreal.

The lounge chair creaked under me and a shadow fell across my plate. I looked up. Donovan Reilly had sat down, rather close to me. "Hello," he said.

"Hi."

Jason wandered over with his plate and glass and took a seat nearby.

"Soooo, nice view, huh?" Donovan stretched out an arm.

"Mmm-hmm." I ate a forkful of food.

"This your first time in LA?"

"No. I was here last fall for a symposium."

"A sym-po-si-um." He sing-songed the word. "What was the symposium on?"

I sipped my lemonade and put the glass down again. "Diplomatic considerations in antiquities preservation."

"Diplo-what?"

There was no point repeating myself. I just ate more food.

He leaned over and put his arm behind me. Not exactly around me, but enough to give me the general idea.

I turned and stared at him.

His smile faded. He sat back and gave me some more personal space. "You do... what was it? Antiquities preservation?" So he had heard me when I told him the symposium title.

"No, but I co-wrote a paper on digging artifacts in an active warzone."

"Have you done that?" Jason asked.

"I screened some dirt in Chiapas, during a big teacher's strike that led to some deaths," I said.

"Screened dirt?" said Donovan.

"Yeah, like sifting it," said Jason. He mimed shaking a screen back and forth. "I got to do that one afternoon. Went to a Roman dig while we were shooting. It was really interesting."

"I did it for a whole summer," I said.

"Really? You were on a dig in Chiapas as an undergrad?" said Jason. "And you authored a *paper?*"

"Co-wrote. Yeah."

"So we got ourselves a smart one here," said Donovan.

I just ignored him then. My food was way more interesting than his condescension.

He was silent for a long time. When I looked up, he and Jason were looking at each other, levelly. Jason had a slight smirk on his face.

"I'm Don, by the way," Donovan said to me.

"Right, Donovan Reilly. I recognize you."

"Yeah... that's my stage name. It's just Don. Short for Donald. Smithers."

"Oh, okay." I looked at Jason.

"I use my real name," he said.

A few minutes later, Don got up for seconds and Jason pulled his chair closer. "So how've you been since I saw you last?" he asked.

"Been good. Getting ready for school to start."

"Yeah, I'll bet." He looked down at my leg.

I followed his gaze. My scar was easy to see in this light. My hand tightened on my fork. He went to a Roman dig when he did *New Light*. What other research had he done for his roles? I moved my leg and, stupidly, revealed the scar on the other side of my calf.

He blinked.

I froze.

"You taking all classes for your major senior year?" he asked. "Or, I should say majors?"

"I have to do a ton of biology credits, since I only just added that major."

"A lot of people just take an extra year for two majors."

"I'm ready to be done."

"That's impressive, that you can just add in another major like that and still finish on time."

"Shows I didn't really know what I was doing," I said. "I assumed a BS in archeology would've been good for forensics. You know, lots of digging and dusting and collecting evidence. I shoulda explained what I wanted for grad school to my career counselor sooner." I hadn't really understood what a career counselor was for. I'd never met with one in high school. Little things like that made an enormous difference to me now. Book learning wasn't enough; college required me to learn a whole new culture. As it was, I'd only just talked to the grad schools I wanted to attend, and while they assured me a minor in bio would be enough to meet their science requirements, I was taking no chances.

"I'm sure the archeology will still help," said Jason, "because what you said isn't wrong. And it'll make you unique."

It was kind of him to say. I ate the last of my vegetables and rice.

"You get any time to read on the side?"

"Hmm?"

"Did you get a chance to read *Danger Fields?*"

I nodded. "Yeah, I always read the book before I watch the movie." I'd checked it out from the library that week.

"It was such a good book, I hope the film doesn't screw it up."

"You haven't seen it yet?"

"No, not the whole thing, and-" he shrugged as he put his empty plate down "-what I see when I watch a movie isn't what you'll see. I know what's fake and how they did each effect and that there's the DGA trainee just outside the shot who's fanning smoke across the newly dug foxhole I'm in and all that. I don't really see the narrative anymore. The one thing I really, truly regret about my career. It's rare that I can just watch a movie."

"That would be rough," I agreed. "Worse than the screaming fans?"

"Yeah. Fans won't be around forever. Twenty years from now, *New Light* will be some campy old movie trilogy that teenagers mock to their parents, if anyone even watches it anymore. The stuff you learn, though, you never unlearn all the way."

"Right."

"Which isn't all bad, when you also take time to do stuff like visit Roman archeological digs." He smiled at me. "You want more food?"

"I'm good."

"Lemonade?"

"No thanks."

He ignored that, though, and took my glass. At least Don had moved back to Lori. She didn't seem to find him anywhere near as annoying as I did.

"Uh, Chloe?" said Lori as we walked into our hotel room. It was a cheap room, but a clean one, with two queen sized beds and a fluorescent light with a really annoying flicker that made me feel like I was under a strobe.

"Hmm?"

"Jason Vanderholt... really likes you."

"What? No he doesn't." I switched off the light and switched on an incandescent floor lamp.

"Yes he does. You can't see it?"

"He's dating Corey Cassidy."

"I don't think he is."

"You're the one who told me that."

"Maybe they broke up. Or maybe he's a player. I don't know, but he was definitely looking at you."

I brushed that aside.

"No, seriously," Lori pressed. "What are you going to do?"

"Do? Nothing. Even if what you say is true, and I don't think it is, what would I do?"

"You don't like long distance?"

Now Lori was talking craziness. I rolled my eyes. "There's more than geographic distance between us," I said. "The guy's from a whole different planet."

"One with nice houses-"

"Whatever."

"*Chloe*, ohmigosh. You can't just not care."

"And yet, I don't. First of all, you're wrong about him being interested. Second of all, even if you were right about tonight, we leave for Albuquerque the day after tomorrow, and I probably won't ever see him again, and third of all, he is all wrong for me in every possible way. He's a lot older; he's used to female adoration. He'd put up with me for a week, tops. And the big house and fancy life and stuff, who cares?"

"Yeah, I think that's it," said Lori. She sprawled out on her bed.

"What?"

"I guess you really offended Donovan-"

"Good. He's a jerk."

"He came over after he tried to talk to you and said something about how you were impossible to impress."

"Mmmm."

"I mean, I think you really got to him. I think he thought you were, like, one of Jason's fans or something and he thought you'd fawn over him, but then you didn't care who he was. But the thing is, when he came over to talk to me, all grumpy, that's when Jason pulled his chair over to you. I think he likes that about you, that you don't care about his money and fame and stuff."

"Well, whatever. There are other girls who don't care about fame and stuff. I'm sure here in LA there are a lot of people who spend a lot of time around the movie business and don't get all into whomever's hot at the moment."

"Maybe."

"I'm sure of it. Let's talk about something else. Let's plan something fun for tomorrow."

THE following morning Lori and I went to see the Getty Museum, then did lunch at California Pizza Kitchen in Westwood, then went back to our hotel and spent a couple of hours getting ready. I steamed the little black dress I'd brought – the one nice dress I owned – while Lori clipped the tags off her floral print number that she'd bought at a boutique in Old Town. I never shopped that neighborhood, but hey, it was her money. At least she was removing the tags, which meant she wasn't doing the buy, wear, and return routine. I had no idea what to wear to a movie premiere, but Lori and I both thought it would be fun to dress up.

I showered and blew my hair dry. My phone rang as I was applying mascara.

"It's hiiiim!" said Lori.

"Then answer it," I said. I dipped the mascara brush back into its tube and pulled it out again.

"Ms. Winters's phone. Hiiii! Uh-huh. Okay, hang on." She pressed the phone to her chest. "There's an afterparty, he wants to know if we want to go to it."

"Oh... um."

"Here." She stuffed the phone at me.

I put my makeup down and pressed my phone to my ear. "Hi."

"Hi, Chloe," said Jason. "So there's an afterparty at a private club, if you want to go."

"Well..."

"Not your kind of thing?"

"Not really."

"That's cool."

"I want to go!" Lori called out.

"Yeah, she can come, of course," said Jason. "Which means I guess one of you will need a ride."

"I can drop her off and get her. It's no problem."

"Well, okay. Let me give you the address. You got a pen?"

I fumbled around on the counter for one. "Yeah." I took it down and handed the paper to Lori. "Thanks for the invite."

"Of course. Look, I may not get much of a chance to see you guys tonight."

"Totally understand," I said. "I assumed it would be like that."

"Cool, but I hope you have fun."

"Yeah, this'll be great. Good luck."

"Thanks. Meh. The red carpet walk."

"Can't say that would be my thing either."

"Yeah. I'm not sure it's anybody's thing. Not after the first few times. If my smile is looking kind of painful and forced, that would be because it is."

I laughed.

"Don't get me wrong. I do love my fans and everything. I love my job. I love opening a new movie. I just have trouble sustaining the love for the whole length of that dang carpet."

"Right. Can't say I've ever had to do anything like that."

"What? You've given papers at a symposium."

"That's paper, singular, and I didn't have to pose and mug for cameras."

"I think my job's easier, really. Okay, I gotta run. Talk to you later."

"Yeah, later." I put down the phone and picked up a tube of lipstick.

The premiere was a mob scene. We parked our car in a nearby lot and walked over to the theater, which had screaming fans and about a million photographers and reporters out front. At least the weather was fantastic. Seventy degrees, no wind, the sun casting long shadows across the streets of Westwood Village. The theater scene looked daunting, but I found that with my ticket in hand, I was ushered along to the red carpet. Fortunately, the red carpet had a line of barriers down one side and an alley that Lori and I could walk down. It was the entrance for normal people, so the reporters knew to ignore us. We made it about halfway down before Jason showed up and the crowd erupted with earsplitting screams.

I clapped my hands over my ears and turned to look. Jason had stepped out of a limo and had Heather Reynolds on one arm.

"She plays his love interest," said Lori.

"I know."

"She's married to an Olympic skier."

"Mmm-hmm." I turned to keep walking.

"Man, it's going to take him half an hour to get down the carpet," said Lori. "They keep stopping him for pictures and he's signing autographs."

I didn't bother to look. We got to the theater and found a crowd in the lobby. Roughly half the people were all dressed up like we were, then the other half were just in jeans and t-shirts. Lori asked around and came back to report, "We wait here until the VIPs go in, but meanwhile they've got really nice d'oeuvres and, like, cocktails and stuff in the concessions area."

"I just want popcorn."

"I think I'm going to get a cosmo." She held out her hand for money from me and disappeared back into the crowd.

I didn't time how long it took for Jason to walk the red carpet, but once he and Heather made it into the lobby, it didn't end. The ticket-holders wanted his autograph and a chance to say hello too. He and Heather quickly worked the room, an army of attendants hovering behind them. I saw Dave, Jason's assistant, but he didn't see me. He probably wouldn't have recognized me anyhow.

My feet were starting to hurt in my heels. I shifted my weight as the rest of the cast made their way into the lobby, along with some guys in suits whom I took to be the producers and director and suchlike.

"Hey," said a voice behind me.

I turned to see Steve and his wife coming in through the doors. He was in a suit, she was in a long cotton dress. I waved back at them.

"Crazy, isn't it?" said his wife. "What level ticket did you get?" She peered at my hand. "Oh, yeah, same as ours."

"Means we don't get reserved seats," said Steve. "But it's all good."

Lori emerged then, with a cocktail in one hand and a bucket of popcorn in the other. The whole flow of the crowd shifted as the stars were ushered into the theater and people began to line up.

"We're going to get food," said Steve. "See you guys."

I waved at them and followed Lori. We let ourselves get swept along into the theater and just took the first seats that looked good. They were towards the back, and the theater didn't have stadium seating, but we still managed a decent view.

Once we were settled, Lori clamped down on my arm. "So cool!" she whispered.

As the movie began, I was able to relax. This was what I'd driven out to LA for. This was fun. The movie was good, the action was exciting, the love story was touching. Lori turned to look at me during the kissing scene. Jason in his combat fatigues swept Heather Reynolds, in her suspiciously clean nurse's uniform, into his arms.

I turned to look back at my housemate. "What?"

She raised her eyebrows.

I rolled my eyes and resumed watching the movie.

When the film was over and the lights went up, everyone gave it a standing ovation and several guys in tuxes filed to the front of the theater, where someone had set up a mic. "Thank you, thanks everyone," the first one said. He introduced himself as one of the producers and the others as other producers and the director. They each took a turn to thank everyone for coming and the cast for doing such a great job.

I glanced at Lori. I wondered how long this would go on.

Not long, fortunately. They all said their little soundbyte, then they had the cast all get up and come to the front to take a bow, and we all stood up to applaud them again, and then it was over. People started filing out of their seats. All in all, a great evening.

"After part-ay," said Lori. "Sure you don't want to come?"

"Yep. But I'll take you. You okay alone?"

"Heck yeah. You don't want to part-ay, you can just miss out."

Hours later I was in my pajamas, watching CNN. My hair was up in a towel, my face was clean and my toes were happy not to be smushed in those heels anymore. I wasn't really paying attention to CNN, but I found the calm, newscaster voices soothing.

There came the sound of the keycard slipping into the lock, then the metallic clunk of the latch. Lori waltzed in, a paper bag from Jack-in-the-Box in one hand.

"Hey," I said. "I thought you were going to call me?"

She flopped down on her bed and opened the bag, an amused smile on her lips. "Got a ride with Jason."

"Oh, okay."

"I think he wanted to come see you. Buuut, he didn't know we were staying here." She laughed. "No interior hallways, and we were pretty sure there were some photographers on our tail. He didn't want pictures of him escorting me into a cheap hotel room to get posted on the internet."

I had to laugh too. That was pretty funny.

"So he dropped me off at Jack-in-the-Box and told me to ask you to call him if you were still up. Which you are. So call him."

"What, now?"

"Or in the next little while. I don't know how long it'll take him to get home. You want a fry?"

"No. How was the party?"

"Awe-some. You missed out, except it totally wasn't your kind of thing. Talked to Donovan some more and met Rick Lucero."

"Don still a jerk?"

Lori threw a fry at me. "I had fun, okay? Call Jason."

I got out my phone.

"Hello?" he answered on the first ring.

"Hey, thanks for bringing Lori back." I dodged another fry. "I think. Stop throwing stuff at me!"

"No problem," said Jason. "She said you wanted to get going early tomorrow?"

"Yeah, I want to try to beat the heat. Like that's possible."

"I hear that. Good luck crossing the Mojave."

"Thanks."

"Sooo, yeah, I guess I'll see you next time I'm in Albuquerque."

"Yeah, okay. Thanks again for the tickets."

"I'm glad they didn't go to waste."

"Well, I'm about to turn in. Good night."

"Night."

I hung up. To Lori's inquisitive look I said, "Pretty sure he's just being friendly."

WHEN we pulled into our driveway the following day, Matthew was sitting on our front stoop. My spirits lifted at once.

6
MOM'S ISSUES

"Hey!" I called out to Matthew as I got out of the car. He looked good. His hair was shorter, and his cheeks were sunburned. Dappled shade from the cottonwood in the neighbor's front yard shielded him and the front of our house from the intense sun.

He got to his feet and smiled.

"When did you get in?" I asked him.

"Ah, just a little while ago. Where you been?" His eyebrows shot up when Lori hauled her duffel bag out of the trunk.

"We saw *Danger Fields*. It's good, but probably not your thing."

"And it's not out yet. Not until next week," said Lori. "We saw the premiere!"

"Oh." Matthew looked even more confused now.

I got my suitcase and went over to him. "I need to go for a run. You want to go for a run?"

"Sure."

"Meet you in an hour?"

There was a big, open sports field on campus, right along Central, where Matthew and I jogged. We did our laps, then walked to cool down. By then the sun was sinking low and the air was cooling off.

"So, yeah, I went to LA for a couple of days," I said. "Saw a movie premiere, that was fun."

"Why'd you go to LA?"

"Just for a vacation. You were right. I work too much."

"So you bought tickets to a premiere?"

"No, I got the tickets from Jason Vanderholt. He had some extras."

"You called-"

"He called. I've never contacted him. He was just being friendly, is all. Really."

"He's been calling you?"

We were both sweaty, but Matthew's sweat had a nice, clean scent to it. I hoped I didn't reek too bad. "He called once. And Lori's already given me a hard time about all this, so please don't you start."

"Well, did you see him in LA?"

"We kind of had dinner at his house, with a bunch of other people and... It was one of the most random things that has ever happened to me."

He lifted one eyebrow and looked at me. "Every girl's dream, right?"

"Not mine, and no, nothing 'dreamy' happened. I met his brother and his wife and kids. They seem nice."

Matthew only stared.

"Please don't give me a hard time about this. Lori was telling me I should flirt with him, and... no way. I'm not interested."

That earned me a half smile. "This would happen to you."

"What's that supposed to mean?"

"Of all the people for Vanderholt to go after."

"He hasn't gone after me."

"You hope he hasn't. I get it, I do." He put a hand on my shoulder and squeezed.

I put my hand over his and squeezed back.

That seemed to settle things for Matthew. He left his hand on my shoulder as we walked back to my place.

"Hey, Chloe, it's Jason. Just calling to wish you luck. Class starts tomorrow, right? Hope you've got at least a couple fun ones. Anyway, just saying hello. Talk to you later."

That message was on my voicemail when I finished work Sunday night.

On Tuesday was my first Media Studies class, one of my only non-science classes. Matthew had talked me into it. He and I found seats near the front of the lecture hall and he turned to scowl at the hordes of students packing in behind us.

"Well," I said. "Watching movies and television for credit, you know?"

The professor, a harried looking man in a tweed suit, stepped up to the podium. "Hello!" he shouted. "Everyone quiet. Quiet now! All right, welcome to the most grueling class you'll ever take. Not a joke, people. Every film, every television show, every commercial we watch, you will write a report on, and you'll need to log your own media consumption habits, including internet, every week."

"And that," I said to Matthew, "probably just cut the class size down 75%."

Matthew's eyes, however, had lit up. He was an English major. Essays and reports were his life.

"This morning we begin with YouTube. We're going to look at their copyright policies, their business model, and some of their top videos, beginning with Smosh and LonelyGirl15 and then Justin Bieber."

There was a collective groan. We were all a little old for Justin Bieber.

"Get out your notebooks, people. I also do quizzes without notice."

I already had my notebook out and took a deep breath. This was not my kind of class at all, but Matthew, on the other hand, looked like he was in heaven.

On Saturday night, I woke from a deep sleep. "Chloe? Chlo? Wake up. Please?" Someone had my shoulder in a death grip and was shaking me.

I pulled away and rolled over, my sheets twisting around my waist. I was in my bed, in my bedroom, and it was dark. No one else should have been here to bother me.

"Chloe?" It was Lori.

"Hmmm?" I groaned.

"Please. Your mom's here, and she's, like, freaking out."

In my exhaustion, it took a moment to process that. When I did, I extracted myself from my covers and sat up. A frame of light showed around my partially open door. Lori sat on my bed, still fully dressed.

"What time is it?" I whispered.

"One. Charles and I just got back. She was in her car in the driveway."

One o'clock on a Sunday morning. "Okay." I dug my legs out of the tangle of sheets and got to my feet. "What's she doing?"

"She's just crying."

I opened my door and blinked so my eyes could adjust. I could hear my mother now, sobbing like someone had broken her heart.

"I'm going to go to my room, okay?" said Lori.

"Yeah." I cleared my throat, smoothed my pajamas, and padded out to the front room. Mom was on the couch, wearing a sweatsuit. Her face was devoid of makeup and her blond hair was disheveled.

"What's going on?" I asked.

"Oh! Oh, honey!" She blew her nose in a tissue. "It's... it's... it's..."

"Breathe," I said. I sat down next to her on the couch. "Now talk." I tried to keep the annoyance out of my voice, but with her, it was always hard. Especially at times like this.

"It's... it's..."

"*Mom.* Just talk."

"I'm trying!" she wailed.

"Did Dr. Winters call?"

"Huh? No. No. Nothing like that."

"Some other guy-"

"My windows are broken!" She hiccupped another sob and buried her face in her tissue. Her shoulders heaved.

"What windows? On your car?"

"No."

"On your house?"

"Yes!"

"What happened?"

"Someone broke them!"

This late at night, I did not feel like working this hard to put together a puzzle of events. "*Mom.* Come on. Just talk. Who broke your windows? What do they want?"

"I don't know!"

"Which don't you know?"

"Either."

"Will you just tell me what happened?"

"I was-was home, talking on... and... a rock came through the window, and someone broke the kitchen window too, and I got down on the floor. I didn't see who it was."

"Did you ask the neighbors if they saw?"

"No."

"Did you call the police?"

"No."

"What time was this?"

"I don't know. A while ago."

"How long? Was it dark when it happened?"

"Yes, but I don't know what time. I just waited to see if there were any more rocks and then I came here, but the lights weren't on, and-and..."

"So okay, you left the house, with a broken window. Any idea if the people are coming back? Maybe going to break in?"

"Oh! Really? I don't know. I don't *know!*" Her voice rose to a shriek.

Lori's voice, which had been talking softly in her room, went silent. I heard Charles laugh nervously.

I went to the kitchen, grabbed another box of tissues, and threw it at my mom. "I'm calling the police."

She dodged the tissue box rather than trying to catch it. "I was so scared. It was awful."

"911," answered the operator on my cellphone.

"Hi, I'd like to report someone breaking windows in my mom's trailer home."

"Who was it?"

"Don't know. Not sure if there are any witnesses. I wasn't there."

"Can you put your mother on the phone?"

I looked over at Mom, who now lay on her side, a throw pillow clutched to her stomach. She still sobbed, like a little girl who'd lost her puppy.

"Probably better if you just talk to me. I'm coherent."

HALF an hour later, I stood outside Mom's trailer home. Its white siding flashed blue and red, the reflection of the police car lights. Two cruisers were parked out in front. The air was chill and I shivered even with my windbreaker on.

"No forced entry," one of the cops said. "Just looks like vandalism."

Another cop strode up from the direction of the neighbor's. "No one saw anything. They heard the breaking glass, but just assumed someone had dropped a dish or something. They say it happened around ten."

"This been a problem before?" The first cop asked me.

I shook my head. "No."

"Well, no one else in the neighborhood got hit. Your mom get in a fight with anyone recently?"

"Let me get her."

Mom was seated in the passenger seat of my car. She'd stopped crying, but her eyes were huge. Even if she'd been my age, the expression would have looked immature. On an almost forty year old woman, I thought it looked like she was missing a few marbles. "Mom, come out," I ordered her. "Talk to the cops."

She scrambled to obey and came to stand right beside me, her eyes still wide.

"Ms. Hanson," said the first cop. "Do you have any idea who this was?"

She shook her head. "No."

"You sure?" I said. "Who've you been dating recently."

"No one."

"No one – no one or no one you think would do this? Come on, Mom!"

"Could you calm down please?" the cop said.

"No one who would do this. I've been talking to a guy on e-Harmony..."

I rolled my eyes.

The cops exchanged a look. "All right," said the second one. "Tell us all about that."

"He's in North Dakota."

It was all I could do not to grab her by the shoulders and shake her. E-Harmony! Her extramarital affair with my father hadn't worked out, so then she'd jumped into a series of other similar affairs, and now she'd turned to internet dating. Great.

I paced around while the cops examined the house for clues, packaged up the rock (which I doubted they'd bother to fingerprint) and wrote up a report.

I didn't get home again until five.

When I woke up again, it was to my phone ringing. My bedside clock told me it was eleven. I grabbed my phone and cleared my throat a bunch of times before answering, "Hello?"

"Oh, did I wake you up?"

Dang it! My voice had still given me away. "Um..."

"It's Jason."

"Hey."

"I didn't mean to wake you up."

"It's okay. Just had a weird night last night. Someone vandalized my mom's house."

"Oh, really?"

"No big deal. Broken windows. Probably just some kids."

"Wow. That's awful."

"It's Albuquerque. You know." Well, he probably didn't. That kind of thing was less common in the Northeast Heights.

But much to my surprise he said, "Yeah, unfortunately. Someone tagged Steve's house a couple of weeks ago. That was fun, wondering if there was a gang moving their boundaries into his neighborhood. He says nothing else has happened."

"Where's he live?"

"West side. Over by Montano Bridge."

"That's not too dangerous, is it?"

"Like you said, it's Albuquerque. There's a reason they filmed so many episodes of *Cops* there. Anyway, I was just calling to say that I'd be in town next week. You want to meet up?"

"Um, sure."

"Turns out I know the guy who runs the Sandia Tram these days. He says I could get a ride up the first ride – when they take the restaurant staff and visitors center staff and everyone up, before they let on passengers. It'd be really early, but, you want to do that?"

"What time?"

"Six a.m. Really early, but I dunno when sunrise is? The views should be amazing."

It did sound nice. I hadn't been on the tram in years, not since a class trip in middle school.

"If that doesn't appeal," he went on. "My sister's taking over as chef at a restaurant and the family's all going there to celebrate the night before. You're welcome to-"

"Tram sounds nice." Way nicer than meeting all the Vanderholts at a family event.

"All right, cool. I'll call you later this week, then."

"Sure."

"Bye."

"Bye."

I put my phone down on my nightstand and rubbed my temples to clear my head. The air in my room was thick with moisture, I was sure, but I couldn't really smell it because I'd woken up in it. If I left and came back, I'd probably want to crack open the window.

Going up on Sandia Peak at the crack of dawn with a guy sounded romantic. It sounded like a date. Had I just agreed to a date?

On Thursday, I missed Jason's call because I was in class. "Hey," went his voicemail message. "Okay, so... I know this is seriously early, but we should be at the tram at a quarter to six. I can come pick you up if you give me your address. Call me?"

I dialed as I walked across campus towards home. It was a gloriously sunny day with the deep blue sky above and the warm brown, adobe style buildings of campus all around. There was the faint scent of roasting chile in the air, probably from one of the little groceries across Central. They'd have their big wire mesh roasters out, full of chiles, which they'd spin over an open flame. "This is Jason," said a recording. "Sorry I missed you. Leave a message after the beep."

"Hi," I said. "It's Chloe." I tried to think of what to say next. Should I cancel? Say that something had come up? As tempting as that was, it wasn't very nice. Not if he'd already talked to the guy who ran the tram. I'd have been annoyed if someone had done that to me. I couldn't help but wonder, though, had I missed the opportunity to hint that I was not interested in him? Did he mean to tell me, by asking me on this tram ride, that he was single? Or a player? "Why don't I just meet you at the tram?" I said. "I'll see you there at 5:45." And maybe I'd figure out an intelligent way to parse the subtext of this situation before then.

I called Matthew.

"Howdy?" he answered.

"Hey."

"What's wrong?"

"I did something stupid."

"What?"

"I kind of agreed to go on Sandia Tram at the crack of dawn with Jason Vanderholt."

"What?"

"There might be other people there. Or... not."

"Chloe!"

"He called right when I woke up. I'm an idiot."

"What did he say exactly?"

"Just asked if I wanted to hang out. I think he said hang out. I don't remember. It was the tram or dinner with a group at a restaurant-"

"Oh, naw, you're good. He said 'hang out.'"

"I am?"

"I think so. But no blaming me if I'm wrong."

"Would I do that?"

"How does this happen to you? Of all the-"

"I know, I know."

"You want to go to the movies sometime?"

"Yeah. Sure. There something you want to see?"

"Victorian period drama?"

"Okay, I'm game."

"This weekend I've got a ton of homework, but if we go Sunday evening, that'll be my incentive to get it done."

"Works for me."

"Cool. I gotta run to class. I'll see you."

"See you."

Saturday morning, I woke up bright and early and jumped in the shower before my brain could snap into gear. I figured the best way to handle this morning was to just go with it. Odds were, Jason would bring some other people, and I'd be laughing at myself for ever having worried about this being anything but a friendly outing.

7
SANDIA PEAK

The Sandia Tram parking lot had a few cars in it when I pulled up. I got out of my car, wearing a long sleeved shirt, jeans, and sneakers, my warm jacket draped over my arm. It was chilly at the base of the mountain and sure to be frigid at the top. The sky was overcast and shone a light peach, but the sun wasn't quite up yet. The air was so still, that it was almost like being indoors, except for the scent of sage and pine.

A blue Prius pulled up beside my car and Jason hopped out, wearing jeans and a t-shirt, a sweatshirt tied around his neck. "Hey!" he said.

"Hey," I replied.

"Yes! No fans. No photographers. I feel almost normal." He started in the direction of the tram terminal.

I jogged to keep up.

"Sorry," he said. "I know this is stupid. I just feel really exposed out in the open."

"No, it's fine." The terminal was dark and I wondered if the doors would be locked, but no, the first one opened when Jason grabbed the handle. We ducked inside, past the gift shop and up the steps to where the trams left. It was odd to be traipsing through while the lights were off.

At the tram dock, there was a small crowd of people, most of whom were in some kind of work uniform, either for the tram company or the restaurant or the Park Service. Jason waved at one guy who waved back and just called out, "We'll take off in about ten minutes." The tram car was in the dock; it looked like an enclosed ski lift, and some people used it as such, to reach Sandia Ski Area on the other side of the mountain.

"Cool!" said Jason. I noticed he kept his distance. In the dim light, no one seemed to notice who he was.

He turned to me. "So how've you been? How's school?"

"School's good. You?"

"Been doing more press stuff for *Danger Fields*. I was on *Letterman* the other night."

"Oh, I don't watch him."

"You didn't miss much. I made up a story about how hard it was to learn to fire a gun without flinching. You ever seen how some actors do that? They're in a big action movie or something and they fire a gun and flinch?"

I shook my head. "Not into action movies."

"Looks pretty stupid, and I figure if I'm running around shirtless and pretending like I know something about war strategy and how to live in military barracks, I should at least look like I can shoot my fake gun with blanks and totally fake sound effects they put in later, you know? I can only ask so much of the audience."

The tram door opened with a clunk and he fell silent. I watched as he put on some shades and a baseball cap. His whole demeanor shifted from confident and outgoing to quiet. He shuffled his feet and glanced around like he was shy as we made our way to join the others.

We got on with everyone else and he turned to look out the window. The tram had panes of glass that went all the way around, so we had three hundred and sixty degree views.

Everyone craned their necks to get a good look at him. I could tell they knew he'd be there, and they were trying to be polite and leave him alone, but they each had to get an eyeful. It was like they were observing an exotic animal that would take off into the underbrush at any moment. The tram was big enough to hold the twenty, or so, people who were on it, with room to spare. I positioned myself between Jason and the rest and joined him to look out the window, while they shut the door.

The motors buzzed to life and the tram lurched, swayed a moment, then pulled away from its dock. The view, once we were clear, was spectacular. We were hoisted up towards the first tower and got to see the entire city of Albuquerque laid out on the desert plain. The streetlights were still on, and car headlights cruised up and down the tiny streets. A tiny cluster of highrises marked downtown, off in the distance, by the snaking strip of moisture that was the Rio Grande. Not much standing water in it this time of year, and definitely not enough for it to flow.

We went up and up and then the entire car shook as we went over the rollers of the first tower, then we sailed across a shallow mountain valley. A footpath zig-zagged beneath us and something, a coyote or a deer – I couldn't see from this distance – bounded away behind a rock. The twisted wreckage of an airplane lay strewn out across the boulders.

At the second tower, everyone turned to look out the front, and suddenly, we were gazing out across a deep valley. The tram seemed smaller and more fragile as the ground dropped sharply away. The path below shrank to the width of a thread, and another plane wreck lay half hidden in the jagged rock.

The sky was lighter ahead – east was over the Sandia Mountains and the sun hadn't yet peeked over, but it was close. The tram swayed slightly in the breeze as it passed the other tram car going the opposite direction. All the staff waved at it, even though it was empty.

"This the longest tram in the world?" Jason asked. His voice was soft.

"Mmm-hmm, think it still is," I said.

"Been ages since I've been on it."

"Me too."

The tram finished its journey and slowed to slide into its dock at the top. I put on my jacket and Jason put on his sweatshirt before the crew pushed the door open. Sure enough, the air that whooshed in was cold and crisp, like winter.

"Hey," said a guy in a restaurant uniform. "Give us twenty and we'll serve breakfast, okay?"

"That's great." Jason clapped him on the arm.

The guy smiled like he'd been bestowed a great benediction.

"Oh, breakfast?" I said.

"Yeah. Sorry, I should have spelled that out. Did you already eat?"

I shook my head. I'd had my coffee and that usually kept my stomach quiet.

"Just fruit and pancakes and stuff," said Jason. "That good by you?"

"Sure." But I knew I didn't sound sure. Everyone else had let us precede them out from the swaying tram onto the firm decking. Now they all trooped past us to get to their jobs.

Jason and I were definitely the only non-staff, which meant we were basically alone, at the top of Sandia Peak. The sun rose behind us, painting the sky a deep watermelon pink. He was looking at me, his expression uncertain.

"Um... okay," I said, "really stupid question-"

"Is this a date or isn't it?"

"I thought you were dating Corey Cassidy."

"Oh." He shook his head. "No, the hot tub scene was purely professional. Except... I need to not say stuff like that to normal people."

But I laughed, which seemed to make him relax.

"You got a boyfriend?" he said.

"Not exactly. I'm sorry. I'm inept at this kind of stuff." This was not the conversation to have while the sun rose and birds sang and the city beneath us woke up, the streetlights all winking out in a wave that ran from one end of town to the other.

"You? I'm not even remotely ept. Look, I'm sorry if this is awkward. Really. It doesn't have to be anything."

"We're friends?"

"Yeah. Friends is fine."

I nodded. "Sorry to make-"

"No, no. Way less awkward when things are clear, you know? I'm freezing, though. You okay with going inside?" He nodded in the direction of the restaurant.

I couldn't help but smirk at him. "But you're not even in a t-shirt or eating ice."

He laughed. "Wearing a coat between scenes just makes me colder when I have to take it off. I don't suppose I can get you to believe I suffer for my art sometimes?"

"Yeah, I saw the whole red carpet thing. I believe it."

He smiled, his blue eyes sparkling.

We headed inside the wood frame building which also had windows all the way around. It smelled like pine and mountain air even inside. A waiter showed us to a seat by the windows on the east side, where we could watch the sun come up. The cloudy sky cut the glare nicely.

I tried to think of something normal and conversational to say. "So what's your next project?" The table we sat at had a plain white tablecloth and nothing else on it.

"I play a criminal. A murderer. You know, good fun family entertainment." He ran his fingers through his hair. "That shoot starts up in Vancouver in January. Until then, I don't really have anything. Just meetings and interviews and stuff."

"What's the film?"

"No title yet. The working title is *Killer*, which they won't keep. I hope they don't keep it. Research has been interesting."

"Dare I ask?"

He smiled. "Just been talking to cops, profilers."

"That useful at all?"

"Some. You sound doubtful."

"Well, movie villains and real criminals don't have much in common. Movies tend to make them look like heroes." This was one of Matthew's pet peeves, which he ranted about often.

"Yeah, you sound like the cops I've talked to." He gave me an appraising look. "They say stuff like, 'You'd never want to watch a real criminal for two hours. You'd want to lock them up after fifteen minutes, then run.'"

Yep, I thought. "So you don't talk to criminals?"

"I don't know any."

"Well, that's good, right?"

"Yeah." More of those blue eyes sparkling with amusement. "Listen," he said, "you sure you don't want to come to my sister's new restaurant? Tia Anita's?"

"Oh..."

"You heard of it?"

"It's my favorite restaurant."

"Last chance to eat with the old chef in charge. You sure?"

"It sounds really nice, but no thanks."

"It's a non-date, so we're clear. And I'll make sure my family knows."

"I'm sure your family is very nice," I said. "But meeting them, given my family situation, would be weird."

"Well, here's the thing, my parents already know who you are. And they're tactful."

They knew who I was?

"Aaaand, I love my sister and the way she cooks, but she's very individual about it. Very avant garde. The food'll still be good there, but it will definitely be different. Just come."

"When does she take over?"

"Monday. Tonight's the last night with the old chef. Oh, and the restaurant's fully booked. Solid reservations from opening to close."

"Okay, okay, no need to torment," I chided him.

"Am I getting to you? I am, aren't I?"

"You're being cruel."

"I am so terribly *not* sorry. Come with us. My family's cool. You know, Steve's a dork, but-"

"He's nice."

"Well, if you like him, you'll love everyone else."

"Your parents know Dr. Winters *and* know about me?"

"Yeah, I don't know how they found out, but when I said your name to them and that you were kind of related to Chris and Beth, they looked at each other and my dad said, 'We know the rest of the story there.'"

That was strange. Mom hadn't had much contact with Dr. Winters's social circle.

Jason fixed those blue eyes firmly on mine. "They don't care okay? You're an innocent third party, and even if you weren't, it's not like they'd say anything."

I tapped my finger against the tablecloth. "What do they know about Chris and his situation?"

"I don't know. What is his situation?"

"He got into drugs and is now in prison."

"Oh, really?" He looked surprised, but not mortified. "No, they never said anything about that. I think they lost touch with the Winters when I moved to LA. They stopped going to Dr. Winters for their teeth not long after that, and Jen and Steve didn't hang out with Chris or Beth at all. Steve's wife and Beth went to different high schools. Look, am I doing a thorough enough job here? No one's going to care that your father's a cheater and your brother's a junkie. No one. It doesn't matter. Come eat with us."

I put my elbows on the table and my head in my hands.

"Chlo-e," he sing-songed. "You know you want to. It's Tia Anita's."

"You've already been so nice to me-"

"What? So? There a limit on nice between friends? C'mon, it's all cool."

"But you're always doing the nice stuff-"

"Well, okay, look. That's unfortunately how it goes in my life. As much as I'd love to go and hang out with whomever, whenever and do whatever, I can't. I've got to plan ahead and sometimes I need security guards and sometimes it'll have to be six o'clock in the morning. You did something very nice for me, getting up this early. Ever look at it that way?"

That, I had to admit, was smooth. Smoother than I could ever pull off.

"So, you coming tonight?" he asked.

"I..."

"You hesitated! Just say yes."

"Well..."

"Okay?"

I shut my eyes. "Okay," I said.

"All right! You can help defend me against Kyra."

"Who's that?"

"My sister's stepdaughter. She hates me."

"How old?"

"Sixteen."

"There's a sixteen year old girl in America who hates you? Does the media know?"

He thought that was hilarious. "Well," he said, after he caught his breath. "She knows me. Too well."

Our breakfast arrived then. Plates of whole wheat pancakes and fruit. I was pretty sure this wasn't on the restaurant's menu. I tried not to feel too uncomfortable as I ate what Jason piled onto my plate. First class just wasn't my style.

8
THE VANDERHOLTS

Jason's phone went off as we were headed for the tram. The first flight of tourists would depart soon, and we wanted to be in the tram car going the other way. "Uh-huh," said Jason. "Oh." He hung up and frowned at me. "Sooo, I guess there's a crowd at the bottom. Someone must've called someone and word's out that I'm here."

He'd taken the time to go sign autographs for all of the staff on the peak, and although he was gracious about it, there was a strain around his eyes that let me know his heart wasn't really in it. On one hand, it seemed only fair that he take the time, because these people had all done us a big favor, but on the other hand, I couldn't imagine having to spend my life asking for such favors and signing my name on pictures of myself in gratitude. It was so bizarre.

As we stepped onto the tram, he tapped his phone and put it to his ear. "Yeah," he said. "Yep. Really sorry. Thanks." He hung up. "I've got some security guys on their way," he said. "They can escort you to your car too."

"Or I could sneak off and pretend not to know you."

I meant that as a joke, but he nodded. "Yes, if you want to make absolutely sure no one follows you."

I thought about my car with two flat tires. "Do you mind?"

"I don't. I'm just sorry my life is like it is."

If we'd known each other better, I might have put my hand on his arm. As it was, I tried to nod sympathetically.

Jason stared out the front of the tram the entire way down. The city grew larger and larger in front of us, its scum of brown smog dissipated as we descended down into it. He seemed so lonely and isolated, just him silhouetted against the cityscape on the desert plain.

When I got home, Lori was just getting up. "Where have you been?" she asked. She looked me up and down, at me fully dressed with makeup on, my hair windblown.

"Up on Sandia Peak."

"Sandia *Peak?*" She looked at the clock on our microwave. "There some kind of school thing up there?"

"Be honest with me about something?"

"What?" She poured herself some coffee.

"If I went up for a morning ride on the tram with a guy, and I'm meeting his family tonight, am I-"

"Whoa, what?" She nearly dropped her coffee mug.

"Yeah, okay. That answers my question."

"Who?" she called after me.

"No. It's no one."

"Who the heck did you meet and when? Is he cute?"

I ducked into my room for refuge.

"Chloe, come on!"

I stuck my head out. "Lor, please. I screwed up."

"He must've been real smooth. Or real smart or something, to get you in this situation." She laughed.

Her door opened and Charles stepped out. "Hi," he said to me.

"Hi." I retreated back into my room.

I considered canceling on Jason, but again decided I couldn't. Not on the very day. I dressed neutrally in a gray skirt, white blouse, and black flats. My phone rang while I dusted my nose with powder. It was a local number I didn't recognize.

"Hello?"

"Hey, it's Steve. Vanderholt."

"Oh, hi."

"Listen, do you mind if Shan and I drive you tonight? I guess there's a rumor out that Jason's going to be at Tia Anita's, so the parking lot might be especially bad."

Tia Anita's didn't have a big parking lot as it was. "Sure," I said. "I'm on Cornell, between Silver and Lead. You know where-"

"Sure, yeah, I know where that is. What number?"

I gave it to him. "But if you live out by Montano Bridge and we're going to Corrales..." My house was a good half hour to forty minutes out of the way, depending on traffic.

"Oh, my brother's giving out where I live, is he?"

"Well-"

"I'm at UNM right now. I can pick you up when you're ready and I just need to get Shan from her sister's house. That's who's got our kids tonight."

"Okay. Well, I can be ready in ten minutes."

"I'll see you then."

SHANNON and Steve drove a minivan with two car seats in it and crumbs ground into the upholstery seams, which they kept apologizing for. To get to Tia Anita's, we drove parallel to the river until the regular buildings of Albuquerque gave way to the alfalfa fields and farmhouses of Corrales, then turned towards the river onto the little dirt road that led to the restaurant parking lot. As soon as we were close enough to see the restaurant's windows, glowing with honey colored light, we could see the hordes of people that choked the entrance.

"Oh no," said Shannon.

It was worse than it had been this morning, at the base of the tram.

"I just hope they don't mistake me for him," said Steve.

"Mmm-hmm. Sure, honey."

"You hear that?" He turned around in his seat. "My own wife!"

"You're much better looking, my dear."

"Nice one. Very smooth. You taking notes on this, Chloe?"

I rarely met people who were more sarcastic than me. It was great.

"I'm glad you're smiling," said Steve. "We should probably tone down the Vanderholt snark, huh?"

I shook my head. Matthew would have thrown a fit.

He nosed the car through the crowds of people and into a parking space. "This is for cars," he said, as if they could hear him. "Outta the way. Move! This is insane."

"This worse than usual?" I asked.

"Oh yeah," said Shannon. "Or it might be the new usual. But back when he was just the top rated show on Disney, he could go out to dinner in peace."

"It was *New Light* that did this," said Steve. "But *New Light* is over, and it just won't quit. We all thought it would, but he keeps getting more famous. *Danger Fields* broke the record for its opening weekend, and it's still number one."

Shannon's cell phone rang and she answered it. "Side entrance," she said to us.

I hadn't known Tia Anita's had a side entrance, but a short trek through the tall grass on a flagstone path took us there. I also hadn't known Tia Anita's had a private room at the back. The restaurant was in an old farmhouse, or a building built to look like an old farmhouse. I didn't really know the history. Rather than one dining room, it had a series of little ones. This one was the smallest I'd seen, with only one table for about ten people.

The wooden floor creaked under our feet and a chandelier overhead threw little pieces of rainbow prismed light all over the room. Candles guttered on the rough hewn wooden table and the chairs all made heavy scraping sounds as we took our seats. No one else had arrived yet.

A gangly busboy stuck his head in. "Guess you know where you're going," he said.

"How is it, tonight?" Steve asked.

He grinned. "All Chef Armijo told us was that her brother's a public figure. We were expecting the county clerk or something."

Steve and Shannon cracked up.

"Manager's talking to the people in the crowd, asking them to disperse," he went on. "We'll see if it works."

The sound of more hard soled shoes on the floorboards let us know others were coming. Jason strode in first and came straight over to me with a smile and a "Hey!" He was followed by an older couple that I assumed were his parents.

"Lillian," the woman introduced herself to me. She had her son's eyes.

"Doug," said his father. They each shook my hand and smiled.

By the time they took their seats, three more people had arrived. "I'm the mean sister," announced a woman who was very obviously Jason's sister. She had the same eyes, same shade of hair, just slightly paler skin. She was gorgeous. "Name's Jennifer."

"Nice to meet you," I said.

Her husband was quite a bit older than her and had dark hair and eyes and skin the color of coffee mixed with milk. "Kyle Armijo," he introduced himself. "And this is Kyra." That last was directed to a young lady who looked me up and down as if sizing me up for some kind of competition. Her hair was tied back in a ponytail and she wore eyeliner and red lipstick that she probably thought was sophisticated, but made her look even younger than sixteen, like a little girl playing dress up.

"Hi," I said to her.

Her dark eyes narrowed at me and her mouth twitched up at the corners. "*Hi,*" she said.

"Kyra," said her father.

She shot Jason a venomous look.

He didn't react. "Hi, Kyra," was all he said.

With a chorus of scraping chairs, everyone sat down and the servers brought out baskets of sopapillas. Jason reached across the table and deposited one on my plate before passing the basket along. The warm, fluffy pillow bread was still crackling a little from being pulled out of the hot oil. People passed the jar of honey around and I tore off a corner of my sopapilla and spooned a little in. The flakey exterior and warm, sweet honey was heavenly.

"You aren't allowed to change these," Jason said to Jennifer.

"Shut up," she replied. "You get one?" She put a second one on his plate.

"Hey-"

"No advice from you!" She smiled as she said it.

"You see how mean she is to me?" He tore his second sopapilla down the middle and put half on my plate.

"Awwwww," said Kyra, under her breath.

"Kyra," said her father.

Jason was right. This kid really had it in for him. She batted her eyelashes at her father.

Food started to arrive, then. It looked like there would be no menus tonight, either. The family had ordered ahead. Not that I cared. There wasn't anything at this restaurant I didn't love. As it was, I found I had a combo plate with an enchilada, a relleno, and a three taquitos. Way more than I could eat, not even counting the generous sides of Spanish rice and refried beans.

"You want my taquitos?" Jennifer asked her brother.

"No."

She put them on his plate.

One of them ended up on mine. The older Vanderholts asked if it was okay if we said grace, so we all held hands while they did that, then tucked in. I had been away from this restaurant for too long. As I worked through my relleno, I worried that I might, in fact, be able to eat my entire plate.

"So who *are* you?" Kyra asked me.

"Kyra. You aren't too old to have to sit in the car," said her father.

She scowled at him.

"My name's Chloe."

"Are you from here?"

"Yeah. I'm local. I grew up here."

"Which high school?" Kyle asked.

"Rio Grande."

"All right, Rio." He winked at me. "Good school."

"Rio Ghetto," said Kyra under her breath.

"You trying to get sent to the car?" I replied, under my breath. "It that bad, sitting next to me?"

She bit her lip and shrank away, like I'd poked her in the cheek.

"Howabout you?" I asked her.

"The Academy."

That was a private school in the Northeast Heights, and a very, very well funded one at that. "Hey," I said, "then you need to be nice."

"Yes you do," agreed her father.

Kyra slouched down in her seat, picked at her food, and gave up on us. Jason looked over at me as if to ask whether or not she was bothering me. I shook my head.

Everyone else made small talk for the rest of dinner. Kyle asked me about school and told me about the construction company he owned. Given how small Albuqerque was, I knew the name and had seen his trucks around town. I ate half my dinner and had the rest put in a takeaway box. The servers set out goblets of flan for desert. I was so stuffed I couldn't eat more than a few bites, even though it melted to almost nothing on the tongue.

"You can't change this either," Jason told his sister.

"Quiet! No bossing around from you."

"I don't boss you around."

"No, because I usually beat you to it. Now be quiet."

"It's our little competition," said Jason, "to see if we can be the most immature people at the table."

"Shhhh!" Jennifer swatted his arm.

Kyra rolled her eyes. I wondered if this was what she didn't like about Jason, that he brought out her stepmother's silly side. Or maybe she just didn't like her stepmother either. It had to be hard. Jennifer couldn't be more than a dozen years older than Kyra.

After the desserts were cleared away, I excused myself to use the bathroom.

The restrooms had thick walled cubicles, tiled in saltillo tile.

When I stepped out of mine to wash my hands, I found Mrs. Vanderholt, Jason's mother, waiting by the door. I expected her to head into my empty stall, but instead she came to put her hand on my shoulder as I washed my hands in the sink. I looked up at her, surprised.

"Chloe, honey," she said. "I don't know if you know this, but my husband and I used to both work in the DA's office."

It felt like the temperature in the room dropped twenty degrees. So that's how Jason's parents knew who I was.

9
THE DRIVE HOME

Mrs. Vanderholt saw the look on my face and said, "I'm sorry, dear. I didn't mean to put you on the spot."

My throat was dry, so I could feel the walls of it rasping together as I swallowed.

Her expression, though, was all kindness and concern. "We didn't say anything to our kids, if you're worried about that."

"I'm not protected anymore," I whispered. "I don't think? Isn't my name in the public record now?"

"It doesn't matter. We know better than most what it's like to be defined by one thing in your life. We're the parents of Gladius, the hero of *New Light*." Her eyes twinkled.

I let myself smile.

"I really am sorry to put you on the spot. It's just... you look fantastic, honey. Not even a limp."

"Thanks."

"So how are you?"

"I'm good."

"It is just so good to see you." Her eyes were moist. "All grown up, and very beautiful."

I shied away from that remark, but I couldn't turn my head without catching our reflections in the round mirror on the wall in front of us.

She gazed down at me like a proud mother and squeezed my shoulder.

"You know who else has applied to work at the DA's office?"

"No, who?"

"Beth. Your sister."

"You know Beth?"

"We do. Lovely, lovely girl. Finishes her law degree at University of Chicago in the spring."

I realized my hands were still sudsy. I rinsed them off and plucked a paper towel from the stack on the counter. "I don't keep in touch with any of the Winters," I said.

"Well, who does? Your father's moved in with another woman." She said this as if it was a recurring thing. "His wife is... well. She's had it rough, but is still his wife."

I dried my hands slowly and deliberately.

"How is your mother?" she asked.

"Do you know her?"

"No. Which... this is a terrible question. Which one was she?"

"Started out as the student intern, ended up the receptionist."

"Oh. Oh... see I didn't even know-" She shook her head. "Enough about that. Have I embarrassed you too much to go back out again?"

"No, it's fine." I threw the towel away.

Mrs. Vanderholt swept me up into a hug. It came as such a surprise that I nearly tripped, but I managed to hug her back. She smelled like lotion and vanilla. It was a nice combination. "Sorry," she said, when she released me. "Did I tell you I'm happy to see you all grown up and well?" She pushed the door open and motioned for me to precede her out.

Back at the table, everyone was clustered into a loose huddle, conferring. Jason turned as soon as I walked in and came over to me. "Can I drive you home?" he said. "The crowd's dispersed, they tell me."

"Okay." I wasn't sure where Jason was staying, but logic suggested that his parents and sister were in the Northeast Heights. Their children all had gone or went to schools over there. My house wasn't quite on the way, but it wasn't too far out of the way either. Much more convenient than it would be for Steve.

Everyone was moving in the direction of the door. I picked up my take home box of leftovers off the table. "Can I pay for-"

"No," said Jason. "All taken care of. Come on."

"Well, thank you."

He put his hand on my shoulder and guided me out through the side door, then left it there as we walked across the parking lot to his blue Prius. The way looked clear, until three girls stepped out from behind a parked car.

Instinctively, I moved away from him. He took his hand off my shoulder. "Hi," he said.

The girls were high school age, and unable to say anything coherent in reply. Two giggled, one just shook and looked like she was going to cry. It was so strange.

"Having a nice night?" he said. He kept walking. They all turned to stare and continued to giggle. I followed a few paces behind him. As soon as we were past, one of them said, "He looks just like he did in *Danger Fields*."

"I know, isn't he hot?" replied another.

A sniffle let me know that the shaking one had, in fact, started to cry.

Jason glanced back at them, nervously, as we approached his car. He opened the passenger side door for me, then got in the driver's side and started the engine. "Sorry about that," he said.

"That happen to you a lot?" I asked.

He shrugged, non-committally. "Right after a movie comes out is when it's worst. But it won't last forever, you know? Just comes with the territory." He put the car in reverse.

"So, thanks. Really," I said. "Dinner was nice."

"I'm glad you came. Kyra wasn't too mean?"

"She's fine."

"My mother didn't give you the third degree in the bathroom?" We headed out of the parking lot and down the road.

"No. Huh-uh. Why?"

"I did tell her and Dad that you're a friend, but you know, I think they like you, so I'm sorry if she insinuated anything."

"Nope."

"Good. I'm proud of her."

"So, are they both lawyers? Your parents?"

"Mmm-hmm. Like Steve said, it's the family trade. How'd you hear they were lawyers?"

"Your mom."

"When'd she tell you that? In the bathroom?" He gave me an odd look.

"Yeah, I guess Beth's also a lawyer, or will be soon. She was telling me about her."

"Huh, okay. And she didn't make you uncomfortable? Talking about the Winters?"

"Not at all. Your family is all very nice."

"Yeah, I like them. I lucked out in the whole genetic lottery thing. Means I don't have deep childhood traumas to draw on when I act, but I'm cool with that."

I laughed, even though I wasn't sure he meant to be funny.

His grin let me know I wasn't over the line. "I'm glad you met everyone."

Since I'd already said they were nice, I couldn't think of a non-repetitive response. I gazed out the window instead. We'd stayed late, so it was pitch dark. This part of town didn't have streetlights. Beyond the glow of Jason's headlights was just a wall of black.

"Soooo," he said.

"Hmmm?"

"About... yeah..."

I turned to him.

His hand fidgeted on the steering wheel. "Can I just ask something?"

"What?"

"If I say something in the next five minutes that offends you, can I get a take-back? Just, can we erase it from memory?"

"What are you planning to say?"

He glanced at me and then looked right back at the road. I noticed the car was alone. The road stretched off into blackness behind us. "I told everyone you're a friend, but I really want to kiss you good night."

"Oh..."

"Yeah... Can I have a take-back?"

"No, it's fine... it's just... um..."

"Who is he?"

"What?"

"Or, make someone up. It's a male ego thing. Tell me there's someone else."

"I... am going to the movies with my best friend tomorrow."

"Is he better looking than I am?"

"He's not bad. We've been friends for years."

"Oh. No surpassing that, then." He glanced at me. It wasn't a lecherous look, but it was definitely a look.

In fact, it was a rather flattering look.

"Well," he said, "I hope I didn't make you too uncomfortable just now."

"It's fine."

"Fine, like I can keep calling you and we're still friends fine?"

"Yes."

He breathed a sigh of relief. "Okay. Good."

"And I'd be okay with a hug tonight. That sound all right?"

"Yeah." He didn't look at me, just smiled at the road ahead.

Usually, after a conversation like that, I would just cling to the door and count the miles until I was home and able to get out of the car, but this was different. Things really did seem okay between us. I couldn't, for the life of me, imagine kissing Jason, but I could definitely imagine talking to him some more.

When we pulled into my driveway, we both got out and I asked if he wanted to come in.

"Nah, it's late," he said.

"Yeah, okay." Perfect, I thought. I'd only asked him in because it was polite, but it was also past eleven. I held out my arms.

He didn't just hug me. He sort of enfolded me in an embrace. For a few moments I felt the rough stubble of his chin against my cheek, and his very muscular arms around my waist. He smelled like moisturizer, and lots of it. I rubbed his back before letting go. He was such a genuinely nice guy.

With a smile and a shy wave, he got back into his car and was gone.

The next morning I woke up to a knock on my bedroom door. "Chloe!" snapped my housemate. "Care to tell me why there's a picture of you hugging Jason Vanderholt in front of our house on TMZ?"

10

I ROLLED out of bed and yanked open my door. Lori stood there with her hair still up in its messy bun, her laptop in one hand, the screen angled towards me. Sure enough, there it was, a big picture of me and Jason locked in an embrace.

"This is who you had two dates with yesterday?" she said.

"They weren't dates."

"Um, sure they weren't."

I spun around and hunted for some clothes to put on.

"Where are you going?" Lori asked.

"I wanted to go to the library today."

"There are, like, fifty million reporters on our doorstep."

"What?" I turned to her again.

"Okay, more like four, but they're staked out, waiting for you. They keep knocking."

"Oh no..."

"Chloe, you bring a movie star here and engage in PDA, what do you think is going to happen?"

"We are just friends. This is all a misunderstanding."

"Does he think you're just friends?"

"Yes! We talked about it."

"You had a DTR?"

"A what?"

"A Define The Relationship talk? Lemme guess, he was the one who started it?"

"Sure. Something like that."

"And you told him you want to be friends?"

I pushed past her and went into the front room. Sure enough, there were shadows moving across the front windows. The curtains were drawn, so the room was dim. Sitting on our couch, one leg up, was Charles. He had the television on and wore sweats and a v-neck t shirt. Two nights in a row. He and Lori weren't wasting time.

He twisted around to look at me. "Hey. You want me to go out there dressed like this? Say I was here for the night?"

"I don't think that'd make them go away," I said. "I think that'd do the opposite."

He shrugged. "Offer's open."

I made straight for the coffeemaker and poured myself a mug.

"Okay, Chloe, let's talk," said Lori. "Jason Vanderholt wants to go out with you."

"I don't care. How many people on campus are going to recognize me in that picture?"

Lori shrugged. "No one. But some people might recognize the house."

"This is a disaster."

"You don't want people to know-"

"No!"

"Why not?"

"Because why would I? You want people camped out in our front yard all the time?"

"You're being pursued by *Jason Vanderholt*."

"Whom you barely even know. Just lay off, all right? There's more to life than fame and money."

"If you say so."

Charles cleared his throat.

"I mean, right. Totally true," said Lori. "But he's also hot."

"Not to me he isn't. He looks like a Ken doll."

Charles burst out laughing. "That's a good one."

I looked at the clock. It was eight, plenty of time to get started on my homework and be done by mid-afternoon. I downed my hot coffee just as my phone rang.

I tore down the hall to my room to answer it. "Mom" flashed on the display. Oh great.

"Mom," I said.

"Honey?"

"It's all a misunderstanding. I am not involved with Jason Vanderholt."

"That's not you in the picture?"

"It is me, but we're just hugging. He's a friend. That's all. Okay?"

"There's a reporter here-"

"You aren't talking to him are you?"

"Her."

"Send her away. Seriously. Do not give any information about me to the press."

"But she's such a lovely-"

"Put her on the phone now! Or send her away, *now!* How did she even find you?"

"I don't know."

"We don't even have the same last name! How on Earth-"

"Are you okay, honey?"

"No. Get rid of that reporter now and don't talk to any more of them."

"Okay. Okay. One second."

I heard the muffled sound of voices, then my mother saying, "No comment. No comment. You have to leave now." I breathed a sigh of relief. Mom could have a backbone. That was good.

"She's gone, honey. What happened?"

"I hung out with Jason this weekend and hugged him. That's it."

"Were you really out with his family last night?"

"As a friend, Mom."

"The Vanderholts were always so nice. She was so well dressed and her nails-"

"Mom!"

"I used to see them at the office every six months. Even Jason. Did you know that?"

"I could guess, given you worked for their dentist. But keep perspective here. He's a friend. Yes he's famous. No, we don't let the media invade our lives over this."

"Okay."

"Okay?"

"Sure, honey."

"Really? You're okay with that?"

There was a long silence on the phone. When she spoke, it was clear she chose her words carefully. "I do know how to keep quiet about who I'm with and when. I know that's how it is sometimes. Attention can be a bad thing."

I never thought I'd have this in common with her. "Thanks," was all I could manage in response. We said our goodbyes and I then downed another mug of coffee and tried to think of how to pass the time until the paparazzi went away. I still had to write my weekly Media Studies report. That, I figured, would be easy. I got out my netbook, opened a new document, and launched into a diatribe about how many stupid, irrelevant facts people tried to collect on celebrities.

At noon, I got a Skype request. A "jvan3872" wanted to talk to me. "It's Jason" the little text message said. I was skeptical, but I added him and the chime went off, indicating I had a video call. I accepted, but didn't turn on my own video.

"Chlo?" It was Jason. He was sitting on a leather couch somewhere, blank white wall behind him. From the angle of the webcam, I guessed he was talking to me through that sleek, hi-tech phone of his.

My netbook could only just run Skype, and the video was choppy and grainy. I turned around to neaten up my bed a little before I switched my webcam on. "Hi," I said.

"My publicist just called. Told me about TMZ."

"I've got a front yard full of reporters."

"Oh man, I'm sorry." He rubbed his face. "How long?"

"Since at least eight this morning."

"So they're being persistent. They been knocking and ringing the doorbell?"

"Oh yeah."

"I am so sorry. I should've gotten Jen or someone to give you a ride."

"No, it was nice of you to drive me. You didn't do this."

"Not on purpose. Glamorous life I have, huh?"

"Strange life. Why do people care so much?"

"I'm not sure care is the right word. Feel entitled? And I don't know."

"This must be awful for you, to get this all the time."

"It's my career. It comes with the territory. You on the other hand, didn't do anything to ask for this."

"They'll go away eventually, right?"

"Right. Yeah. And how many are there? In Albuquerque, you don't usually get a crowd unless they followed someone big into town."

"Four."

"Yeah, okay... that's kind of a crowd... They'll leave when they figure out you're not going to give them a picture or a soundbyte, or when someone else does something that interests them more."

"What lovely people they are."

"Aren't they, though? You know the type. We all went to high school with them."

I chuckled at that. "I'll just stay indoors then. There's nowhere I have to go."

"Well, that's good, I guess. Anyway, I've gotta hit the gym. I just wanted to call and see if everything was okay, and again, I'm sorry."

I waved that away and we signed off.

By four, our front yard was empty. I stole out to my car and had my key in the lock, when someone said, "Miss?"

I pivoted on my heel and looked towards the house. Standing right next to the wall was a short, blond guy. He had a camera around his neck, which was all I needed to know. I unlocked my car.

"No, I'm not trying to interview you. Can I just tell you something?"

I paused and wondered if that were a ploy.

"You've got some guy driving past your house every hour or so. Goes real slow, looks at your front door. You know what that's about?"

There was no way I'd utter a single word. Who knew how this guy would use anything I said?

"He's in a little sedan. Driver's wearing sunglasses, has a buzz cut. Brown hair. That ring any bells?"

Sure, I thought, brown hair. That's so distinctive. My guess was that this guy was lying to make me talk to him.

"I just wanted to let you know, in case you didn't. It just doesn't look good. But enough about that. I don't suppose you'd let me-" He reached for his camera.

I ducked into my car, slammed the door, and started the engine.

When I saw the guy again in my rearview mirror, it looked to me like he was laughing.

The drive to Matthew's was short. Soon I pulled into a space in his building's parking lot. It didn't look like the photographer had followed me, but I darted across to the stairs anyway. Seconds later I was at the top landing and knocking on Matthew's door.

He tugged it open, a microwaved Evol burrito in his free hand. "Hey," he said to me.

"Hey," I said.

His face fell. "What's wrong?"

"You don't read tabloids do you?"

"Oh no, what? Come in."

His apartment was a studio, a futon in one corner and a television in the other. The kitchen was just a little square of tiled area with some cabinets, a microwave, and a couple of electric burners. The refrigerator had more storage space than the rest of the apartment put together. The whole place smelled like freon and old carpet, and right then, a chicken, cilantro, and lime burrito.

His futon was folded into a couch and his blankets and things were piled at one end.

"Sorry 'bout the mess," he said.

"No, sorry to just barge in."

"You can always come here. I don't mind."

I plopped down on the futon. "You remember that picture of me and Jason in the paper?"

"Yeah." He bit into his burrito.

"Well, now there's another one of us on TMZ. I hugged him and it was a friendly hug, that's all. But they caught it on film."

"What's TMZ?"

"A tabloid website, I guess. I don't really know."

"Oh, okay. You hungry?"

"No thanks. I just came here to hide, really."

"How was the tram?"

"It was a nice non-date, and then I did meet his family last night. Turns out his parents know all about me and are really cool about it."

"Met his family, huh?"

"He was crystal clear. Non-date."

"But then he did get you to hug him."

"Aw, you want a hug? That what this is about?" I winced. Matthew hated sarcasm.

But this time he tossed his burrito wrapper in the trash and wiped his hands on the kitchen towel. "Maybe," he said.

My phone rang.

"Hello?" I answered it.

"Okay," said Lori. "Someone just busted our front windows."

11

SKYPE CALLS

I don't know what made me angrier, the property damage, or the fact that I missed the chance to go to the movies with Matthew because I had to be home to answer questions for the police. Matthew came over too, and he and Charles watched WWF so that Matthew would have something to write about for Media Studies. In hindsight, that's pretty funny, but at the time I was too annoyed to laugh.

"So you had reporters in your yard all day and one of them warned you about a suspicious vehicle?" the cop asked. She was a young woman with red hair pulled up into a bun and freckles all over her face.

"Yeah," I said.

"Driving slowly past your house?"

"Yep."

"Any idea whom that would be?"

"No, no idea."

"Any guess?"

"Nope."

"Have you fought with anyone recently, or seen anything-"

"I hugged Jason Vanderholt-"

"Really?"

"He is a *friend*. But once, after we had coffee, someone slashed my tires."

"So you think this is a jealous fan?" said the cop.

"Given the timing, yes."

"I'm concerned about that car, though. This is near the War Zone here, where you live." The War Zone was a bad neighborhood many blocks away that was dominated by drug violence.

"It's not that close," I said.

"And this, the University Area, can be very unsafe."

"We've never had any problems," said Lori. "No one on this street has, that we know of."

"Miss Winters, do you, or have you ever had any contact with anyone in the drug trade who might hold a grudge?"

Yes, but he's in prison, I thought. I shook my head. "I'm pretty sure this is a fan. Some girl who wants to marry Jason Vanderholt and thinks that I'm competition or something."

"You really know him?" asked the cop.

I rolled my eyes. "He's from Albuquerque. People know him. It's no big deal."

"Still-"

The look on my face must've silenced her, because she turned back to her notes real fast. "Okay, I'm going to write this up, and has your landlord called back yet?"

"She'll be here in ten minutes," said Lori.

"We can wait for her, then."

I looked at our front windows. One had a fist sized hole in it. The other just had a big spiderweb of cracks. The police had put one rock, the one found inside the house, on the windowsill. There was no telling what rock had made the other break. It was with the hundreds of others in our rock garden.

Lori put her head to one side. "What's that sound?"

It was my computer chiming. I darted down the hall and saw that Jason was calling again. "Hey," I answered.

"Hey, reporters go away?"

"Yeah, and now someone's broken our windows."

"*What?*"

"Some jealous fan-"

"You're kidding me."

"No."

"You're sure it was a fan?"

I told him about my tires and his eyes only got bigger. "Chloe! I had no idea. *No* idea this was happening to you."

"It's only happened twice."

"That's terrible. I'm paying for the windows."

"There's insurance-"

"I am at least talking to your landlord. What's his number?"

"Hers. Not necessary."

"No, listen, I don't want you to get in trouble for associating with me. I'd hate it if you got evicted or something because one of my fans is breaking her property. You have to let me talk to her. What's her number?"

"She'll be here in a few minutes."

"Even better. Let me talk to her on Skype."

"Chloe?" Lori called from the front room. "Eli's here."

"That's our landlord," I said.

"Carry me out."

"You don't-"

"Do it. Please?" His eyes were narrowed, his expression was all stubborn resolve.

I gave in, picked up the netbook, and carried it out to the front room. Eli blinked at me from behind her thick, round glasses. Her graying hair was piled on top of her head. She was a dance instructor who lived in Nob Hill. I held the netbook screen up to her. "Eli, Jason, Jason, Eli."

"Jason Vanderholt?" said the cop.

Lori stuffed her hand in her mouth to suppress a giggle.

"Here," I handed the netbook over.

"Please let me pay for the windows," I heard Jason begin.

I turned my back on that conversation and went to sit by Matthew.

"He called you?" Matthew moved over to make room for me.

"He called about the tabloid stuff today. Normally, he doesn't call."

He slipped an arm around my shoulders. I leaned against him. "Thank you," I said.

"For?"

"Being you. I needed a good friend today."

That evening, after the cops had left and Eli had nailed plywood over the broken window, someone else knocked on the door. I was eating my leftovers from Tia Anita's.

Lori was gone. She and Charles had taken off for the evening, and I couldn't blame them. I peered through the peephole to see a Hispanic man in plain clothes who looked vaguely familiar. I opened the door.

"Miss Chloe," he said. "Jesse Baca. Officer Baca." He stuck out his hand.

"Oh, hi." He was the cop who'd written up the report on my slashed tires.

"I heard about what happened here."

"Yeah, I think we're okay. Just-"

"I wanted to let you know, you're gonna be safe. We'll be patrolling your street for the next little while, all right?"

"Thank you. You don't have to-"

"It's been ten years, but I won't ever forget that phone call when we heard you were gonna pull through. It was a miracle, the shape you were in." He patted my shoulder. My right shoulder. "You're going to be all right, you hear? Can't help it if a pretty girl like you is attracting movie stars. And two incidents this far apart? That's not good."

"That is going above and beyond, really."

His smile was fatherly and kind. He gave my shoulder another squeeze and stepped down off our front step. Sometimes it paid to be from a city that was such a small town in so many ways. Even though I hadn't admitted it to him, I would definitely sleep easier knowing that some crazed fangirl wasn't going to climb in my window and take me hostage.

Jason had seemed able to sweet talk Eli into being sanguine about all this. I was grateful for that too.

"Any more break in attempts?"

"No. The windows are fixed. It's all good."

"Your landlady wouldn't let me pay."

"I'm sure she's got insurance, but thanks for offering."

"So you're okay?"

"I'm fine, really."

"I really am sorry. The whole fame thing can be pretty stupid."

"Well, you said it."

"And you don't disagree. That's refreshing."

"So it doesn't look like there's any more media coverage of you. No wild rumors about you carrying my love child. All good."

"I'm so relieved."

"Had enough Hollywood glamour in your life?"

"To last several lifetimes, yeah."

"How's Matthew?"

"Huh? He's fine, I think. I still owe him a movie sometime."

"He around a lot?"

"Yeah, he doesn't live all that far. Walks past our house on the way to campus."

"Oh, okay."

"How are you tonight, Chloe?"

"I'm good. You?"

"I'm eating celery, and I keep wanting to offer you some, but I don't think I can find a way to stuff it through the internet."

"I'm not hungry, thanks."

"What's that you're working on?"

"Drawing diagrams to understand how the Golgi apparatus works."

"Oh, that thingy in cells where proteins get assembled? Is it proteins?"

"Don't you start quizzing me too."

"Sorry."

"Yeah, you sound really sorry."

"You usually work until after dark?"

"Three nights a week, yeah. Matthew walks me home, though."

"Seems extra nice of him."

"He's Texan. Very chivalrous."

"Oh, okay."

"You seem very interested in Matthew."

"I've never had a female best friend."

"Well, you've got me. I'm a friend."

"True..."

"I've talked to you twice this week. I think that's way friendly."

"Yeah."

"No more vandalism on your house?"

"Nope. There was a cop car cruising the neighborhood pretty regularly for a while. They're being vigilant."

"Really? I'd think your incident was pretty minor compared with other stuff they deal with."

"Yeah, I think that's true. But this one they nipped in the bud, it looks like. Seems to be working."

"That's great. I'm relieved."

"I need to go. Matthew's coming by any minute."

"Oh, right. Talk to you later, then."

A month after the window break, Matthew and I were seated on the floor of the living room with printouts of web pages strewn all around us.

"I'm not even sure what I'm looking for," I said. "Themes in the types of web searches I do when not studying? I don't hardly do any."

"You search news stories. You think you have it hard? I don't even have internet at home." He reached for my netbook. "May I?"

I handed it over and turned back to my mess of papers. Matthew was right, I did search news stories. Usually crime ones. I didn't want to talk about that to my Media Studies professor. I liked the guy – on my paparazzi report he'd written, "Mind if I share this with the class? Just kidding!" - but that didn't mean I wanted to open a vein and pour out my heart in a class I only took for the company.

Matthew was clicking away on my computer.

I reshuffled my printouts, then gathered them all together and tried to sort through them again.

A few more minutes and a few more clicks and Matthew hadn't said a word.

"You find what you need?" I asked.

"Um..."

"Hmm?"

"How often, exactly, do you talk to Vanderholt?"

"I don't know. He calls whenever. He's very chatty."

"He calls you every other day, Chlo."

"Well, I don't answer all those."

"Okay, he calls you every day. Every other day is about how often you answer."

"What are you looking at?" I looked up at him.
"Your Skype call log."
"Why?"
"Because... Sorry. You're right. This is none of my business."
"I've been stupid again, haven't I? I'm totally not picking up on his signals and being more than friendly."
"I dunno."
"Just be honest."
"You don't talk to me that often."
"What?" Before I could catch myself, I laughed.
Matthew got very quiet.
"Wait... what?" I said. "Am I missing something? Because that whole myth about females being able to read minds? We can't."
"He bothers me."
"Jason?"
"Yeah. He's too forward with you." Matthew leaned back against the couch and rested his hands on his bent knee.
"What do you think might happen?"
"He's trying to charm you."
"Maybe, but it isn't working."
"So why do you talk to him so much?"
"I dunno. Now that you point it out, I'll cut back. You're right. It's probably giving him the wrong idea. I just never thought someone like him would want to get any ideas about me, you know?"
"Why not? Don't insult yourself, Chloe."
"Because it's random. I'm not insulting myself. I seriously doubt I'm the only girl he tries to charm, though. He's got to have how many fawning over him?"
Matthew nodded. "Yeah, that's smart that you know that."
"Why thank you. Okay! Sorry, that was irony and I know you hate that. Lowest form of humor and all that."
"Well, I guess I was patronizing, so I deserved it."
I nudged him with my elbow. "Thank you for looking out for me."
"Yeah... sure."
He wanted to say something else, that was obvious, but I didn't quite know what. Despite how close we were as friends, Matthew could be quite shy and reserved. I didn't push the issue, but I did steal a lot of

glances at him that evening. He was seriously cute. And he was my best friend. I purposely didn't follow those thoughts too far, in case I was misreading.

But I did note that he was the opposite of my ex-boyfriend, Jon. Jon was popular and outgoing, and Matthew was quiet and introverted. Jon was on track to make good money, while Matthew dreamed of becoming a high school English teacher in a small town somewhere. Jon was several years older than me, but Matthew was my age. Matthew wasn't anything like any guy I'd ever been interested in before. Not a bad thing.

The following Friday, Matthew went home for the long weekend. I was at work, wiping down the counter when someone slid their purse right into the path of my cloth. It was a nice leather purse too, not something I'd want to risk getting bleach on. I looked up.

The woman who looked back at me had my face, or close enough. Same heart shape, except she didn't have a cleft in her chin. Same big brown eyes, same thin lips. "Beth?" I said.

She glanced around. It was clear she wanted to be anywhere but here, with me. "Chloe," she said, "you know that Chris got paroled, right?"

12
CHRIS

It took me a moment to process what Beth had just said. Chris was paroled? He was out of jail? A shiver went through me. Calm, I told myself. Who cares? It's not like he's going to bother you now.

"Okay. Thanks. For telling me."

More fidgeting. Beth ran her fingers through her hair and flipped it back from her face. "Lillian told me someone vandalized your house and your car."

"Lillian?"

"Vanderholt."

"You talk to her?"

"She called to say she'd seen you."

"She did?" Why? That wasn't a good idea.

"You know how to get a restraining order?"

"Against Jason's fans?"

"I don't know that it was Jason's fans. Chris has been cruising your mother's house. Maybe he found yours. He still blames you, you know, for ruining his life. Dad's got him at his house right now. I talked him into taking away the car, but I don't know how strict Dad is about that."

My head spun as I processed this. He'd hit my mother's house? I'd assumed her broken windows had to do with her e-Harmony habit, or the fact that she lived in not the greatest neighborhood.

But Beth saw the stricken look on my face and picked up her purse. "I can't help you any more with this, okay? Don't tell anyone I came here. Please. My family's been through enough..." She gave me another nervous glance. "I know that sounds selfish."

"I won't tell."

"I'd better go." She slung her purse over her shoulder and clip-clopped her way out of the restaurant without a backwards glance.

Those were more words than I'd ever exchanged with her in my entire life.

The next day was the beginning of Labor Day Weekend, which meant the District Court was closed. According to their website, that was where I ought to go to pick up information on how to file a restraining order.

Skype rang while I surfed. I right clicked the icon and shut it off. Then I went into the program's settings, and switched it so that it wouldn't be on every time I booted up my computer. I needed to not give Jason so much attention. As nice as he was, he wasn't that good of a friend.

First thing Tuesday morning, I was at the District Court, with its arching, blue roof high overhead. The day was overcast, so the broad expanse of concrete in front of the doors wasn't quite frying pan hot. As soon as I stepped in the glass doors, I had to go through security, just like I was getting on an airplane. I put my purse on the conveyor and took off my shoes. I still set off the alarm so I had to take off my belt and my earrings too. That thing was sensitive.

It took me five minutes to dress myself again on the other side. "Where do I go to find out about restraining orders?" I asked the uniformed guard.

"How to file one?"

"Yeah."

"I think you talk to the clerk." He pointed across the rotunda to a low doorway.

"Thanks," I said. The front lobby of the court had a ceiling clear up at the top of the building, which drew the eye up and up. Curved staircases invited people to climb them towards whatever lofty things happened in the chambers there.

The way to the clerk's office felt like going down a little rabbit burrow. I joined a line of people wearing polo shirts with law firm logos on the breast and waited for a clerk. They were all behind glass windows, like bank tellers. When I finally got one, I told him what I wanted. He scratched his nose, handed me a stapled packet, and said, "You need anything else?"

"I don't know."

"Well, get in line again if you do."

I took the hint and moved off to one side. The packet instructed me on how to fill out the enclosed paperwork and file it with the court. It was a fill in the blank sort of form, where I put in who I was, Chris's name, what had happened, and why I wanted a restraining order.

This seemed simple enough, but I knew at once that it wasn't simple at all. This was what people without lawyers used. Chris, if he was still his father's son, would have a lawyer. I couldn't just fill this in with a pen and expect to win against the reams of professionally typed documents that would be filed in response.

Think, I told myself. How would I make this professional looking? Well, I would first need to cite the court case that had put Chris in jail. I had no idea how to find it. I assumed my name wasn't confidential anymore, since I wasn't a minor, but I really knew nothing.

Last time I'd faced Chris in court, the DA had been on my side. This time I needed to at least find a non-profit attorney. The line for the clerks was long, though, and snaked out the door. My car was being charged by the half hour in the lot across the street. I decided to head home and try an internet search. But first, I had class.

That evening I typed "Legal Aid" into Google and found that the New Mexico office dealt mostly with housing issues. I didn't think vandalism was what they had in mind. I wracked my brain for other ideas. "Non-profit lawyer" yielded a bunch of names, but how would I know if any of them were good?

My gaze slid to the Skype icon in the lower right hand corner of my screen. It'd been a week. Maybe if I logged in, Jason would call.

And then what would I do? He wouldn't want to be dragged into all this. The person I really wanted to talk to was his mother, but I didn't really know her. Steve's name sprang to mind, but I didn't really know him either.

But Beth's visit had set my heart racing. The very idea of Chris out of jail was enough to make me break into a cold sweat.

I launched Skype and logged in. Jason was online, and his call came at once. I blinked in surprise.

"Not to be rude," I answered, "but don't you have a life? You can't possibly be watching Skype all day." The video resolved itself into an image of him sitting in his kitchen chewing on what looked like a carrot. From the angle of the video, I surmised he was on his laptop this time.

He smiled at my comment. "Nope, no life. I just work out and work on my tan. I take it you're busy?"

"Actually, I was just going to try to call you."

"Oh yeah?"

"Yeah. Do you have a minute?"

He sighed. "I *guess* so. Though I'm afraid this tan might flake." He rubbed his arm. "What's up?"

"Well..."

Those blue eyes searched my face. He put his carrot down.

"It's a long story."

"I do actually have time, if you need."

"And a very personal one."

"Okay."

"Except your parents already know it."

"My parents?"

I buried my face in my hands a moment. "Okay, so... ten years ago, I'm the one who sent Chris to prison."

He blinked. "For drugs?"

"For what he did while on drugs."

"What did he do?"

I fiddled with my pen. "Got into a steroid rage and attacked me."

"Ten years ago, you were a little kid."

"Yeah."

"This isn't why you've got a gunshot scar on your leg, is it?"

"You recognize that, do you?"

"Holy..." He sat back. "I had no idea. *No* idea."

"Well, my name was kept out of the public record. I was only eleven, you know. But if your parents worked for the DA, they would have known it. And if they know the Winters…"

"They never breathed a word. This wasn't when Chris was in high school was it?"

I shook my head. "After he dropped out."

"Oh, I didn't know he dropped out. I guess that's why Jen and Steve don't know anything about this. So, you said Chris was in prison. He's not anymore?"

"I've just learned. And I think him getting out might have something to do with the broken windows on my house."

"But I thought that was a fan."

"Me too, but the thing is, my mom's windows also got broken. I didn't connect the two incidents because she was conducting a relationship on the internet and I just kind of jumped to a conclusion there. But one of the reporters who was at my house said he saw a guy cruising past. I didn't think anything of it because… you know, it's been ten years and I thought Chris was still put away and this guy was a reporter who wanted me to talk about you."

"You really think your brother would come after you again?"

"Well. Yeah. Beth came to warn me. She came to visit me at work – though I don't think she wants people to know about that."

"Who was the pap?"

"Huh?"

"The photographer. I wonder if he took a pic."

"I don't know. Short blond guy."

"I'll get Dave on it. I can't believe I used to hang out with Chris. You must think I'm the shallowest-"

"Well, I assume you never got involved with his drug binges or anything like that."

"No. Nope. I don't do stuff like that. Never have."

"So, listen, I want to get a restraining order against him, but I'm in over my head here, and I can't afford a lawyer so-"

"I'll call my parents, if that's okay?"

"Do you think they can recommend someone?"

"Yeah, much better than I can. I know nothing about this kind of stuff."

"*Thank* you."

"For what? Being related to my parents? I didn't have any choice about that."

"For talking to them for me."

"Well, of course. Gimme a minute here." He cut the connection.

Fifteen minutes later, my cellphone rang. A 505 number I didn't know flashed on the display.

"Hello?" I answered it.

"Chloe?"

"Yeah."

"Doug Vanderholt."

"Oh, thank you for calling."

"Steve and I are going to help you out with this, okay?"

"Sorry? Wait I-"

"Listen to me. I happen to know that if you take Chris to court, you'll be up against Gloria Garcia, and she's the very best criminal defense attorney in the state, so you can't do this with a nonprofit lawyer. No offense to them, but Gloria and the Winters with their money would run circles around you. Nonprofit lawyers have heavy caseloads and limited resources, and no amount of talent quite compensates."

"But-"

"The State Bar requires me to do a certain number of pro bono hours a year. I don't have mine yet. Steve wants some clinical experience while he's in law school. That kind of thing is invaluable and would give him a real edge when he applies for jobs. Please. We'd consider it a personal favor if you'd let us do this."

Typical Vanderholt logic, let us give you stuff worth more than you can afford and we'll thank you for it. Now I could see where Jason got it from.

This wasn't a predawn tram ride, though, or a catered dinner at Tia Anita's, or free tickets to a movie premiere. Lawyers made hundreds of dollars an hour. Just the time it would take to do the hearing would empty my checking account. My savings would drain down fast in the time it took to prepare the documents. What Mr. Vanderholt was offering basically amounted to a the value of my car, and then some.

"Take your time," he said. "Think it over, but please understand, this is a very serious offer."

"I appreciate it-"

"Did my number show up on your phone?"

"Yeah."

"Save it, and call me back whenever you're ready, okay?"

"Thank you."

"Chloe, you've overcome way too much to let this creep jeopardize your safety. You don't deserve to ever have to even look at him again. If someone did something like that to one of my kids, I don't think he'd even be alive. You call me back, okay?"

"Right, okay."

"Take care now." He hung up.

THAT night, as I drifted off to sleep, I caught a whiff of dry, desert air. Not the kind that we got in the city, the really scorching stuff that blew around the open desert. In an instant my throat was parched, my eyes burned, my shoulder felt like it was seeping blood. A loud *pop* jolted me awake, and I was back in my bed, the soft sheets pressed to my cheek. A tear slid from the corner of my eye, leaving a little trail of wet.

I couldn't face this. Not alone.

I got up and dialed the police department's non-emergency number on my cell phone.

"Hello?"

"Hi, can you tell me how to reach Officer Baca? Jesse Baca?"

"Are you in danger?"

"No, I don't need to talk to him now. Is there a department phone list or something I can get?"

"I'll pass on a message to him. Give me your name and number."

I did, then thanked her and hung up.

Five minutes later, much to my surprise, my phone rang.

"Hello?"

"Hi." It was the woman I'd just spoken to. "He's on patrol and he's going to stop by your house, okay?"

"Oh, okay, thanks."

"Bye now."

I threw on some sweats and a t-shirt, went to the front room, switched on the porch light, and sat and watched out the windows, already dusty and dirty, despite being new. Within ten minutes, a police cruiser came around the corner, its headlights criss-crossed with the push bumper and all the other equipment it had mounted on the front.

It slowed in front of my house. I put on my shoes and went out to the curb to meet it. It already had one window down. "You all right there, Miss Chloe?" It was Officer Baca's voice.

"Yeah, I just wanted to ask you something." I peered into the dark cab. "I just heard that my brother, the guy who shot me? He's out of jail. He might have vandalized the house."

"He's out?"

"Yeah."

"Get a restraining order."

"You think I should?"

"And if you can, move house. If he's breaking your windows, that's no good."

"Okay."

"Let me call some people at corrections. They have Victim Services... I may have the number for that here somewhere." I heard him rustle around in the cab.

"That all I can do? Get a restraining order and run away?"

"You've already been the hero. This isn't your fight. You stay well away from it and let us do our job. Here." He handed me a business card. "They'll tell you his incarceration and parole status. But you get a restraining order right now."

"Will that help?"

"It won't stop him coming to bother you, but it'll give me the right to throw his butt in jail the moment he does. Also, anything you dig up to support a restraining order, I want to see it. Maybe there'll be some parole violations there we can use to get him back in jail before he bothers you again."

"Do I need a lawyer? He's got Gloria Garcia."

Officer Baca cursed. "That's not good."

"Do you know Doug Vanderholt?"

"Nope. Vanderholt... wait... DA's Office? Yeah, sure, heard of him. Or was it a her?"

"They're a married couple."

"DA's Office beats Gloria sometimes, but she's hard. She don't lose often. You want the best attorney you can get, all right?"

"Okay."

"Meanwhile, I'll keep watching your house. I'm on duty all night."

"You don't have to-"

"I haven't been around lately. I assumed it was an isolated incident, but if some guy's still mad at you after ten years, that's really not good."

I shivered. "Thank you for helping me."

"I hear you're on track to be valedictorian?"

"Yeah... looks like it." Seemed like an odd change of subject.

When he spoke again, his voice was thick with emotion. "Good for you. Couldn't be prouder if you were my own. No one's gonna stop you walking across that stage, you hear me? Now get some sleep."

13
DIGGING UP THE PAST

Steve and Doug Vanderholt met me at the District Court two days later. I still felt consumed with guilt. I felt like I should at least bake cookies for them, but I wasn't sure if that was an insult. I couldn't make thousand dollar cookies.

I followed the two of them, both in their suits, through security and back to the clerks' windows. Ten minutes later we were in a little room with a wooden table, a small bowl of paper clips, and manila folder stuffed to bursting. We sat on rickety plastic chairs that creaked every time we so much as breathed, or so it seemed.

"Your original case," said Mr. Vanderholt, who insisted I call him Doug. He patted the manila folder. "Is it okay if Steve reads this?"

"Of course."

Steve flipped it open and started to skim. His eyes went wide and he blinked a few times and he started over again from the beginning. This time he took his time and read.

"It's not a pretty case, son," said Doug.

"I'll say." He flipped a couple of pages, read some more, then flipped the entire stack of papers and read the very last one. "They sued for attempted murder. How did they not get it?"

"She healed too fast," said Doug. "And the Winters paid a king's ransom on attorneys."

"Was there ever a civil suit? For damages?"

"Chris doesn't have any money or assets of his own, I'm guessing," said Doug.

"This why we stopped getting our teeth done by Dr. Winters?"

"No, we stopped going there when I learned Dr. Winters ran around on his wife. Found it hard to look him in the eye after that."

"Whoa, wait." Steve reread something, then covered his eyes for a moment. "Sorry. Chloe, I had no idea."

"Good," I said. "I don't want to be known as the girl who went through this for the rest of my life."

"I hear that."

Doug clasped me on the shoulder. "Thank you for letting us do this."

"Thank *me*?"

"When you have kids," said Steve, "you will totally understand. I can't read this and not work on your case, Chlo."

"Exactly."

I thought back to my mother's reaction. She'd cried a lot, but she hadn't tried to do anything about it. In fact, she'd just gotten drunk for a week. Whenever we talked about it, in the very rare instances when we did, she just got all wide eyed, like she'd been the night her house got vandalized. It was as if all of this had happened to her, not me, and that still burned me up inside.

"Okay, kidnapping-" Steve jotted this down on his notebook "-assault with a deadly weapon, battery, reckless endangerment of a minor... and we add in the fact that it's been ten years and there is evidence that he's still taking an interest in her."

"Right, good," said Doug.

The two were on a roll, and I'd been right, I had no idea what I was doing when it came to writing up the documents I'd need.

"I FEEL guilty," I told Jason that evening over Skype. "They're doing so much for me." I was sitting on the floor of the front room with my notebook and a biology textbook open in front of me.

"Chloe, when I told my dad Chris was out of jail, he swore. He never swears. Ever. This is my dad really angry: 'Son, I am very disappointed in you. I would like you to take a moment and think very hard about what you've done wrong.'" Jason tapped the table in front of him like a patient kindergarten teacher. "If I'd wrecked his brand new car, that's the lecture I'd get. Not that I... let's not talk about that."

I smirked at him and carried on drawing my diagram of a cell membrane.

"Matthew know about this?"

"No. He's been in Texas over the weekend and into this week and I don't want to have this conversation over the phone."

"Lori?"

"I told her enough to convince her to stay with Charles for the next little while, but she's going to want to know details eventually."

"That's gotta be rough."

"I'm just lucky your family already knew. And are amazingly, incredibly charitable."

"Yeah, they're nice, but my dad's not lying about needing pro bono hours. It's required for the bar. And hey, you gave them free coffee today."

"Because coffee is all they would order!"

"Let people be nice to you. Someday you'll be out solving cases and saving lives and putting bad guys behind bars. The karma will more than even out."

"But-"

Someone knocked on the front door.

"One sec," I said. I got up and opened it. Matthew stood on the doorstep, a sheaf of papers in one hand. "Matthew! Hey!" I hugged him.

"You got a moment?"

"Yeah, sure, come in."

"I'll call back later," said Jason from my netbook.

"That Jason?" said Matthew.

"Yeah, he and I were talking about-"

Matthew went around to my netbook, knelt down, and held out the sheaf of papers.

"Am I being served?" Jason asked. "You must be Matthew. Chloe talks about you all the time."

Matthew took a few deep breaths. His knuckles were white and his mouth pressed into a thin, firm line.

It was a moment before I figured out he was angry. I'd seen him upset before, but this was something more extreme.

"I should go," said Jason.

"We had an internet assignment, for Media Studies," said Matthew.

"You talking to me or her?"

"I decided to do some searching on the web, for stuff about you."

"Who?" I asked. "Me or him?"

"That'd be *whom-*" Matthew was a bit of a stickler for grammar "-and I'm talking about him. You'll want to read this, Chloe."

"I can't imagine I'd care."

"Ye-ah. Anything you want to talk about, Chlo," said Jason, "we can. You can ask anything."

"Like the all night sex party you held at your house?"

"Stuff like that. Right. I am going to hang up now, okay?" The sound of the line cutting out whistled from my netbook.

"Matthew?" I said. I'd never heard him raise his voice or accuse anyone of anything. He was the quietest, most withdrawn guy I knew.

"That's only the beginning."

"Okay."

"He's a scumbag. If you got involved with him-"

"What? Wait a minute. I am not interested in anything like that."

"After you read this, you won't even want to talk to the guy. He's a user. Him calling you all the time? It's probably just a game to him, to see if he can put another notch in his belt."

I sat down on the couch. "Some stuff happened this weekend. He's being the opposite of a user right now. I owe him – not that I'll put myself at risk of... you know... whatever's in there." I nodded at the stack of papers.

"He got sued for statutory rape. You got many other friends who can say that?"

"You know the press isn't always accurate."

"Yeah, check my research."

"Okay. Can I tell you about this weekend? Because I really need to tell someone."

"Yeah." Matthew put the papers down. "Of course." He turned to me.

I related the whole story, beginning with Beth's visit and ending with Doug and Steve gathering evidence for a restraining order. "I need to tell Lori more details. I need to move house. I've waited too long as it is."

"What did your brother do to you ten years ago?"

"Um, he shot me a few times..."

"Go stay with someone, now. Tonight. You're right, you shouldn't be here."

"It would put whoever I stayed with in danger."

"Whomever. You think he'd find you?"

"I have a rather distinctive car."

"Oh, right. So stay with someone who doesn't live in the area. I'll drive you to school if you want."

"I hate having to rely on other people for help with my problems."

"Chloe, I don't see how any of this could possibly be your fault. You have a psycho relative. No one's going to blame you."

"I guess I could ask Val if I could stay at her place." Val was an archeology graduate student I'd done some work for. She lived clear out in the Four Hills area and was doing her fieldwork right now, so her apartment was empty.

"You do that." He handed me the sheaf of papers. "Take these. And read them. And by the way, it's good to see you again."

"You too."

He slipped his arms around me for another hug.

I hugged back and tried to gauge whether this was a friendly hug or something more.

But he let go of me before I could decide. "I gotta go run some errands. I'll call you later?"

"Yeah, okay."

I MANAGED to reach Val on Skype and she told me I could of course stay in her apartment and gave me her housesitter's phone number. While I waited for the housesitter to call me back, I read the sheaf of papers that Matthew had left. I reminded myself that Jason liked to lie in his interviews.

But these weren't interviews. The article on statutory rape was testimony by a woman who said this had happened to her friend, and that Jason had paid her friend a quarter of a million dollars to keep her mouth shut. The website this was from wasn't a tabloid, it was a mainstream news outlet.

The interview with Donovan Reilly wasn't about Jason at all. His comment about Jason's "after hours activities" was an aside, a corollary to the story went on to tell about why no one else from the cast ever hung out with him much while they shot the first *New Light*.

The all night sex party was out of a police report that they'd broken up a party at his house and arrested four people for indecent exposure. Jason, apparently, was so drunk he couldn't even stand up to take a breathalyzer test.

And then there was story after story of Jason out partying at all hours and leaving clubs with one or more women in tow. There was a complaint from the director of *New Light* that Jason's wild ways interfered with the movie shoot. There were pictures of Jason with scantily clad women getting in and out of his car. It looked like he drove a gray Prius in LA. There were dozens of pictures like this.

My netbook rang. Jason. I wasn't sure I wanted to answer.

But I did. "Hi."

Jason looked at me, and at the papers I held, then at me again. "Hi."

"So... yeah. I told Matthew about Chris and-"

"That really what you want to talk about?"

"Um..."

"Well, I guess I'd rather not talk about *that*-" he nodded to the papers I held "-over Skype. But I do want to talk about it. Tell you my side of things."

"Are any of these true?"

"I'm not sure what you've got there."

I dropped my papers. "Okay, you know what? Never mind."

"Chloe, I don't know what you think of me right now, but it can't be good."

"I'm not interested in you as anything more than a friend, so I don't really care about this stuff."

"Okay."

"Except the rape case."

"I can tell you everything, but I'd rather do it in person."

That meant it was true. There was no way I wanted to meet up in person to discuss it.

"Sorry," I said. "I should go."

"Sure. Right." He didn't move as I cut the connection.

14
THE HEARING

Steve and I met up again in the UNM law library the following day, and continued to work off the outline he'd drafted under his father's supervision.

"You don't have to do this," I said to him. "I can try to look up statutes and-"

He shook his head. "I need to know how to do this stuff. You, I hope, don't." He looked sidelong at me. "You still have scars?"

I nodded and pulled up one pants leg. There, in the side of my calf, was a silver dollar shaped scar. I twisted around so he could see the identical one on the other side. "That's one of them."

"Yeah, I won't ask to see them all," said Steve. "But can you take pictures? In case we can enter them into evidence?"

"Sure."

He shook his head and launched his internet browser. "Statutes are online... here. Okay, a lot of them are going to be the same as in the old criminal complaint." We had a copy of that on the table between us. "But we always check. I don't want to accidentally cite to some farm subsidy statute or something."

I laughed.

"Right, so... kidnapping..." He clicked hyperlink after hyperlink until he found it, then jotted the statute number down in another window.

"False imprisonment... right. Battery... okay. Assault with a deadly weapon... okay. I guess assault goes first, really. Um... right, endangerment of a minor... not sure what that'd be under. I still can't believe they didn't get attempted murder."

"I wasn't in bad enough shape."

"The heck you weren't." I got the impression that the Vanderholts weren't big on swearing. "I'm looking up the criteria, just to see." His finger tapped away again and again at the touchpad on his laptop.

He paused and looked up at me. "How are you, by the way? Here my dad and I have been so absorbed with this, we didn't ever ask. How do you feel about getting this restraining order?"

"I'm fine, I guess. Stressed."

"Yeah, Jason said you guys hadn't talked much about it. He did get these, by the way." Steve dug out a stack of pictures. I stared. Sure enough, the guy behind the wheel of the little sedan looked like an older, fatter Chris. His hair was buzzed and his eyes were behind sunglasses, but I could see his distinctive, tapering jaw.

Guilt welled up inside of me like blood from a wound. Jason had put me in touch with his family and gotten me some evidence, and I'd cut him off last night.

"I don't mean to pry, but... my brother did call me yesterday," said Steve.

"What did he say?"

"That your 'friend,'" he curled his fingers in the air, "dug up a bunch of dirt on him and made, like, a little case file."

"He's just trying to protect me."

"From what, exactly?"

"Matthew thinks Jason's trying to hit on me or something. And I don't know, maybe I talk to Jason too often. Maybe it does look bad."

"Oh, well." Steve scrubbed his fingers through his short hair, his wedding ring glinting in the late afternoon light that shone in the windows. "Jason's always on his phone. That thing's going to grow onto his ear. He gets real lonely in LA and doesn't relate to the people out there, even after all this time. But all of us in the family know you guys are just friends."

"Well, so I'm sorry if last night really upset him."

"You should talk to him, okay? Give him a chance to tell his side of the story."

"The stuff that Matthew brought up, I don't usually talk about with my friends."

"Sure, but can I just say, it's hard enough for Jason to have his personal life always under the microscope. Let him tell his side, even if it's awkward. It would mean a lot to him. And for what it's worth? My brother's a good guy."

I nodded.

"Not that your friendship with Jason affects us wanting to help you with this case, okay? This kind of thing? It's what all of us went to law school for."

"It's why I'm going into forensics."

"And it's probably why Beth's applying to the Albuquerque DA's office – well Bernalillo County's that is."

"Really?"

"Yeah. I don't know her very well, but she and Mom still talk sometimes. I guess this case really affected her. She's providing us with an affidavit."

"What is an affidavit?"

"A statement under oath. She can't come out from Illinois to testify, but she provided an affidavit that says she heard Chris bragging about slashing your tires and knows he cruised your mom's house."

"Your dad must've twisted her arm."

"I don't think so."

"But this is her brother."

"And you're her sister. Come on, who do you think she's gonna side with? Her older, drug addict, convicted felon brother or her little, defenseless, class valedictorian sister?"

That didn't match the awkward, uncomfortable Beth I'd seen in Flying Star at all. It seemed then like she'd have done anything to get away from me.

That Monday, I dropped all the paperwork off at the courthouse, and got a hearing scheduled for Thursday. Steve had located an address for Chris, and the clerk said that their process server could notify him for a small fee, which I paid on the spot.

I then walked over to the police station and dropped off copies of the pictures and Beth's affidavit. The receptionist promised to get them to Officer Baca, who wasn't on duty just then.

On Tuesday, Jason called again. I stared at his name on my phone for several rings before I answered it. "Hi," I said.

"Chloe."

"How are you?"

"How are *you*? Things all set for Thursday?"

"I think so."

"Is there anything I can do? At all? Anything you need?"

"I think I'm okay."

"Anything at all?"

"I've already had more Vanderholt kindness than I deserve. I'm fine. How are you?"

"Just glad you picked up the phone."

"Yeah..." I didn't know what to say to that.

"I really want to talk to you."

"I know."

"I really want to see you. We had that awful conversation and then you're facing down a guy who shot you this week and... this is crazy. I want to be there."

"Well, thanks."

"Can I?"

"What, seriously?"

"My friend got *shot*."

"Ten years ago."

"And has to face the guy who shot her. Come on, you wouldn't buy a bus ticket to go support a friend at a time like that?"

"It'd be a long bus ride."

"I'd spend the same proportion of my income on a plane ticket across a couple of states that you'd spend on a bus ticket across town. Yeah, my life is weird, but it is what it is."

"Jason..."

"I'm sorry, okay? Maybe I'm too emotionally involved, but I am emotionally involved. I care about you. Matthew will be there for moral support, right?"

"No, he-"

"No?"

"He's got class."

"Class? He knows what this is, right?"

"He knows the gist."

"Then I don't get why he isn't cutting class. Tell me someone's going with you. Lori?"

"Doesn't know."

"Your mother?"

"No, and I don't really want to talk about that right now."

"You're going *alone?*"

"I'll be fine."

"Are you sure?"

"Yeah, I'm sure." I'd done this before, been to court against Chris and this time I wasn't a little girl. I could look him in the eye, though the very idea made me sick.

"If you hadn't seen those printouts about me, would you still feel the same way?"

"I don't know, okay? I'm a little distracted right now. I haven't talked to anyone, not even Matthew or Lori, in a couple of days. I haven't been out of the apartment except to go to class."

"Right, sorry. You're completely right. Not the time for me to be all obsessed about me. Just... promise you'll call me if you need anything?"

"I'll be fine."

"I'm your friend, no matter what you think of me. Call anytime. I mean it."

"Thanks. I'll talk to you later."

"Sure. Later."

We hung up and I felt the sudden urge to cry. I dialed Matthew.

"Howdy?" he answered his phone.

"It's me."

"Chloe. I been meaning to call. You sure you don't want a ride to school tomorrow?"

"It's way out of the way for you."

"I don't know where you're living these days. I'd like to come see you."

"My hearing is on Thursday."

"Oh... What time?"

"During Media Studies."

"You... want me to take notes for you or..."

"Sure, that'd be great."

"You okay? You want company right now or you want to be left alone or-"

"I'm at Val's. You know where she lives?"

"Give me the address."

I did.

"Okay, I just put in my laundry, but I'll come by right after. Unless you want me to come now?"

"Later's fine."

"I'll bring dinner?"

"That'd be great."

Two hours later, Matthew came with Chinese take-out. I greeted him with a hug and offered to pay for the food, but he shook his head.

"You okay?" he asked.

"I'm fine. It's all good." I went to get plates. Val's apartment was a small and cozy one bedroom with practically no windows, and I felt like an intruder, living there. The place still smelled like her, like hairspray and herbal soap. I hadn't talked to Eli yet about breaking the lease on my house. I didn't want to. It felt like letting Chris win, again.

"Chloe, you want me to come to the hearing?" Matthew asked.

"I don't," I said. "Don't take this the wrong way, but I want to keep my past in the past."

"Okay." He sat down at the little dining table and began to pull out white boxes of food. "You want to talk about other stuff, then? Distraction?"

"Yes, please."

"You got it. What do you think of having to watch the pilot of *Glee* for Media Studies?"

Thursday took both a hundred years and the blink of an eye to come. Steve picked me up and drove me to the courthouse. He was in a suit and tie. I wore my sensible gray skirt and a blue blouse. My heart felt like it was in my throat, choking me each time it pulsed. My head felt light and my hands were dripping with sweat.

"You going to be okay?" Steve asked.

"I'll get through this."

"You're allowed to panic, hyperventilate, whatever you gotta do, okay?"

I smiled at him. "Thanks."

We parked, crossed the street to the courthouse, went through security, and made our way up the stairs and into the chambers. Inside loitered a guy with slouched shoulders and a sullen posture. He stepped towards me and I leaned away. He was no doubt one of Chris's friends. He might even have helped slash my tires and break my windows.

"Chlo?" the guy said.

I nearly jumped out of my skin. "Jason?"

He pushed up his baseball cap and stood up straight.

Just then, Doug walked in. "Jason, what are you doing here?"

"That's what I was going to say," said Steve. "When did you get here?"

"If the media tailed you to this-" Doug began.

Jason held up one hand to ward them off, took me by the arm, and pulled me aside.

"I can leave if you want," he said. "I just wanted to at least show up long enough to let you know I'm here for you. I don't have to stay."

I was speechless.

"You can be mad."

"Uh..."

"Okay, I'll leave. Just-"

The door of the chambers swung open again and in walked a woman with silver hair and a tailored suit, and a guy in jeans and a t-shirt. My heart felt like it'd stopped. The guy turned to scowl at me and I stared back at the face I hadn't seen for ten years. He had a tapered jaw just like me and Beth, and dark brown eyes that ought to have seemed deep and insightful, but just looked mean.

Jason turned around. Chris's gaze flicked to his face. He stopped in his tracks. "Jason?"

The lawyer looked at him, then at her client. "Who is this?"

"We knew each other in high school," said Jason. His hand on my arm tightened a little.

The lawyer gave him another uneasy look, but she didn't say anything else. She went to her table, got out her briefcase, and started laying documents out neatly.

"So, you're like a movie star now," said Chris.

"How are you?" said Jason.

Chris turned his gaze back to me and scowled. "Been better." He shifted his shoulders in a move to look intimidating and angry.

My first instinct was to shrink away, but I didn't. That wasn't me. It never had been. I looked him over and sized him up. Last time I'd seen him, he'd looked like a giant. Now he just looked like a guy, and a slightly chubby one at that.

He flinched. Like a dog who'd been stared down by a house cat, he looked at the wall as if to say, "Never mind. I wasn't looking at you. Go away now, all right?"

"Right," said Jason. "Leaving now-"

"No," I said. "Stay. Please."

"You sure?"

"Yeah." My mouth was dry.

The chambers were small, with seating for only about twenty people. In front of that was a low wooden banister, then a table for each party to the lawsuit. The front of the room was dominated by the hardwood stand where the witnesses and judge sat. The jury box was empty. There were no windows, just fluorescent lights bleeding the color out of everyone and everything so that the place felt anemic. The judge was a youngish Hispanic woman with gorgeous eye makeup that went so well with her robes that I couldn't help but stare and wonder how she'd applied it.

I sat in my chair and only half listened to Chris's lawyer blather on about how Chris hadn't done anything and had served his time and felt real remorse for the past.

Doug's intro had been short and sweet. He just said why we were here, thanked the judge, and sat. I liked that. It wasn't until I glanced over at Steve's notepad and saw it covered with doodles, that I picked up on the fact that he was nervous.

Chris's lawyer sat down. Doug looked over at me. "You ready?"

I nodded.

He got up. "First witness, your honor, is Chloe Winters."

The judge nodded and Doug motioned for me to take the stand. I did. The padded seat was quite comfortable and the microphone moved easily into position as I manipulated it. The court reporter gave me a small smile while I composed myself.

"What is your relationship to Mr. Winters?" Doug began.

"I am his half-sister."

"And would you care to tell us a little about your history?"

"We grew up estranged, and about ten years ago he kidnapped and tried to kill me-"

"Objection," said Chris's lawyer. "There was never a conviction for attempted murder."

"Fine, strike it," said the judge.

"You can go into more detail in a moment," Doug assured me. "He attacked you, though?"

"Yes."

"Did he cause bodily harm?"

"Yes."

"Objection. Leading."

"Sustained."

Doug frowned. "How did he make you feel during the incident?"

"Like my life was in danger."

"Objection!"

The judge waved it away, lazily. "I understand your position," she said. She nodded at Doug, who turned back to me.

"Okay, Ms. Winters, why don't you tell us about this incident?"

"Objection. Relevance."

"Your honor," said Doug, "the reason she is asking for this restraining order is because the defendant's previous history of violence towards her is so severe, it warrants special precautions."

"My client hasn't done anything. Not since he served his time. This whole request for an order is frivolous."

"Your honor, you've read our complaint and this testimony lays the foundation for our current claims, that Mr. Winters vandalized my client's vehicle and house and her mother's house."

"I'll hear it," said the judge.

Chris's lawyer sat down, not looking particularly surprised.

"Go ahead, Miss Winters," said Doug.

"I was eleven," I began. "And I was on the playground at school, when my brother drove up to the fence." I didn't look at Chris, but as I spoke, he seemed to grow larger and larger in my peripheral vision, until he towered over me once again.

15
TEN YEARS AGO

I'd never been a sociable kid. Just like now, I had only ever had a few close friends, and during recess in elementary school, I'd played by myself. That day I was playing right by the fence. There was a clump of dandelions there and I'd been trying to weave them into daisy chains, only I didn't really know how to weave a daisy chain.

Witnesses would later say that Chris's truck drove past three times, but I was oblivious. I was sitting on the grass, surrounded by decapitated dandelions. Their flowers kept popping off their stems when I flexed them too hard. One minute I was tying two stems together, the next a hand was clapped over my mouth and I was hoisted into the air.

I watched the dandelions fall out of my hands and scatter onto the pavement while I was jostled so hard I thought I'd throw up. The ground pitched and sprang away, beneath me. Looking back, I can figure out that Chris had thrown me over his shoulder and jumped the fence, but at the time I was just aware of being gripped so tight that it hurt, people shouting in the background, and feeling seasick.

Chris vaulted into his truck with me still over his shoulder. My head hit the doorframe, hard. Dark spots swam in my vision. He threw me down into the passenger footwell and I landed on a pile of garbage. Potato chip wrappers, an old t-shirt, some broken CD cases. Before I could get my feet under me, he'd slammed his door and hit the gas. I was thrown against the base of the passenger side seat. A siren started up behind us, but it seemed like a small and distant beacon of safety that faded fast. Chris drove like a maniac, and swore an unending stream of epithets.

He said he'd kill me, that I had to be quiet, that he'd bash my head in.

He was a steroid user, and this was one of his rages.

I was being kidnapped, just like they warned us about in assembly. And none of the safety advice they gave us applied. I could scream, but no one would hear, and Chris would probably kick me in the head. It was too late to run. It was too late to do anything.

We were going so fast and he was jerking the steering wheel so hard that I kept getting thrown against the car door, the dashboard, the seat, the gear shift. I tried to brace myself, and I started to cry.

"Shut up!" he shouted. "You shut up!"

But I didn't shut up, so he cracked me across the head so hard that I blacked out for a moment. I don't know what he hit me with, but it made my head throb like a sub-woofer. I could even hear the thrum of blood through my ears, like the sound of bass tones reverberating through a car body. I put my arms over my head and curled up tight.

The floor of his truck was filthy. It reeked of stale cigarette smoke and red and black wires dangled down from beneath the dashboard. I heard more sirens in the distance. Come get me! I thought.

I don't know how long we drove. The problem with being so little was that I just couldn't know that much. Things were happening to me and I had no control. We left the paved road and were now jouncing over a dirt road. Or maybe it wasn't even a road. Maybe it was a field. He didn't slow down, though, so I just stayed curled up tight, bouncing like a lotto ball.

"Chris?" I whimpered.

"You know my name?"

Well, of course I knew his name. I'd seen his picture at Dr. Winters's dental office. I'd even seen Chris, himself, a few times there.

"You know my name? Answer me!"

"No," I lied.

He brought his fist down on my side, a glancing blow that startled me, but didn't hurt. I pulled in tighter into my fetal position, though, hoping that if I bluffed like it hurt, he wouldn't hit me again.

We tore across the desert, off to some unknown destination that I would later learn was out on the West Mesa. We drove and drove until Chris slammed on the brakes and got out of his side of the car. Warm air rushed in and cool, air conditioned air streamed out. A moment later the door on my side opened and Chris grabbed me by the collar and hauled me out onto the dirt and dry grass. I landed on my hip and skinned the heels of my hands. Dust swirled up and made me sneeze.

Okay, I thought, here's my chance. I'd run, I decided. I'd just take off and scream and-

Click-*clack*.

I lifted my head and found myself staring up the barrel of a shotgun, Chris's face was a blurry pink mass way beyond it.

"N-no..." I whimpered. "No!" I guess most people would have begged for mercy, but I was still a little kid, and my mind was in a strange place. Maybe I'd been hit in the head too hard, but what I was thinking wasn't, "Please don't kill me," but rather, "This isn't fair! You can't do that. These aren't the rules! You don't just haul people off and shoot them for no reason. This is *wrong*."

"Go away!" I shrieked. "Leave me alone! Go away!" I put my hands over my head, as if that would somehow save me from a bullet.

For what felt like an eternity, nothing happened. The sun beat down, scorching the skin of my hands and neck. An ant crawled across my shadow, antennae rooting around in the loose dirt. Chris breathed a hard, panting breath. Then I saw the shadow of the gun lower.

I looked up.

Chris pulled a handgun out of the back of his jeans and, *pop*, a dull, burning ache hit my calf. I looked down and saw blood spilling out onto the dirt. *Pop*. It felt like he'd shoved a hot poker right through my shoulder. I fell back and my head hit the ground with a thud. Warm, sticky liquid soaked its way across the back of my shirt. *Pop*. My stomach blossomed with fire. I didn't fully understand that I'd been shot. The gun didn't sound like what I'd heard on television.

He stared down at me then, and I glared back up at him. "Go away," I whispered.

I wondered if blood would bubble from my mouth, like it did in the movies, but it didn't.

"Leave me alone," I rasped.

Chris wiped the gun off on his shirt, polishing away fingerprints, and threw it as far as he could. I heard it land in the distance on the dry grass. Then he turned his back on me, got into his truck, and drove off, leaving me to stare up at the deep blue, New Mexico sky, my life's blood streaming out of me onto the dust.

An ant walked across my throat, but I didn't even move to shoo it. All the color was leaving the world. The sky went pale blue, then gray, then black. There were sirens, but they were impossibly far away. The last thing I had been aware of was the sound of my racing pulse and the feeling that my entire back was soaked through with blood.

A RINGING silence had descended in the courtroom. Doug looked back at Jason, who just stared down at his hands.

Chris had his eyes closed, and his lawyer did not look happy.

"Your honor, as you know, I've entered into evidence some pictures of her gunshot wounds," said Doug. "Ms. Winters, do you feel that the defendant might hurt you again?"

"He kidnapped me and shot me multiple times without warning and without provocation," I said.

"Do you anticipate seeing him in the future?"

"Not if I can avoid it. And that's why I'd like this restraining order, to avoid it. I just want to get on with my life."

"Why didn't they go for attempted murder?" asked the judge.

I looked up, startled. Was she allowed to ask questions like that?

But Doug didn't seem to think it was odd. "They did, your honor," he said. "But the jury found him innocent of it."

The judge shook her head in disbelief and turned to me. "How did you survive a gunshot wound at close range, to the stomach?"

"The police were right behind us, your honor. There was a cop at my school who followed my brother and radioed for backup, so that by the time I was out in the desert, they had four cars and a chopper on his tail. They airlifted me to UNM Hospital within minutes."

"Still."

"And I was lucky, I guess. If that term applies to someone who's been shot three times by her own brother."

Her mouth quirked in a smile. "All right, is that all?"

"That's all from me, your honor," said Doug.

"Fine, your witness, defense."

Chris's lawyer got to her feet and fixed me with a very determined glare. "Ms. Winters, yes or no, has my client contacted you since he was released from prison?"

"I don't think so."

"Yes or no?"

"He might have slashed my tires."

"Yes or no!"

"There's been a lot of vandalism and he drove-"

She slapped the table with a bang. "Yes," she said, "or no."

"I can't answer that."

Doug nodded.

"Have you seen my client, since his release?"

"No."

"Has he called you?"

"No."

"Has he emailed you?"

"No."

"Facebook message?"

"No." I got her game now. She just wanted a long list of "no's" to make my testimony look trivial. Fine, I thought, I could keep answering these questions. My story had made its impression. All the lawyer tricks in the world wouldn't dilute it.

Chris put his head on his hands, as if even he were embarrassed by this whole charade.

AFTER everyone had made their case, the judge directed us to one waiting room and Chris to another. The decision, she promised, would be made shortly. I turned to Doug and Steve and smiled. "Thank you," I said.

"You can smile. I'm still traumatized," said Steve as he packed up his papers. "And now you're laughing."

And I was. What could I say? Some days it was good to just be alive, and this day, watching Chris so ashamed that he couldn't look at me, was one of those days.

We got up and moved towards the back of the courtroom. Jason was on his feet and turned to look at Chris as he went past.

Chris paused, looked at him, then me, then him again. "What?" he said. "You got something to say?"

His lawyer took him firmly by the arm and steered him on.

Jason just shook his head.

"Oh yeah, *that'll* get you laid," said Chris. He shot me a leer before his lawyer dragged him out the door. She looked like she was digging her nails into his arm.

I giggled. "Did you get that, Jas? Research for your next role. What a real criminal sounds like when he's trying to be manipulative and witty."

"You feeling okay?" asked Steve.

"Maybe a little giddy."

"Come with us, Jason," said Doug. "I think you belong in our waiting room."

16
FIRST KISS

WE all made our way down the hall, only Jason hung several steps behind. I fell back so that we could talk.

"Chlo, I'm really sorry," was the first thing he said. "I didn't know how bad it was. I should never have barged in on that."

"I'm glad someone was here. I thought I could do this alone, but it was dumb to even try."

A woman in a skirt and blouse came around the corner and planted herself in front of Doug and Steve. They both turned to wait for me to catch up.

"You've got your restraining order," the woman said. "So the way this works is that it's effective immediately. You need to leave the courthouse now, and once you're away, we'll let Mr. Winters know that he can leave."

"Thank you," said Doug.

"Can I drive you home?" asked Jason.

"Jason," said his father. "Chloe gets seen leaving the courthouse with you, the press might go find her old case."

"Wait a minute," said the woman. "You're… you're…"

"Yeah, hi," said Jason.

She blinked and looked at Doug and Steve.

"There aren't that many Vanderholts in Albuquerque," said Doug. "You're looking at about half of them."

"We have a back exit. Would that be better?"

"You know, it would. Thank you," said Jason. He turned to me. "You go out the front and meet me at the car, it cuts down on photo opportunities."

"Jason," said his father.

"Dad, I left my house in a car with tinted windows without telling anyone, besides Dave, where I was going."

"Does that usually work?" his father asked.

Jason frowned and looked at the floor.

"It's okay, really," I said. "I'll go meet you in the parking garage. Where's your car?" If Jason wanted to talk to me this badly, I could talk to him. If there were more paparazzi photos, well, I'd deal with it.

"Third level," Jason said. "By the stairs."

"Well, in that case." Doug turned to Steve. "Post hearing powwow?"

"You got time?"

"I do."

"Then yeah, that'd be great."

"This way." The woman gestured for Jason to follow her down the side hall. He tugged forward his baseball cap and got his sunglasses ready. The rest of us headed for the front door.

"So," said Jason, as we pulled out of the parking lot in his Prius, "after they airlifted you, what happened?"

"I don't know. I was unconscious. I woke up two days later in a room that smelled like a flower shop."

"And Chris was in jail?"

"I don't know all that. They arrested him, don't know if he posted bail or what. But there was a woman in my room who asked me what I remembered and was really happy that I could name Chris. She was from the DA's office, and you know, it might've been your mom."

"Maybe. Your testimony must've really clinched it, then."

"I dunno. It helped, but the forensics people were amazing."

"Even though he wiped his prints off the gun?"

"Even though. First the cops noted that the gun was still hot from being fired. Then the forensics people matched the gun to the bullet that was buried in my shoulder, and found fibers from Chris's t shirt on the handle. They found powder burns on Chris's hands and residue on his clothes. The prints didn't matter. With some relatively simple tests, they had him nailed. And there was no one else out on the mesa, the cops weren't suspects, and everyone knew I couldn't have done that to myself."

"So that's why you want to do forensics?"

"Yeah. I'm not sure I want to deal with the action that cops deal with, but I want to be part of the process."

"Sure."

Jason was driving to my house off Central, and I decided that was for the best. If there were any media following us, the last thing I needed was for them to track me to Val's. Since the house was close, we were there in no time. Jason turned to me. "You got time to talk?"

"Yeah, okay."

Jason strode from his car to the front door and stepped in the moment I opened it. Only when we were inside did it occur to me to feel embarrassed. My house was so small. The carpet was dingy. It all smelled like dust. Books and papers covered the coffee table. Jason went and sat on the couch without batting an eye.

"You want a glass of water?" I said.

He shook his head.

"Orange?" I tossed one to him from the bowl on the counter and he caught it with one hand.

"Where are the printouts?"

"I'll get them." I got myself a glass of water, set it on the coffee table, then tried to think. Where were those printouts? I'd taken them out of the front room so Lori wouldn't find them. "Be right back," I said.

It took me a couple of minutes of rummaging around my room before I found them in a stack of notes. I carried them back out to the front, where Jason had peeled his orange in one great big coil, and tossed the peel in the trash.

I sat down opposite him and held up the papers. "I don't care about most of this stuff-"

He took them from me and started to go through them. I watched him sort them into two piles.

"What are you doing?"

"True and false."

"Like I said, I don't care."

"Well I do, okay? I do." He paused to put one orange section in his mouth and to lay a second one on the couch cushion next to me. While he worked, he ate, and made a line of orange sections between us. They were like a little set of rock markers that Boy Scouts used to mark the edge of a trail.

Finally, he stuffed one stack towards me. It was the bigger stack.

"Some of those are exaggerated, but they aren't complete lies."

The one on the top was the sex party story.

I set the stack aside. "Look-"

He grabbed it from me again and went through it. "Okay, this one," he held up the statutory rape story, "sort of... is the crux of the issue. This one got me banned from coming home for the holidays for a year."

"And it's in the true pile."

"Well, right. I don't know if the charge was ever true. It happened a long time ago, when I was eighteen. I thought she was seventeen, but she later said she lied about her age and... long story short, it was right when my career was taking off. I'd landed my first big movie deal that wasn't tied into my Disney show. She told me she was going to press charges, my lawyers met with her, they told me the way to deal with this was to buy her off."

I ate a section of orange, and stared down at the cluttered coffee table.

"People file frivolous lawsuits against me all the time. I've paid out settlements before, but this one's different, way different. For one thing, I don't know if it was frivolous, but you know, what really bothered me was that here was someone I'd loved, and she accused me of rape. Statutory rape, but still, it's a word that I don't ever want any woman who's been with me to think, you know? No guy wants that." He paused as if waiting to see if I had something to say.

I didn't. I had no idea what to say.

"I went to talk to her about it. I asked her what I'd done wrong and told her I was sorry and that I hoped she didn't hate me. She basically told me she just wanted the money. Not that she needed it, wanted it. Bought herself a house and a car and never looked back. I mean, she didn't put it in so many words, but... yeah."

"That's pretty awful," I agreed.

"It's not an excuse for the way I acted afterwards. I got burned, and the way I dealt with it was to decide not to care about any girl that much again. I messed around. Got a reputation as a party animal. I did not host a sex party, but I did have a party at my house where some girls decided to streak down my road and the police weren't thrilled about it. I did stuff like that off and on, I guess, for several years. Then one day I woke up and realized I was lonelier than ever, so I just swore off dating for a while."

"Well..." This was way more detail than I cared to know.

"I was over all that stupidity by the time this happened." He held up the statutory rape article. "The girl's friend came forward for her fifteen minutes of fame and told the world how I bought my ex-girlfriend off to avoid a public court case. That was a few years ago. Jen called to ask if it was true, and when I said it partially was, she told me I wasn't welcome to stay with her for Christmas. She said that was just too much bad press from me. She was trying to raise a very confused teenager and I wasn't a good influence."

"That why you call her your mean sister?"

"No. She wasn't wrong, you know? She put up with a lot for a long time, and Kyra is pretty confused about it all. I understand where Jen was coming from. A criminal charge is serious. That was a really lonely Christmas."

I nodded and looked down at the huge stack of pictures of all the women he'd been with.

"So now you know," he said. "I have had normal relationships since then, okay? I haven't done the one night stand thing in years."

"Look," I said, "you and I are friends, and I don't usually pry into the, um, sex lives of my friends."

He nodded. "I take your point. Sorry to delve into that. Guess I feel like I learned so much about you that ought to be private today... never mind. This mean we're still friends?" Maybe it was an act, but he really did look like he cared about what I thought.

"Yeah, we are." I reached for another orange section and found they were all gone.

He sat back. "Okay. That's all I needed to hear."

"Thanks for coming today."

"It wasn't over the line?"

"It's not what I would have done, but... I am grateful you did it."

He smiled with relief.

The door behind us swung open and Lori walked in, followed by

Matthew. "Hey," said Lori. She glanced at us but didn't really look. She got herself a glass of water and started to gulp it down. "I just need to get some things and then we can go to the gym," she said to Matthew.

Matthew stopped dead in his tracks.

"Hey, you," I said.

His gaze was fixed on Jason.

"I didn't know he was in town today," I said, "and he came by-"

Lori dropped her glass and it hit the tiles with a bang and shattered. I looked past Matthew at her and saw that she was staring, bug eyed, at Jason. "Sorry!" she said. "Sorry, sorry. Getting the broom." She went down the hall.

"You can say hello!" I called after her.

"Hello, Jason!"

"Hello, Lori." Jason turned back to Matthew. "Hi," he said.

"Hi. Was he at the hearing?"

"I wasn't invited," said Jason. "But I showed up anyway... she was nice about it."

Matthew pressed his mouth into a thin, firm line.

Jason got to his feet. The tension in the air was palpable, as if their stares were radiating waves of distrust and fury.

"You know?" said Lori. "I'm going to go to my room for no reason and just stay there. Ignore me." She leaned the broom against the wall and beat a hasty retreat.

"What..." I began. There was some kind of guy turf war going on here, and I didn't get all the nuances. All I could grasp was that Matthew felt threatened by Jason in some way, so I got up and put my hand on Matthew's shoulder. He slipped an arm around my waist.

Jason looked down at Matthew's hand, then up at me. "You propose to him?"

"It's a purity ring," said Matthew.

"Oh, right, okay."

"It means-"

"No sex outside of marriage, I know. I used to work for Disney. Several of their actors wear those. Look, I'm sorry I just barged in today, I am. Chloe's been charitable, but I know I'm out of line."

"Why are you here?"

"Because... coincidence. My parents worked on Chloe's old case.

I knew it was bad and I just... okay. It was a mistake. I shouldn't have come."

"I don't just mean today. Why do you keep calling her?"

Rather than answer that, Jason walked over to the door. "I should go."

I wasn't sure what to do. It seemed rude to just let him leave, but it also seemed important to Matthew. "Thanks for all your help today," I said.

"Yeah, no problem." He let himself out.

I looked up at Matthew, who still stared angrily into the air. "What's wrong?"

"He was at the hearing?"

"I didn't invite him. Like he said."

"Need a ride home?"

"Sure, but are you Lori's ride?"

"Lori will be fine!" Lori called out. Clearly she'd been eavesdropping. "Go. Take Chloe home!"

The first half of the ride to Val's was in stony silence. Matthew's truck was so high off the ground that all I saw out the window were the roofs of other cars slipping past. "Are you mad at me?" I asked.

He didn't answer that immediately.

"Okay, what did I do?" I turned to him. The front seat was so wide, there was quite a bit of distance between us. I put one knee up on the seat, my seatbelt digging into my hip. Matthew had an evergreen tree air freshener dangling from his rearview mirror that spun lazily as we drove.

"I'm not mad at you."

"What did I do? I'm lost."

"I just don't get it."

"Get what?"

"Why you talk to him."

"He talks to me. He takes the initiative. I don't."

"Why do you let him? Why'd you let him come to your hearing today? I offered, and you said no."

I'd already told him I didn't invite Jason. Clearly that wasn't the issue. Somehow, by not throwing Jason out, I'd upset Matthew.

"And what were you guys talking about just now?" Matthew went on.

"He was telling me about his past. I told him I didn't care- okay, what is this about? I feel like I'm missing something."

"I just feel like he's taking advantage."

"Of who? Me?"

"Whom."

"Matthew."

"Yeah, you."

"Taking advantage how? I only ever talk to him. What exactly is he getting away with, in your opinion?"

"He takes you places and buys you stuff."

"Not recently. Not since that last little mix up. Look, you think he's dating me? Even though I've told him I'm not interested?"

Matthew gave a half shrug.

"Because it doesn't work like that," I said. "No guy can just decide he's with me. That's my decision too. You know that, right?"

"Why don't you just tell him to get lost?"

"Hey, when he said he wanted to kiss me, I said no. No way. Not interested. We are not romantic, ever."

"He said what?"

"It's not like I'm clueless. I have talked to him. I've laid out my position and he has to respect it. If he still wants to call, well... even that, I've been turning my Skype off. So whatever you think he's getting away with, you could give me a little credit here."

"I don't mean to not give you credit."

"Then what's with this anger? If you have issues with Jason being in town, talk to me. No point fighting with him over it. What do you want? For me not to be his friend anymore?"

"I'd never try to control your life like that."

"Then what do you want? I'm confused."

"I want him to go away. I want him to leave you alone."

"So you want me-"

"But I don't want to tell you whom you can and can't talk to. I know it's not right, and besides, I know that if I told you it was one or the other of us, I'd lose."

"Why do you think that? You're my best friend. He's just some random guy with way too much free time on his hands."

"You don't put up with getting bossed around."

"No, but if you have an opinion to express or feelings that are getting hurt, you can tell me. You know that, right?"

"I... feel," said Matthew, as we pulled into the parking lot of Val's complex, "that I want you all to myself and want him gone. Okay? That's how I feel, and I know it's stupid and childish and wrong and-"

"Fine, look. I'm not going to call Jason right now and tell him never to talk to me again."

"I know."

"But I can do this. Will this help?" My pulse edged up as I unbuckled my seatbelt and moved over to him. I wasn't normally forward like this, but just then, it felt right. I put my hand on Matthew's rough, unshaven cheek and touched my lips to his.

The sensation was strange, but not in a bad way. On one hand, this was Matthew, my best friend. The guy I talked about school with and saw every day, or near enough. On the other hand, this was a gorgeous guy with a sexy Texan drawl and down home manners that would drive any girl to distraction. I'd just never put all that together before.

Matthew's reaction was immediate. He grasped me around the waist and pulled me in for another kiss, a much longer one. I'd never, ever seen this side of him. I had no idea he wanted this, but right then, there was no mistaking his feelings.

A small lifetime elapsed during that kiss, where everything I'd ever known or thought about him shifted. *This* was the guy I'd been sitting next to in class? This was my annoying friend who chastised me for being sarcastic? When he broke off the kiss, he was breathing hard.

I stroked his hair. "How long have you wanted-"

"Forever, Chloe. Since I met you."

"Then why didn't you ever say anything?"

"Because I was sure you'd say no."

"Matthew..."

"You sure this is okay?"

I nodded. "Yes. This is more than okay."

He gave me a fierce hug.

We spent the evening on the couch. I wasn't sure how far or how fast Matthew would want to go. It wasn't the kind of thing we'd ever discussed, but he was clearly okay with making out. We didn't say more than ten words to each other, just held each other and kissed. Strange thrills of excitement sparked in my stomach as he kissed my neck and pressed my body close to his.

I ran my fingers through his hair, feeling the kinks in the individual strands, and stroked his back, feeling the long, lean muscles. For the first time ever, while this close to a guy, I felt safe. I wasn't going to have to stop to ask what he planned next. I wasn't going to have to break things up and launch into the Talk. He wasn't going to try to undress me. I could relax and just be with him. It was the most liberating experience I'd ever had with anyone, and the only way I could describe it was intimate. I was able to lay my feelings bare and have them accepted for what they were, rather than as the opening bid in a back and forth to see how far he could push me.

The whole rest of the world receded into nothing and I could just focus on him.

Afterward, we lay there with our arms around each other. I had wondered what it would be like to kiss him, if it would be an awkward experience that I'd have to rationalize. Instead, it had opened the floodgates to feelings I'd never even known I had. I'd thought I'd been in love before. That was nothing compared to this. I was with someone who knew me better than anyone, and found me desirable. I didn't want to ever let him go.

"So," he whispered in my ear, "guess things are different now?"

I chuckled.

"You're okay with this?"

"I wouldn't do this if I wasn't okay with it," I told him.

"I had *no* idea."

"What?" I said. "You were the one holding out. You should've said something sooner."

17

That night, after Matthew left, I saw I had a text from Jason. "Everything okay?" he asked.

"Matthew and I are together now," I replied.

The answer came half an hour later, as I was brushing my teeth. "Ok." And that was it.

The next day, when I didn't see Matthew in class, I called him and got voicemail. "Hey," I said. "It's me. Just, call me whenever, all right?"

Afternoon rolled on into evening, and he didn't call back. At first I panicked, but then I reasoned that he must've gotten really sick or something. He wasn't the kind of guy to bail on me. I tried calling again, got voicemail, and resolved to go visit him the following day. In the meantime, I ordered flowers for Doug and Steve. It seemed like a pathetic thank you, given all they'd done for me, but it was better than nothing. I wasn't sure what to do for Officer Baca, but decided I'd send him a thank you note in a graduation announcement once I got those in.

Matthew's truck wasn't in his apartment complex parking lot the next day. I wondered if there had been a family emergency that had called him home. I called Lori.

"Hmmm?" she answered her phone.

"Do you know where Matthew is?"

"Um, I haven't seen him since math class."

"What? He was in class?"

"Uh-huh."

"He wasn't in Media Studies."

"Weird. Well, I dunno. I'm sure you'll see him tomorrow." Her tone was light.

"Did he say anything to you about me?" I said.

"No... why?" she asked.

"We kind of hooked up."

"Oh..."

"What?" I said. "Why do you sound like that?"

"I'm sure it's nothing."

"What's nothing?"

"Give him space, Chloe. See if he comes around."

"It wasn't like it was a bad thing."

"Sure, right-"

"He said he wanted-"

"Deep breath. Breathe. Just calm down. I'm sure it'll be fine. You want to go to dinner tonight or something?"

I shook my head, even though she couldn't see that. She had to be wrong. She hadn't been there. She was making assumptions on incomplete information. "Nah, thanks. I'm busy tonight."

"Okay. I'm sure it'll all be fine," she repeated.

I said a quick good-bye and hung up.

A FEW days later, Officer Baca called my cell phone late in the evening, a gleeful tone in his voice. "So, Miss Chloe," he said, "guess who's back in the Big House?"

"Chris?" I said.

"You gave me a picture of him driving. He doesn't have a license, so we went over to his house to confront him about it and he let us search his room without a warrant. He's not the brightest bulb. We even checked with Ms. Garcia first, but she told us she no longer represented him."

"What did you find?"

"Drugs, and a firearm."

"He had a gun?"

"Felon in possession. My partner took him in while I had a little talk with his father. Told him how much trouble Chris was already in, and I suggested he not bail him out of jail." Officer Baca chuckled. "I dunno if he'll listen to me. I was probably over the line, but we got him, Miss Chloe."

"So do I need to move house?"

"Well, keep in touch with Victim Services and see if he gets out of jail. If he's out, you better not be at your house."

"Right."

"This'll never be over, you know that, right?" said Officer Baca. "I wish I could call you up some time and tell you that he's put away for good and you never have to worry, but unless he kills someone or gets killed, these things just go on and on. For the rest of your life, maybe."

"I know."

"Don't ever get a listed phone number, and be real careful with your privacy."

"Yeah, I understand. Thanks."

"You take care of yourself."

"Yeah, I will. *Thank* you. For everything."

"Been an honor, Miss Chloe."

AFTER a week of no Matthew, I waited until ten at night and drove over to his apartment. Sure enough, his truck was there and his light was on. I force marched myself up the stairs and knocked on his door.

I saw the pinpoint of light in the peephole wink out, then there was a long moment of nothing. I was ready to start pounding on the door again when he opened it. "Howdy," he said. He was in sweats, with a worn sweatshirt and socks with a hole in the toe.

I folded my arms across my chest.

"Yeah, I know." He shut his eyes a moment. "I know. Stay there. I'll come out." The door stayed open as he went to get his slippers on. I found a seat on the top step of the stairs and stared off at the horizon. The sky was jet black out beyond the city limits and the stars were thick as speckles on a hen, almost.

I heard, rather than saw, Matthew come to sit next to me. "I'm sorry," was the first thing he said.

"For what, exactly?" I asked. Now that he was here, within striking distance, I wanted to grab him and shake him and cry. I wanted to tell him I'd fallen for him and demand to know what his game was. He was the last person on earth I'd ever have expected to betray me.

"For not calling you back," he said. "For what it's worth, and it's probably not worth much, I needed the time to think." The fluorescent lights on his walkway cast deep shadows in his features, making him look even more stern than he was.

"You done thinking yet?"

"I dunno."

"Well, shall I go away-"

He put his hand on my arm. "No."

I shook him off. "What did you conclude, while *thinking?*"

"Well..." He sighed and put his head down on his hands.

It occurred to me to just get up and leave. Just walk away and never speak to him again, but I wouldn't get answers that way, so I waited. He was going to talk. I was adamant.

"So, I made a mistake," he said.

"That what you call it?"

"A big one. The worst."

"I can't believe you!" I said. "How on Earth-"

"Just, let me say my piece, all right? Then you can scream at me and hate me forever or whatever you want."

I pressed my lips together and turned to look at him.

He stared down at his hands and fidgeted. "I've spent a long time thinking it over. First of all, I didn't expect things to go as far as they did. I thought you'd be more... reserved."

"That," I said, "is not my fault. I trusted you. If you wanted to slow down, you should've said something."

"Well..."

I'm not a violent person, but I was sorely tempted to slap him. As it was, I just glared. "I'm not a mind reader. Pretty sure I told you that."

He looked back down at his hands. "I've liked you for ages. I just never thought it would go anywhere, and... so when it did, I had a lot to figure out."

"Like what?"

"Like whether it was love or just a crush. Whether I wanted to be with you, seriously, or whether it was just one of those daydream things.

The thing is, you are amazing. Truly. There's no one I admire more than you. And you're beautiful."

"But," I prompted.

"It's just a crush. And what we did this week... I pushed things way too far."

"Okay, so what do you want? Just to slow down, or not to even be together?"

Matthew didn't answer, just fidgeted.

Anger went supernova in my chest. "Why would you do that if you don't even want a relationship? What's the matter with you?"

"I'm not proud of my reasons."

"Which are?"

He shut his eyes and his lip quivered a little. "I've thought about it from every angle. I just... I didn't want Vanderholt to win."

"I never made this about Jason."

"I know. I did."

"And you really don't know me at all, do you? I am not interested in the random movie star guy with all his free time and a Skype connection. I'm nice. I let him talk to me. That's *it*."

"He's got it bad for you, Chloe. Anyone who sees him with you could tell you that. I dunno if he always gets this into his scams or if you're different to him but-"

"So what?"

"So? I got jealous. I wanted to be that into someone, and it's not like I couldn't see what he likes about you."

"Yeah, yeah. You like me, I'm wonderful, but don't even want to try dating me-"

"It's not like that."

"I'm like a sister to you?"

"You're not religious." He looked right at me as he said that.

I opened my mouth and shut it again.

"You're a good person," he went on, "but your wiring's fundamentally different from mine. A lot of things that really matter to me, I can't talk about with you."

"I totally fell for you."

"Chloe..."

I got up and headed down the stairs then. I didn't let myself look back. Matthew didn't say another word.

Jason picked up on the third ring. "He-ey!"

"I shouldn't have called you. I'm not in my right mind." I was driving home, my bluetooth device in one ear.

"What's wrong?"

"Nothing. Everything. I don't know. You're not whom I should talk to."

"You know you can talk to me. Talk to me."

"Jas…"

"Talk."

"I kissed Matthew."

"Uh-huh."

"And he bailed on me."

"What?"

"Blames himself at least. Calls it a mistake."

"Man, I'm sorry, Chlo. Really. I know what it's like to get burned."

"Yeah. But I shouldn't have called you."

"Why not? We're friends, right?"

"I lean on you enough."

"You've never leaned on me. Ever. Though you can, if you need."

"I should go."

"Hey, don't-"

"I need to go now." I hung up. I was at my house, not Val's, mine. This was home. This was my refuge, and Chris was locked up for the night, at least. I parked my car and went inside.

The kitchen yielded up no potato chips when I searched, and the freezer was devoid of ice cream. I couldn't find a scrap of junk food anywhere. I cursed Chris and the inconvenience he caused me. But gorging myself wasn't the answer.

Hiding in my room felt like the answer. I shut the door and curled up on my bed in fetal position. My bedclothes smelled a little dusty, but they also smelled like me. I couldn't imagine leaving my little cocoon of sheets and blankets to venture out into the world again.

Two hours later, the doorbell rang. I looked at my clock. It was midnight. Too late for a casual visitor. It had to be Matthew. He'd probably gone to Val's and was now here. He wanted to find me. He'd put real effort into the search.

I rolled off my bed and padded out to the front door. Okay, I thought. I'm ready for this. It'll be good. I twisted the knob and pulled the door open.

Jason stood on the doorstep, a grocery bag under one arm, his Prius parked behind him in the driveway. "Hey," he said, "you all right?"

18
SOMEONE ELSE'S FAIRYTALE

For a minute I just stared. "You're here?" I said.

"Yeah," said Jason. He looked like he'd just stepped off the set. His hair was styled. He'd shaved.

"How did you get here?"

"It's called an airplane. Invented over a hundred years ago." He glanced over his shoulder. "I don't think I was followed, but-"

"Come in," I said. I stepped back.

He came inside and dumped the grocery bag on the counter. "So are you all right?"

I nodded.

He held out his arms to me.

Now that he offered, I realized I could use a hug. His strong arms wrapped around my waist and he pressed his cheek against mine. As always, his skin smelled like moisturizer and with his body pressed close, it was natural for me to relax. I felt safe now. He kissed my cheek.

That felt good, really good. It was tempting to turn my head and kiss him back. No, I told myself. You're not thinking clearly. This is Jason, not Matthew; be smart. I pulled back.

He let go of me and turned to the grocery bag on the counter. "I don't know your favorite flavor, but I know chocolate's supposed to have magical properties in a situation like this." He pulled a carton of ice cream out of the bag. "This work?"

"Definitely."

He reached over the counter and tugged open the silverware drawer. I wondered how he knew which drawer, or if it was just a lucky guess. He extracted one spoon and led me over to the couch. Alarm bells went off in my head, and they only got louder as Jason sat me down, peeled the lid off the ice cream and dug out a spoonful. "Here," he said. He fed it to me.

It wasn't cheap, generic brand ice cream. This was the good stuff. It made me melt inside. I wanted to let him feed it to me and pour my heart out to him in return. I wanted him to put his arms around me and erase this whole nightmare with Matthew. And I wanted to kiss him and gaze into his dreamboat eyes. I had no doubt that he'd let me.

"You okay, Chloe?"

I shut my eyes. It seemed natural to lean against his shoulder, but I didn't. This is *Jason*, I reminded myself. He had more ex-girlfriends than I had college credits. "Give me a second." I got up and made myself walk to the bathroom, where I shut the door and took several deep breaths. Chloe, I thought. Get a grip. Think clearly. Do the right thing.

I splashed some cold water on my face, which made my cheeks sting like I'd rubbed them with sandpaper. The tearstains hadn't faded yet. Worse, I wanted to start crying again. Jason was being perfect. If I could dream up the ideal boyfriend, I couldn't script a better visit. He clearly knew what he was doing. Because, I reminded myself, he had experience.

Do the right thing, I thought.

I dried my face, squared my shoulders, took a deep breath, and walked back out into the main room.

Jason was back on his feet, by the counter, eating ice cream. At the sight of me he put the lid back on the carton and began to fidget with the spoon.

"I am really sorry," I said.

"You want me to leave."

"I should want you to leave, so I'm going to ask you to leave."

"You should?"

"Okay." I wiped my eyes. "One, I'm on the rebound right now, so as much as I want to kiss you, it's a mistake, and how stupid would it be for me to give in and regret it, given what just happened with Matthew?"

Jason blinked a few times, processing this.

"Two, this was amazing of you. I am overwhelmed with guilt that you did this for me and I shouldn't have called you."

"I'm glad you did."

"I shouldn't have. I feel like an-"

"Don't insult yourself. Please."

I felt like I was going to fly to pieces, this was so difficult. I folded my arms across my chest as if I could physically hold myself together. "This is like a fairytale. Everything with you has been like a fairytale. You've been Prince Charming to a T. You've been attentive and caring and taken me on amazing dawn rides to the top of Sandia and been there for me with Chris and you've got a wonderful family..."

He looked down. "But," he prompted.

I leaned against the counter. "It's not my fairytale. It's not anything I ever wanted. It's the last thing I've ever wanted. I hate crowds. I don't want to be the envy of every other woman on the planet. I never dreamed of being with a guy with flawless good looks. This is someone else's fairytale."

"Yeah," agreed Jason. "I know."

Relief unfolded in me. "You do?"

"It's mine."

Ouch. It would've been easier if he'd just jammed that cold spoon he was holding right through my sternum.

"First time you looked at me, I knew what you saw. A jerk in a t shirt eating ice at four in the morning." He chuckled.

"You're not a jerk."

"You're the most literal person I know."

"Jas..."

"I know that if you like me, I must be a decent guy."

"You are a great guy," I agreed.

"I love you."

Okay, now I definitely wished he'd just end me with that cold spoon. Tears of shock welled up in my eyes. "I'm sorry. Really. I'm so sorry."

He nodded. "Honest to the end. That's so you."

"Jason..."

"Bye, Chloe."

"Bye."

He turned and walked out the door. I shut my eyes and listened as it clicked shut. A moment later I heard his car start up. Three seconds later,

I assumed he was gone. His Pruis was silent, so I didn't hear it pull out.

I wiped my eyes again and looked around. I felt a million times worse than I had at the beginning of the evening. The only consolation was knowing deep down, that I'd done the right thing and dodged another bullet.

Still, a part of me wanted to pick up the ice cream and slam it against the wall, or throw it away. Instead I dumped it in the freezer, locked the front door, and went to bed.

19
POETIC JUSTICE

THE next morning I considered sleeping in, but my routine was a source of comfort. I got up, showered, got my things from Val's, and went to class. Matthew was in Media Studies, but he sat at the front and I sat at the back. At noon, I called Victims Services and learned that Chris was still in jail. Apparently Dr. Winters still hadn't bailed him out.

LORI was at the house when I got back. "Chloe," she said, "I want to talk to you."

I seated myself on the couch and waited.

The light from the window framed her silhouette. She stood, hands on her hips, head tilted to one side. "Um, you look like you expect me to chew you out."

"I'm listening."

"You didn't ruin my floral dress, did you?"

I shook my head. "I haven't touched your stuff. What do you want to talk about?"

"Are you feeling okay?"

I took a deep breath. "You were right about Matthew, and I'm sorry. Really. I was stupid."

"What happened?"

"He wasn't actually interested in me. We went too far."

"Ouch."

"My fault."

"Yeah, I can't really imagine you throwing yourself at a guy," said Lori. "Not your style, so I'm betting it's not your fault. But now I feel really bad."

"Why? Did you hook up with him too?"

"No." She laughed. "No way. Chlo, I'm moving in with Charles for good. We talked it over. I'll pay up the rent on the rest of my share of the lease-" She held up a hand to cut off my protest. "I'm really not ready to explain all this to my parents yet, so this is easier. Charles's used to paying his full rent, so it'll be cool. I just... I hope you're not mad at me?"

"Why would I be?"

"Be-cause... I'm leaving you alone to deal with your psycho brother. But things are going really well with Charles. They're perfect. I love him so much and living with him has made us so much closer."

"Well, I'm happy for you."

"You sure you're okay?"

"I'm fine."

"Not feeling abandoned?"

That was exactly how I felt, but telling her that meant explaining what I'd done to Jason, so I just shook my head and smiled.

I THOUGHT the worst was over, I really did, only three weeks later, I walked into my Media Studies class and heard the professor announce, "Well, the big event is here."

I didn't know there was a Big Event.

"The reason many of you ladies signed up for this class."

I glanced around the lecture hall. Several of the girls were giggling. Matthew, sitting in the front row, lounged back. I couldn't read his expression. He never so much as looked at me.

"Today, we begin the *New Light* series, the biggest blockbuster of modern times. Okay people, these movies are long so I'm not going to open with a lecture. Let's just get started." He switched off the lights, and started the movie.

All right, I thought. No worries. I can handle this. I settled myself in my seat and resolved to watch.

The very first shot was of Jason, with shoulder length hair, shirtless.

He was working in a corral, or whatever the Roman equivalent was, with white horses. It was an absurd, Hollywood shot, and he looked so young. He'd been what when the movie was made? Twenty four? Twenty three? Not all that much older than me.

What hit me, though, wasn't how stupid and generic this opening shot was, or the stilted dialogue when Gladius's slave owner yelled that he wouldn't ever amount to anything. It was Jason's steely eyed, cover of a million magazines, perfect pose response. Jason looked... well... fabulous. My knees felt weak and my palms started to sweat.

I missed him. A month with no one to talk to was killing me. I'd thought Matthew was my best friend, but when it had really mattered, it was Jason who'd come through. Now I could hardly remember anything Matthew and I talked about from day to day. I could, however, remember that Jason ate celery after a visit to the gym and that he'd known what a Golgi apparatus was. I remembered how he'd sit, rubbing lotion on his arms while we talked, and explain how much the lights on set took their toll. I remembered how eager he'd always been to talk to me. I remembered how he'd wanted to kiss me after dinner at Tia Anita's, and his hugs. I couldn't forget his hugs. I wondered how many women he'd charmed with his hugs alone.

I too, was now a fangirl. Great. Against my better judgment, I got swept up in the absurd plot of the movie. I watched Gladius earn his name (though my mind kept inserting the word "sword" whenever anyone said it), saw him catch sight of Caesar's beautiful daughter and become smitten with her at once. I went with it as he dreamed about kissing her and I broke out into a cold sweat as I imagined what it would have been like to kiss him myself. I refused to notice how disturbing it was that I was watching him stalk a woman who'd never met him. He sneaked into her camp at night and peered into her window to watch her sleep. (If any guy actually did that to me, I'd get a restraining order *so* fast.) I wanted him to go into the gladiator ring and earn enough money to buy his freedom so that he could pursue her. He had me convinced this was a love story even though the woman didn't know about him, let alone love him.

We got as far as his second major challenge in the ring, and then class was over. The lights came up and everyone gathered their things. I needed a moment before I could get to my feet. My heart was still pounding. I was still afraid for Gladius, that he might get killed, even though I knew this was the first in a three movie deal for Jason.

I shook myself and gathered my books. A walk outside would help me return to my senses, I was certain.

I was early to my next Media Studies class two days later and immediately picked up where I'd left off, my heart in my mouth, willing Gladius to overcome his enemies and become a champion.

When the princess showed up to his final challenge for the movie, I wished I could shoot poison darts out of my eyes at her and step into her place. I watched as he hacked his way gorily through the trial, emerging triumphant against all odds. I thought it was sexy that he was dripping with sweat and covered with a few streaks of blood. I would have run right into his arms, just like the princess did.

Only, that turned out to be a daydream for Gladius. The movie finished with him winning enough for his freedom, but still gazing longingly at the princess, who left the coliseum without a backwards glance.

The lights came up and the professor started his lecture. I tried to focus and take notes, but I kept reliving parts of the movie in my mind. I imagined being there at that final fight and dropping some kind of token onto the battleground (even though that was an idea from a different era). I imagined breaking into his slave quarters to make him forget all about the princess. After all, I had been that girl for him, for a little while at least. I daydreamed in a way I hadn't done since I was a little girl, before Chris's insanity had brought an abrupt end to my childhood.

I missed the end of the lecture and had to gather my things while everyone else filed out. I knew I had to write an essay on the movie, and that, for once, wouldn't be hard. As soon as I got home, I got out my netbook and got to work. I pointed out every ridiculous misogynistic trope in that film and then analyzed how a good Hollywood actor got the audience to look past them all.

I certainly had.

Two weeks and two more *New Light* movies later, and I was in even worse shape. I watched Gladius enlist in the Roman army and make a name for himself in *New Light: A Call to Destiny*, then watched him lead the armies to a great and strategic victory in *New Light: Glory's Reign*. I sat on the edge of my seat when he met the princess for the first time and declared his undying love for her, and my heart soared when he returned from battle to find that she'd spurned her betrothed and pledged to be with him instead.

I watched their wedding and a very stylized sex scene and the beginning of Gladius's reign as emperor. The princess was madly in love with him, and he convinced me that he'd be true to her forever, and thus the movies ended on the perfect note. Provided one could ignore the fact that the Romans were shouting "All hail Gladius Caesar!" at the end, and nothing in the historical record supported the idea that they'd had an "Emperor Sword".

But the unit was over.

I wished my daydreams would end that neatly. After the last class I went to work. One of the magazines on the magazine rack, across the room from me, had a picture of Jason on the cover and boasted a seven page interview. I tried to distract myself by thinking about how I really had done the right thing that last night I'd seen him. He'd have moved on ages ago. I was now just another face in the screaming legions. A fangirl.

A customer stepped up to the register. "Y-" I meant to say "Yes?" but I choked. Standing across the counter was Steve Vanderholt. "H-hi," I said.

"Hey, Chloe."

"Hey, Chloe." That, I realized with a start, was Jennifer, standing right next to him. The two siblings faced me, both smiling. Next to them was a very bored and disgusted looking Kyra.

"Yeah... hi." My face burned hot. I wondered how often they'd been in before I'd ever met Jason. How many people around town saw them and served them and had no idea. "Um... so... can I uh..."

"How are you?" Steve asked.

I wanted to slink away. To morph into someone else or have someone knock over a table or start a fight so I'd have a reason to take off at a run.

"Ye-ah," said Jen. "We heard what happened."

"I'm sorry," I said. "Really."

"For what?" said Steve. "Jason made a pass at you, and you, by his account, were real decent about it."

Now that my head had cleared a little, I saw they weren't

uncomfortable. If anything, they looked like they felt bad about how things had turned out. But I knew Steve independent of Jason. He and I were still friends.

"So how are you?" he said.

"I'm real good. The evidence you got for my case? The cops followed some leads and took him into custody for parole violations. I think I can move home again soon, so I'll never be able to thank you enough."

"That was all you. You took the initiative and got the whole process rolling."

"Steve said you were amazing," said Jennifer.

"Can I get you guys anything?"

They placed their orders and I handed them a number to take to their table.

Steve looked confused, "Wait, what about-"

"You're not paying," I said, curtly. "Go sit."

Jen gave my arm a squeeze before they went to find a table. I looked after them wistfully. Jason did have a great family. I was glad more customers flooded in so that I could forget they were even there.

Only, when I returned from the back to fetch something, there stood Kyra, by the milkshake line. She didn't look like she was in line, though. She was at the counter, next to the people placing orders.

"Hi," I said to her.

"Hi..."

I paused to see if she wanted to say anything else.

"So... um..." She shifted her weight like I was the one who'd put her on the spot. "Can I see your scar?"

I had a pitcher of juice in one hand, and the counter was too high for me to show my calf. I pulled up my shirt and showed her the one on my stomach, a glossy circle of scar tissue.

"Whoa," she said.

"Hope you don't know too many people with those." I moved on.

Only, she stayed. I took a couple more orders. Jen and Steve were seated at the edge of the dining room, and Jennifer glanced over now and then, but didn't call her stepdaughter back. I went over to stand across from Kyra again.

"Jason said you were the strongest woman he'd ever met."

"Well, he never saw that scar," I said. "I've got another one on my leg."

"Oh... really?" Confusion clouded her expression.

I laughed. "Yes, not that it's any of your business. Really."

"You were just his friend?"

"I was."

She looked down. There were customers in line, but my coworkers seemed to be on top of it. I waited.

Kyra said nothing.

"So how've you been?" I asked.

"Fine."

"Family treating you all right?"

She shrugged at that and pulled a face. "Who, the Vanderholts?"

"They would be your family."

"They treat me fine."

"What's that mean? Jen been feeding you too much?"

"She doesn't do that to me."

I nodded.

"They don't like me."

"I happen to know that isn't true."

"They're always telling me what to do."

"Well, that's what's really not fun about being a teenager. It gets better. 'Scuse me a sec." I went to help out by putting bread rolls on plates. "Sorry," I told the guy who was manning the Red Stuff machine. "Don't mean to be slacking." He just waved that away. I dished up a few slices of cake and cookies, then returned to where Kyra still stood.

"They like you," she said. "They still talk about you. They all think I'm messed up."

"You got into the Academy, which I happen to know isn't easy. I graduated from Rio Grande and have bullet holes in me. There's no way they think I'm okay but that you're messed up. Gimme a break."

She blinked a few times in surprise, then giggled.

I made as if to look her over critically. "You seem all right to me. How do you like school?"

"It's okay."

"What's your favorite class?"

"Drama."

"Really? You ever talked to Jason about that?"

"No..."

"You should. I bet he doesn't even know."

"Nobody knows."

I didn't get why she would tell me, then, when she had such a close knit family, but the girl standing across the counter from me looked lonely. I wondered if I would have been that way if my mother had married my father, and I felt the rest of the Winters family didn't approve of me. Not exactly the same situation, but close enough, it seemed.

"Kyra?" Jen called out. Kyra and I both turned and Jen pointed to the plates of food that had just been delivered to the table.

"I gotta go," said Kyra.

"Nice to see you," I said.

"Thanks." She said it awkwardly, and scurried across the room.

AT closing time, I had a moment of weakness and bought the magazine with Jason on it. I took it home, stared at the cover for about half an hour, then flipped open to the interview. The first page had a two page picture of Jason lying on a couch, gazing at the camera with the loneliest expression I'd ever seen. It was the way he'd looked at me just before I'd kicked him out of my house, and right then I wanted to put my arms around him and tell him I was sorry, and that I wanted to take it all back.

But the stack of printouts that Matthew had made was tucked under the couch. I'd put it there in a moment of laziness when I ought to have cleaned. Jason would most certainly have moved on. Even if I had kissed him that night, it'd probably all be over by now. I was no one special to him.

I shut the magazine and tossed it on the table.

MOM showed up at my house a couple of weeks later. No tears, no crisis, just Mom. I let her in and she sat down on the barstool, and said nothing. I took a deep breath and said, "What?"

"How are you?"

"I'm fine. How are you?"

"I'm good. I hear you got a restraining order against Chris?"

"Yeah."

"I should do that."

Guilt hit my like a wave of cold water to the face. My mother's house had been vandalized, and it hadn't occurred to me to have her join me in the petition. "Sorry, I should have told you. But, he's back in jail now. He got five years."

"Oh. Okay."

"I just..." There was no good way to finish that. I'd been so worried about myself that I hadn't thought of anyone else. But why, I thought, should I have to think of anyone else? I was the one who'd been shot and left for dead in the desert. It seemed only fair that I got to be a little self-centered about it.

"A friend of mine works as a court reporter," said Mom. "He said you were amazing."

I shrugged.

"Always so tough." She smiled with pride.

"It's not like I ever had a choice." The words came with a flash of anger.

Mom blinked in surprise, then got her wide-eyed look. She didn't ask what I meant or try to defend herself. My outburst hadn't provoked a fight. Her reaction was far worse than that. She started to cry.

"Mom," I shouted. "For once in your life, act like a grown up!"

"Honey?"

"Chris's attack happened to me, not you. To *me*."

"I-I know. I was there when they brought you in..." Her voice faded to a whisper, then choking sobs. If she were making an Oscar clip, it would have been perfect, but given this was real life, it made me want to throttle her.

"Well how come I don't get to cry about it? How come I've got to be the strong one? Why did you even come here to talk about restraining orders? Do you expect me to help you out with yours? Because it should be the other way around!"

Mom didn't reply, just kept staring at me with those wide, vulnerable eyes.

"I can't take this," I said. "Mom, I love you, but I don't want you around right now. I can't comfort you-"

"I don't want you to comfort me-"

"Well you sit there sobbing and what am I supposed to do? Just go read a book?"

"I don't expect-"

"What would any normal person do if they saw you right now? What would they feel with all the tears? The 'I'm so scared' look?" I gestured at her. "You may not be asking directly for comfort, but I can't just ignore you. When do *I* get to be scared and get comforted and all that? Huh? In ten years, that has never happened."

My mother blinked several times, fat tears running down her cheeks. She took a deep, shaky breath and looked, as always, like a scared little girl. One who'd just been yelled at by her mother. She took another deep breath. "Okay," she said. "I can try to... to understand that, but I'll never forget what it was like, seeing my baby like that."

"Yeah, try to imagine what it's like comforting your baby through that."

"Honey... I don't... I can't..." She rested her forehead on one hand as if bracing herself against a headache. She heaved some more deep breaths.

I went and flopped down on the couch and stared at the blank gray television screen. There was no point yelling at her. It had only made me feel worse.

"Have I ever told you how proud I am of you?" she said.

"What?"

"I don't think I have. I hear you're on track to be valedictorian?"

"Mmmm."

"Amazing. I think I got one A once in a class. PE."

"Mom..."

"So you think I'm silly and inadequate. Compared to you, I am. I always will be."

"Come on. No martyr stuff."

"Most people are weaker and stupider and less capable than you. I can't help you there."

I shook my head.

"I'm sorry," she said.

"Don't. You're making me feel guilty."

"Well, I don't mean to do that either."

"I'm sorry too," I said. And I was. I was sorry for provoking a fight.

"Well... anyway... I didn't come to talk about restraining orders," said Mom. "I shouldn't have even brought that up. I'm moving, honey." She bit her lip, again, as if she were the daughter and she were looking to me for approval.

"Moving where?"

"North Dakota."

I sat up. "What?"

She shrugged and began to fidget by flicking her thumbnails against each other, *click, click, click.*

"What's in North Dakota?"

She didn't respond.

I took a deep, bracing breath. "Who's in North Dakota?"

"His name's Ron."

"And how did you meet him?"

She stopped clicking her nails and pressed a hand to her forehead again. "On e-Harmony."

Calm, I told myself. "Have you ever met him in person?"

"Yes, honey, he's been down here twice. I didn't introduce him to you because I wasn't all that sure what I thought of him yet."

"But now you're moving in with him?"

To my utter shock, she shook her head. "No. I've got a little apartment up there, and a job. I'm going to work at a hotel reception desk. I figure... there's nothing really keeping me here. Other than you, I mean, but you're all grown up and don't need your mother hanging around."

"I like having you around."

She was kind enough not to correct me, only gave me a tolerant smile. "Thank you. I figure I should go explore this..." She waved her hand. "Opportunity. He treats me very well. And he's unmarried." She bit her lip again.

"That's a plus."

"Yes it is. He's a widower. Has two girls in high school. Owns a garage and seems to do real well for himself. I'm not really sure what he sees in me."

"Oh, come on."

"I don't."

"You're young, and even for your age you look good. You take care of yourself. You're good to your boyfriends. Way better than they deserve. What's not to like?"

She shrugged. "I'm not you. You're the one who attracts the rich men lately."

I shook my head. "Nothing ever came of that."

"Oh." She looked at my coffee table.

I sat forward and swiped the magazine with Jason's picture on the cover, and tucked it under my arm. "I haven't spoken to him in months."

"That issue only came out last week."

"Well, yeah. I..."

"He broke it off and you still miss him?" She nodded. "That's rough."

"Nothing happened. I broke it off, Mom."

"So did he send you that?"

"No."

She didn't raise an eyebrow or smirk at me or anything, just sat and waited.

"I'm pathetic," I said. "We watched *New Light* in Media Studies and now I can't get over it. They're such stupid movies, and I'm a fangirl."

"I love those movies."

"Yeah, well, so... What Jason liked about me was that I didn't care about that stuff. Turns out, I do. He wouldn't be interested in me now."

"What? That's harsh. Those made him famous."

I tried to shrug like I didn't care.

Mom didn't buy it. She got off her stool and came to sit next to me. "Honey, why don't you call him?"

"He'll have forgotten about me."

She tugged the magazine loose from under my arm. "How do you know that?"

"He gets around, Mom. He's probably had two other girlfriends by now."

She looked up from paging through the magazine. "Have you tried calling him?"

"No... but-"

She'd reached the interview, and the two page picture of him reclining on a couch. I averted my eyes.

"He just makes up stories for interviews. There's nothing in there that's him."

Mom paged past the photo, and the next, and the next. "'Do you believe in true love?'" she read.

"Mom..."

"He says, 'You know, in all seriousness, I do. Fairytale endings aren't just for normal people. Us abnormally famous guys want them as much as the next person.'"

"Stop," I said.
"Why? Like you said, it's just made up, right?"
"But-"
"They ask him, 'Have you ever met your fairytale princess?'"
I snatched the magazine away. "Stop."
"Maybe he'll mention you. You don't want to find out?"
I clasped the magazine to my chest and folded my arms. "No."
Mom didn't buy it for a second. She burst out laughing.

20
PHONE CALLS

"Give me the magazine, Chloe," said Mom.

I shook my head and kept my arms clasped over the magazine. I knew I was scrunching Jason's picture, but I reminded myself that I shouldn't care.

"Are you scared?" Mom asked. She started to giggle.

"What? What's so funny?"

"Honey, I've never seen you scared of anything. You've faced down being murdered, and you're afraid of *boys?*"

I turned away from her. Why couldn't she be a wise, caring, mother? Why did she have to act like one of my high school classmates? She was full on laughing at me now.

"Well," she said, "that got you through high school without incident, but you've gotta let it go someday, honey. It's okay to get your heart broken. It doesn't hurt worse than multiple gunshot wounds."

"How do you know?"

"Well, it doesn't hurt worse than seeing your daughter with multiple gunshot wounds. Not even close. I can tell you that."

I shook my head.

Mom held out her hand for the magazine. "Come on," she said. "I can read it and tell you if it's good or bad." When I didn't move she wiggled her fingers. "Come on. What if he tells the world he's in love with you?"

Tears sprang to my eyes. I let go of the magazine to swipe the back of my hand across my cheeks.

"Oh, what, honey? You love him?"

"He told me he loved me."

She yanked the magazine out of my arms. "I'm reading this."

"Mom-"

"You want me to read it aloud or no?"

"I..."

"If I leave it here without reading it aloud, you going to read it, or you going to do your stoic thing and throw it away?"

I folded my arms across my chest, as if they'd form a shield between me and her.

"I'm reading it aloud." She cleared her throat. She was just right there. I could still grab the magazine. "They asked if he'd ever met his fairytale princess, and he says, 'Well... maybe.'

"Then the interviewer says, 'That a yes?'" Mom gave me a significant look. "Shall I go on?"

I grabbed a couch pillow and hugged it to my chest. "He'll probably tell some story about some other girl."

"Which, according to you, could be a total lie. He lies in interviews, right?"

"Sure."

She squeezed my arm. "Be strong. He says, 'Well, I've met someone who deserves to be the fairytale princess. Beautiful, intelligent, and, like, the strongest person I've ever met. Knowing that she doesn't have someone in her life who loves her for the amazing person she is, that's what breaks my heart. No one deserves a Prince Charming more than she does.'" Mom inclined her head. "Think that's you?"

"I don't know."

"It's this month's issue of the magazine."

"Could be an old stock interview, from a year ago."

"He looks like he did in the interviews he did for *Danger Fields*."

"Maybe they do the photoshoots at a different time."

Mom dropped the magazine on the coffee table. "Call him."

"I can't."

"Now."

"Mom!"

"Just do it."

"No way."

"Look, you can't tell me off for never helping you through a crisis and then refuse my help now. I know this isn't you lying near death, but it's as close as you're likely to ever get again. I hope." She sat forward.

"Mom-"

"There's no 'Mom-ing' your way out of this. Where's your phone?" She swept her gaze around the room and spied it on the counter. Before I could move, she'd crossed the room and snatched it up. "You call him, or I will. How would that make you feel, having your mother call him up?"

"Just stop, okay?"

She sat down next to me and held out the phone. "No. You may know more than me about just about everything, but not men. I've got enough bad experiences to have a doctorate in this, and I'm telling you, you don't let this one go. You'll always wonder. You *will* regret it. If you love someone, and it's a healthy love- no... extramarital issues or anything like that -you tell them. You have to."

"When have you ever gone through this?"

She frowned. "A guy asked me out when you were about five. A nice guy. Really good looking, knew about the situation with your father and everything and told me he wanted to show me what it was like to be treated the way I deserved. I said no."

"So you call him!"

"He's married now, honey. Got four kids. And the thing is, I wasn't attracted to him at all, but I've always regretted passing up the opportunity to find out what he meant. If I regret that, you will definitely regret this a million times more." She pushed the phone at me. "Someday you'll thank me, even if some girl picks up the phone and you hear the shower going in the background."

"Mom..."

She waved the phone back and forth, enticing me to take it. "And if it goes horribly wrong, you can turn around and yell at me. Just let it all out. Blame me for everything. You won't get a better opportunity."

I looked at the phone.

"You do love him, don't you?"

"I hate his life."

"Well, it could be worse. He could be married."

"Yeah, I'll remember that." I snatched the phone from her and keyed to my directory. "I will totally blame you when this goes wrong."

"Fine."

"And I may not even give you credit if it goes right."

"Yes, I hear that's often how this mother/daughter thing is supposed to work."

I called up Jason's number and hit "Send" before I could talk myself out of it. Then I held the phone to my ear as if it were a live grenade. I screwed my eyes shut and clenched my teeth.

"Chloe?" he answered. It was him, his soft, deep voice.

"Hi."

"Hi. What's up?" He sounded distant, like he didn't want to talk to me.

I wilted inside. "I'm just... just calling, to see how you are."

"I'm good. How are you?"

"I'm fine."

"Yeah... that's good."

Our ability to talk about anything or nothing was gone. There was just dead air.

Mom waved the magazine at me but I pushed it aside. "I'm sorry," I said. "I shouldn't have bothered you."

"Do you need anything, Chlo?"

"No, I'm good. Just... just saying 'hi.'"

"Oh, well, it's good to hear from you."

"Yeah, you too."

"I'll be out in Albuquerque for the holidays. Maybe we could get together?" It didn't sound sincere, just polite.

"Yeah, sure. That'd be great."

"All right. Yeah, well, I'll call you when I'm in town." The clear meaning, I was not to call him.

"Okay, cool. See you then."

"See you. Bye." He hung up without waiting for my response. I let the phone drop from my fingers and tears welled up in my eyes.

"What did he say?" Mom asked.

I waved my hands dismissively. "That he might call when he's in town for the holidays."

"That's good!"

"No, he was just being polite."

"You should have told him how you feel."

"Mom, I know him; he wouldn't have wanted to hear it."

She looked like she might argue, but put her hand on my shoulder instead. "You did all right," she said. "You might still wonder what if-"

"Mom, don't."

She pulled me in for a hug. "It'll be okay, though."

I wished I could hit rewind on my life, go back to that night with the ice cream, and take another road, but I couldn't. That moment had passed and was gone. For the first time ever, I cried in my mother's arms.

Mom left town the following weekend, full of apologies about not spending the holidays with me. She was going to meet Ron's family and that made her a nervous wreck.

When she arrived in her new apartment, she called me on Skype. That surprised me.

"What?" I said when I answered. "You have a computer?"

"Yeah." Behind her was a plain, white wall and the edge of a door frame done up in dark wood. Her apartment was definitely a little dated.

"Since when?"

"Since I bought one from Best Buy." She looked at me like my question was strange. "That okay with you? I'm not that old. I can download from the internet. They did have the internet when I was your age, you know."

"I just wondered if Ron got it for you." Then I remembered that internet was how she'd met Ron. I was slow. Obviously she'd had a computer for quite some time.

"Oh, no. He did give me a present when I moved in. He gave me this." She held up an ice scraper, the kind that people used on their windshields in the winter.

"Nice," I said.

"It's got a brush at the other end." She flipped it over for me to see. "And a mitt for me to put my hand in to keep it warm."

"That's what he got you?"

"Yeah... he's a little different from Bill."

Major understatement. Dr. Winters had given her spa weekends and romantic retreats and new clothes. I don't think he even knew how to use an ice scraper.

Mom smiled at it. "It's cold here. There's ten inches of snow on the ground."

"Oh, wow."

"So I can really use this."

"So he's a good kind of different?"

"I think so." She put the ice scraper down. "We'll see."

"But you're happy, Mom?"

She nodded. "How are you?"

"Um... heartbroken, but I'm okay."

"Oh, honey. I'll send you all the virtual hugs I can."

"Thanks."

"You need ice cream?"

"No! Sorry, didn't mean to yell there, but no. I'll stick with french fries."

"All right." She raised an eyebrow.

"He... the night I told him I wasn't interested... he flew out on a private jet and brought me gourmet ice cream. He even started to spoon feed it to me..."

Mom blinked.

"Yeah, shut up."

"I didn't say anything."

"I should look for a guy who'll buy me an ice scraper instead, right? Practical. None of the mushy stuff."

"Mushy stuff is okay when it's sincere. This-" she held up the ice scraper "-is sincere. He wants to make my life better, but if he sincerely wanted to give me foot rubs and peeled grapes, that's okay too."

"Peeled grapes?"

"You ever tried to peel a grape?" She looked defensive.

"Noooo. But you're not supposed to make me feel stupid. You're supposed to support me. I told him no because I was on the rebound over some other guy and I wasn't thinking clearly."

"Okay."

"I'm hanging up now, Mom."

"I love you, honey."

"Love you too. Bye." I cut the connection. The magazine with Jason on it was still on the coffee table. I picked it up and flipped to the first, two-page spread of him. He's all wrong for you, I told myself. After everything that was right about Matthew, this guy is a step in the opposite direction.

My mother called again. "Yes, hello," I said.

"Sorry," she said.

"No, it's fine."

"That the magazine?"

Dang it! I hadn't noticed that it was in the video frame. I dropped it on the floor. "Maybe."

"You could call him again."

"I can't. No. I just need to get over him."

"It's all right."

"It's not! I'm reading interviews by him, looking for messages to me. I'm like a million other girls, looking at his picture and fantasizing about him kissing me... or... well..." This was my *mother* I was saying this to. I had to get a grip.

But Mom looked at me like I was nuts, not inappropriate. "Let me explain this to you," she said. "Millions of other women fantasize about what he's like and read interviews by him and imagine he's talking to them, and they're wrong. They've never met him. They don't even know what he looks like without airbrushing."

"I don't think they had to airbrush much, Mom."

"But you know that. You actually know him. He may, in fact, be talking about you in his interviews. How is it that all those other silly girls can think they're sane and *you* think you're crazy? That's backwards."

"I just want to be over him."

"Well, I'm sorry. He won't be the last guy to fall for you."

"Thanks."

"You're not mad at me?"

"No. I gotta do my homework now, okay?"

"Isn't it the weekend?"

"Mom, it's *me*."

"Oh, right. Well, have fun then."

"Thanks. Bye." I cut the connection again.

On Christmas Eve, which was also my birthday, Mom called again, wearing a silly green and red dunce cap, decorated with glitter. She blew a horn and sang to me.

"Did you get my present yet?" she asked.

"No."

"Oh. Well, it might make you mad."

"Why? What'd you get?"

"The *New Light* trilogy, boxed set."

"Mom!"

"Okay, okay, send it back if you don't want it. It'll come from Amazon. As will your Christmas present, which is just a gift certificate, so you can buy textbooks or something."

"I sent you some rock salt," I told her. "Just so you know how much I care. You can de-ice your walk with it."

That sent her howling with laughter. "Really?"

"Yeah, really."

"Oh, that's too funny. I've gotta run to Ron's house, but just wanted to say Happy Birthday."

"Thanks. Love you, Mom."

"I love you too."

"Now for this scene," came the director's voice, "I wanted to get that rock into the shot. Look at that rock. Isn't it just craggy and fabulous?"

"What do you think it adds to the story here?" said the writer.

"I dunno. Which part of the story is this?"

It was the day after Christmas and the cellophane from the *New Light* movies was crumpled on the floor. I had already watched all three and was now watching them again with the director's commentary on. I was that pathetic.

On New Year's Day, Jason called. My heart just about stopped.

"Hello?" I answered the phone.

"Hi."

"Hi."

"Sooo, me and some friends are going out to eat tonight. You want to come?"

I felt torn right down the middle. Of course I wanted to go, but at the same time, I knew I'd be a total wreck and probably look like an idiot.

"Chloe?"

"Yeah... yeah, sure. I can come."

"Okay. It's at Tia Anita's at seven. See you then?"

"Yeah, see you."

"'Kay, later." He hung up.

I put my phone down, my heart thundering. It was this or not see him at all, and I didn't know which was worse. Tia Anita's, of all places. What would Jen think? I looked out the front windows and saw that the sky had grayed over. A few flakes of snow drifted down.

21 DINNER

For once, I hated myself for my lack of wardrobe. I'd worn my gray skirt around Jason a couple of times, and I wasn't sure if he'd seen me in my black dress. I decided that if I was going to make a fool out of myself, I'd at least try to look stunning too. I went shopping and got myself a fitted, burgundy dress with a shawl. That plus some new pumps helped bolster my confidence.

I showered and took half an hour to blow dry and style my hair, curling the ends the way I'd seen Beth do it. (Why not? We did have the same shape face and it'd looked fabulous on her.) I did my eyes up dark and smoky, which would be a disaster if I started crying. One more reason not to cry. My lips, I did up with a light plum lipstick under lipgloss. Matthew had once told me it looked very kissable, and I hoped that was good advice, even considering the source.

I timed the drive so that I could sweep into Tia Anita's at 7:05, only there was a huge crowd of fans at the door, and no one to call me and give me access through the side entrance. I had to muscle my way through the crowd to get inside.

It was probably more like 7:10 when I presented myself to the host, who looked a little surprised when I told her what table. My already low self confidence sank another notch. "One second," she said. She disappeared back into the restaurant, with its smells of green chile, queso blanco, and warm sopapillas.

I waited, feeling like the most pathetic fangirl on the planet, until the host returned and waved me on back. I followed her around the corner and down a small hallway to the private room, where Jason, Donovan Reilly, and Rick Lucero all sat. The table had either been switched out, or had some leaves removed. It was big for four people, but not enormous. Rick Lucero was another actor around Jason's age, with similar dreamboat status. His eyes were hazel gray, his hair dark brown, his tan perfect, his body toned. Not remarkable at this table. I had no idea what he was doing here in Albuquerque. When I walked in, all three guys looked up. Rick raised his eyebrows.

"Chloe, right?" said Don.

"Hi," I said.

"Hey, have a seat," said Jason. The only seat was at the far end of the table, opposite and facing him. I slid into it and crossed my ankles. There was a hint of surprise in his gaze as he looked at me. "You look nice."

"Thanks."

"How've you been?" asked Don.

"Good. I'm surprised you even remember me."

He gave a self conscious chuckle. "Of course I do."

"What brings you to Albuquerque?" I asked. As weird as it was to have him there, it was nice too. I could just turn and talk to him, rather than making calf eyes at Jason.

Jason sat back in his chair and turned to Rick. The two of them started talking.

"Rick and I have a shoot starting here next week, and we just came out early to hang with Jason," said Don.

I nodded.

"'Cause, you know, he's got his shoot starting tomorrow in Vancouver."

"Oh." I shrugged. "No, I didn't know."

A look of confusion flitted across Don's face, but it was gone as fast as it came. "How're your studies going? Dig up any good bones?"

"Not recently. Saw your cover on *People*. Very suave."

"Oh really?" He pretended to preen. "Ye-ah... prepared for days for that one, you know. Practiced the look."

I laughed.

Jason and Rick paused and looked at me. Jason's expression was unreadable.

"So, your high school was called La Cueva?" said Rick.

"Yep." Jason smiled.

"Nice name."

"Well, you know, it's actually in a cave."

"Seriously?" said Don.

Jason nodded, then shook his head. "No." He laughed. He was being smooth and charismatic and silly, just like he was in his interviews. There was little hint of the quieter, just as crazy, self effacing guy I knew. I wondered if that was because he was with his famous friends, or because that guy was gone.

The waiter came in and deposited a basket of sopapillas on the table.

"Are you going to show us how to eat this food?" asked Don.

"I'm sure you can figure it out," said Jason.

Don turned to me. "You know how to do this?"

"Yeah. It's not rocket science."

"Can you teach me?"

"I can try."

"Can I trust you not to make me look like an idiot?" asked Don.

"I dunno, how hard is that to do, usually?"

"Ouch," said Rick.

"Yeah, well," said Don. He grinned. "Now you've met Chloe." He raised his glass, and I realized he was flirting with me.

He was my mother's age. I handed him the basket of sopapillas. "Tear off a corner and put a couple of spoonfuls of honey inside." Talking was fine. Flirting, no way.

Jason pressed his fingers to the bridge of his nose, as if he had a headache. I decided to tone down the sarcasm, though he'd never been embarrassed by me before. That hurt.

Rick leaned forward. "How do you know Don?"

"She knows me," said Jason. He didn't look at me as he said it. He was looking everywhere but at me.

"Oh."

"We're both from here," he went on.

"So did you go to high school in the cave?" Rick asked.

"No, that's where the spoiled rich kids go. My high school is a bunch of mud huts at the west end of town."

"I can't tell if you're kidding."

"Okay, cinderblock," I said. "And portables."

"Aw, we've got those in LA," said Don. "Public schools without enough funding. Not to... I don't mean to knock your education. Chloe's... don't get into an intellectual argument with her."

"Noted," said Rick.

Jason fidgeted with his menu and scowled at it as if it were a bad review of one of his films.

And then Jennifer came out, wearing her white chef's uniform and apron. I wished I could just crawl under the table and disappear.

"Hey, it's my mean sister," said Jason.

Everyone exchanged hellos. I managed a sheepish wave. Jen tried to look me in the eye but I feigned interest in the menu instead. While the others made small talk, I sensed her gaze on me. Yes, I thought. I'm pathetic. Those piercing, Vanderholt eyes seemed to peel back all my bravado to examine the scared, clueless girl underneath. My new clothes now felt frumpy and my makeup clownish.

"I'll try not to drop your food on the floor too many times," she said to her brother as she left.

"See how mean she is?" said Jason.

"Brutal, having a chef for a sister," said Don.

"Brutal on the waistline, yeah," said Jason. "I'm supposed to be in shape for this role."

"She married?" said Rick.

Jason nodded and took his cellphone out of his pocket. He read something on it and keyed in a response.

I noticed that Rick glanced at my left hand. I slipped it under the table. This meal could not be over fast enough. Jason clearly did not want me here. The waitress arrived soon after to take our orders and the food came mercifully fast. The problem was, I couldn't eat. I picked at it diligently, stirred the black beans and rice around the plate so that it looked like I was eating, and traded more barbs with Don, but I was sick to my stomach. The food was fabulous, though as Jason had promised me, very different. The sopapillas were now made with whole wheat flour, my chile relleno was a poblano chile, and there wasn't a refried bean in sight. The black bean side was slightly sweet.

Jason stayed quiet, though he didn't eat much either. He kept glancing at his phone. He kept it under the table so as not to draw attention to it, but I noticed. He glanced at me, too. It was as if he too wondered why I'd come. It was a disaster. This guy wasn't my friend. He was a megastar who didn't have time for the likes of me.

I was thrilled that no one ordered dessert. Jason seemed ready to be done, so no one ordered coffee either. When I reached for my purse, he held up his hand and said, "Chloe, I got this."

"Are you sure-"

He nodded. "Guys, we can use the side exit."

"Thanks," I said to Jason as I pushed back from the table. "I think I can use the normal person exit."

"Rub it in," said Don.

"Eh, let me walk you to your car," said Jason.

I paused, unsure what to make of the offer. "Okay."

Don and Rick exchanged looks. Well, Don never seemed to like anyone else getting attention from any female in the room. Rick I didn't know, but it looked the same for him. I let both of them go ahead of me, while I walked in front of Jason down the hall. We all turned to go out the side exit and stepped right out into a snow shower. Clumps of flakes floated down all around, landing in our hair and clinging to my eyelashes. I wrapped my shawl more tightly around myself and dug in my purse for my keys.

Jason put his hand on my arm. "Where's your car?"

I did my best to seem nonchalant and nodded in the appropriate direction. We set out and I waved good-bye to the other two guys.

"Bye, Chloe," they each said in turn.

Jason's hand, on my arm, flinched.

"They seem nice," I asked.

"Sure." The word came out clipped.

All right, I thought. I'll get out of your world now. I get it.

The gravel had a layer of ice over it, so I focused on staying on my feet. High heels that I had not been broken in were not the ideal footwear for this. We made it to my car without being spotted, but a scream about thirty yards away let me know Don and/or Rick hadn't been so lucky.

I stepped up to the driver's side door and turned to Jason. "It was good to see you," I said.

"Yeah." He put his hands in his pockets and looked away. "You too."

The appropriate thing to do would have been to shake his hand, or just say goodbye. This was it, after all, probably the last time I'd ever see him. Impulse took hold of me and I held out my arms.

He paused, then pulled me in for a rough, informal hug. One squeeze and he let go.

Only, I didn't.

Chloe, I thought. You are being an idiot. Still, it felt so good to hug him again. His toned muscles, the lotion scent of his skin. Okay, stop being a fangirl, I told myself. I made my muscles relax and released him. "Bye," I said. I didn't look at him as I unlocked my door and climbed into my car.

He stood next to the door for a second longer, looking annoyed or confused, I couldn't tell which. I waved at him as I pulled out and he lifted his hand in reply. In my rearview mirror, I saw him head back towards the restaurant, a crowd of girls in hot pursuit.

WELL, I thought on the drive home, you're stupid. Everything was going less than disastrously until you clung to him like that. The tears were flowing long before I pulled into my driveway. I dabbed at them with a tissue and smeared my eye makeup all over my face. I could have been worse, I reasoned. I could have done that in the restaurant.

Boy did I feel terrible. I went to the bathroom and washed my face twice. The water ran first black, then gray as the eyeliner and eyeshadow swirled away down the drain. When I looked at myself in the mirror, I just looked like me, with puffy, red eyes. I changed into a t-shirt and sweats.

And I was starving. The fridge was empty. The freezer still had that carton of gourmet ice cream in it. I rolled my eyes. I hadn't touched it and Lori had moved out before she'd eaten it, so it'd just sat there for two months. The thing was probably hard as a rock, and I needed to get rid of it. It would only remind me of Jason.

I picked it up and looked around. The kitchen garbage was out. It'd melt and go rancid. I had to take it outside, in the snow. I headed for the front door and opened it.

Jason stood on my doorstep. I had to stop short in order to not run into him.

"Hi," I said. I hid the carton behind my back.

"Yeah, hi." He still seemed distracted and annoyed. He pushed past me and stepped inside. Snow was melting in his hair and clung in little drifts on his jacket. His Prius, which had pulled up silently, was in the driveway. "I gotta ask you something, and then I'll leave you alone, for good. I promise."

"Okay." I shut the door behind us.

22
HIS QUESTION

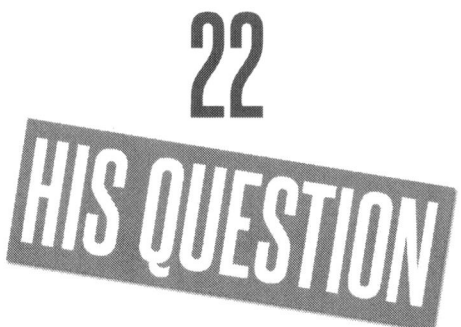

"So... yeah," Jason said. He paced my living room.

My hand was going numb from holding the freezing container of ice cream, so I sidled on over to the counter and put it down. I tried to keep myself between him and it.

"One question," he said.

"Okay."

"It... you can blame my sister. I... she... I just spoke to her and..." He scrubbed his hands through his hair, wiping away the last of the snow.

I waited.

"Did the rules change?" he asked. "You know, between you and me? Would... would kissing be allowed now?"

My heart just about stopped.

"You know what? Never mind. Stupid question." He turned to leave.

I had seconds before he stepped out the door and was gone for good. "Wait," I said, only it came out as a whisper. A mass the size of a grapefruit had formed in my throat. I coughed. "Jason," I tried again.

"What?" He had his hand on the knob, but he turned to look at me.

"Yeah." Saying the word felt like stepping off a cliff and going into free fall, plummeting without knowing if he was going to catch me or just leave me in a crushed heap at the bottom.

"Yeah what?"

Come on, Chloe, I thought. English is your first language. Try to speak it coherently. I pressed myself against the counter. It only provided a narrow ridge of support across my lower back, but it was better than nothing. I felt like I was plunging farther and farther down into the abyss, picking up more and more speed while I tried to piece together a sentence.

He let go of the doorknob and came over to me, stepping way closer than we'd ever stood as friends. He kept his gaze locked with mine and slowly, as if he wasn't sure what he was doing, he reached out and stroked my hair, gentle as a butterfly. All the while he looked like he was waiting for me to either jerk away or punch him.

I was a mess, and still tumbling headlong. He looked at me as if both desperate to hear what I had to say and terrified of breaking the tension, because he didn't know what lay beyond it.

Don't screw this up, I thought. Speaking was out of the question. It'd release a torrent of nonsense, so I put my hand on his chest and leaned up to kiss him.

He kissed back and his hand spasmed against my cheek. His lips were cold from the chill outside.

When I broke it off, he looked down at me, still uncertain, though now there was a flicker of hope in his expression.

I couldn't believe that I was *still* in freefall. The kiss hadn't ended the sensation. But this was Jason Vanderholt. Women threw themselves at him for all kinds of reasons. The man who looked into my eyes right now was smart enough to wait for me to explain myself, rather than take the kiss as an answer. He wanted to know what I wanted, in concrete terms.

My thoughts scrabbled in a vain attempt to come together. "I love you," I heard myself say.

His hand grasped my shoulder and he took a breath that sounded like something between a gasp and a sob. "I love you, too."

That, finally, put a stop to my headlong plunge. I took a breath, then another. Yes, he was all wrong for me. Still, those eyes were now searching my face as if I were Venus in all her glory.

He leaned in and, with a pause to look me in the eye for permission, kissed me again, first hesitantly, and then as if he never wanted to stop. A flood of emotion spilled loose inside of me. I slipped my arms around his neck and felt his arms go around my waist. It was a million times more intense than I'd imagined, even at my loneliest times when I'd hugged my pillow and wished he were there. His mouth warmed against mine as the kiss went on and on, making my heart race and my head spin. When he broke off, there were tears in his eyes, real tears!

"I'm sorry," I said as I dabbed them away with my fingertips.

"For?"

"For taking so long to figure out what's what."

He just shook his head. The disbelief still hadn't faded from his expression. "Why?" he said. "What changed?"

"I dunno. I don't know what I'm doing right now. I just... I've missed you so much. I was sure you'd be over me."

"No. Are you kidding? I *love* you."

It was incredible to hear him say that again.

But now he looked past me and his expression turned quizzical. I felt him reach for something on the counter.

"Yeah..." I shut my eyes. "It's gotta be like concrete now."

"Seriously?" He hoisted the ice cream with one hand.

"My mean roommate moved out without eating it, so it's been there, tormenting me for two months."

"I am so terribly *not* sorry about that." He stepped away from me and went to fetch a spoon from the drawer.

I turned and watched him dig into the ice cream. It looked okay. He held out the spoon to me. I tried it.

"Okay?" he said.

"Yeah, it's still fine."

"Sooo, I'm still kinda hungry. I didn't eat much."

"I'm starving."

He held up the carton. "What do you say?"

As we sat on the couch, working our way through the ice cream, Jason told me his side of things. "It was Jen," he said. "When she went back to the kitchen, she texted me."

"What'd she text?"

He pulled out his phone to show me. "What's up with C?"

His response was, "What do u mean?"

"U guys getting 2gether?"

"What???"

"So then," said Jason, "here I am trying to eat dinner and Jen's stopped texting me and I just don't know what to think." He grinned at me and licked the back of the ice cream spoon we were sharing. "Then I walked you out to your car, and you were asking me, 'Are your friends usually that charming?'"

"I didn't say that."

"That's what I heard. I heard you sigh wistfully, too."

"You're losing it."

"I was, I totally was. Then you hugged me and... yeah."

"Clung to you like a pathetic fan."

"You held me. For, like, a whole fraction of a microsecond."

"More like a million years."

"Now *you're* losing it."

"It was long enough for you to notice."

"Okay, yeah, it was. But I was desperate. So I went back into the restaurant and barged right into the kitchen and pinned Jen down. I asked her about the texts and she just said, 'I thought maybe Chloe changed her mind.' And I said, 'What? Really?' And she said, 'Why would she go out to dinner with you looking like that? She doesn't look like she wants to be friends.'"

I blushed.

"And I said, 'I think she's flirting with Don.'"

"What?" I shook my head. "Are you serious?"

"Yeah, well Jen said you weren't like that. She said, 'Go over to her place now, before she gives up on you.' So I did, even though I expected you to laugh at me." He leaned in and nuzzled my cheek.

I traced an idle pattern on his chest with my finger. I wished this moment would go on forever. Right now, things felt perfect. We were in love, we were in each others arms, we could talk and kiss and hold each other. I wondered how long it would take for it all to become complicated.

"Everything okay?" Jason asked.

"Everything's more than okay."

"You seem preoccupied."

"Just thinking."

"About?" He dabbed ice cream onto my nose and when I pulled away from that, he used the opportunity to kiss it off. Then he put the ice cream and spoon down, slipped both arms around me, and kissed me again.

Okay, I thought. Here we are, on the couch. We've had our dramatic reunion. What's he going to try next? Do I need to start the Talk now? But he was the one who pulled back. "Rules aren't changing back, are they?" he asked.

"No."

"Good, because this still hasn't sunk in yet for me. I'd like it to last at least a little while longer."

"Me too."

"Make that a long while." He stroked my hair.

"I hope we can make that work."

"You hope?"

"There's a lot you don't know about me."

"Is it worse than the stack of articles you know about me?"

"Well, no, but-"

"Hey, if you can get over that, I think we'll be okay. I'm no hypocrite. Why? What's your deepest, darkest secret, that you're scared of?"

I leaned against him.

"You don't have to tell me. But you can, whatever it is."

I'm a virgin, I thought. And you're not. You think you like me, but I'm not the kind of girl you want to date.

He reached down for the ice cream again and fed me another bite.

"I cheat at solitaire sometimes," I said.

"Oh... whoa... maybe we should hold back on this whole honesty thing." He chuckled.

"I'm sorry."

"I love you. I mean that. I risked the wrath of Jen tonight, and I don't even care."

"I owe her one," I said.

"She likes you. I guess you helped Kyra?"

"Helped her with what?"

"I dunno. The girl doesn't talk to many people, but I guess she talks to you."

"I talked to her once at work, for, like, five minutes."

"More than Jen has, then. She's a confused kid."

"Yeah, she is."

"What did she say to you?"

"Not much. She doesn't feel like part of the family."

"Well, yeah. She is, though."

"She likes her drama class."

"Oh really?"

"I told her you'd be interested to know that."

"She hates me."

"Well, she thought it was weird that I'd never shown you the bullet scar on my stomach. Even though your whole family knew we were just friends."

"Right. Like I said, she's confused. She knows all my bad press and thinks I'm still like that, and more than one guy has seen... more than her stomach. She had a miscarriage when she was thirteen." I felt a shudder go through him. "Kyle and Jen don't know what to do with her."

"Thirteen is young, even for around here."

"Yes it is. It's scary young. And now she's in love and talking about running away with this guy."

"Poor Jen."

"Yeah, exactly." He finished off the last bite of ice cream and put the carton down on the coffee table, then reached down to grab something from under the couch. The magazine with his picture on the cover.

"Oh, yeah, that," I said.

"Did you read it?" It fell open at the first page of his interview.

"Um... yeah." Enough times to warp the spine of the magazine, I thought.

"I talked about you in it."

"I thought you always lied."

"Almost, but I slipped. I was vulnerable. It was two days after you told me it wasn't going to happen." He frowned at the picture of himself. "They usually make you pose exactly how they want, but they used this picture when I was just, you know, looking how I felt. It was kind of embarrassing." He tossed the magazine onto the coffee table and put his arms back around me. "So how have you been? I haven't spoken to you in forever."

23
SURPRISE

I woke up to the sound of Jason answering his phone. His voice was clear. He hadn't fallen asleep. I was lying next to him on my couch, my head pillowed on his chest. His arm was firm around my waist.

"Hello?" he said, softly.

"Where are you?" I heard Jen's tinny reply.

"At my girlfriend's." He grinned.

"That better be Chloe, or I will kill you."

"Of course it is."

"What do you say?"

"You were right. I owe you one, mean bossy big sister by three minutes."

"And did she hear you say girlfriend?"

I looked up so he'd see that I was awake.

"Yes. And did you hear me get slapped? No."

"You are *lucky,* mister."

"I know."

"And you have a plane to catch at six a.m."

"I know, I know. I'll come. Gimme a few minutes."

"I'm sorry-"

"No, you're right. Again. Doesn't that make you feel good?"

"Guess we don't get to see Chloe again this trip…"

"Next time. 'Kay, bye."

"Bye."

Jason put his phone in his pocket and sat up. "I am really sorry."

"How long did I sleep?" I smoothed my hair.

"I dunno. Look, this shoot's going to be seven weeks."

"It's okay. You've been gone before."

"This is different. Promise me the rules won't change back? We'll figure out sometime when you can come up and visit and-"

I kissed him, drawing it out long enough that I felt some of the tension go out of his shoulders. "I promise the rules won't change back." He'd give up on me long before I got over him. I knew this for certain.

"I love you." He gathered up the ice cream carton and the spoon.

"Love you, too. You don't have to do that," I protested as he went to wash the spoon in the sink. I grabbed the carton and tossed it in the garbage.

Jason picked up his jacket from where he'd draped it over the couch, then paused to kiss me again before he left.

"C'mon, lie to him, he totally deserves it." Jen whispered so forcefully that it came out like a hiss. I was at her parents' house with Kyra lounging on the couch nearby, Steve's kids running riot outside, and Jason's parents sitting across the table from me. Jen sat right next to me. It was just over a week since Jason had left for his shoot.

"You're busy all break?" said Jason over the phone.

"Some people got laid off at work," I lied. "It's extra shifts for everybody."

"You can't come at all, for the whole shoot," said Jen.

I shook my head. "No," I mouthed.

"Can you come for a long weekend in February, maybe?"

"Yeah, I can't do that. I'm so sorry."

"It's okay. Can't complain about your job when mine's got me up in Vancouver."

"Look, I'll figure out my work situation as soon as possible and let you know."

"Okay. I love you." Normally, on Skype, this was when he would stroke the screen with his fingertips.

But this wasn't Skype so he couldn't see that I was sitting in front of his whole family. I took a deep breath. Yeah, this was embarrassing. "Love you, too."

"Bye."

"Bye."

"He is *lucky*," said Jen.

I put my phone away, not able to look his dad in the eye, but I got the impression both his parents were smiling at me. My face must've been beet red. It felt like my skin was burning up.

"Okay, so I booked flights for next Thursday to the following Tuesday," said Jen.

"And Chloe," said his mother. "We can cover hotel if you'd like?"

"I can cover the hotel," I said. "I found a place not too far from his."

"What my parents mean to say, is if you are getting your own room, they'll pay for it in Jason's hotel."

I put my head in both my hands. "Yes, I will be in my own room."

"We aren't judging," said his mother, brightly. "You're both adults and-"

I cleared my throat. "Um... yeah." Jason and I hadn't ever even been on a real date and this is where they thought the relationship was at?

Kyra rolled her eyes and I found myself exchanging a rueful smile with her. She burst out laughing.

"And Dad will be calling your room every night to check- just kidding," said Jen. "Yeah, that was really not handled well, was it? Okay, so you need anything else for the trip?"

I shook my head.

"You've got a passport and all that?"

"Yeah, I do." Thanks to that dig in Mexico, I'd gotten one years ago.

"See if he remembers *my* birthday," said Jen.

The sliding glass door rolled open and Steve and Shannon came in with plates of hamburgers and buns. "Not as nice as what you cook," he said to Jen.

"Shut up. Anything I don't have to cook is delicious."

The Vanderholts had invited me over for a barbeque, and to plan out their collective birthday gift to Jason. The snow that had fallen over New Year's was gone as fast as it had come, leaving only chilly days and the occasional gray sky behind.

While everyone else bustled around to arrange a buffet on the counter, Kyra slipped into the seat next to me. I turned to see if she'd say anything, but she just smiled. I didn't know whether to get up and help, or stay with her, and before I could decide, the family had finished their arranging and Doug asked for everyone to bow their heads for grace. We all did, then everyone went up to get food. Kyra and I both got behind everyone else in line. She still didn't say anything. She seemed perfectly happy just to hang out near me. She even sat with me through the meal while she texted someone else on her phone and shot dirty looks at Jen when she tried to intervene.

It was hard to sit still for the flight up to Vancouver. On one hand, I was excited to see Jason. On the other, I was nervous. Part of me wanted to just call him and blow the surprise, but his family had seemed so excited about it that I didn't want to let them down.

A long layover in Seattle and a mechanical problem meant I didn't get in until past nine o'clock at night, so it was dark. I'd taken taxis in Mexico, so I tried to tell myself that this would be easier. The driver would speak English. I had Canadian dollars in my wallet, this would be fine.

And it was. I walked up to the taxi stand, gave the driver the name of the hotel, he helped me put my bag in the trunk, and we were off. The drive revealed a skyline of tall buildings and winking lights. It was hard to get a sense of much else other than how foreign the place was, not because it was in Canada, but because it was populated. As a New Mexican, I just wasn't used to that.

The taxi pulled up to the gleaming glass and metal doors of the hotel. I got out of the cab, paid, went into the hotel, and tried not too look like I was gawking at the plush lobby. The Hyatt Downtown in Albuquerque had nothing on this. The couches and carpets were *white*. I felt for their cleaning crew, and wondered if anyone would curl their lip at my jeans and casual sweater.

The woman at the front desk didn't bat an eye. She had pale blond hair and gray eyes. "I'm Chloe Winters," I told her. "I've got a reservation?"

She tapped that into her computer terminal with a set of perfectly lacquered nails. "Oh... right. Okay, I've got your room key and then Mr. ah, Kevin Douglas-" that was the name Jason had checked in under "-says we're to give you one of his room keys."

"He's not supposed to know that I'm coming."

She tapped something else into the computer and shrugged. "He set it up when he checked in."

"Okay." I was confused. I wondered if this meant that he assumed I'd stay in his room with him when I came up for another visit later. That was moving fast.

"You need a key to get up to his floor." She pulled out two plastic cards and jammed one into a slot on her computer. A few more key taps and she pulled it out and handed it to me. "That's yours." She repeated the process. "That's his."

This way, at least, I could sneak up on him, if he was in. He often was on set until late. I took the elevator, which looked like it had a marble floor, up to my room, dumped my bag, then continued on up to Jason's. His floor had a key reader slot next to it and the button wouldn't light up until I inserted the room key. I'd seen those buttons on elevators before, but never used one. That gave me a little thrill.

The doors opened onto a hallway every bit as plush as the lobby. Rather than the utilitarian buff carpet that was on my floor, this had more white carpet and a chandelier right outside the elevator. I followed the brass signposts to Jason's room and marveled at the space between doors. These were some seriously big rooms.

I could hear Jason's voice coming through the door of his room and I picked up my pace, only to slow down when I heard another, female voice as well.

"It's late, and yes, I think you should go back to your room." Jason's voice.

"You're sure?" A woman's voice.

I looked at my watch. It was past ten o'clock. Part of me wanted to flee, just go back downstairs and hide in my room. But that was never the part of me I listened to. I jammed my key in the lock, and pushed the door open to reveal a plush sitting room.

Jason was sitting on the couch across from a gorgeous woman, Gigi Malone, his costar. "Do you mind?" she said.

"Chloe?" His face lit up and he got to his feet.

"Am I interrupting anything?"

"No-"

"Not at this exact moment," said Gigi.

Jason shot her an annoyed look as he crossed the room to me.

She laughed. "Oh, does she not know about us?"

"When did you get in?" he asked.

"It's the surprise visits that get you in trouble." Gigi looked back over her shoulder at me, one arm outstretched on the back of the couch and a mocking smile on her lips.

"Whatever. Gigi, Chloe, Chloe, Gigi, who is a *friend*..."

"Mmmm-hmmm."

"...who cracks some really lame jokes sometimes."

"Oh, riiiight, we're just joking." She winked at him.

"C'mon," he snapped.

"If she'd arrived any later, you couldn't get away with claiming it's all just a joke."

"Gi, quit it." He looked a little panicked. His hand, resting on my wrist, trembled slightly.

"What? It could be worse. I could've been like this when she walked in." She got up on her knees on the couch and, facing me, started to unbutton her blouse.

"Yeah, okay." Jason dragged me through a door, into the bedroom, out of sight of Gigi. "She's joking, okay? I swear. I *swear*."

"I often undress as a joke," Gigi chimed in.

"Just quit it, okay? This isn't funny!" Jason turned back to me. "I promise you, I am not a cheat. I've done a lot of really stupid things, but I'd never stoop so low as to-"

"Whee!" A bra flew past the open bedroom door.

"Seriously, Gi. Cut it *out*."

"What, honey? Nothing you haven't seen before."

Jason gazed past me at something on the other side of the room, then shook his head and looked at me. "I promise you, she is joking and just taking it way too far." He raised his voice. "I'm calling Phil."

"What?"

Jason patted his pockets, glanced around, then said to me. "Wait right here." He made a point of looking away from Gigi as he stepped back into the other room, as if a single glance in her direction was lethal.

I turned around and tried to guess what he'd looked at just a moment before. Behind me was the bed, neatly made, and next to it a nightstand. Jason's computer lay on the floor, probably where he'd left it the night before after we'd signed off Skype.

"Give me my phone."

"Come get it."

"I am not reaching there. Seriously. Stop it. I can't believe you."

"What, you ashamed of us, sweetheart?"

On the nightstand was a stack of papers, which turned out to be call sheets. Under them was a spoon, which I picked up. It was my spoon, or one of my spoons, at least.

Jason stormed back into the room and grabbed the hotel phone off the nightstand on the opposite side of the bed. He muttered to himself as he jabbed the buttons, only to freeze when he saw what I was holding.

I dropped the spoon onto the bed and hunched my shoulders with guilt. "Sorry, I shouldn't go through your stuff."

"Yeah... I stole the ice cream spoon. And go ahead." He gestured around the room. "Dig all you want. I've got nothing to hide from you, other than a little petty theft. Go through my email if you want." He pointed at his computer. "Hey, yeah, hi," he said into the phone. "Gigi's taking a joke waaay too far and, I'm sorry to bother you. Dave's got the night off, my guys are downstairs, and I just want this to end now... Yeah... my girlfriend's here and Gigi thought it'd be funny to take all her clothes off... Thanks." He hung up and came around the bed to me. "Please believe me. I *swear,* I would never cheat on you, or anyone. Especially not you. I love you."

There came the sound of a knock.

"Sec," said Jason. He strode back out to open the door. "Phil, hi."

"Dangit!" There came a thud, which I assumed was Gigi falling down. "Jason-"

"Need this?" said another male voice. The bra flew the other way past the door.

"I am really sorry to bother you," said Jason.

"You're not the one being a bother, here."

"I was just kidding around!" protested Gigi. "Come on? Can't you take a joke?"

"It's not funny. Not now, and not with her. I can't believe you."

"All right. I'm leaving. I'm *leaving,* okay?" Gigi bustled past the door, holding her blouse to the front of her bare chest. She had her jeans on, but that was about it. The door opened and slammed shut.

I poked my head around the corner and saw Jason was conferring with a dark haired guy who had a middle aged paunch sagging over his belt.

"Ah, hi," the man said to me. "Kelly, is it?"

"Chloe," said Jason. "Chlo, this is Phil, one of our producers. And he can tell you, there is nothing going on between me and Gigi. She just thought it'd be funny to... did you ever hang around the drama club in school? We're a little uninhibited, sometimes..."

"Everything going to be okay here?" Phil asked. "What do you need to have happen?"

"I need to miraculously not get dumped in the next five minutes."

"I mean with regards to the shoot."

"No, I know what you mean. Nothing. Like I said, I'm sorry to bother you."

Phil clapped him on the shoulder. "It's all right. About tomorrow-"

"I'll be on time. Won't even throw a tantrum. It's all good."

"All right. Nice to meet you, Chloe." He turned and left.

Deafening silence descended as the door clicked shut. Jason turned back to me. "Chloe-"

"She admitted it was a joke."

"Right. Yeah."

"And Phil knew my name, even though you didn't tell it to him. You just said your girlfriend was here."

He nodded. "True."

"He even got it slightly wrong, which would be pure genius if you planned that ahead."

"And I'm not that smart. Please don't think I'm that smart." There was a glimmer of hope in his eyes now.

"You didn't panic when I barged in. You seemed happy to see me."

"I was. I am."

"And you gave me your room key, which would be pretty stupid if you wanted to hide anything from me."

Jason breathed a sigh of relief. "So you believe me?"

"Yeah."

"I love you."

"Love you too. Things always this eventful?"

"Not in that way, but yes, unfortunately. Gigi's discovered Vicodin, or is it Valium? I dunno. Something with a V. I think. She's a mess, the shoot's a mess. This whole project's a nightmare."

"I'm sorry."

"You hungry? I'm starving, and I'm going to ignore my nutritionist right now."

"I could eat."

He strode over to the entertainment center and got a binder out of the drawer. "Room service menu," he said, as he handed it to me. "Tell me what you want."

I blinked and looked down at it. My head still spun a little.

"Or we can split a pizza? You want to split a pizza?"

"Since I'll end up with half your pizza on my plate anyway, sure."

He laughed, flipped to the pizza menu, and plied me with questions about what I wanted, but I just told him to order. "I don't care," I said. "Really, I don't." I flopped down on the couch while he called in an order for a Tuscan pizza with prosciutto. Now that I had a moment to look at his suite, I saw it was nicer than any hotel room I'd ever been in. The sitting area was larger than most hotel bedrooms I'd rented, and the couches were so plush I wondered if I'd be able to get up again. I felt like I was still sinking into the cushion. The carpet was cream colored and the furniture a deep, chocolate brown.

"So... yeah," Jason said, once he was off the phone. "Had enough of my glamorous life yet?" He sat next to me on the couch.

"You really do have the weirdest job."

"The recreational drug use and spontaneous nudity are not part of the job. I'm just glad you're here. Especially when you said…" He raised an eyebrow. "You lied to me, didn't you?"

"Jen's idea."

"She is so *mean* to me."

"She paid for my ticket. Happy birthday. Make sure you remember hers."

"I don't ever forget hers. I sent her a lump of coal like I always do." He reached for me.

I moved closer and put my arms around him. He nuzzled my neck and took a deep breath. It had felt good to be held by him the first time; this time felt even better.

"Where's your suitcase?" he asked.

"My room."

"Oh, okay. You staying at this hotel?"

I nodded.

He didn't bat an eye. "I'm paying for your hotel room when you come up next month too-"

"Jason-"

"You want one on this floor?"

"No..."

"It's not that expensive. Not for me. Dave's got a room up here."

"Not my kind of thing at all. I just want a normal room, and I will-"

"Let me pay for it."

"Look-"

"No, you look," he said. "I want to see you, and I want to be able to see you regularly, and it's my job that has me running all over the place. Just let me do this."

"I don't like the idea of a guy spending money on me, okay? I don't. Dr. Winters bought my mom stuff all the time, and I just have issues with it now."

Jason nodded. "Fine, so you don't want me to send you out for spa days and shopping sprees and exotic trips, though you can have those if you want."

I shook my head.

"But this is spending money on me, okay? And it's not very much money. Not with your tastes. And I don't know exactly what you make at Flying Star, but really, you shouldn't be blowing any of your savings that you could put aside for grad school."

He knew me too well. He'd found the one argument that would impact me. Grad school was going to clean me out and require me to take on loans. I wasn't entirely sure how I'd pull it off.

"Yes?" said Jason.

"Just a normal room."

"Yes. And plane ticket-"

"Jason-"

"Economy class, if that's what you want. You can have first-"

I shook my head.

"Economy it is." He smirked at me. "Of all the things to have our first fight about."

I leaned my head against his shoulder and felt his arms tighten around me. "I don't mean to fight with you."

But he was laughing now. "Especially after what just happened. You show up and find me with a half-naked woman in my room, *alone,* and you handle that just fine. Then I try to pay for stuff, and that makes you mad." He kissed my forehead, my cheek.

I lifted my head and he gave me a long kiss on the lips. When it ended, he gazed at me as if he still couldn't believe he was allowed to do that. "Been too long," he whispered. "Wish we could do this on Skype. How long you here until?"

"Tuesday."

"Nice," said Jason. "You can come to work with me tomorrow. Only, I kind of have to do a love scene. Not an extreme one where I have to be naked but... um... yeah. With Gigi. I hate my job right now. Please don't break up with me over this."

24
LOVE SCENES

"Get out of here!"

"Make me."

"Hit your mark, Gigi."

I sat and read an article while Jason shot his "love scene" the next day. It was, according to him, "very mild". I wouldn't be allowed to watch a serious love scene. They closed the set for those.

As it was, I wasn't allowed to watch this one either. Once the cameras started rolling, everyone was supposed to look down. I read my article for organic chemistry while Jason and Gigi yelled at each other and tore at each others clothes.

The lights were hot, even from where I sat, out of their glare. The set was Jason's character's "apartment", which was actually the corner of a warehouse with a fake window and a rumpled bed.

"Cut! Hit your *mark*." The director pointed at a taped mark on the floor where Gigi was supposed to stand when Jason lunged at her in his romantic, leading man kind of way. I flipped another page of my article. The first assistant director had made it crystal clear that if there was so much as the hint of the sound of paper rustling, I'd get thrown off the set, so I was careful.

"Had enough of this yet?" said Jason. Without my noticing, he'd come up to stand next to me. "Because I have. I just want this to be over."

It didn't show in his performance. His job was strange, but he was very, very good at it.

Gigi had been late to work, which meant everything else had started late, and as Jason explained to me, guild rules required twelve hours off between shifts, so starting late one day guaranteed they'd start at least as late the next. "I'm getting a lot of work done," I said.

"I know. What's that say about my performance? You aren't riveted? Don't answer that. I'm glad you're not riveted."

I tugged the cap off my highlighter with my teeth and ran the felt tip over some text.

"I'll make this up to you, I promise," he said.

I wasn't sure what he meant by that, but before I could ask, the director summoned him over and he went back to yelling at Gigi and then collapsing onto a nearby bed with her. Then the shots moved on to kissing scenes, which I had to admit, weren't even remotely romantic. Not with the director making them tilt their heads this way and that so that they didn't cast shadows on each others faces and Jason breaking it off the very second he heard "Cut!"

I carried on reading.

When the director shouted, "That's a wrap!" I'd finished one article and moved on to another.

"Okay," said Jason. "Let's get out of here." Dave, his assistant and a handful of other people gathered around and Jason conferred with all of them a moment while I packed up my things and stretched my legs.

"Have a nice night," Gigi Malone said as she glided on past. She looked fabulous. Her skin was translucent and radiant. Her hair was glossy and styled. Her eyes even sparkled. Jason ignored her completely.

I RODE back to the hotel in a car with Jason. He had a driver and Dave in the front seat and several other guys in tow. Everyone went up to his room and talked business until Jason sent them all away.

Okay, I thought. Now what?

"You want to watch TV?" Jason asked.

"Sure."

He handed me the remote and we settled down on the couch. He slipped his arm around my waist and seemed more interested in me than watching anything. I found a news channel and then turned my attention to him. He kissed me a couple of times, but it didn't escalate. He was more intent on scanning my face, as if trying to read my thoughts, rather than establish a mood.

"I know," I said. "I'm boring, huh?"

"No." He smirked as if I'd said something funny. "Not even close."

I leaned against him and rubbed his chest with my hand.

His arms tightened around me and we held each other like that for the whole evening. Like before, I dozed off and woke up to him stroking my cheek. "It's midnight," he whispered.

"I should go."

"Okay. I'll come pick you up in the morning. I love you."

"I love you, too." That was no exaggeration. I was already in deep, and we'd only been together a month.

When I got back to my apartment in Albuquerque late on Tuesday, my mailbox was jammed full. I pried out all of the junk mail and coupon offers from grocery stories and found, wedged in the back, a large envelope from Loyola University in New Orleans. It wasn't easy to extract; it'd been stuffed in so that the paper tore as I wiggled it loose from the corners of the box, but in about five minutes I had worked the wrinkled mess free.

The envelope was ripped open, but the acceptance letter inside was intact. There was also a prospectus and a housing brochure. I sorted through all this as I called Jason.

"You got in?" he said. "Is that a good school?"

"It's one of the best. It's the one I wanted."

"New Orleans is a really nice city."

"I've never been. I don't know if I'm going, though, yet. I need to find out the financial aid package and that's not in this."

"Oh. Well, I'd be surprised if that were a problem. I mean, no offense, but I'm guessing you don't have a ton of assets for them to go after."

"Me, no. My mother, no. My father-"

"Never gave you a dime."

I rubbed my forehead and dumped the whole mess of papers from Loyola onto the coffee table. "Problem is, schools still want to take his assets into account because I'm under twenty-six. They try to, at least. I just have to keep after the financial aid office to understand my situation.

It's not like I even know what his assets are." That had never been a big problem at UNM, given I was on the state lottery scholarship, but grad school would be different.

"Oh, you're kidding."

"It'll work out."

"Surely you could get merit scholarships, Chlo?"

"I'm applying for a couple of fellowships, yeah."

"And loans?"

"Sure. But my mom's credit record is awful, so she's not much use as a cosigner."

"This is ridiculous. You're brilliant. There's gotta be a way for you to go to the school you want."

"It'll all be fine. This stuff is complicated for everyone. It's no big deal."

"You know I'd give you the money in a heartbeat."

"No way."

"I know, I know... But it'd be small change for me."

"Thank you, but-"

"Back off. Yeah. I know what you're saying. I do."

"I shouldn't have even told you about all that."

"No. Hey. We're just talking, right? About your life and all that. I want to know."

"I know New Orleans is even farther from LA than Albuquerque."

"It's also August we're talking about, right? Or September?"

"Yeah." I bit my lip. I was getting way ahead of myself.

"Let's talk about next month instead. You able to come Friday through Monday, or is that going to interfere with school too much?"

"No, that works."

S INCE I arrived in the middle of the morning on Friday, Dave just took me straight to the set, where a cluster of people, including Jason, stood and argued. The crew had moved to an abandoned office building, and the set was a room full of cubicles, meant to look like the police department. The desks had office phones and paper trays and documents scattered around. A half read newspaper rested on a chair.

"We can't reshoot that whole sequence," the director said as I walked up.

"I think we might have to," said Phil. He looked tired and haggard. Jason caught sight of me and came over, grinning. "Hi!"

"Hey," I said. "Everything going all right?"

"No, it's all falling apart. Horribly." He hugged me. "She finally did it."

"Did what?" I didn't have to ask whom. Gigi wasn't the only woman in the movie, but she was the only one people talked about, it seemed.

"Showed up wasted and ruined a day's shooting."

"So why are you on set right now?"

"Good question. Ben-" that was the director "-wanted me here, and then he and Phil started talking. It's a train wreck."

"Because she messed up one day?"

"It's been building." He had a script tucked under his arm, which he tugged loose and held out to me. "I know you have a ton of schoolwork," he said, "but do you have time to read this?"

"This for this movie?"

"No. For another one. I planned to take the summer off, but I think this might be one of the best scripts I've ever read. I need a second opinion."

Two hours later, I was in Jason's trailer dabbing tears from my eyes. Jason sat next to me on the couch, his arm around my shoulders.

"Yes?" he said.

"It's amazing." I couldn't put my finger on what was amazing about it. On the surface, it was a pretty simple story about a young stockbroker who discovered an insider trading scandal. There were no love scenes, no chase scenes, nothing traditionally Hollywood, just a good solid story.

"Well, dang it," said Jason. "They had Barry Waitrose for the lead, but he just quit on them and they offered it to me. I wanted to take the summer off and be in New Mexico. That's in New York."

"I don't think you can pass this up."

"But it's in New York. When are we ever going to spend time together? I don't want to miss out on being with you, either."

"Well, maybe I can get a job in New York. They have coffee shops there too, right?"

"You would do that?"

I considered it carefully. A whole summer in New York was a commitment, but not a huge commitment. Presumably I could find other people to spend time with if and when things fell apart with Jason. Really, it sounded like a nice change of pace. I'd never been to the East Coast.

"Yeah," I said.

"Will you let me rent you an apartment?"

"No."

"Hotel-"

"No. Not for a whole summer. I'll find something."

But Jason shook his head. "You know what real estate runs in New York? They're filming this in Midtown, and you see what long hours a shoot can be. I'd like you somewhere close."

"I'll find a roommate or something on Craig's List."

He kept shaking his head, though. "Please let me-"

"No. Thank you, but no." I flipped back to the beginning of the script and skimmed the opening scene again. It was so simple, but so good.

I sensed the Vanderholt stare, though, and looked up again. Jason seemed tentative, like he was about to step out onto thin ice. "I'd like you in a building with security," he said.

That statement, coupled with his demeanor, made no sense to me. "Sure. Fine. I'll make that a-"

He leaned forward and snagged his computer off the table. After a moment of typing, he showed me the screen. A page from Craig's List. "That is how high rent is in Midtown."

"Well, how close is Midtown to a more affordable neighborhood?"

"Not close enough."

"Why are you pushing this?"

"Okay, okay... sorry."

"It's all right. I'll be all right. Just need to do some research."

"Chloe?"

I put the script aside. I was missing something. He wanted to have a serious talk, and I wasn't picking up on the clues that led to this.

"Does it bother you that I care this much about seeing you over the summer?"

"No. Of course not."

"Because whenever we talk about the future, you get real quiet."

"It gives me a lot to think about, I guess. That's all."

He fidgeted a moment. "I'm very serious about us. That all right with you?"

"Yeah..." I tried to think ahead to where this conversation was going. "If I have to choose between time with you or this movie-"

"You don't have to choose. Why would you think that?"

"Other movies will come along. Someone like you-"

"What are you trying to say? Because I keep telling you to do this movie and that I'll go to New York, soooo..."

He shifted his gaze to the wall. I glanced at my phone to check the time. He had to be on set in a few minutes. I wracked my brain. What was I missing? "You want me to live with you this summer?" I hazarded.

"Do you want to?"

"I don't not want to. I just... it's not..." The Talk. It had sneaked up on me.

"Yeah, okay. No, that's not what I was driving at."

Or maybe it hadn't. "Then what are you driving at?"

"I like how things are right now, this weekend. I like seeing you every day and having all my free time with you. I'd like to, once this shoot is over, move to Albuquerque and have it be like this. Would that crowd you?"

"No..." Not if things were exactly like this. I liked it too. We spent time together, but we lived our own lives in the process. I could do homework in his trailer just as well as I could do it in my house. He wasn't clingy. He just liked to share the same space. It was ideal, really. But if he wanted to do it every day for weeks on end, I sensed that would speed up the whole relationship. He'd want to move past cuddles in the evening before too long.

"You having to find your own place in New York, is that you trying to get a little more space?"

"Oh. No. It's what I told you. I don't want you to buy me big stuff like that."

"Well, we've been together two months and seen each other twice. It's a little hard to gauge where we're at. Are we a couple who's been on two dates or one who's been together for a while?"

"I don't know."

He frowned. "You want to see the house I rented in Albuquerque?"

"You've already got a place?"

"Yeah. I don't know what you want, but for what it's worth, I want to be with you. I want to invest some time in us." He looked like I'd jammed a knife in his gut and was twisting it, slowly.

Instinct took over and I kissed him. "I love you," I whispered in his ear. "And yes, I want to spend time with you. This trip has been one of the best weekends of my life."

He shut his eyes and breathed a sigh of relief. Someone knocked on the door.

"I gotta go."

"Yeah. Break a leg."

25
THE TALK

Two weeks later, I met up with Lori for lunch in the student union and she greeted me by whipping out a picture of Jason and me walking down the street in Vancouver.

I swiped it and hid it away. She knew that Jason and I had gotten together, of course. She and I still saw each other regularly, even though we weren't housemates anymore. But Jason and I were careful about the rest of the world. We never hugged or held hands in public. I often walked next to Dave to imply that we were together – which Dave's boyfriend thought was hilarious. From that vantage I watched everyone and everything female hit on Jason, the ones who could form coherent sentences in his presence, at least. There were still a lot of girls who just stood in front of him and shook. Some of the paparazzi had no doubt figured out we were together, but they didn't have any juicy images to prove it, so there weren't any stories about the two of us – at least, not any stories that weren't complete and total fabrication.

"Rumor has it, he's in Albuquerque now?" said Lori. The place was so loud, she almost had to shout. The television was blaring, someone was doing some kind of drum performance further down the mall, and the tables around us were packed with people chattering and laughing.

I leaned in closer so that I wouldn't have to yell. "Yeah. He moved in the other day."

"Oh. My. Gosh."

"He's got family here. I'm not the only reason-"

"You are totally involved with Jason-"

"Shhh!" I said. "Do you know how lucky I am that no one else has picked up on this?" I looked down at the picture of the two of us in Vancouver. I was paranoid that any day now, despite how careful Jason and I were, people would start to point at me and whisper behind their hands whenever I walked by. Apparently the UNM student body didn't read a ton of tabloids. No one had even asked if I knew him. Everyone else in the student union just now, ignored me.

"Have you heard the rumor he's with Gigi Malone?" said Lori.

"Yes, and I know Gigi, whom I'll bet started that rumor."

"What about the one where he picked up three girls at a night club?"

"The night that he was Skyping with me all evening, yeah."

"The one where he hooked up with a camerawoman?"

"Okay, I don't have a direct disproof of that one. I'll make sure to hack into his computer and check." I rolled my eyes.

Lori, laughed. She looked fantastic. Her eyes practically shone and her skin had a healthy glow. Life with Charles had just lit her up from the inside. I'd never seen her so happy. "Well, I have news," she said.

"Hmm?"

"Charles is taking me to Hobbs to meet his family next weekend."

"Nice. He met yours yet?" Lori's parents lived in Moriarity, just over the mountains from Albuquerque. Technically it was close, but they hardly ever came into town.

"Not yet. But soon. I've never felt like this before, Chlo. Things are *so* good."

"I'm hap-" Over her shoulder I caught sight of something that brought me up short. Matthew came up the stairs, with his arm around a girl. She had lustrous blond hair, like a lion's mane, and catlike, green eyes.

Lori turned to see what I was staring at.

I looked away, fast.

"Michelle," said Lori. "Her name's Michelle."

"Right."

"Goes to his church."

"Mmmm."

"Are you... okay?"

I wasn't. My palms had started to sweat. "Yeah," I lied.

Out of the corner of my eye, I saw Matthew's figure slow and stop. It took all my courage to look at him again. He offered a small smile and a wave.

I turned away. "Can we go somewhere else?"

Lori raised an eyebrow. "Sure. Fine. But... he really wants to be friends again, you know? You've both moved on. Why can't you just put the past behind you?"

Jason's rental was a converted farmhouse on three acres of land off Second Street. He'd tried to go low key. The front gate required a security code, which I tapped in with shaking hands, and the house was set well back from the road and shielded by cottonwoods and poplars. The whole property was fenced, with alarms and security cameras. I pulled up to park in front of the garage and went around to the front door.

It was definitely springtime again. My nose and eyes itched with all the pollen in the air. A cottontail rabbit bounded away from me across the weedy field.

The door was slightly ajar and I could hear Jason talking on the phone inside. I went in and shut and locked it behind me.

"This one will break the streak, Ange," he said. He was talking to his agent. "It's going to be a turkey. Everything fell apart during the shoot, so seriously, now is not the time to talk about an increase in- No, listen. I don't care who's making what, I want to have a career three years from now, so I say be conservative. I've gotta stay bankable." He was in the other room, so he hadn't seen me yet. I wasn't sure if he'd heard the front door.

The front room was the living room with a cathedral ceiling and hardwood floors. I tossed my backpack down by the couch and sat. I had studying to do. I had a late shift at Flying Star, so I needed to work ahead on some things. But tears were already running down my cheeks.

Get a grip, I thought. I put both hands over my face. A sob bubbled up from my chest, followed by another. I felt like someone had ripped my heart out.

"Yeah... yeah... Just send that part to Keith. I already talked to him about it. Right... Okay. Talk to you later."

I dabbed my eyes with the backs of my hands. It didn't work. More tears kept on coming.

Gentle footsteps came towards me and the couch cushion sank as Jason sat down. His arms were around me now, his hand stroking my face. "Hey, what's wrong?" he asked.

"Nothing. Nothing. It's just... it's stupid."

"Tell me."

"I saw Matthew with his new girlfriend. It's nothing. It's... I'm just..."

"Oh." Jason's took his hand from my cheek. "Yeah. You don't ever talk about him anymore."

"I'm being dumb. The whole thing happened last term."

"But clearly it still gets to you."

I shrugged and tried again to clear the tears from my eyes. I was glad I hadn't put on much makeup that day.

Jason snatched a tissue from a nearby box and gave it to me.

"I'm sorry," I said.

"You still have feelings for him, Chlo?"

"No. It isn't that. I wouldn't cross the street to talk to him now."

"Hate's just the other side of love."

"That isn't it, okay?"

Jason waited for me to continue. Obviously, I had some explaining to do, given I was still crying.

"He was different, is all," I said. "It's something that's stayed with me."

"Because he was your best friend?"

"Because up until he was a total jerk, he accepted me for who I am."

"What do you mean by that, exactly?"

I dabbed my eyes. I wasn't sure this was the best time for the Talk, but I realized now that I needed it, even if it precipitated the end of us as a couple. Having Jason here in Albuquerque to be with me was stressful. I loved him, but I didn't see where this relationship could go. Any day now he'd invite me to spend the night and I'd have to tell him. "I've never been with a guy," I said. "Intimately. I don't want that in my life right now."

Jason stopped stroking my hair and sat back. "Okay." He sounded uncertain, which wasn't the worst reaction I'd had. Rather than launch into questions, he waited for me to say more.

I dabbed my eyes again. The tears had stopped. "All my relationships dead end on that issue. Matthew-"

"Wears a purity ring."

"Right. Being with him felt... comfortable in a way that... I dunno how to explain it."

Jason ran his fingers through his hair with one hand. His other arm was still around me. For a long moment, he said nothing.

Well, I thought, here we go. Now he'll ask me what "right now" means and what exactly was and wasn't allowed. I braced myself for negotiations.

"So does my past bother you?"

"I'm not like everyone else you've been with-"

"Whoa, wait. The tabloids like to embellish, and people make assumptions and... yeah... I've done some crazy stuff too, but I'm not that guy, okay? You think Jen would still talk to me if I was? Or my mother? My dad would kick my butt."

I took a deep breath and shifted my weight. "I don't know what you expect-"

Jason grasped my wrist, as if afraid I would pull away. "I don't expect anything. Whatever pace you're comfortable with, it's fine."

"But, look," I said, "you can't be indifferent-"

"Well, no." He shrugged, but his eyes belied amusement. "That's not the word I'd use." He pulled me closer, nuzzled my cheek and caressed the inside of my wrist with his thumb. "I love you. I mean that, all right? I don't know what kind of guys you've been dating in college, but I'm over the novelty of not living with my parents and having my own king size bed. Really."

I couldn't help it. I laughed. That was a new twist in the Talk I'd never heard before.

Jason moved his hand from my wrist to my cheek and gave me a long, lingering kiss. For the first time, I let myself unwind all the way in his arms. He kissed my forehead. "So... we okay?"

I nodded.

He pressed his lips against mine again.

Matthew receded to the dark recesses of my memory. This, I now knew, was what it was like to be in a relationship with my best friend.

THREE days later, when Matthew sidled up to me in Media Studies before class began, I turned to him and said, "Yeah, you're a jerk."

"How are you?"

"Really, really good. Jason won. Deal with it." I kept my voice pitched low. This was *not* the class to let my secret out in. It was teeming with Jason's fans. "I'd ask how you are, but I don't care."

He pulled out the chair next to me and sat down.

"I'm not going to stop making comments like that any time soon," I said. "And I don't want to hear any more cracks about my boyfriend being a player."

Matthew got out his notebook and a pen and set up for class.

"I'm also going to be sarcastic whenever I feel like it."

"The horror."

"Yeah, like that. You know what's funny? It wasn't the guy with the wild past who turned out to be the player. It was *someone else*."

"So you're talking to me again?"

"Like it or not."

He gave me a lopsided smile. "I am still sorry, okay?"

"Good thing you aren't that great of a kisser, huh?"

"Good thing I know you like to use irony."

"Dream on."

"He'd better deserve you."

"I love him."

Matthew nodded. I knew he had a girlfriend now and that our little encounter had been ages ago, but the gesture still looked like an acknowledgment of defeat. That made me able to smile at him. "Okay, I'm out of insults for now. I'll have to think of more."

"Take your time. You know where to find me."

26

A COUPLE of weeks later, while I was cramming for a biology exam in the evening at Jason's house, someone pulled up in the driveway. A moment later, I saw Jen walk past the front window and I got up to let her in. She already had her hand raised to knock and looked baffled for a moment.

"Hi," I said.

"Hi. Jason here?"

"Yep!" he called out. He'd been sitting on the couch, with Steve's old Securities Law textbook. I now knew how he filled his brain with so much random knowledge; he studied every spare moment he wasn't working, working out, or talking to me. He capped the highlighter in his hand and set it aside as he got up. "You hungry?"

"I'll make you something," she said, absently. She walked right through the front hall and back to the kitchen.

"Hey." Jason tailed her. "That is not what I asked."

"Do you have a moment?" She sounded exhausted.

"Sure."

I went back to my studying. Whatever had Jen so distraught was none of my business.

Jason's floors were all tile and hardwood, though, so I could hear their conversation clearly a room away.

"I'm out of ideas," said Jen.

"About?"

"Kyra. That girl's going to kill me."

"Kyle know you're here?"

"He's taken her a on a long drive. Up through the Jemez. I don't think this'll work any better than the last three times, but at least it keeps her tied up for a couple of hours."

"What's going on?"

"She's in love with this guy. Name's Nate. No good, does nothing, good looking-"

"Like me?"

"Please, I'm not in a joking mood." There came a clank, like someone putting something down on the stove.

"Jen, you don't need to cook-"

"It's what I do, okay?"

"It's your job. Take a break."

Water ran in the sink. "I've got to get her out of Albuquerque. I wish there was a military school in Alaska I could send her to-"

"I'm sure there is."

"But she'd probably just run away from it. She's almost eighteen. She will be eighteen in less than a year. Our options are dwindling, and I'm so afraid she's going to get herself pregnant."

"You talked-"

"Yes, yeah. She's on the pill. Doesn't stop me worrying. At that age, people just don't know any better."

My mother sprang to mind.

"So you want me to help? You need money for tuition in Alaska?"

"No."

"Just tell me what you need. And you really don't need to be cooking right now. I'm not hungry."

"Maybe you can talk to her."

"She hates me. You've noticed that, right?"

"No, she hates me. She thinks I've got a double standard because I've put up with you all these years and tell her she needs to stop it with all the guys. But she knows you're not screwing around anymore, so maybe you can say something that'll get through to her."

"I don't think she and I have the same problems, Jen. She's throwing her life away. I never did that. Can't understand it at all."

"I know, that's the problem, isn't it? I can't understand it either. At her age, all I wanted was to get into culinary school."

"Her mother won't help?"

"Her mother hasn't returned any of our phone calls or emails for six months. Not even Kyra's."

The two fell silent while Jen continued clanking around the kitchen. After about ten minutes, Jason came back into the front room. "You want pasta primavera?" he asked.

"Sure." I got up.

"Don't ask me why she's cooking. Do I do that, just start acting when I'm stressed?"

"I don't know, do you?"

"Pretty sure I don't."

I had to agree there. Jason was the most undramatic person I'd ever met in his personal life. Jen was arranging pasta onto plates when we returned to the kitchen. "I gotta go," she said.

"Jen," said Jason.

She gave him an awkward hug. "Thanks for letting me vent."

"Hey-"

"I'll talk to you later." She bustled out of the kitchen, continued out the front door, and was gone.

I looked after her. "She really stressed?"

"Yeah." He looked at the plates of pasta and frowned. "And I'm not hungry. Are you?"

"Not really."

A LITTLE over a week after that, I was on Jason's service porch, hefting my laundry from the washing machine to the dryer. I still felt a little guilty, taking advantage of his facilities like this, but as he pointed out, he couldn't exactly come to the laundromat with me without creating a mob scene.

"Hello?" I heard Jason say in the kitchen. I glanced through the door and saw that he had his cell phone to one ear. "Hmmm? No. No. Whoa, what? Slow down."

I tore off a fabric softener sheet and tossed it in with my clothes, pressed the door shut, and started the dryer. The whoosh of its motor drowned out Jason's words for a moment. But when I went into the kitchen, he was frowning. "What can I do? You want me to call someone or... something?" At the sight of me, he took his phone from his ear and tapped the screen.

"-don't know!" came Jen's voice on speakerphone.

"She's still a minor. You can call the police and have her brought home, right?"

"And have her hate me."

"She can't move out of your house at seventeen, Jen."

"She just did!"

"Well, what can I do?"

"Nothing. I'm just calling to stress. I'll figure this out."

"Where's Kyle?"

"On the phone with her. He's doing his best, you know?"

"You talked to Mom and Dad?"

"Yeah, yeah, they just told me to 'hang in there'. You know how they are."

Jason looked over at me. "Okay if we go over to Jen's house?" he asked.

I nodded.

"Chloe and I will come over. Don't cook anything."

Jen's house was a sprawling ranch style in the foothills, not too far from Sandia Tram. We pulled into the driveway at the same time Kyle and Kyra did, and walked into a scene of pandemonium inside.

The house reeked of cooking smells. Spice and tomato sauce and warm bread. Jen's kitchen wasn't quite as state of the art as Jason's in LA, but it was several grades better than the usual home kitchen. Despite Jason's admonition not to prepare anything, she had a basket of crisped tortillas and a spinach artichoke dip set out for everyone. The other smells, I surmised, were left over from dinner.

Jason and I came in the front door and Kyra came storming in through the back. She burst into the kitchen and screamed, "I hate you!"

"Fine," said her father. He followed behind at a more sedate pace. "But you will live at home until you finish high school."

She whipped her purse off her shoulder and made as if to throw it, then caught sight of me and froze.

To say I felt like an intruder was an understatement. Everyone else looked at me. In a gesture of defeat, Kyra tossed her purse on the counter and shoved both hands into her pockets. She was wearing a short little denim skirt and cute sandals. I couldn't help but notice the similarities to how my own mother dressed. Mom had probably looked cute too, at seventeen.

"Hi, Chloe," she said.

"Hi," I said.

She glanced around at the rest of her family, shuffled her feet, then marched out of the room and down the hall.

Everyone turned back to look at me.

I took a hesitant step after her, then, because it seemed to be what everyone expected, I followed her. It felt like a real intrusion to go back down the back hall of Jennifer's house, but it was easy to find Kyra's room. The door was shut and the light was on inside, making a thin strip of brightness at the bottom of the door. I knocked. "Kyra?"

"Yeah. Come in."

I opened the door and found Kyra sitting at a desk, staring out the window at the twilit scrub brush and desert expanse outside. The house was set quite a ways back from the road, but had no landscaping. The girl's bed was neatly made and her room tidy. The walls were painted a powder pink and decorated with framed photographs, mostly of landscapes.

"You probably think I'm really stupid," she said.

"Honestly? I have no idea what's going on and feel like I don't belong here at all."

"Me neither. Jen hates me."

"Hardly."

"I'll never be good enough for her."

I didn't have any well thought out answers to that one, so I just went to sit on the bed.

After a moment, Kyra turned around, and I saw there were tears in her eyes. "What are your parents like?"

"Um... my mother was your age when she had me, and my father was a philandering loser. Really, your situation is much better."

"You coulda gone to the Academy. You're smart."

"Even if I had a full scholarship, Mom wouldn't have driven me. Jen may be a little neurotic sometimes, but it's because she cares." I didn't feel like I was saying anything Kyra didn't already know. I was at a loss. I knew nothing about how to talk to a teenager.

"So because I'm lucky, I should just be happy?"

"You've got a lot of people who want to help you be happy. If you could do anything, what would you do?"

"I don't know."

"What would you try?"

"I don't know."

"You still like your drama class?"

"Set design."

"You want to go with Jason next time he does an interview? Or a photo shoot?"

"Maybe…" Her eyes lit up a little. "That'd be kinda cool."

"Or see a movie shoot this summer?"

"That would be way cool."

"Means putting up with Jason, though."

"He's different now."

"Is he?"

She nodded. "He used to be, I dunno. Really shallow. Thought he was all charming and funny all the time. Now he's just… himself." She looked at me as if I should appreciate the significance of this.

"He's a good guy," I ventured. "And he cares about you."

Kyra pulled open a desk drawer and tugged out an artist's portfolio. "Do you want to see some pictures I took on our trip to Elephant Butte?"

"Sure."

I emerged from her room an hour later, fifty minutes of which I'd spent looking at pictures. If it was a miracle intervention that Jen had hoped for, I hadn't pulled it off. Jason, Jen, and Kyle were all seated around the table, eating tortilla chips and dip. When I walked in, they looked up and fell silent.

I shrugged. "I learned all about camera lenses."

"Oh, her pictures," said Kyle. "Yeah, she's got a good eye, and a very nice camera, as of last Christmas."

"I'm sorry," I said.

"For what?" said Jen. "She won't even talk to anyone else. For some reason, she really likes you."

"And it's ten p.m., and she's still here in the house," said Kyle. "I call that a win."

"We should get home," said Jason.

"Yeah, yeah, of course." Jen got up to walk us to the door.

Once we were in his car, Jason was all apologies. "I'm sorry you get dragged into my family stuff."

"No, I don't mind," I said. "I just don't feel like I did any good."

"Like Jen said, she talks to you. That's more than anyone else can manage. Jen and Kyle want to send her away somewhere for the summer. Get her away from that guy and try to get her to think about the rest of her life."

"Well, I can't help with that last part, but if they want to send her to New York for the summer, I can be her roommate."

"Don't joke about that. People will take you up on it."

I shrugged. "It's not a joke. Provided I could send her home if there are any problems, I don't mind."

Jason glanced at me. "Really?"

"Sure."

"Would you let me rent the apartment?"

"Jas-"

"She's still just a kid. Jen would want her in a safe building with a doorman and... I bet I could get her a job of some kind on set. Wait a minute, why am I talking about this? You do not need to spend the summer babysitting my wayward niece."

"I really don't mind. The moment it became a babysitting job, I'd want to send her home."

"Totally reasonable..." He looked sidelong at me. "I'll talk to Jen. And I'm renting the apartment."

I didn't want to fight about that right then. The truth, though, was that I'd searched high and low for an affordable apartment in the neighborhood Jason wanted and come up with nothing.

27
LORI

Jen showed up towards the end of my Saturday afternoon shift at work. One minute I was ringing up an order, the next I was face to face with her. "Hi," she said.

"Hey."

"You get off soon?"

I nodded. "Ten minutes."

"Okay... can we get coffee or something, then?"

"Sure."

Jen went to find a seat and page through a magazine. I finished off my work, signed out, poured two cups of coffee and went to join her. "So how are you?" I said as I put her cup of coffee down in front of her.

"Oh, I was going to go order. I didn't mean for you to-"

I waved that away. "You want something other than coffee?"

"No, no. This is great." She took a sip – I noticed she drank it black. "Okay," she said, "I gotta ask, you taking Kyra to New York, is that a serious offer?"

"Sure. Though I'll need a way to get one of you out there or send her back if things go wrong. I might be in over my head."

"Of course, yeah, of course. Are you sure, though? I mean, that's not exactly a romantic summer away, having her around."

"Well, what would she need?"

Jen fidgeted with her coffee cup, exactly like Jason did when he was on edge. I wished I'd gotten her something other than coffee, or cut it with decaf or something. "I've got an old classmate in New York who knows the people who are doing the catering for Jason's movie. I could probably get Kyra a job."

"I'm sure Jason could-"

"I never ask Jason for favors like that. I know he'd help, but-" She shrugged. "Seems dumb that I deserve anything for being his sister. My friend in New York, now I helped her through culinary school. She owes me one. Think Kyra would do catering?"

"I barely know her."

"Right, me too. Kyle and I are also hiring her an SAT prep coach who'll help her with her college applications."

"Sounds nice."

Jen gave me an odd look. "Really? Doesn't sound neurotic and over the top?"

"I wish I'd had one of those."

"Make sure you tell her that. Basically, we'd just need somewhere for her to live. She and Jason aren't a good mix. I mean, I think they get along now, but only up to a point, and we need someone to just make sure she's... spending the night in her bed. Alone. That sounds awful."

"If I had a daughter her age, I might have her chained to the floor."

"The thought has crossed my mind, but I think that's illegal. I'm being unfair, though. Her problem isn't guys, plural, right now. It's one guy. This one guy we can't seem to keep her away from."

"And you want her to go to college and get a life."

"Exactly. But I've gotta ask, are you *seriously* offering-"

"Yeah, it's a serious offer. I don't think I can fix your problems here, but I can be her roommate and keep tabs on her. And this resolves my little discussion with Jason about apartment rental. He can rent the apartment and I'm not just his girlfriend, whom he has out there."

"I get what you're saying, but it's not like that. Here's the other thing, though, and it may be the deal breaker. When you spend the night with Jason, I need you to be discreet about it."

Ye-ah, I thought. I kept a straight face and nodded. "Sure. I understand." I wondered, though, how clueless Jen thought her stepdaughter was.

"I feel guilty," said Jen, "just dumping this on you. Kyle and I are at the ends of our respective ropes, though. I mean, we've sent her to the Academy and funded her going to speech competitions and track and field and drill team and whatever else she's been interested in, but she won't stick with anything. She and that guy- his name's Nate, by the way -are talking about getting married as soon as she graduates high school. She told me to be glad she's waiting until she graduates. Maybe this summer she'll meet some other guy, and not get into this obsessive, unhealthy relationship with him."

"Or maybe she'll find something she wants to pursue as a career," I said.

"Right. Yeah." Jen drained the rest of her coffee. "I'm sorry to be so crazed. I just feel like I'm really bad at this. Kyle's asking me if I want more kids and... I just don't know! I can't seem to keep Kyra in line."

"Well, that's not really your job," I said. "All you can do is try, right?"

"But it means failing sometimes. Do you know how scary that is? Someday you'll have kids and you'll know what I mean."

And for a moment I imagined that, having a family the way Jen did. Would I ever really get that?

"Kyra's lucky," I said.

"Try telling her that."

I just nodded.

"I'm so glad you're with Jason," said Jen.

"Thanks... I know he's dated a lot..."

"Mmm, I guess." Her tone was noncommittal. "You're what he needs, though. Stable, normal, still able to put up with his crazy family."

"I never did get to thank you, for what you said to him on New Year's."

"Oh." She laughed. "I'm just glad I was right. After he tore out of the restaurant I wondered if it was just wishful thinking on my part. Anyway..." She shrugged.

After a little more small talk Jen got up to go, and it was decided, Kyra and I were bound for New York in a few weeks.

"So what was it like, filming in Albuquerque? That's home for you, right?"

Lori and I were at my house, watching *The Tonight Show*, while I also did my homework. Jason had started the press junket for *That Day*, which had, like his last five films, opened at number one. He wore a casual blazer over a button down shirt and matching slacks. I did like his stylist. Lori munched potato chips, transfixed.

"Yeah, Albuquerque's home," said Jason. "I grew up there."

"Until when? You were doing your Disney show by the time you were, what? Sixteen?"

"Well, right. I moved to LA in high school."

"But your family's out there?"

"Yeah, yeah, they're all out there."

"High school friends?"

"I wish I still had my high school friends, but they're all too cool for me now."

"Won't return your calls, eh?"

I flipped to another page in my textbook and started scanning down the text. I didn't get how people could watch this show every night. My own boyfriend was on it and I found it dull.

"Maybe I should try that, calling them, yeah. No, seriously, a lot of them have moved away. One of them's in the film industry. He's a key grip. Worked on set with us."

I shook my head. "That's made up," I told Lori.

"A key grip, eh? What does a key grip do?"

"You know, I'm not sure. Every time I saw him, he was just sitting around eating nachos."

Lori and everyone in the studio laughed, including the host.

"Maybe we should ask these people." Jason gestured off camera. "Hey, are any of you guys grips?" There was an inaudible reply. "Yeah?" said Jason. "Are you a key grip or just a grip? Is there a difference? Do you have to have, like, special ninja skills to be a *key* grip?"

The crowd was eating this up, roaring with laughter.

I went to get some water. This was a more productive study evening than I'd anticipated.

"So did you get to spend time with your friend-"

"Oh, not my friend. He was way, waaaaay more popular than I was in high school."

"But he's out getting fat, eating nachos and you're a movie star."

"Right, the moral of the story is, stay in school kids... except I didn't. I had tutors. Does that count?" Jason feigned a thoughtful look.

"He graduated from La Cueva," I told Lori. "Transferred his credits there."

People were howling with laughter.

"Does key grip guy have a high school diploma?" asked the host.

"You know, he probably has a college degree..."

By LA studio audience standards, Jason was being a riot. Lori kept giggling too.

"All right, tell us about this clip."

"This clip is interesting because it uses no special effects."

"This is the clip with the aliens invading right?"

"Yeah, isn't that interesting? I guess the director had connections with some aliens or something. It's all real."

"Is it now?"

"But if you ask me, the aliens aren't the best actors."

"Well, let's see. Let's roll it."

The scene shifted to Jason, huddled in the dark with Corey Cassidy, next to the anthropology building, only it wasn't supposed to look like an anthropology building. I did notice, though, that their breath did not fog the air as they gasped with wonder. Lights shone across their faces as they watched something descend in front of them. The scene shifted to a bulbous craft, touching down, blasting the ground with gouts of what looked like dry ice. Definitely not anything that would actually slow down a descending spaceship.

Jason looked at Corey, who looked back. "They mention this to you in the evacuation order?" he said.

And the scene cut back to Jason on the set of *The Tonight Show*. Everyone burst into thunderous applause. I went back to my reading.

"So do we ever get to see the aliens?" the host asked.

"Hey, go watch the movie."

More applause.

"All right, all right. Last question."

I glanced up to see Jason sit up straight, as if bracing himself to be grilled.

"Are you seeing anyone?"

Lori nudged me.

"No comment." He grinned.

"Look, you can't say 'no comment' and then smile like a cat who just ate a canary."

"I never share my personal life."

"Maybe, but I think we all know the answer, don't we?"

The whole audience booed. Jason's grin widened and he laughed.

"See?" said the host. "They know you're not available."

"Not even remotely. But I'm not divulging any details, sorry."

"Oh. My. *Gosh*," squealed Lori.

My netbook chimed. Mom was calling on Skype. I went back to my room, away from the television noise, and answered it. "Hey."

"Things are going well?" She smiled at me.

"Hmmm?"

"I just saw your boyfriend on television."

"Oh, right. I think so. He's telling the world about me, kind of."

"I *know*. He never says anything like that in interviews."

"I wouldn't really know."

"Well, I would. Not that I can blame him for letting it slip."

"Uh, thanks." I brushed that comment aside. Now was a good time to tell her I'd be in New York for the summer, but I couldn't bring myself to do it. Despite the fact that I'd be there with Kyra, and that Jason wasn't a married man buying me off, I still felt embarrassed to admit that he was renting me an apartment. "Are you coming out for graduation?" I asked instead. It seemed innocuous enough.

"Am I invited?" She blinked in surprise.

"Um, *yeah*. You remember how you gave birth to me and all that?"

"Well, sure but-"

"Of course you're invited. You're my mother. But it's okay if you can't come. I know how it is with work-"

"When is it?"

I clicked over to the calendar. "Second Saturday in May."

"I'll be there!"

"Okay... great." I had the feeling this was supposed to be another mother-daughter bonding moment, but I just had the overwhelming sense that I didn't get her. She'd never cared about school before. What had changed? Then it hit me. "Mom, Jason can't make it. His movie opens in Australia that day and he's going to the premiere in Sydney."

"Oh... Well that's okay, right?"

"Yeah, but just so you know."

She smiled, brightly, but I could see it was forced. "I'll still be there. You'll be doing a speech, right?"

"Yeah, yeah." It was official now, I was the class valedictorian.

My cell phone rang.

"That him?" she asked.

I looked. "Yeah."

"Then I'll let you go. Bye!" She cut the connection.

I picked up my phone. "Hello?"

"I love you."

"Nice interview."

"Yeah? You okay with me talking about you?"

"I don't think it'll make your fans any less aggressive."

He laughed. "One more day of interviews, then I'm coming home."

I felt guilty all over again for missing the premiere of *That Day*, but the timing was awful. I had two big projects due for school, and since I never interacted with him in public, it'd just be me sitting in the back of the theater, though I knew Jason would have liked even that. "I miss you," I said.

"Miss you too. I know it's late. Just wanted to call though. And I emailed you the info on your New York apartment."

"Yeah, about that-"

"Please, let's not argue."

"It's just-"

"I wanted you guys close. It's right by my hotel."

"Jas-"

"C'mon, you wouldn't pick for yourself, so I picked. Just let me be nice to you for once."

"You're always nice."

"You never let me spend money on you."

"Because-"

"You don't want to get used to it?"

"Sure. That's part of it."

"Why not? You still have reservations about the future?"

"Okay, you're right. Let's not argue."

"I love you."

"Love you, too."

"Night."

"Night." We hung up and I went back out to the front room. The commercial break was over and Gigi Malone, of all people, was being interviewed about another movie she had coming out. "She is crazy," I told Lori.

"I can't believe you know these people."

"Me neither. Random, right?" I sat back down in front of my book. "She is messed up, and she's got a thing for Jason."

"Well who-" Lori bounded to her feet and ran out of the room to the bathroom.

"You okay?" I called after her.

I heard the sound of her retching.

"Whoa, Lori?" I said. I got to my feet.

"Sec." The toilet flushed and the sink ran. A moment later she opened the door, her expression grim. "Well, guess that kind of gives it away, huh?"

"What? You're pregnant?" I was half joking.

She gave a sheepish smile.

"Really?"

"Yeah." A broad smile spread across her face. "But we aren't telling anyone yet, so keep it quiet, okay?"

"Charles knows?"

"Oh yeah. He was there when I took the test. I think he's even more excited than I am." She came back into the living room and sat on the couch, beaming.

Lori pregnant? That made my head spin. "Congratulations."

"I know, I'm doing this out of order." She shook her head. "But, it's kind of cool like this. It's an adventure." She bit her lip. "Sorry... I know you didn't love having an unmarried mother."

"Different situation."

"You're not judging me?"

"I'll leave that to Matthew."

"Yeah, I won't be telling him about this."

"But Charles is supportive?"

"Oh yeah. I mean, we were already talking about marriage, and this just makes it more certain. We'll make it formal *after* the baby and graduation and starting our new jobs and all that." She shrugged.

She didn't know the details, but she knew her long term future was secure with Charles. Despite my background, I envied her right then.

28

"This is going to be *so cool*," Kyra was bouncing in her seat next to me on the plane. "You are the *best*." We were on our way to New York and had just taken off from Albuquerque. The passenger on the other side of me, a middle aged man with a laptop case not all the way under the seat in front of him, shot Kyra an annoyed look.

And I wanted to throw up. This was all wrong. Kyra and her issues aside, Jason was paying more for this apartment than I'd paid in three years of rent on my house.

"You okay?" Kyra asked.

I tried to nod, but she wasn't stupid. I shook my head. "I'm nervous." I forced a smile. "I hear you're a real handful."

It was meant to be a joke, but she didn't take it that way. The bouncing stopped. Her shoulders slouched. She turned to look out the window. Her hair was done up in two pigtails silhouetted against the powder blue sky outside.

"No," I said. "Okay, bad joke. I'm sorry."

She dismissed me with a flick of her chin.

"People pick on you a lot?" I asked.

"What did Jen tell you about me?"

"Not much."

"Liar."

"Hey, come on. I don't lie to you. She's worried about you, and she's got you a catering job-"

"And she hates Nate."

"Nate your boyfriend?"

"Yes."

"I know nothing about him."

Kyra turned her head enough that I could see one made up eye, looking me over. "He's your age."

"What?"

"You really didn't know that?"

"Are you serious? How long have you been together?"

"Two years, almost."

"That's not legal."

She smiled, amused. "Ten years from now, it won't matter."

"You sure you'll make it ten years?"

"Why not? You think I'm too young to know?"

"Well, yeah. The odds are against you."

"Everyone thinks-"

"Okay, look, I'm not everyone. I was raised by a woman who started out like you, seventeen and in love. When she was your age, her relationship seemed like a fairytale to her and it was all going to work out. Suffice it to say, it didn't. I wouldn't wish my childhood on anyone."

"I'm not pregnant."

"Fine, but even if she'd had me three years later, or four, it wouldn't have mattered. She never grew up. Same problems."

"And my guy isn't married."

"No, but he's too old to be looking at you."

"Jason is way older than you and my dad is way older than Jen."

"Yes, but Jen and I aren't jailbait. We're grown women with degrees who know how to do stuff like pay bills and support ourselves. We're adults. You're not there yet."

Kyra scowled at me and I realized that I'd said the wrong thing. I wasn't an expert on teenagers, but I was pretty sure they didn't like being called little children. Still, I was being truthful. That had to count for something.

"What's Nate do for a living?" I asked.

"Right now he's a mall security guard."

"Okay."

"But he's going to be a doctor."

"He in med school?"

"No, he's still working on college."

"Where."

Her gaze darted from my face to the seat in front of her to the airline magazine tucked into its pouch. "This online program."

"Stop right there. You're not talking sense. That's fairytale logic, not real world logic. He's not going to be a doctor."

"Just because I'm young-"

"Youth has nothing to do with it. You've got to have a grip on reality. Doesn't matter how old you are. My mom, when she was Jason's age, still thought Dr. Winters was going to leave his wife for her, and it was just as delusional then as it was when she was your age."

"Yeah, well, not everyone can date a movie star."

"Which is good for them. Not that I don't love Jason, I do, but his career and money and all that..." I shook my head. She had me thinking about that dang apartment again.

"You don't like it?"

"It's just... I don't hold it against him. It doesn't matter. It shouldn't."

Kyra looked me up and down. "You ready for a whole summer with him?"

"Yes."

"Because here's reality for *you*. What do you plan to do when you go to New Orleans?"

"I don't know." I shrugged. "We have to be long distance a lot of the time-"

"He hates that and you know it. You're going to have to get used to his lifestyle eventually, because he's going to want to share it with you. You can't live in your stupid little rental house off Central forever."

Why not? I wanted to say, but she was right. She'd turned this conversation on me fair and square.

"What are you hiding from, anyway?" she asked.

"I like being a normal person," I said. "That's all."

Dave met us at the airport, his spiky hair wilting slightly in the heat. I had no idea New York was so hot, or humid, but once we stepped out of the air conditioned interior of La Guardia, we hit a wall of superheated air. I put on my sunglasses, which almost slid off my nose, I was sweating so much. It was disgusting.

"So how was the flight?" he asked.

"It was good," said Kyra, brightly.

I nodded.

Dave didn't see, because he was tapping away at his phone. "Car will be here in a sec." He put the phone away and rested his hands on the pushbar of our luggage cart.

My awkward, nauseated feeling edged up a notch when a shiny black limo pulled up to the curb, long and sleek and silent as a cat.

"Oh *cool*," said Kyra.

"Yeah, stylin', right?" said Dave. He and the driver loaded some of our bags into the trunk and the rest inside. I climbed in and settled myself as best I could on one of the plush seats while Kyra bounded in next to me. "A fridge?" she said, pulling open the square appliance set into the wall. "And a computer terminal? And a television?"

I just stared out the window and craned my neck upwards to take in the skyscrapers. The limo slid away from the curb and we were underway. I swallowed hard, a rich liquid rising in the corners of my mouth.

THE apartment was in a highrise. I had no idea where we were in the city. The building had a doorman who helped Dave and the driver with the luggage. All of my attempts to chip in were rebuffed.

They loaded everything onto the elevator and the doorman handed me a set of keys and said, "Fourth from top floor." He nodded at the other elevator. I wondered if I should tip him, but before I could fumble for my wallet, Dave slipped a folded couple of bills into his hand. This was just not my kind of place.

I followed Kyra into the elevator and up to our floor. Each apartment on this level had a pristine white door, gleaming brass knocker, and peephole. Our door was already open and Dave had moved our suitcases from the other elevator into the sitting room.

Much to my relief, the apartment was small. The sitting room barely had enough room for the three of us and the luggage; the overstuffed couch and chair hogged the rest of the floorspace. There was a tiny kitchenette and then two bedrooms with double beds. Mine had an en suite bathroom, Kyra had access to another bathroom off the sitting room. It looked just like the virtual tour Jason had emailed.

"You all right?" said Dave. He was looking right at me.

"Yeah," I said. "This is great. Thanks."

Kyra went to open the windows and took a deep breath of smoggy, city air.

"Okay," said Dave, "well, just call me if you need anything. Kyra, I'll pick you up in the morning."

"Yeah, thanks," she said.

He left with another unsure glance in my direction. Once the door shut, I sat down on the couch, my head in my hands.

"What's wrong?" said Kyra. "Isn't this cool?"

"It's very nice. Way too nice."

"What do you mean, too nice?"

"Nothing." I got up. "I'm going to lay down for a while, all right? I'm tired."

A KNOCK on the door woke me up. The light that diffused through the window shade was dim and dusky. The clock said it was seven pm. I sat up. "Yeah?"

Jason stuck his head in. "Hey."

"Hi." I rubbed my eyes.

He came and sat down on the bed, the mattress tilting under his weight. "This place okay?" He asked.

"It's great."

"I know it's more than you want, but I wanted you close and Kyra needs her own space and it isn't real expensive for the area-"

"Jas, you were right. I'm not going to complain about this amazing apartment. I don't want to argue."

"I've really made you uncomfortable, haven't I?"

"Did Kyra say something?"

He didn't answer that, just kicked off his shoes and lay down next to me.

I put an arm over him and rested my head on his shoulder. He hugged me around the waist. "It's all me," I said. "I have issues. My mother still doesn't know I'm here, because I don't really know how to explain it to her."

"She wouldn't approve?"

"She'd totally approve. She'd think it was the most romantic thing ever." I rubbed my cheek against the smooth cotton of his t-shirt. Even now, the image of my mother back from one of her spa days, her eyes glowing, made me cringe. She'd always had a hungry look when Dr. Winters bought her things, like she couldn't get enough of it, and to me it seemed so sick.

"You know I don't expect anything in return, right?" He rolled onto his side so we were facing each other. I propped myself up on one elbow as he stroked my cheek. "I'm glad you tell me how you feel, and I do get it, okay?"

"I *am* grateful."

"If I wanted to buy you off I'd, I dunno, give you a big gift certificate to Amazon or something."

I laughed.

"I just need to have you close. The more time I spend with you, the more I want."

I felt the same, only having him here, on my bed, that was different. This would be our private space, now, with Kyra in the picture. It could get pretty cozy. I'd been attracted to all my boyfriends, but none of the others had had personal stylists or those unreal, blue eyes.

"What?" he said. He looked me right in the eye.

"Nothing."

"No, c'mon, what?"

"I didn't go for my run today."

"Yeah, about that. I did get you a gym membership too. I know you didn't want it-"

I really didn't want to fight right then. "Fine. We can spend more time together that way."

"You want to get dinner? Though I'll warn you, I'm paying for that too."

I punched him lightly in the chest. "Okay."

Kyra walked past my door, talking on the phone in a low voice.

"It's the guy," said Jason.

"Nate?"

"Whatever his name is."

"She's not going to get over him in half a day," I told him.

29
MY QUESTION

Two weeks later, I was much more put together. I was done with work for the day – I'd found a job as a barista at a coffee joint within walking distance of my apartment. The tips I got in that neighborhood were something else. I'd stopped by the apartment to get the mail, then caught a cab over to where Jason was filming. They were shooting a bunch of scenes at dusk this week.

The cabbie gave me an odd look when he pulled up to a crowd of gawkers. "You gonna watch them shoot this movie?" he asked. He had an accent I couldn't even guess at. Nigerian maybe? Ghanaian?

"Something like that," I said. "My roommate works in catering."

"Catering?"

"Provides the food for the cast and crew."

"Can you get autographs?"

I tugged loose enough bills to pay for cab fare plus tip. "You want one?"

"My wife is a Jason Vanderholt fan."

I reached into my purse and pulled out an autographed picture. I had to use my big purse to carry the mail, as there were several large envelopes. "Here you go. I can't get it personalized, I'm afraid-"

"No, no, you keep this."

"I can get more. Don't worry about it." I paid him and got out into the sweltering heat. The pictures were the last of a stack I'd gotten for the people at work. Kyra had come by one day, full of stories about life on set, and they'd hounded me for autographs ever since.

I texted Dave as I jostled my way through the crowd. "I need to get past," I explained to the scowling faces that turned my direction. "Let me through, please."

Dave met me partway through the crowd and ushered me the rest of the way in. I went from the press of bodies to the open, empty street beyond – a narrow side street. "You know you can call me for a car," he reminded me.

"And you know that if you send one for me when I don't call, I don't like it," I replied.

We walked in the cool shadow between the highrises and then got blinded by the sun again as we rounded the corner. The catering truck was right in front of us and Kyra stood outside, chatting with a woman who munched a sandwich.

Dave lifted his hand to wave goodbye and darted off in the direction of the trailers.

"So, why is she working at a coffee shop?" the woman asked.

I hesitated.

"Well, she's not going to just hang around here."

"Why not? If her boyfriend's here?"

"That's how she is. So not interested in being a famous guy's arm candy. She's into having her own life."

"She's weird."

"No she's not. She's really cool. She's just not into this lifestyle."

"But you guys live with Jason, right?"

"No... he's at the hotel. We've got an apartment."

"She doesn't even eat here. She could if she wanted to."

"No, she buys her own food and does her own laundry-"

"Now that's just a waste of time."

"I think it's cool."

"Vanderholt could pay for laundry service, easy."

"I know, but they hang out in the laundry room. He carries her basket up and down the stairs. It's way cute."

"She clearly doesn't know how this works."

"No, she does. She just doesn't like it."

I cleared my throat. Kyra looked over at me and ducked her head in embarrassment.

"He-ey!" Jason strode on over, wearing his stockbroker costume, which was a rather nice, gray suit. Dave had found him and let him know I was here. He gave me a hug. "You hungry?"

"I'm fine." We stepped into the shade of the truck.

"What do you want?" Jason asked.

"I'm not hungry, really."

Kyra rolled her eyes.

We sat down in some cloth chairs and I pulled my hair up off my neck. The air felt cool against my sweaty skin. Gross, I thought.

Jason leaned forward, his gaze fixed on my upper arm. My shirt sleeve had ridden up to reveal the edge of my scar. I pushed it all the way up to show him. "That one's the nastiest looking," I said. "Had to have two surgeries."

I dug the mail out of my purse and waved it at Kyra. "Looks like a bunch of college prospectuses," I said.

"Because your parents are really subtle," said Jason. "Let's see, Canada, Alaska, Outer Mongolia. I hear that's nice this time of year."

Kyra came to sit with us and swiped the stack of envelopes. "Colorado College, UT, UCLA. You are such a liar. Oh, this one's yours." She handed an envelope back to me. It was a small, business sized one, but it was fat.

Sure enough, it was addressed to me with a yellow forwarding sticker, and it was from Loyola. "My financial aid package," I said. I'd meant to call them to find out about it.

Jason glanced around. "You want to open that here, or you want some privacy?"

I shrugged. "Won't change what's inside, will it?" I tore open the envelope and unfolded the first page. I read over the letter once, twice.

"Well?" said Jason.

"I got one."

"A fellowship?"

"Yep, with stipend." I smiled up at him.

"Nice, so you are definitely going this fall?"

"Looks like it, yeah. I gotta start looking for somewhere to live."

"Lots of flood and hurricane damaged real estate goes cheap," quipped the woman over by the catering truck. She was staring at me like I had beamed down from Mars.

"Thanks..." I said.

Jason frowned at her and shrugged apologetically at me. "I need AC," he said, getting up.

He needed to shoot a scene at any minute, according to his call sheet, but I followed him anyway. He just wanted to get away from the woman, and to tell the truth, so did I.

The next day I got home to find the apartment door open a crack. Someone, Kyra I assumed, was sobbing inside. "Wait," I heard Jason say, "this about me, or you? You sure your fights with Nate have nothing to do with this?"

I peered through the crack and saw him sitting with his arm around Kyra, who was, in fact, crying. "I just don't get it," she said.

"Don't get what?"

"You haven't even seen her scars?"

"Okay, you know what? Any society where it's normal to say, 'Oh, gee, she has gunshot scars. Wait, what do you mean her boyfriend hasn't seen them?' is messed up, all right? Sick."

"I thought you guys were serious."

"We are serious. You're conflating some concepts here."

"Not as serious as you think."

"Now you just need to mind your own business. We should talk about Nate and whatever he said to you today that made you lock yourself in the bathroom for an hour."

"But you've been together seven months."

"Yes. And?"

"Don't you worry that she's freezing you out?"

"People are different, okay. You leave her and her decisions alone. They're between her and me."

"You've changed."

"Maybe. Not necessarily. I was never like, say... *Nate*, for example. He's a creep."

"He's not a creep."

"Yeah, he is. I'm just saying."

"You haven't ever done *anything* with Chloe. At all?"

"Kyra. I love her, way more than Nate loves you. More than you can understand, okay? As is obvious from the stuff you've been saying."

"That's not going to make her want to be with you."

"Nothing will make her. This isn't about control."

Kyra looked over towards the door. She craned her neck, peering at the crack. "Chloe?"

My face burned hot. I pushed the door open. "I just got here," I said. "It looked personal. I didn't want to barge in." I stepped inside and shut the door.

Kyra wiped her eyes and got up. "I'm going to my room." She slipped out.

"She okay?" I asked.

Jason looked up at me. "Yeah, I think she's fine."

"You okay?"

"I'm good." He was distracted, though.

I hesitated and deposited my purse behind the couch. "Okay," I said, "I heard what she was asking you about... you want to talk?"

"About what?"

I glanced towards Kyra's door. "Let's find some privacy." I went back into my bedroom and Jason followed.

"Okay, so let's talk," I said. I turned to face him.

"Am I supposed to say something?"

"Well, do you have questions for me?"

"Like what?"

"Like... are you wondering if I'm not interested in men or-"

"What? No."

"Or why it's been seven months-"

"I'm supposed to have you on a time limit? Gee thanks, Chlo. Any other selfish, immature behavior I'm supposed to exhibit here?"

"Please don't get mad at me. Look, I know our relationship isn't normal for people our age."

"Says who? And who cares if it isn't?"

"Jason, come on-"

"Why do you think I'd ever, in a million years, sit you down and ask you stuff like that or pressure you or-"

"We never talk about this."

"We did talk about it."

"Months ago, and only a little."

"Yeah. You expect me to harass you? You think I'm like that?"

"No." I wasn't sure how this had turned into an argument. I was trying to give him a chance to tell me his feelings, and he was raising his voice at me.

"All of this is up to you," he said. "You want to wait, fine. You want to switch gears completely, fine. It doesn't affect how committed I am to you or much I love you or anything like that, we clear?"

"Look. You are amazing at respecting my feelings. You're ideal, and I guess I worry about that becoming one sided. I want you to know that I respect your feelings too, okay? I don't want you to hide stuff from me. It's a two way street."

"What do you mean?"

"Well, how do you honestly feel about how things are going? Because most guys do have a time limit and-"

"Chloe, stop. Please. Look, I know you, okay? Your dad was a cheat and your brother tried to kill you. If you take your time trusting men, there're logical reasons there."

"Um... what?"

He sat down on the bed and shrugged. "Well, that's my take on it. Too much psychoanalysis? I'm an actor. I try to take people apart and understand how they tick."

I sat down next to him. The rest of the apartment was quiet. Too quiet. I nodded in the direction of the door.

Jason got up and tugged it open to reveal Kyra, who tried to look as if she was just passing by.

"Do you mind?" he said.

She bit her lip and sidled away.

He shut the door and came to sit down again. "So, okay, bad analysis of how you think?"

"Well... I never thought about it that way. I just really, really don't want to risk having a kid out of wedlock at this point in my life. Especially not with a guy from a really high profile Albuquerque family-"

Jason chuckled. "Projecting much?"

"Yeah, completely. I know I'm not my mother and there are ways to make it almost impossible to get pregnant and people raise kids alone all the time nowadays." I thought about Lori and how happy she was.

"I'd never leave you alone in a situation like that. Ever."

"Well, okay, but I've never regretted not sleeping with an ex, even when I really thought I would. Maybe for all those reasons you listed. I don't know. That why you're so patient? Because you think I'm messed up?"

"No. You know my past. My first love sued me for rape."

"I'd never-"

"No, I know. You wouldn't try to extort money out of me. It's a fight just to get you to let me buy ice cream, but there were a lot of stops on that whole emotional journey and none of them were fun. For a while I really thought she felt I'd forced things with her. It was awful, and I don't ever want to feel that way again."

I leaned on his shoulder.

"So if it's a choice between risking regret and abstinence," he said, "abstinence wins. We've both been burned in our lives and had reasons to think about this stuff. We're not so different."

"You're a hundred percent happy with our relationship? There's nothing you'd change? At all?"

"I don't think so."

"You don't *think*?"

"It's a hard question."

"No it's not. It's not supposed to be. Look, you once said this was like a fairytale for you."

"Yeah."

"Is it still?"

He was silent.

I put a hand against his chest and he slipped an arm around my waist.

"I want to be your Prince Charming," he said.

"I'm not a knight in shining armor kind of girl."

"But... it's what I've been practicing my whole career. How many guys have more experience than me, honestly?"

I laughed. "I don't need you to rescue me."

"I know." He seemed disappointed by that. "You've slain all your dragons already."

"Anything else you want?"

"That's a hard question. It's like you're asking me to be selfish."

"I want to know."

"Let me think about it." He frowned and looked at me, like he was debating whether or not to say something more.

"What do you mean you don't get it?" Kyra said on the other side of my door.

Jason and I exchanged a look. He rolled his eyes.

"There's nothing to get. I texted you, deal with it." Though she stepped away from my door, her voice got louder and louder. "Yeah, I can change my Facebook status if I want. Shut up, okay? Just *shut up!*" There came a crash, which I suspected was the sound of her phone hitting the wall.

"I'll go deal with her," he said.

"You sure?"

"Yeah. After the talk I just had with her, this'll be a piece of cake." He went into the living room and shut the door behind him.

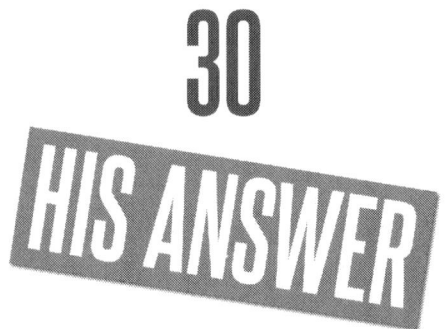

30 HIS ANSWER

"What? You're crazy."

"Kyra..."

"No way. *No* way."

"Just, okay, keep your voice down at least."

Jason's conversation with Kyra was not going well. I stayed in my room and debated whether to stay put and stay out of it, or try to intervene.

"You want to give me advice on *my* love life? You don't even know what you're talking about." Kyra was angry.

"Yeah, thanks."

Well, I wasn't a psychologist, but I was pretty sure that Jason getting defensive would only cause the fight to escalate. I went out into the main room.

Kyra was standing inside her door, looking at Jason like she thought he was an idiot. Her arms were folded across her chest.

Jason just looked frustrated. He leaned against the wall and kept running his fingers through his hair.

Kyra nodded in my direction to let Jason know I was out of my room and he turned to look at me. "Yeah, sorry," he said, before he turned back to his niece. "Please let's not fight. Just, come on. I'm trying to talk to you like another adult. Think you can help me out here?"

She raised an eyebrow at him.

"I'm serious. I wouldn't talk to you about this if I didn't trust you, or if I thought you were a dumb kid."

I watched Kyra struggle then. I could see that she wanted to just roll her eyes and withdraw, but Jason's words had a marked effect. She chewed her lip a moment, looked at him again, then dropped her arms and stalked across the apartment to me.

"Everything all right?" I asked.

She glanced back at Jason. "Yeah."

"Anything I can do?"

"Can I borrow your green shirt?"

"Sure."

"And that silver necklace you have?"

I waved her into my room. "You can borrow whatever. Go ahead."

She ducked inside and Jason just shrugged at me. Clearly he'd tried. At least she'd made a graceful exit. No slammed doors, no yelling.

Jason, however, looked defeated. I went over and gave him a hug.

"I'm bad at this," he said. "Maybe it's better if she talks to you?"

"Yeah, sure if she wants." I always waited for Kyra to come to me, though. I wasn't sure if that was the best idea, but it was the only strategy I had.

That evening, after Jason left, Kyra knocked on my door.

"Yeah?" I said. I was cross-legged on my bed, my netbook in my lap.

She opened it, but didn't come in, just leaned against the door frame. "Sooo, I borrowed your lapis ring and pendant."

"Yeah, fine." I shrugged. "You always take good care of your stuff. You can borrow whatever. Just ask."

She traced an idle pattern on the carpet with her toe.

I looked up at her and waited.

"I'm sorry I eavesdropped on you and Jason," she said.

"Sorry we didn't have anything juicy to say."

Clearly not the answer she expected. She giggled.

"I kind of eavesdropped on you too, this afternoon," I said. "When I got home. I didn't mean to be nosy. I just wanted to figure out whether or not I should come in."

"It's okay."

"I promise, I won't pry into your life," I said. "But if you ever do want to talk to me, you can."

She nodded and turned to leave. "Okay, thanks."

The next day, when I showed up on set, I found her talking to the same woman I'd seen her with before. This time the woman was picking her way through a bag of gummy bears. I wondered how she didn't get fat.

"Well, he's having a crisis and she's doing this all wrong," the woman said. "She's with Vanderholt, the most desirable man on the planet, and she's out pouring coffee while he's just puttering around in his trailer most of the day. She doesn't warm his bed at night. No wonder he's losing his mind."

Crisis? Losing his mind? I waited around the corner and eavesdropped, even though I knew that was a major breach of faith after Kyra's apology the night before. Then again, Kyra was telling this woman stuff that was none of her business.

"She's saving money for grad school," said Kyra.

"He's got money!"

"Well, she's not gonna just let him give her money."

"So she lets him buy her stuff. Jewelry. Clothes. A new car. Seriously, she's weird. It's not like she's off working as a model or something. She can put off drudge work for one summer and actually *be* with the guy. I've never seen anyone behave like she does."

"I know. She won't give up being normal."

"She's not normal! Normal people do not date Jason Vanderholt."

"Yeah, I know. He's just lost it, though. I mean, seriously."

"Well what does she expect him to do? She's gotta know he's going to crack at some point."

"I don't know. I keep telling him he's totally misreading the situation, but he won't listen to me."

That evening, Kyra had an appointment with her SAT tutor and Jason and I went back to his hotel. "I overheard Kyra talking to that woman again today," I said.

"Who? Maxine?" He looked exhausted. When we stepped inside, he went straight to his bed and laid down. While he didn't exactly look like he was having a crisis, he did look like he had a lot on his mind. He'd been quieter than usual the last few days, but I'd just chalked it up to work stress.

"Is Maxine the woman who works in catering and is always eating by the truck?"

"She doesn't work in catering. She's a grip."

"And what does a grip do, exactly?" I jibed as I sat down next to him.

"They're in charge of the electrical equipment and wiring and all that." He put an arm over his eyes.

"Is there anything you want to talk about?" I asked.

"Hmmm?"

"At all?"

"I'm working late Friday. Me and Kyra are. We'll meet you in the apartment afterward."

"Okay... anything else?"

"There something *you* want to talk about?" He lifted his head.

"No. I just wondered if you had something. That grip woman says I don't 'get' how to be your girlfriend because I don't just... I don't know, hang around you all day and spend your money."

"Well the grip woman needs to get a grip, and mind her own business. She's used to seeing actors carting women around who do just that. Ignore her. She probably just wants some rich guy to fall for her and pamper her and keep her in a mansion somewhere."

"So you're okay with how I am?"

"Why you worried about that all of the sudden?"

I laid down next to him and propped my head on my elbow. "I don't know. You don't ever wish I were different? In any way?"

He rolled over to look at me. "No. What kind of question is that?" His gaze was guarded, though. There was something he wasn't telling me.

"So things are okay? Really?"

He stroked my cheek and nodded.

"It's just-"

He cut me off by reaching past me and pulling open the drawer of his nightstand. His hand came back with the ice cream spoon in it.

Not what I expected. "You still have that?" I said.

"Yeah. You know why?"

"Because you never clean out your suitcase?"

He tapped me on the nose with the back of the bowl. "It reminds me that you kept that ice cream I brought you. And, I have this story I like to tell myself about that, so don't ruin it by saying you just never got around to throwing it out."

"If I'd thrown it out, I'd have to remember what I did to you."

That earned me a smile. He slipped his arm around my waist and tickled the spoon between my shoulderblades. "You mean how you heartlessly-"

"Don't," I said. "Please. I'm sorry, okay? Just... yeah..."

"Hey, it's all right. It was my mistake."

"It wasn't a mistake-"

"Yeah, it was." He let go of me, rolled onto his back, and rested his head on his arm. "I acted first and thought later."

"I am sorry."

He smiled. "Look, once upon a time, what I did was cool. I was a professional actor with my own TV show, and all my friends at La Cueva were jealous. Then I got older and realized that I'm the weird one in my family, not the cool one. My siblings grew up and got jobs and lives while I still play make believe for a living and the media writes stories about what restaurants I go to and whom with. Some days I think it's all downhill from there. Once you make a certain amount of money, everyone around you is on your payroll, and they'll do whatever they have to do to keep in your good graces." He looked at the spoon. "So sometimes I wonder if I'll get weirder and weirder until I'm posting incoherent rants on Youtube or having my bathwater flown in from Greenland or-"

"That's not you."

"I hope it isn't. But-" he looked me in the eye "-neither is some of the other stuff I've done." He focused on the spoon again. "About a year ago I had Dave escort a woman to my trailer and she let me know in no uncertain terms that it was out of line."

"I misread the situation. I was stupid and oversensitive and-"

"You were normal. Being summoned? It's not normal, and your reaction was a wake up call. If I wanted to talk to a normal person about normal stuff, I had to be normal, so I went to your work... with a security detail in tow."

I shrugged.

"Also not normal," he said, "but you were polite about it, at least. When I invited you out to my house in LA to dinner without a caterer or a chef or anything like that, Don tried to put the moves on you." He rolled his eyes. "You were polite about that too, but that was not at all normal. Then breakfast on Sandia-"

"Was really nice."

"But still weird. Not the kind of thing you'd ever done before."

"True."

"I hadn't realized how Hollywood I was until I tried not to be. It was like you and I were from different planets, and I thought I hadn't let the industry change me. But, dinner with my family? That worked. The date that most couples have to work up to and is usually all uncomfortable? Things went fine, even though we barely knew each other."

"Your family's nice."

"Yeah." He spun the spoon between his fingers, making the reflection of the light in the room slide over its surface like liquid. "Then after I dropped you off at home, the paparazzi showed up. So much for normal that time."

"It's okay."

"But you let me talk to you on Skype." He flicked his gaze in my direction. "Sometimes."

"Every other day, almost."

"And then you found out about my past. It was like, no matter what I did to bridge the gap between us, there it was again."

"Hey, non famous people do that kind of stuff too."

"But I'd like to think I wouldn't have done it if I wasn't famous. You don't see anyone else in my family behaving like that. I'm just glad we were able to talk about it... after I crashed your restraining order thing."

"That was okay. More than okay, and that was my weird life, not yours."

"My dad told me off over that. He sat me down and said, 'Look, I don't know what your intentions are, son, but let's be clear. If you ever hurt Chloe, you and I can't be friends anymore.'"

"That's harsh."

"He was stressed out after that hearing, and feels protective of you. Not everyone can face down an attempted murderer and laugh about it. I think he just wanted to do something to make your life better."

"He did. He got me a restraining order."

Jason stopped spinning the spoon and held it in front of his face. "I thought we were getting along pretty well by then, only when I showed up at your place with ice cream and tried to kiss you that night-"

"Like I said, don't remind me. I'm sorry, okay? I had all of this other stuff going on."

"I screwed up. Normal people don't fly out in private jets just to share a carton of ice cream. You summed it up when you said it was someone else's fairytale. Extravagance puts you off, and you never daydreamed about Gladius feeding you ice cream."

"I hadn't seen the *New Light* movies before then."

Amusement lit his eyes for a moment. "I went to Jen's after you shut me down and she laid it out for me. She said she could tell that you liked me as a friend, but if the spark wasn't there, it wasn't there and I should be grateful that you weren't into my fame or money. I should respect your honesty, and know that you honestly weren't interested. Of all the things she's ever said to me, that's one of the most hurtful."

"She was wrong."

"She's never wrong – but don't tell her that. I spent a month trying to get over you and move on but that didn't happen. I met a lot of people who claim they don't care that I'm rich or famous, but that's never entirely true, and there are a lot of strong women in the world, but few people have to face their brother in court after he's tried to kill them. That requires something rare."

"Yes," I said, "really bad luck."

He chuckled. "Okay, the fact that you can be sarcastic about it?" He traced the spoon across my forehead and looked me in the eye. "The fact that you could say no to me meant that if you ever did say yes, it would mean something. I mean… it wouldn't just be because I'd charmed you, but Jen told me it was friends or nothing, so I tried nothing, and I hated it, so I called you up on New Year's to try friends, and I hated that even more. Watching Don hit on you *again,* and Rick."

"They weren't hitting on me, and even if they were, who cares?"

"Yes they were."

"No-"

"Yes, Chloe. They both asked me afterward if you were seeing anyone."

"They did?"

"Yeah. You looked more gorgeous than ever."

"It's not that nice of a dress."

"What dress? I don't remember what you wore. I'd thought I'd gotten a little bit over you, but I hadn't. I was still in love with you. That whole evening I felt like you were cutting my heart to pieces with kitchen shears."

"It wasn't fun for me either."

"And then Jen suggested that maybe you'd changed your mind, not that I get how that works. All of the sudden the rules change? I drove to your house, certain that you'd shut me down again, but if there was any chance..."

I kissed him. As always, he kissed back, as if he'd been waiting for me to make the first move.

"Yeah," he whispered. "So that happened." He kissed me again. "*And you told me you loved me.*"

"I do."

He shifted onto his side so that we faced each other. His arm was around my waist again. "When you fell asleep that night-"

"In the middle of our conversation. Real romantic."

"It was. Gave me a chance to hold you and just... be in that moment. I told myself that maybe you'd kept the ice cream because you liked me enough to be okay with my weird lifestyle, with the private jet and all that. Then the next morning when I flew up to Vancouver, I panicked. Remember when I called you?"

I didn't. "Um..."

"Left you a message, something stupid like, 'Hi it's me, call me if you want to,' or... I don't remember. Dave asked me if I was okay, and I just said something nonsensical. I don't even know what. And then you texted me back. You said you were in class, but you'd call me after, and that you loved me. You hadn't woken up the next morning and regretted it all."

I ran the tips of my nails across the back of his neck. "Of course not."

He half closed his eyes, like a cat having its ears scratched. "Dave asked me who it was, and when I showed him, he told me he'd beat me up if I wasn't due to start work the next day. You know, he couldn't leave a mark on me just before I started a shoot."

"Beat you up?"

"He thinks my karma's got to be way out of balance, and I agree. It is. He was just trying to even things out."

I didn't know whether to shake my head in disbelief or laugh, so I did both.

Jason kissed me again, and again. His hands worked their way down my back. I slipped my arm around his waist as he moved to kiss my neck. It was easier to relax now. Things are fine, I thought. My worries were baseless. I let myself melt in his arms and he shifted half his weight onto me. I ran my fingertips down his spine, returned his kisses as fervently as he gave them, and whispered, "I love you." I felt completely secure, able to let go and just be with him.

As spontaneously as his kisses had started, they stopped. He put a hand on my shoulder and pressed me away. "Love you too," he said as he extricated himself from my embrace.

"Sorry, I didn't mean to push things-"

He shook his head, levered himself up to hunt around on the bed for the ice cream spoon. Once he found it, he dropped it back into his nightstand with a metallic thud. Then he lay back down, but kept his distance and took my hand in his. Right then, I really wanted to be held. This time it wasn't him and his life putting the distance between us.

Friday night, I sat in the apartment, reading a book, when Kyra burst in through the door.

"Kyra," Jason called after her.

"You aren't *listening*," she snapped.

"Hey, please." He rounded the corner and came into the apartment.

She looked over at me.

"Hi," I said.

Tears welled up in her eyes.

I vaulted up out of my seat and went to hug her. "What's wrong?"

"Promise me something."

"What?"

"If Jason does something really, *really* stupid, you'll forgive him."

"Kyra." There was a warning note in his voice.

"Like what?" I said.

"Like unimaginably, unbelievably-"

"That's enough!" he snapped.

She just cried harder, let go of me, and ran into her room. Jason rested both hands on the counter and hung his head a moment.

"Um... rough day on the job?" I asked.

"Sure."

"Dare I ask-"

"Please don't."

I nodded. "You're not cheating on me, are you?"

"What? *No.* Absolutely not."

"You didn't get someone else pregnant?"

"Huh?"

"You aren't planning to hurt yourself?"

"*What?* Chloe."

"I think I forgive you then."

I expected him to laugh. He usually found me funny, but this time he just ran his fingers through his hair and shook his head. "Don't speak too soon. I've gotta... I've gotta get home. They want us in early tomorrow."

"But you just got off work." It was eleven o'clock. "You get twelve hours off, right? Guild rules?"

"Um, usually, but they're... it's a site rental issue and... so... I get not this Monday, but next Monday off. You, um, you able to take next Monday off work?"

"Sure. I'll arrange that. Care to tell me-"

He cut me off with a kiss. A long one that made spots swim in my vision. "I love you," he said. Then he ran out the door like he couldn't escape fast enough.

31
THINGS FALL APART

I STARED at the closed door for a minute, trying to make sense of what I'd just seen. Something was definitely wrong, and I was lost. I patted my pockets for my cellphone. Surely if I called Jason, he'd explain, but out of the corner of my eye, I saw Kyra standing in her doorway.

"Care to tell me what that was about?" I asked.

"I heard what you asked him."

"What? When?"

"When you wanted to know if there's anything he'd change about your relationship."

"Right. And?"

"Well, he's been doing a lot of thinking."

"And?"

Her eyes looked very big and very lost right then. "We're friends, right? No matter what happens with Jason?"

"What exactly do you think is going to happen?"

"I just want to finish out the summer here. Things are going good."

"Why wouldn't you?"

Her eyes stayed big and round. "Why don't you ever spend the night with him?"

"Um..."

"Is it because you don't love him?"

"No. I do love him, very much. Look, if you have some personal reason of your own to ask about my sex life, like something you're going through with Nate, I can talk about this, but if you're just being nosy, it's none of your business."

She fell silent for a moment, then said, "I don't think you're gonna like his answer to your question. Promise me you won't get too mad about it?"

"Are you going to tell me what it is?"

"No way."

"Okay, well, then I can't answer you. But we'll still be friends, okay?"

She nodded.

"I'm gonna get ready for bed, but you know where to find me." I went to my room.

Kyra stared after me.

Once in my room, I sat down on my bed and rubbed my temples. I'd known what his answer to my question was going to be. Of course he wanted to sleep together after seven months of dating. A part of me wanted that too. But my other issues wouldn't leave me, and he and I both knew it.

I was twenty-two, way older than the average virgin. I was with my best friend who'd stayed devoted to me for seven months and never complained. A guy who could have any other woman on the planet, literally. Was I just being selfish? The thought of letting go of my chastity felt like breaking a solemn promise to myself. I wasn't where I wanted to be in life before I re-evaluated my feelings on that. I didn't feel ready. I wondered if there was something wrong with me.

THE next day, Jason was working when I arrived on set. Right afterward, he had an interview with a reporter out in front of his trailer. I didn't get a chance to talk to him until after nine, after we'd gone back to his place, and he was in a foul mood. But I was confident we could talk things through anyhow. We communicated well. One good sit down and everything would be okay.

"Jas," I said.

"Hmm?"

"Can we talk?"

He looked up. "Yeah, sure, of course." He went to sit on the couch and pulled me down to sit next to him. "What is it?"

"I talked to Kyra last night."

He tensed up at once. "What did she say?"

"That she heard me ask you if there's anything you'd change about our relationship. And that it made you think about a lot of things."

"It did."

"Do you have an answer for me yet? Because-"

"I'm still working on it."

"Jas, be honest. Do you want me to spend the night? I won't be at all offended if you do. If you're getting frustrated with me, I want to know."

"I'm not... just.. enough about that, okay?"

He'd never snapped at me before. I did my best to pretend like it didn't knock me off balance, though it did. "I love you," I said, "and I want you to know that and I... I don't want to lose what we have, okay? So be honest with me."

"Do you think sleeping together will prevent our relationship going in a direction you don't want?"

"Um... Well, yeah."

"It wouldn't change anything, all right? Not with..."

"With what?"

"What else did Kyra tell you?"

"Nothing."

"Really?"

"Yeah, really."

"You look like you're dreading something."

"Should I be?"

He didn't answer that.

Well, now I felt dread. "Jason, I really love you. Seriously. If there's something wrong and you're considering anything drastic-"

"Chlo, I'm under a lot of stress at the moment and this conversation is pushing all my buttons. I know it's probably not intentional, but I don't know how to respond right now. Let's just... just watch television or something, okay?"

I felt like I was being strangled, my throat was so tight. "Okay," I whispered.

Jason turned on the TV, but didn't watch it. He put his arm over his eyes and lay back instead. I stroked his chest and he patted my hand, absently.

But my fear grew, like a yawning chasm in my heart. Our conversations *used* to solve our issues.

Lori didn't answer her phone when I tried to call, and I tried six times. I had other friends, but no one who knew about Jason. I'd kept him secret. Well, except for one: Matthew. That was a crazy idea, and I was desperate.

"Howdy?" he answered.

I burst into tears.

"Something wrong, Chloe?"

"I really, really need a friend right now."

"What happened?"

"I think the Talk broke us up."

"Jason dumped you cuz you won't sleep with him?"

"Not yet, but soon, I guess. I shouldn't have called you."

"Well... I dunno if I can help here. I'm just... you know. Just a religious hick. But did you hear about Lori? She's expecting?"

"Yeah, I already knew about that."

"You're making the right decision. I know Lori's all happy and jolly, but sheesh."

I ignored his judgment. "I thought we'd moved past the issue. We had the Talk months ago and he was fine with it, but then I asked him if he was really, truly, honestly happy with our relationship, and he won't answer me. He's gotten all quiet and-"

"Aw, why did you do that?"

"I thought it was only fair."

"What are you, nuts?"

"Matthew!"

"Sorry. I'm just sayin', though, you don't ask that. You trying to torture the man?"

I sniffled. "How's Michelle?"

"Naw, we broke up."

"Oh. Sorry."

"It's okay. I got me a teaching job in Houston and she doesn't wanna go there. Breakups happen. I'm good."

I cried even harder.

"Look, you sit down with Jason and you tell him you love him and you just be you. If he dumps you, he's the world's biggest idiot. Which... maybe he is."

"I always said he was someone else's fairytale. Maybe it's literally true."

"Chloe…"

"He always planned ahead for us to see each other, in Vancouver, and Albuquerque, and New York, but he hasn't said word one about New Orleans."

"Did you seriously ask him whether he was okay with your chastity?"

"Well, kind of."

"You'll push a guy to crisis that way. Seriously. What did you think would happen?"

That Friday, I was alone in Jason's hotel room. Jason was on his way with Kyra. They had supposedly left the set forty minutes ago, but there was no sign of them. I'd seen one of the producers in the hotel lobby, and she never left while anything was going on, so I knew everyone was done for the day. Jason and I hadn't had a serious talk in almost a week. I was petrified that would prompt him to tell me that, as much as he loved me, it was time to move on. And who would blame him? If anyone in his circle knew that we weren't sleeping together-

And then I realized, everyone in his circle knew that. His assistant, his stylist, his security guys, they all knew his schedule, and they knew mine too. They knew where I was spending the night. He probably had half a dozen other men wondering why he was in a long term relationship with a nun. All he'd have to do was mention that he was having doubts, and it was obvious what they'd tell him. They'd point out that this was the twenty-first century, and what I wanted wasn't normal. If he broke up with me, he'd have an instant support network of people who wouldn't blame him one bit. They'd think he was noble for hanging around as long as he did.

No, I thought. Stop. He had Monday off. We'd talk Monday. I'd turn this around, somehow.

My phone rang. "Hello?" I answered it.

"Hey, Chloe?" said Jen.

"Yeah, hi."

"I am really sorry about this. We've got a family crisis on our hands."

"What's wrong?"

"It's Kyra. I need you to bring her home as soon as possible. I've got a flight booked for Sunday."

"Is everything all right?" A wave of guilt went through me. Kyra was my responsibility, and here I was worrying about myself.

"No." Jen sounded flustered. "We just need her home aaand, she and Kyle just had a really bad conversation. I hate to impose, but I'm begging you, can you fly back with her and make sure she gets home?"

"You think she'd run?"

"I think she'd stall. Miss her flight and hold out for a while. Things are worse than ever. We can fly you back the next day. I know it might screw up your work schedule and all that."

"Actually, it won't. I already had Monday off, because Jason does."

"And we'd make you miss that. I am so sorry. Really I am." She sounded more desperate than I'd ever heard her sound though, which was saying something.

I couldn't turn her down. "No, that's fine. I just, I'm really sorry about Kyra. I thought things were getting better."

"This is not your fault in any way. Your idea to have her in New York was brilliant."

"And she's all excited about a career in film."

"I know. She's already starting on her essays to apply to UCLA, USC, and NYU. Aaand a whole bunch of fallbacks since she won't have the best GPA even if she aces her senior year. It's her new passion. We'll see if this one sticks. Or at least keeps her distracted for a few months."

"And it sounded like she was getting tired of Nate."

Jen fell silent.

Oh no, I thought. I counted dates. Kyra might be over him now, but if she'd slipped up before we left New Mexico, she could be three months pregnant or more. Her comment about wanting to stay in New York and maybe not being able to took on a new context. Perhaps it had nothing to do with me and Jason. Perhaps these late nights "working" were him taking her to the doctor or something. "I am so sorry," I said. "I'll mind my own business."

Some sniffles let me know Jen was sobbing. "I'm really sorry-"

"I'll go book a ticket."

"No, no, I can. I'll email you. Just, yeah, I'll email you."

She hung up and my phone started to ring again. Jason.

"Hi," I said.

"Where are you?"

"At the hotel-"

"Huh?"

"It's where you said you'd meet me tonight. Listen-"

"Oh... right. We're at the apartment."

"Okay, I can come-"

"We'll come there. Stay put. We'll come there."

"Smooth," Kyra said in the background.

"Love you." Jason hung up before I could reply.

Ten minutes later, a key slid into the lock and a grim faced Jason stepped in, followed by Kyra, who did look a little pinched and stressed. "I need to break a twenty," she said, "so I can tip the doorman and get our laundry." She saw me and caught herself.

"Why would the doorman have our laundry?" I asked.

She winced. "Oh, uh... I sent out our laundry. Hope you don't mind." Jason shook his head.

"You mean Jason sent out our laundry."

"I just thought-" he began.

"Look, don't do that," I said. "Don't do stuff like that. *Please.*"

"I'm sorry. I just thought it might free up some time for Monday."

"Listen..." I looked at Kyra, whose expression was all innocence. "I won't be here Monday."

"Why?" He looked baffled.

Kyra rolled her eyes.

"What?" he snapped at her.

"You really shouldn't have sent out the laundry."

"Yeah," I agreed. "You shouldn't have, but it's okay. The thing is-"

"All right, you know what?" he said. "I really, *really* don't want to fight with you right now. Just... I need a moment." He went into the bedroom and shut the door.

Kyra stared up at the ceiling.

"Kyra, look-"

"Sec," she said. She went over and banged on the bedroom door.

"What?" said Jason.

"Let me in." The door opened and she disappeared inside. "This is stupid!" she yelled.

"You said that already."

"I mean, come on, the laundry. You see how much she hates that?"

Huh? I was lost.

"You may not support me, but you can at least not try to undermine me!" Jason was *angry*. I'd never heard him yell like that before. "Is that too much to ask?"

"But you're messing it all up! Your relationship? Everything was fine until you got the *wrong* idea. I'm telling you-"

"This isn't a sudden thing, all right? Someday you'll grow up and understand that there are moments in life... you know what? I've had enough of you telling me what you think. *You* don't like it when people meddle in *your* love life."

"This is different."

"It is not. Okay, what's different is that maybe, just maybe, you're *wrong!*"

I went over and opened the door. The two of them were standing, shouting in each others faces. When I came in they looked over at me, then at the floor.

Then Kyra burst into tears. "I'm sorry," she said.

Jason didn't look like he wanted to forgive her. He looked like he wanted to punch something. He sat down on the bed and shot her a baleful look.

"I am totally confused," I said. "And I'm guessing this isn't about laundry."

Kyra folded her arms and the tears kept flowing. "I'm *sorry,* okay."

"Is this about whatever Jen called about?"

Jason flopped back on the bed.

But Kyra looked alarmed, and more than a little guilty.

"Kyra?" I asked. "Do you want to talk... about anything?"

"Um... what?" she said.

I glanced at Jason. "Attacking him isn't going to make whatever's wrong in your life go away. Your stepmom wants you home on Sunday, and she wants me to go with you."

"Oh..." She cried harder. "Right... No... *No!* I don't want to talk about that!" She kicked the side of Jason's bed, making him lift his feet to avoid her, then made a beeline out of the room.

I looked at Jason. "What's going on?"

"What did Jen tell you?"

"That it's personal."

"Oh... we-ell... okay." He was dubious.

"I'm really sorry about Monday."

Sniffles behind me let me know Kyra had come back. I turned around and she just about knocked me over with a hug. Awkwardly, I hugged back. "You okay?" I said.

"Maybe you can stay here? I can go home by myself. Stay here."

Jason turned to look at her.

"You guys should have Monday together. I don't want to screw things up."

"Sure, now you don't," muttered Jason.

"All right, I can stay," I said.

But Jason shook his head. "Go with her."

"What?"

"Just... go with her." He gave Kyra a look of sheer disappointment and disgust.

I felt her wilt against me. She blinked and a couple of tears fell. "Yeah, what am I saying? Come with me. It'll be better this way."

"Jason."

He waved me away. "Just go, all right? Forget about Monday." His glare at Kyra had a little less venom this time. She still shrank from it, though, and left me to go curl up on the couch in the other room.

I didn't know whether to go comfort her, or try to talk to Jason. "Jas?"

He took one deep breath, then another. "Yeah?"

"Is everything okay?"

"Sure. Yeah." He still wouldn't look at me.

I stepped inside, shut the door, went over to the bed, and sat down next to him. "You sure?" I said.

Rather than answer, he slipped an arm around me, but not for a hug. He lifted the back of my shirt and ran his fingers across my skin. When he encountered my scar, he stopped.

"Exit wound," I said.

His fingers traced around it a couple of times, his expression unreadable, then he moved his hand around to my stomach, where his fingers located the other scar.

Gently, he folded my shirt to reveal it. He gazed down at it, his expression still unreadable.

I sat still, watching him. I felt like I'd just weathered an emotional earthquake, and all signs pointed to worse to come. I had no idea what to say to him.

"Jas?"

"Yeah?"

"Do you want to forget I ever asked what you'd change about our relationship? We can do that, you know." For the second time with him, I wished I could put my life in rewind and take a different road.

Rather than answer me, he just stared at my scar. "You must think I'm ridiculous."

"What?"

"What I do for a living? How do you stand it?"

"I said it was weird, not that I don't like it."

"I put on fake blood and stand on duct taped markers and pull faces-"

"And do it very well. Really."

"You're for real."

"What do you mean?"

"You're a survivor and a hero-"

"There's nothing heroic about getting shot."

"But overcoming it the way you did. All I do is pretend."

I pressed his hand against my stomach. "That what's been eating you lately?"

"Partly."

"Jason, I love you."

"I don't feel equal to you."

"You've got to be kidding. Please-"

"The mark I've left on the world, is playing a guy named 'sword' in an absurd, inaccurate-"

"I love those movies," I confessed.

"No you don't."

"I do, sorry. They aren't the only movies you've made that I love, but they are the most ridiculous. Somehow you make them work, I mean... you make me not care that they're inaccurate and formulaic and silly, and..."

Jason just stared at me. I wasn't saying this right, and right now, I had no room for error.

I shut my eyes and tried again. "Movies, good ones, with good leads, they give the audience something they need, okay? A release. An escape.

Something that some of us are too broken to give ourselves. Maybe if I'd had a normal childhood, I'd be able to daydream and fantasize and all that on my own, but do you know how many of us can't? People need their dreams. There's a reason why society pays good money for them."

He blinked a few times, absorbing that. When he looked at me again, his eyes were a little misty.

I put my hand over his. "Are things okay, with us?"

"Yeah." He didn't look at me when he said it.

"Look, about my question-"

"It was a hard question, Chloe."

"And-"

"Just give me a little more time."

"Before you do anything drastic, talk to me?"

He lay back on the bed.

"Promise?"

"Can I just hold you? Please? No talking?"

I nodded. "Sure. Of course." I stretched out next to him and he put his arms around me. It was as I rested my head on his chest that my tears started. I blinked them back so he wouldn't notice.

32
BACK IN ALBUQUERQUE

In the apartment that evening, Kyra slipped into my room while I was brushing my teeth and left the jewelry she'd borrowed on my pillow. I scooped it into my jewelry box and wondered if I would get a straight answer if I asked her about what was going on in her life. I was too tired to try, though, so I went to bed.

A very apprehensive looking Jen picked us up at the airport in Albuquerque. She gave us each a hug, and while I appreciated feeling included, I knew I was encroaching on a very private family matter. It was a good thing I'd be flying out again the next day, though what awaited me back in New York was anybody's guess. Kyra had been silent most of the flight, though she did grasp my hand once, and say, "I'm really glad you're with me today. It'll all be good, you know?"

She and Jen didn't exchange anything but pleasantries on the drive home. There was a stiff formality between them that let me know, they weren't speaking freely. I hunched down in the back seat and tried to be inconspicuous.

When we got to the house, Kyle welcomed me warmly and we all ate a dinner of paella and olives and fresh baked bread. I wanted to call Jason afterward, but he was filming that evening. I left him a voicemail and then read my book until I could politely disappear into the guest room for the night.

I'd never felt so lonely in my life. Hearing Kyra and Kyle in the living room as they discussed college applications made me miss them already.

I stayed up late, but Jason didn't call me back.

My phone rang while it was still dark and knocked me out of a fitful sleep. For several minutes I thought I was just dreaming the sound of my ringtone, but then it stopped and started again. It wasn't just any ringtone either. It was Jason's. I'd downloaded the theme to *New Light* for him, which he'd found hilarious.

The clock on the nightstand said it was three a.m. Which meant it was five a.m. in New York. Something was wrong. I grabbed my phone.

"Jas?" I croaked.

"Hi."

"Hi." I rolled over and rubbed my eyes. "You okay? You want to talk?"

"I need you for something."

"I'm in Albuquerque."

"I know. So am I."

"What?"

"Can I pick you up in forty-five minutes?"

"What?"

"Please?"

"Wait... what?"

"Please?"

"Is everything all right?"

"I need to see you."

"Okay, yeah, forty-five minutes. I'll be ready."

I rolled out of bed and fumbled for my little bag where I kept my shampoo and razor and soap. I knew he could be impulsive sometimes, like when he'd shown up to feed me ice cream after Matthew bailed on me, but this was extreme.

Jen's house was dark, save for a little night light in the hall. I tiptoed to the bathroom and shut the door. She'd no doubt wonder what I was doing, but it wasn't like I could tell her. I didn't know myself. The light in the bathroom flickered on when I hit the switch and the fan started up with a faint rumble. I pushed the edge of the shower curtain inside the tub and turned on the shower.

In my bag, I found a rubber band and put my hair up as best I could, then stepped into the stream of warm water. The sensation of it sluicing over me helped me wake up, but that didn't take away the confusion or fear of what was about to come I scrubbed myself with soap, rinsed, and stepped out onto the fluffy bathmat and rubbed myself down with a towel. My hair looked limp and flat even after being steamed in the shower. New Mexico was that dry compared to New York. I brushed it out, then washed my face in the sink and applied makeup. Maybe I couldn't control what happened with Jason in the next few hours, but I was going to look my best for it.

At three forty I was back in the guestroom with the light on. I had only one set of clean clothes. I wasn't equipped for cold weather, but then again, the walk to his car would be short. I put on my jeans and tank top, then put a shirt on over the tank top and grabbed my windbreaker. I felt like I was getting ready to see the Balloon Fiesta, only it wasn't October and I wasn't excited.

At three forty-five I went out to the front room, and almost immediately, there came a soft knock. I flipped on the porch light and opened the door. Jason stood there, wearing a windbreaker and jeans, and otherwise looking like he was ready to do a television interview. His hair was styled. He'd shaved, and he looked tired, like he hadn't slept well. "Hey," he said. "You ready?" The night air was frigid.

"I don't know. Am I?"

"Come on." His Prius was parked in the driveway. At least at this hour we didn't have to worry about photographers or fans. We walked, unmolested, to his car. He held open the door for me and I got in.

It might have just been my imagination, but I thought I saw one of the lights in Jen's house come on as we pulled off down the road. A stab of guilt went through me. I'd tried to be quiet. What would she think when she found my room empty?

Jason was nervous, it was obvious. While we drove, he fidgeted and kept glancing in the rearview mirror, as if expecting to find someone behind us. There was a paper cup from The Frontier in his cupholder, but he didn't drink from it. I looked at it wistfully. I could sure have used some coffee. My brain still wasn't all the way functional. Thoughts moved like they were in molasses. I didn't understand why we were driving. If he had to talk to me, why didn't he pull over and do it already?

He headed towards downtown and turned in at the UNM campus. I looked at him. It felt like I should have some inkling at this point of what was going on, but I was still stumped. We parked by the anthropology building.

"We going to see aliens land?" I asked.

"Maybe." He ran his fingers through his hair, then leaned over and kissed me like he just wanted to hold and kiss me forever. My already addled brain spun out. Whatever semblance of rational thought I'd had dissipated and scattered.

When he broke off, I noticed his hands were shaking. "I love you, okay? You know that?"

"Jas, what's going on?"

He took The Frontier cup out of his cupholder and handed it to me. "Come on."

It was still lukewarm, and it was hot chocolate, not coffee. I drank it down regardless. Sugar was almost as good as caffeine right now. That and the cold outside air woke me up a little more. We got out of the car and I followed Jason up the walkway towards the front doors.

"Okay, here." He stopped and turned to me. "Remember the last time we were here?" He pulled off his windbreaker, so that he was just in a short sleeved shirt.

"Yeah," I said. "It's where we met."

"Right. You were there, and I walked past and I offered you some ice."

"Jason-"

"And you said no."

I wanted to rub my eyes, but I'd put on eyeliner, so I could only scratch the corner of one gingerly with a nail. "Okay, so-"

Jason had disappeared.

No, he was kneeling in front of me. He was down on one knee. "I hope," he said, "this time you'll say yes." He held out a ring box, with a diamond ring.

Reality crashed into focus. The talks I'd overheard between Kyra and her friend, the grip. Jason refusing to give me a straight answer to my question and begging for more time. Kyra's bizarre questions about why we hadn't slept together. The summons back to New Mexico. The tension between Jason and Kyra and their fight over where I should be today. My question hadn't destabilized the relationship at all.

"You want to get *married?*" I said.

"To you, yes." His hands really shook now.

This was Jason, who stood in front of crowds of thousands of people, all screaming at him. Jason the movie star. The guy who'd hosted *Saturday Night Live* three times.

Now he looked like he had stage fright.

Because he wanted this that badly. My head was still spinning. "Oh," I said. The empty Frontier cup fell out of my hand and hit the pavement with a hollow clack. I was trembling. I was about to do what all the other girls had done that morning when I met him. My knees felt weak.

"Chloe?" He was on his feet again, his arms around me. "Chlo?"

"Yes. Of course. Yes!"

"Yes?"

"*Yes!*" I threw my arms around him and squeezed tight. "Ohmigosh! I love you." I wasn't sure if I was sobbing or laughing. I'd lost it.

He kissed me, which helped ground me in the moment. I took a few deep breaths and dabbed my eyes with the back of my hand. "Ugh, I probably look awful right now." My hands still shook.

"Hardly. Are you actually surprised?"

"Yeah, completely."

"You didn't figure this out?"

"No. No way." I sniffled and dug a tissue out of my jacket pocket.

"*Really?*"

"Really. Not a clue."

"Well, I guess that explains why you've been so hard to talk to lately." He looked like he was ready to collapse with relief.

33
THE SETUP

"Kyra practically told you the plan last night," said Jason. "Jen called, I tried to play along, and the kid totally blew it and told me off? What did you think was going on?"

We were walking back to his car and I tried not to stare at the enormous diamond he'd put on my finger. More money than I'd made in my lifetime was mounted on the slim gold band. Though I was no expert, the way it sparkled and seemed to glow from inside seemed more intense than any other diamond I'd ever seen. I hoped this thing was insured.

"I thought she might be pregnant," I said.

"What?"

"Jen was in tears. She was... o-kay, so you're not the only one with acting talent in the family."

"Oh, really?"

"She scared me to death."

"*Really?* Yeah, maybe we overdid it."

"She called about a personal family matter and needed Kyra home. You and Kyra gone in the evening, not working, I thought maybe you were at the doctor. Her all emotional, screaming at you about laundry. Her clinging to me like an overly-hormonal crazy person."

Jason stopped in his tracks and doubled over. "Okay, we definitely overdid it." He laughed so hard I had to steady him. "She thought the laundry was an obvious clue that you hated my lifestyle so much, there was no way you'd say yes."

"So, Kyra's fine?"

"Kyra's good. Kyra's great. Kyra just can't believe that you really love me if you haven't slept with me, not that this is any of her business. She was not in favor of this whole plan."

"She thought I was freezing you out because I didn't want anything long term?"

"Yeah. She's been brow beating me for weeks, telling me that a proposal was way out of line because you didn't even want to live with me. How did you not pick up on this right from the beginning? I've been working overtime to hide clues from you and prevent Kyra from screwing it up, but I knew you were onto something. I thought there was no way I'd be able to outsmart you; you see too much."

"Jason, when I asked if you were going to do something drastic-"

"Yeah, I didn't know if that was a warning or what."

"No, I meant end of the relationship kind of drastic."

"You thought I was going to break up with you?"

"Because things weren't, you know, progressing. Physically."

"*What?* You have been living with Kyra too long. You're not sane. Look, you asked me-"

"What you'd change about our relationship."

"For this to be my fairytale."

"Right."

"How did you not get this? It's the happily ever after that makes a fairytale. I mean, come on. Everyone knows that." We'd reached his car and he held open the door for me. "I gotta call Jen and stuff."

He dialed as he circled around the front of his car and when he got in his side, I heard Jen answer by screaming, "What did she say?"

"She's thinking about it."

"Oh no."

"Just kidding."

"I hate you. That's not funny. That is *not* funny!"

"See you soon."

"She said 'yes'?"

"Yeah."

"*Seriously?*"

"Not you, too. What's with you Armijos? No faith in me."

"This is Chloe we're talking about. She's-"

"Yes she is, don't finish that thought. If there's one day for you not to be mean to me-"

"You want today or your wedding day?"

"Love you too." He hung up.

I looked at my phone. It was four ten. "So she was already awake?"

"Yeah, yeah, everyone is. We're holding a celebration at her house."

"At four in the morning?"

He smiled at me. "They like you."

I looked at my phone again. "I should call my mother."

His face fell. "Should I have called your mother first? To ask for your hand? I wasn't sure. You never talk about her." He started the car and we headed out of the parking lot.

"She's not going to care about that."

"You plan to have her come to the wedding?"

"Yeah of course but…"

"But?"

"It might be really embarrassing."

"My parents don't care, if that's what you're worried about. It's not like they were good friends with Dr. Winters."

"No, but my mom's still the same woman who did what she did all those years. It's awful. I shouldn't be ashamed of my own mother."

"You feel how you feel, and this is your moment, so you do what will make you happy."

I dialed the phone.

"Hello?" Mom sounded startled.

"Hey, it's me. It's good news, I promise."

"Who is this?"

"Chloe, Mom."

"Chloe?" She was still disoriented.

"Sorry to wake you up, but, I'm engaged."

"Engaged? Engaged to Jason *Vanderholt?*"

"Yeah. He just asked me, and please don't tell anyone right now."

"Of course not. You're *engaged?*"

"Yeah, that's kinda how I felt when he asked me." I laughed.

"Oh, *honey!*"

"Thanks, Mom."

Hiccuping sobs.

"Yeah, I did that too. We must be related or something."

"I'm so happy for you." That, I knew, was the truth. I could have tried to guess her reasons and gotten angry, but I took a deep breath and pushed that desire aside.

"Thank you," I said. "And thanks for making me call him back in December."

"Do I get to come to the wedding?"

"Of course. I'll let you know once we figure that out."

"I love you."

"Love you too, Mom."

We hung up.

Jason glanced over at me. "That sounds like it went okay?"

"Yeah, it did."

Back at the house was a crowd, all arrayed in the driveway. Even Steve and Shannon's kids were there, blinking sleepily. When I got out, I overheard Steve patiently explaining that I wasn't Aunt Chloe *yet*, but I would be.

The family all crowded around like fans trying to get autographs, except they were after hugs. Everyone but Kyra, who hung back. I hugged everyone else, then pressed my way through to go to her. "Hey," I said. "When you guys were late home, Friday night, were you out picking this up, maybe?" I held up my left hand.

"Yeah. Jason let me help choose it the Friday before last."

"It fits perfectly. Now I know why you wanted my lapis ring."

She ducked her head, guiltily. "Well..."

"That was smooth. I only just figured it out."

"Are you mad at me?"

"No." I held out my arms to her. "You went along with Jason's plan in the end, so thank you. You guys blindsided me in the best possible way."

She gave me a tight hug. "I was really scared you'd say no."

"I know. You had my back. I appreciate it."

"But I was wrong."

"Look, to answer your incredibly personal question, I haven't ever slept with anyone. That's how I am. It wasn't just Jason."

Her eyes went wide. "Seriously?"

"Yeah."

Jen announced she'd set up a breakfast buffet inside, and Kyra and I followed the others in. Warm tortillas and an assortment of fillings, including real green chile and home made salsa. Jason rolled me a burrito that I could only half finish, and then spent the rest of the meal fending off attempts from his sister to put more food on his plate. Served him right.

"I can't believe you all got up this early," I said.

"Well," said Steve, "we did fear it would be a consolation party."

"*Thank* you," said Jason. "I love you guys too. Man, what did I do to deserve this?"

Kyra tossed an olive at him.

He caught it and threw it back, narrowly missing her head.

She ducked aside with a giggle and the two of them grinned at each other.

I was exhausted. "I don't mean to be rude," I said, "but I think I need to lie down for a little while."

Everyone fell all over themselves to take my plate and usher me to the guestroom. I stopped in the bathroom to wash off my makeup first.

"Oh *no!*"

I woke up. That was Kyra's voice. The clock let me know it was nine a.m. I got up, brushed my hair, and stepped out into the hall. A smaller crowd than had been there this morning was gathered around the dining room table.

"I can't believe it," said Kyra.

I went to see what they were looking at. It turned out they were crowded around Kyra's laptop. On the screen was a picture of Jason on bended knee in front of me. "Jason Vanderholt is off the market," proclaimed the headline. I looked at the time again. "Five hours?" I said.

"How in the heck did anyone find us?" said Jason. His hair was slightly flat on one side and there were marks on his cheek that told me he'd slept on the couch.

"I did not tell," said Kyra. "I swear."

"Maybe they heard you yelling when we went to pick up the ring," said Jason.

"Guys, don't fight," I said. "It doesn't matter. The media was going to find out eventually."

"Someone probably saw you get the ring," said Jen. "If you got it yourself. And yeah, of course the media's all over this. Jason Vanderholt *is* off the market."

"I wasn't ever for sale," muttered Jason.

I looked out the front windows.

"No," said Jen. "That road out there is a private road, so no one comes up this far, usually. We bust them for trespassing if they do."

"Chloe, I'm sorry," said Jason. "I know how much you hate this."

"It's okay. I need to get used to it now, right?"

"This is going to make it difficult for you two to plan a wedding," said Lillian. "How are we going to do this?"

"I dunno." Jason scrubbed his hands through his hair. "Um, let's get back to New York before they do come overrun the house. You two come on the jet with me." He looked at me and Kyra.

"You two go," said Kyra. "I'll take the airline."

"Jet's gotta be more comfortable," I said.

"You guys haven't had any time alone together today, hardly," said Kyra. "No one's going to hound me for pictures. You guys go. I have some stuff I want to do."

THE drive to the airport was not fun. There were several other cars in hot pursuit. At the airport it was a mad dash to the waiting jet, with flashbulbs popping and reporters yelling in our wake, but inside the jet, all was calm. Just a nice, plush interior with couches, rather than seats, and the co-pilot (it looked like, given the epaulettes on his shirt) offered us champagne.

Jason watched out the window as we taxied towards the runway. "They're going to be in New York too," he said. "They know where we're going. You want to just run away to Montreal or something?"

"No. Come on. You deal with this all the time."

"This is different. They're bothering you. Totally not the same thing."

"Like I said, I need to get used to it now, right?" I looked down at the ring, then around at the private jet. My life had changed in the last twenty-four hours. I gripped the back of the seat as the plane shot forward down the runway. Soon we were aloft. I stared at the ring some more.

Jason frowned and turned back from the window. "You can have a different one if you want."

"No way. I want the one you surprised me with. I guess we should get to planning a few things?"

"Will you let me get you a place in New Orleans now?"

"Us a place, yes."

"Well, for you until we get married. When do you want to get married?"

"I assume your lawyers will want to do a prenup-"

"What? I don't want a prenup."

"And I don't want you skinned alive by your lawyers. That would make me sad."

"Chloe, you're missing the point here."

"Sorry... what's the point?"

"You gave me my fairytale."

"Good."

"You sure you don't have one I can give back?"

"Um..." I shrugged.

"Even a little one? Your perfect wedding?"

"Perfect wedding? One without media coverage, I guess."

"Sure, but if you want a real wedding, the media are going to find out about it. They'll figure out where we've booked a site, when we get a license, who we hire for a caterer. Someone will leak the information, no matter how careful we are."

"How do you keep it a secret, then?"

"Well... you do it fast and with as few people as possible, but it's your *wedding*. You don't want to do that. Whatever wedding you always wanted, you should have."

"I'm supposed to have it planned already?"

"Surely you've got some idea?"

"No... Isn't this supposed to be jointly planned thing?"

"Nah. I don't care. I'd go to Vegas and the Elvis Chapel if you want and you are *missing the point*. Think ideal. Wedding of your dreams."

"You can't put that kind of pressure on me."

"Really? There's no dress you always dreamed of or favorite song? Cake flavor?"

I shrugged. "Is that bad?"

"No, it's not bad. But are you serious?"

"My mom was the one always planning her wedding in our house," I said. "I never went near any of her bridal magazines or anything like that."

"But come on. Surely when you were a little girl you have some kind of fairytale you wanted to have come true. What was it?"

"I dunno."

"What daydreams did you have when you were a child? You wanted to be a princess or have a dress with a train. Or..." He waited.

"I never had daydreams like that."

"Not ever?"

"No. The daydream I always wanted to come true was the one where I bought Beth a birthday present and showed up at her party."

"Beth, your sister?"

"Yeah. I dreamed that I'd go buy her a present and wrap it and show up at her party, and she'd be glad to see me. I wasn't invited, but she didn't care. She'd be in her house with all her friends her perfect family and a there'd be balloons and cake and games, and she'd give me a big hug and say, 'I'm so glad you're here!' and then tell everyone, 'Look! My sister came.' And then she'd take me inside and I'd play with her friends and eat cake and just stay with her family forever."

"You used to wish that?"

"Don't ever tell my mother."

"This was before Chris shot you?"

"Yes. That kind of busted that fairytale."

"I also don't see any way to fulfill it. You already got yourself out of that situation. You aren't that little girl anymore. Any way we could update it somehow?"

"Why? What's this got to do with our wedding?"

"Just... is there?"

"Jason, I'd be fine with the Elvis Chapel too, but I think your parents would kill you."

"I want to know your fairytale. Think about it."

I leaned my head against his chest and thought about it.

34
MY FAIRYTALE

THE jet sliced through the air, its engine so quiet, it was little more than a whine. Wisps of cloud formed at the wingtips and streamed away behind us. The sky was deep blue and the ground beneath us was brown, flat, and endless. The little bubbles in my champagne glass zipped upwards and gathered at the surface.

My ears popped as I swallowed a few times. Jason moved to pull me closer. I brought my knees up and rested them across his lap. It was hard to imagine I'd ever wanted to be just friends with him. How many months had I wasted that way?

Now I had a wedding to plan!

"I don't have a fairytale that would apply," I said. "You want to update my childhood fairytale? My new fairytale would be that my kids never, ever have my old fairytale. They may not like me every minute of their childhood. They might wish their real mother was a princess in some mythical land, but everything they wish for, I hope it's stupid."

"Stupid how?"

"Like, that they get chocolate for breakfast and new toys every day."

"Or a boyfriend who also happens to be a movie star with a private jet and a mansion?" He chuckled.

"Right. Stupid stuff. Stuff that doesn't matter, because all the stuff that does matter? Like parents who love them and a safe and stable home? I don't want them to even have a clue what it would be like not to have those things." I shrugged. "Doesn't apply to a wedding."

But Jason's arms were tightening around me. "Yeah, it does."

"What, chocolate and toys?"

"No, the other stuff. I can give you that. I can make that fairytale come true, and I will. You can count on me, okay? I promise."

A strange sensation welled up in my chest and I felt a tear slide down my cheek. I dabbed at it with surprise.

"That happiness? I hope?" said Jason.

And I realized it was. More tears streaked down after that first one. That part of me I'd thought was broken past repair, wasn't so broken after all. I hadn't forgotten how to dream, I'd just stopped paying attention. I'd kicked aside every glimmer of hope and made do with what I had left, which was reason and hard work and all those things that made my life livable, but now I remembered what it felt like to not just look forward to a future of carefully won accomplishments, but to feel excitement, like I was embarking on an adventure and didn't know where it would lead, but couldn't wait to find out.

Jason dabbed my tears away with his fingertips. "You okay?"

I couldn't answer him, only grin. I think he got the idea.

When we landed in New York, the media were out in force. I turned on my cellphone and had five messages. Jason and I exited the cool interior of the plane and descended into the hot muggy air outside. A team of security all closed in around us, making a wall of black shirts, and ushered us to the waiting car.

Jason muttered something about stupid gladiator movies while we climbed back into the cool, air conditioned air. I laughed and ignored the commotion outside while I dialed my voicemail.

"Chloe, it's Kimmie." My boss at the coffee shop. "It's a mob scene here, and I'm sure you know why. Congratulations, by the way. It's going to be very hard for you to keep working here the next couple of weeks. I'm not firing you, but I strongly suggest you quit."

"I lost my job," I said to Jason.

"Sorry."

"No big deal."

"Chloe, it's Lillian," said the next message. "Honey, we're practically on lockdown in our house. I hope you guys are doing all right. The media's just gone crazy with this, and honey... they're also at Dr. Winters's house. They're doing a lot of digging into your past. I hope this doesn't get ugly, but I wanted to warn you. They think it's a modern day fairytale, Jason choosing a non-celebrity that no one really even knew about. Anyway, call us when you get in. We love you."

The next message was her again. "They found your old court case. It's up on the internet now."

The next message after that was Steve. "Hey, Chloe. Um... so your restraining order is up on the internet, and Chris's incarceration status is on TMZ. Just forewarning you. The media finally put everything together, like, from when he was on *The Tonight Show* and said he was dating someone and I guess something from an old magazine interview? They've turned you into a fairytale princess."

The next message was my mother. "Honey? Can you call me? I had this odd dream this morning that I'm not sure was... hang on... Ohmigosh! You're on the news!!!" I had to hold the phone away from my ear for that one.

Jason gave me a questioning look.

"My life is all on the internet now," I said.

He shook his head. "I am so, *so* sorry. This is beyond stupid."

"It's okay. You're worth it. But I'm going into hiding for the rest of your shoot. I'm going to become a clingy fangirl and just hang out in your trailer all day."

"Understood." He grinned.

Jen called after Kyra caught her flight back. We were in my apartment and Jason was on the phone, ordering food.

"Chloe... what did you do to my stepdaughter?"

"Hmm?"

"It would appear that you rewired her brain."

"Did I do something wrong?"

"Wrong? The girl took all of her pictures of Nate and burned them in our kitchen sink. Then she went over to his house and told him never, ever to call her again. Then she came home and apologized to me and to Kyle, and has taken some kind of oath of chastity?"

"Oh."

"She shared more information about you and Jason than you would want, probably."

"Well, whatever."

"But she's adamant. All relationships are now to be on her terms, or not at all."

"This is a good thing, right?"

"This is a mind blowing, incredible, wonderful thing. I mean, I don't know if it'll last. You know how it goes with kids. She may change her mind in a week if she meets some guy she likes, but anyway... thank you."

"I didn't actually do anything other than live my life."

"You amaze me. Jason is *lucky*."

"Well, thanks."

"We love you."

It was weird to say this to anyone other than my mother or a boyfriend, but the words came easily enough. "Love you guys too."

We hung up and Jason asked, "What was that all about?"

"Kyra's on her way back, as a single girl. No boyfriend."

"Finally."

"Mom?" I waited for the video to start up on Skype. It was the first video call I'd made on the new phone Jason had given me.

"Hi, Chloe." She sat at her computer in her tracksuit. It was morning, and the weekend.

"Sooo, do you want to come out to New York to go dress shopping with me?"

"For your wedding?"

"Yes. The wedding isn't going to be much. We're keeping it small, so I don't have a ton of planning to do, but do you want to come for this?"

She blinked. "I would *love* that."

"I'm buying her ticket!" Jason called from the other room.

I rolled my eyes. "He's like that." I couldn't help but grin though. "You want to meet him?"

"And her hotel room." He said that from the doorway.

I crooked my finger and he stood up straight and ran his fingers through his hair before he came over.

To her credit, Mom took it in stride. "Hello."

"Hi," he said. "I'm sorry I keep missing you. It's like every time you've been out to see Chloe, I've had work stuff."

"It's quite all right. I know you're always on the go."

"But I owe you a huge thank you, don't I?" he said. "Something about you getting after Chloe to call me?"

"Mmm, you're welcome." She winked.

And it really wasn't that awkward, having the two of them meet. Not for the first five minutes, at least.

"Yeah, so... let's figure out your calendar," I said.

"You really want me there?"

"Of course I do. This'll be fun, right?"

"This'll be *wonderful*."

"It'll be you, me, and Kyra. Jason's niece. We'll make a weekend out of it, okay?" I patted Jason's arm as he slipped it around me for a hug.

Mom looked like she was about to swoon, she was so happy for me.

Our wedding day was one we purposely picked at random. Jason and I flew to Albuquerque where we planned a tiny, backyard ceremony at Doug and Lillian's house. Only family and close friends were invited, and there were no written invitations. Jen supervised all the food preparation. Doug got his golfing buddy to officiate. We used CDs for the music and bought a tent from Target for the back yard.

I'll never know who tipped off the media.

"They've got a chopper!" Steve announced in the other room. He had to yell because the thrumming of the blades just about rattled the roof off. Lori's baby wailed in protest and I could hear her cooing to soothe him.

"And they've surrounded the house," said Kyra. She peered out the windows of the bedroom where I was putting on my dress. This was Jen's old room, which still had the Hello Kitty wallpaper and her twin bed in one corner, complete with canopy.

Mom sat in on the bed, picking at her new tulip skirt. She'd bought her outfit the same weekend I'd gotten my dress, and it really suited her. The New York stylists knew their business. "A chopper?" she said.

"Sounds like it." I sat down in the chair at the vanity while Kyra touched up my hair. We'd had the hairdresser make a house call hours ago, and that might have been how the media found out. Or maybe they'd seen us apply for a license.

"What a disaster," said Kyra. "This is nuts. I've never heard of any celebrity having it this bad."

"It's Gladius," I said.

"Riiight." Kyra laughed. "You're prettier than Caeser's daughter."

"Awww, thanks."

"Honey," said my mother. "What are you going to do? They'll blow the tent down."

"Plan B. We just hold the ceremony indoors."

"You sure?" Kyra looked out the windows again. "You really want to get married in the living room?"

"We'll all fit."

"We'll have to have the blinds drawn," said Kyra. "This is like an action movie, only it isn't fun in real life, is it? Okay, I think your hair's perfect, at least."

She and Mom helped me into my dress, which was simple, but way more expensive than I'd planned to buy. I'd given in and dug into my savings for a designer sheath dress. The two of them had worked me over, and even now Kyra said, "This is *gorgeous!*"

"He better go through with it," I said. "Because I'm broke now, thanks to you."

Someone tapped at the door. Mom opened it and Lillian stuck her head in. "Chloe? Beth's here. Do you want to say hi?"

"Beth?"

"Yes, we only just managed to get her through the crowd."

I let Kyra finish zipping my dress, then tugged it up so that I could walk.

"Jason!" Lillian called out. "Stay in your room!"

I rounded the corner to the entryway, and sure enough, there was Beth, wearing a straight skirt and blouse, her hair pinned back. At the sight of me she gave an awkward smile. "Hey, I just... I brought you something." On one arm, what I'd glanced at and assumed was a handbag, was in fact a present. "Congrats." She didn't look at me. Just held it out.

"You brought me a present?" I said.

"Yeah. Lillian told me about... all this."

"Are you staying? I mean, you probably don't want to."

She frowned and folded her arms across he chest, like I'd jabbed her. "Um... right."

I didn't understand her irritation just then. She clearly didn't want to be here. Except she was. With a present.

As I tried to look her in the eye, she looked past me. "Hi, Karen," she said.

"Hi, Beth," said Mom's voice behind me. Not angry, not happy, just neutral.

I expected Beth to turn tail and run then, but she didn't, only inclined her head and said to me, "I, um, anyway. You look real good and, congratulations, and, yeah... I'll just get out of your way."

"Out of my way?"

She turned to leave.

"Wait, no," I said.

She paused.

I looked back over my shoulder at everyone bustling around in the kitchen, at the stack of presents on the fireplace, at all my new family talking and laughing, at the Vanderholts' lovely, Northeast Heights home.

"I really wish you'd stay," I said. "I know you probably think this is really stupid, with the media and the chopper and all that. That's all I meant."

"It's kind of weird, yeah." She smiled, her mouth turning up at the corners just like mine did.

With a very odd sense of deja vu, I held out my arms to her. "But I'm so glad you're here."

She stepped forward and hugged me without hesitation, which surprised me. But then again, a lot had changed in twenty years. Her parents had split up. Her brother was in jail.

"Hey, guys?" I called out, as I led her into the living room. Her nervous shuffle and shifting gaze were gone. "Make sure there's a seat for my sister."

"Are you sure you want to get married in here?" asked Doug. He looked over the furniture dubiously.

Lori peered out from the kitchen. Her own engagement ring winked on her finger and her baby was now asleep in his sling.

"Too much hassle?" I asked.

"No, not at all. Just doesn't seem real romantic."

Steve and Maddy came in from the garage. "All right," he said. "We've got bottle rockets. We're going to see if we can hit the chopper. Oh, hey Beth." He waved.

"This'll be way better than outside," I said.

Steve opened the door, letting in a blast of wind and noise, as he and Maddy stepped out.

"But you need somewhere to walk," said Kyra. "You know, to process down the aisle. We need an aisle."

"I have to process?"

"*Yes.* You do."

"This is Kyra," I told Beth. "She belongs to Jen and Kyle."

"And you need somewhere to stand where Jason won't see you when he comes out." Kyra had appointed herself wedding director.

"I could hide behind a couch?"

"Noooo. You can't do that."

"I'm not allowed?"

"And you have to put your makeup on."

I looked at Beth. "Your choice: hang out here, bottle rockets, makeup."

"I'll help Lillian."

I went back to Jen's old room while Doug and Kyle started moving couches. Mom and Kyra helped me with my makeup, and then Lillian was back, knocking on my door.

The front room now smelled like warm crepes, fresh berries, and cream. Jen had brought in the cake, which was a square design with marzipan icing and two action figures: Gladius with his sword upraised and a woman in a lab coat and plastic hairstyle like mine, with a test tube and Florence flask in her hands. My idea. Jason didn't know.

"Okay," said Lillian, "I guess you stand here behind the fridge. Oh, this is just... I hope this is all right?"

"This is fine," I said. "I'll stand here." I positioned myself in the kitchen, the fridge between me and the front room.

"Jason will come in from there. Right. Let's start the music."

I heard a commotion in the other room, then the opening strains of the concerto that Jason had picked out. Kyra came to stand with me behind the fridge, only she peered out into the front room. "So... go now," she said.

All of the sudden, I was nervous. I smoothed my dress, took a deep breath, and stepped out into the living room.

Jason stood over by the fireplace (someone had moved the presents aside) and stared at me with those blue eyes like I was some kind of angel. I focused on him as I made my way across the room, both the shortest and the longest walk I've ever taken in my life. Finally I was there, able to slip my hands into his.

The officiator started to talk, but it all washed over me. I was getting *married,* to Jason Vanderholt of all people. My life had gotten certifiably bizarre, not that I would have changed it for anything.

Jason started to recite his vows, about taking me as his wife to have and to hold. My head was spinning. I couldn't keep track of what he said. At a couple of points the chopper got extra loud, and he paused until the sound subsided again.

Then it was my turn. I just blanked my mind and repeated the words. No one laughed, so I must've gotten them right. I heard a few sniffles.

Steve stepped over and handed us our rings. Jason slipped mine onto my hand, reciting, "With this ring, I thee wed."

I took a deep breath, afraid I'd drop his, but I didn't. I slipped it on his hand and said, "With this ring, I thee wed."

And then the officiator said, "I now pronounce you husband and wife." Just like that, it was over. Jason and I kissed, for the first time ever in public, and then we faced the room while Doug's golfing buddy said, "May I present: Jason and Chloe Vanderholt."

Everyone got up and blew bubbles at us and cried and hugged each other. Maddy yelled out, "Aunt Chloeeee!"

We'd done it, and without a single opportunity for the media to get a photo. Not everyone's idea of a fairytale wedding, but I couldn't have asked for more. Later we'd have to face the hordes of photographers who tried to find us on our honeymoon, and I had the hassle of dodging reporters as I went to school, only to face a bunch of dumbfounded classmates who'd had no idea whom I was engaged to (a lot of people ignore the tabloids, I've found).

But all that passed too. And I didn't much care, because as Jason pointed out, what makes a story a fairytale is the ending. We had our ups and downs over the years, but I'd say those generic words they put at the end of fairytales described our life together pretty well.

AUTHOR'S NOTE

Thanks so much for reading!

If you enjoyed this book, please consider leaving me a review on Amazon, Goodreads, or whichever vendor you purchased this book from. Amazon reviews carry the most weight in the ebook market at this time. To find out the latest news on what I'm writing and when it's coming out: subscribe to my mailing list (eepurl.com/vS_wz). You can also find me on:

my website
www.emtippetts.com

Twitter
twitter.com/emtippetts

Facebook
www.facebook.com/emtippetts

BOOKS BY E.M. TIPPETTS

The Fairytale Series

Someone Else's Fairytale
Nobody's Damsel
Break It Up (spinoff)
A Safe Space (spinoff)

The Shattered Castles Series

Castles on the Sand
Love in Darkness

Standalone Novels

Time & Eternity
Paint Me True

Turn the page for sample chapters from *Nobody's Damsel*.

1
MY GLAMOROUS LIFE

The morning sky was gray and a couple of hot air balloons dotted the skyline like bubbles suspended in Lucite. I took a deep breath of chill air and began my run, feeling the usual catch in my knee for the first several paces and the jolts through my legs as my shoes hit the pavement. My cheeks were soon rubbed raw by the icy air moving past and my breath was ragged for the first twenty yards. Then I hit my stride and everything fell into a rhythm. The sun lit up the eastern horizon, creating a halo of light over the Sandia Mountains. It was good to be home in Albuquerque, with its dry desert air and broad, flat sky. Brown, open fields stretched on either side of the road.

I reached the corner, cut across the road, turned right, and made my way along the uneven shoulder, gravel crunching under my feet. More cold air pumped into my lungs as I pushed myself faster, as if by running I could escape the insanity of the last twenty-four hours and just be me, plain old regular Chloe.

My mother's phone message had arrived last night. When she'd called, I'd stared at my phone, chewed my lip, and felt bitter guilt pool in the pit of my stomach as I hit the "Ignore" button. The picture of her that popped up showed her with her bright pink, glossy lips pooched out and her eyes shut to show off blue glitter eye shadow. Her fake lashes lay curled against her cheekbones.

"Hey sweetie," came her voice in the message. She was subdued, which could only mean one thing, that she had something awkward to tell me. "I'm just calling to see how you and… things are. I know you don't need your old mother snooping around in your business, but I hope everything's all right. I love you."

I'd deleted the message and tried not to stew about it. It was possible, I reasoned, that she just wanted to know how my studies had gone, or what my graduation ceremony had been like, but questions about these wouldn't qualify as "snooping." No, she wanted to know about my personal life, which meant she'd read something in some tabloid, somewhere, that said Jason was cheating on me.

He wasn't. Even if I was new to the whole media insanity that surrounded my movie star husband, his family wasn't. I was staying with his sister right now and she would skin him alive if she had the least suspicion that he wasn't treating me right. The rumors didn't bother me because I thought they were true. They bothered me because they just wouldn't quit. They permeated every aspect of my life these days. A few months ago, I felt like I could just let them slide off me, but I hadn't realized how relentless the onslaught would be.

As I rounded the bend, I looked back over my shoulder and saw a white sedan pull off the side of the road and into the far lane. It took a conscious effort to suppress the shudder that went through me. It was one car. Just because it went the same direction as me didn't mean it was following me.

But the car didn't accelerate or zip past. Instead it went slow and matched my pace. The morning was still too dim for me to get a good look at the driver. I saw the suggestion of a silhouette against the dark interior. A man, perhaps? A glint on something that could have been a camera, or maybe a phone. The window rolled down and a flashbulb went off.

Eyes on where you're going, I thought. With this person taking pictures, the last thing I needed to do was trip and break my neck. I'd lost my rhythm and my breathing came in desperate gasps. I forced my chest to expand, drawing in another lungful of air, now tinged with the scent of car exhaust. I breathed out, stretched my legs to lengthen my stride, and tried to act casual.

If paparazzi were following me, though, and coming all the way to

Albuquerque to do it, then a major story had broken. I wondered how many people had seen it, and how many of my friends now wondered if I was about to get a divorce.

The length of road I ran along still didn't have any houses or businesses along it, only broad flat plain covered in dry grass that was so wide open that I could see clear to the other end of the city in the west. Up ahead, though, was a gas station which promised some cover. Photographers didn't usually follow people inside such places, I'd found, but would wait until one exited again. Maybe I could call a friend to come get me, only at this hour that would mean waking someone up.

That stupid car followed me all the way to the gas station, its quiet motor chugging softly as it paced me. There wasn't any other traffic to honk at it or to stop and ask if I were okay. Surely in Albuquerque people would do that if they saw a lone woman chased by a car. That image gave me chills.

I glanced back and slowed my steps as I reached the edge of the concrete pad, on which stood the gas station and convenience store. Sweat had soaked through my shirt around my neckline and underarms. Great. Just what the whole world wanted to see, I was sure.

My pulse throbbed in my ears as I walked past the fueling bays and crossed over to the convenience store, which was a twenty-four hour place and therefore open even this time of the morning. I shot a glance back at the car and saw it pull into a space, its passenger side window down. With the light behind it, I could now clearly see the shape of the driver and his hand, extended, holding a camera.

Time to get inside.

When I hauled the glass door open, though, the first thing I saw was the current issue of *Entertainment Weekly* with a picture of Jason and Gigi Malone on the cover. Gigi had her blue eyes wide and innocent and bit her lip for effect. She wore a business suit, while Jason stood behind her in a gray t-shirt that stretched over the contours of his biceps. His blue eyes were slightly narrowed and gazed out with smoldering intensity. His dark hair was longer than he wore it now, and with one hand he'd reached around Gigi and was unbuttoning the top button of her blouse. A swirling tattoo snaked up his arm. They'd added the tattoo digitally when someone at the studio decided it would give him greater sex appeal.

Even in a picture, his gaze brought me up short. I looked back at the white car and saw another vehicle pull into the station and park next to it. Two cars at this place at this hour? I ducked inside, only to see what was on the rest of the magazine rack.

Photo after photo of my scowling face burned into my retinas. "Trouble in Paradise?" said one headline. "Jason Vanderholt's Leading Lady No More!" "Yes, Jason, You Can Do Better!" "How Did She Ever Turn Jason V.'s Head?" "Still Working the Backup Plan?" That last one was under a picture of me wearing my backpack, on my way home from classes.

It was official: according to the media, Jason and I were through.

The door chimed behind me and I made myself walk. A picture of me reading the headlines would just be too perfect, so I ducked down an aisle devoted to a hundred different flavors of beef jerky and headed for the glass fronted refrigerator in the back while I tried to collect my thoughts. I had to get home and get ready for work in a couple of hours. Calling someone seemed like an overreaction. This was my life now. I was famous by association, and I couldn't hide from that forever. What I needed to do was just walk out, head back to the house, and ignore that stupid car.

But a glance out of the corner of my eye let me know that the person who'd followed me in was a burly, sullen looking man who stood just inside the door, his arms folded across his chest. He didn't seem like a photographer, and I wished he did. That carriage and the way he looked the room over screamed out that he was casing the store. The last thing I needed right now was to be caught up in a holdup. When I looked over at the person working the register, I saw it was a young woman, likely not even out of her teens. She read a magazine, completely oblivious to the threatening figure in the doorway.

In a play for time, I grabbed a bottle of water, its smooth plastic cool against the palm of my hand, and headed up to the counter, only to remember that I didn't have my wallet on me, just a credit card, and on that credit card was my married name, Chloe Vanderholt. People seemed to think it was an odd decision for me to take Jason's last name (and yes, he used his real name for his career), but my maiden name, Winters, belonged to my absent, married-to-another-woman father and the half brother who once tried to kill me. Much as I hated the harassment that came with being a Vanderholt, I was happy to *be* a Vanderholt. I just wished I had a secret identity I could whip out in a situation like this.

I glanced back and saw the guy was on his way over to join me at the counter. With my thumb, I turned my engagement ring around so that the seven carat stone rested against my palm. It was a stupid thing to wear on a run, but I couldn't bring myself to leave it at my sister-in-law's house. It was worth nearly as much as said house.

The guy was right behind me, now, out of my line of sight. I fumbled my credit card out onto the counter and the girl picked it up, swiped it, glanced at the back, then froze. Her hazel eyes registered shock as she looked up at me.

I took a deep breath. I could handle this.

"Are you related?"

"To?" I played dumb.

"Jason Vanderholt." She said it like I must be a total idiot not to know his name. I wondered if she were from out of town because it was well known around Albuquerque that the Vanderholts were local. Jason visited all the time. That was how he and I were able to have a relationship while I was an undergrad at the University of New Mexico.

"Vanderholt's my husband's name."

"So are you related to him by marriage?"

I shrugged as if I didn't know or much care. "Maybe." I scrawled my signature on the receipt and slid it across the counter.

The man behind me shifted his weight and cleared his throat. I sensed, before I saw, him start to sidle around me and I backed away from the counter, turned, and made a break for outside.

"Chloe," he said.

I skidded to a stop and my hands hit the glass of the door, hard.

The girl behind the counter screamed.

The guy began to laugh and readjusted his baseball cap, his blue eyes sparkling with amusement.

"Jason, what are you doing here?"

"I was trying to find you, but you seem to be avoiding me."

The girl's mouth had dropped open and her gum had fallen on the counter. Red faced, she cast around for a napkin to pick it up with.

"You are getting way too good at that tough guy act," I scolded, crossing back over to him. It was a trick he'd perfected, looking like someone you did not want to make eye contact with.

"Did you seriously not recognize me?"

"I thought you were going to rob the store."

He cracked up and slipped an arm around my waist.

The girl behind the counter stared wide-eyed at the two of us.

"I don't know what this is about us only 'maybe' being related by marriage," he said to her, holding up his left hand and tapping his wedding ring with his thumb. "The guy who did our ceremony seemed legit. I'm pretty sure this is my wife."

"You… you're…"

"Jason." He held out a hand, which she didn't take. "It's nice to meet you."

"Really?" squeaked the girl. "Can I um… get your… uh…"

"Got anything to sign?"

She fumbled around and finally located another napkin. Jason signed it and she stared down at the squiggle of ink as if it were a magical incantation to turn lead to gold, which at least distracted her enough that we could leave gracefully.

As soon as we stepped out the door, the guy in the white sedan got out and began to shoot pictures of us. I kept my arm firmly around Jason's waist as we went to the car, though I knew I scowled. The press would no doubt find a way to use these pictures to add more credibility to the rumor that he and I were done as a couple.

Jason opened my door, and once he'd gone around and climbed in the driver's side he turned to me and said, "So are you okay?"

"Yeah, I'm fine. I didn't expect to see you here."

"You seemed real unhappy on Skype last night."

"I didn't mean to drag you away-"

"From my ever so meaningful press junket? I would've come last night, but my last interview went so late."

"Jas, when I said maybe we should spend more time together, I didn't mean that you should take time off your job."

"What did you mean, then?"

I looked down at my hands. "That maybe I shouldn't even start mine."

"Your job?"

"Yeah. I mean, maybe this is just a bad time and-"

"No way."

"It's fine. I can-"

"It is not fine. There is *no way* I'm going to take your dreams from you."

"I love you, all right?" I said. "And I want this to work."

"What to work?"

"Us. Our marriage."

Here we were, arguing in a parked car while that stupid paparazzo fired away. I didn't want to take this argument back to his sister's house, though.

"You think that's in danger of failing?" he asked.

"You've seen the headlines."

"Oh, gimme a break, Chloe. Those are tabloids. They make all kinds of stuff up. Nobody takes them seriously."

That, I knew for a fact, was not true. Jason's fans took these rumors very seriously. They were all reading the articles and dreaming up how they'd catch his eye once he'd offloaded me. But these thoughts just made me depressed, which made me *look* depressed, which only upset my husband more. I tried to think of a way to change the subject. "Thank you for coming out but-"

"Are things between us… in jeopardy?"

"No. *No.* Definitely not-"

He reached across the console and pulled me in for a kiss, his lips slightly dry against mine, the scent of moisturizer on his skin.

I leaned in, pressing our mouths more firmly together and put my arms around his neck. Let the paparazzo get a picture of *this*.

"Chloe," Jason whispered, "I'll take the whole day off. As many days as you-"

I shook my head. "I don't want you to do that." The press would read all kinds of meaning into that.

"Well I don't want you to quit your job, so decide. Do you need me here? Just say the word."

I shut my eyes and my next breath sounded suspiciously like a sob.

"I take that as a yes," he said.

"No. Jas, don't. I'll be all right. I'm still getting used to all this, and I'm sorry that I don't have thicker skin."

"I love you."

"I love you too. I didn't mean to make you go through all this trouble-"

He kissed my cheek, then my lips again. "It's no trouble. I'm sorry my schedule's been so packed."

"No, it's fine." I rubbed the back of his neck with my thumb. We'd had a short courtship, by modern standards, so the projects Jason was working on now were ones he'd committed to before we'd ever gotten together. Part of why we'd married when we did was to have the wedding and honeymoon out of the way before he shot two movies almost back to back. He'd been in Mexico shooting the first one for three of the six months that we'd been married, and had had press obligations for much of the rest of the time. Unlike most of his colleagues, he was still bankable in big budget blockbusters and had a solid fan base who saw everything he was in, no matter how shoddy the script or direction. In order to keep things this way, he had to pay his dues to his public. I certainly wasn't going to ask him to take a break while other actors' careers hit the skids as the after-effects of the Great Recession rolled on.

And while he'd been shooting films, I'd finished my masters in forensic science. It'd been an intense year of studying, both before and after the wedding, so between my commitments and his, we hadn't had much quality time together.

He looked me straight in the eye and said, "You sure you don't need me to rearrange my schedule?"

I shook my head and forced a smile, "If I put off starting work-"

"No."

I wanted to raise my voice and demand he let me finish a sentence. We were talking in circles because he wasn't even listening to me, but we didn't have time to escalate this fight. In a couple of hours I'd be in the lab and he'd be back in LA. Besides that, he thought he was being nice by staying firm on our decision that I take this job with the Albuquerque Police Department. After all, it brought us back home again and let me work with some of the people who'd saved my life when I'd been a victim of crime, over a decade ago. As stubborn as he could be when he wanted something, he was downright intransigent if he thought I wanted something. The fact that he'd ditched his schedule and flown out here in the wee hours of the morning proved that.

I pushed all my irritations to the side and took a moment to take in my surroundings. We were in his Prius, his old car that he kept at the airport while he was out of town so that it'd be there waiting for him whenever he flew in. I'd wanted this car as soon as we knew we'd be moving here, but he'd insisted I get a new one, because I suppose a new car is the kind of thing most people want. I loved the Prius, though, it was the car he'd driven all the time we were dating. Sitting in its driver's seat gave me a giddy sense of dislocation, a tangible reminder that I'd married the amazing, gorgeous guy who'd driven me home from dinner that one night and begged for a goodnight kiss. I still planned to swipe this car from him, but that was another battle for another time.

We could talk and bicker over the phone or Skype. I looked up into his eyes again and found his gaze fixed on me, intent as ever.

"How'd you know I was here?"

"You weren't at Jen's but your car was. I figured you hadn't gotten far. Then I saw you being stalked."

I shrugged as if that didn't matter, as if I hadn't stumbled into the convenience store a shuddering wreck thanks to the media scrutiny. With the tips of my fingers, I traced a pattern down the side of his neck, then pressed my hand to his chest. His eyes got that faraway look and he put his hand over mine and lifted it so that he could kiss my palm.

Just then another car pulled up on the other side of us. One look let me know it was full to bursting with teenage girls. The cashier had spread the word.

Jason started the engine and we pulled out before any more could arrive.

I leaned across the console, pressed my cheek to his shoulder, and traced my fingers down his arm.

"You trying to get us in a wreck?" he teased.

"Really? That distracting, huh?"

He just chuckled and planted a kiss on my forehead, his way of saying he was going to give as good as he got once his hands were free.

We got back to his sister's house minutes later, and the place was still quiet. If people were awake, they weren't up and about yet. The only one who saw us enter was Boots, the orange tabby with white socks that the family had recently taken in. Jason and I stole across the living room, decorated in the traditional, southwestern style with sturdy, pinewood furniture and punched tin embellishments, including a large mirror with a punched tin frame over the kiva fireplace. The place even smelled like juniper incense.

Once back in the guestroom, I shut and locked the door. Fighting was something we could do anytime. While he was here, it made more sense to focus on what we couldn't do long distance.

"**W**HAT IS that in the driveway?" I heard Jason say in the other room as I stepped out of the shower.

"That's Libby." Kyra Armijo, Jen's eighteen year old stepdaughter. Even though Jason and I owned a house, it was in the middle of renovations. It needed a state of the art security system before the interior decorator got to work furnishing it. Things had run over schedule and Jen insisted that we stay with her.

"You named your car?"

"Shut it, Jason, or I scratch your face."

"*Hey*, come on. That thing's gotta burn gas like anything." The car they were talking about was a bright red Jeep Liberty.

"It was cheap."

"Before you factor in the cost of gas."

"I'll do it. Don't push me." I could just picture her with her fingers hooked like claws, a French manicured nail on the end of each. This, actually, counted as her and Jason getting along. Before they'd achieved this détente, they had spent a lot of time glaring at each other and not talking at all.

"Can I ask why you named your car?"

"Because I've gone off the rails. I bought an SUV, gave it a name, and the cops will be here for me any minute because I'm that out of control." What made her words all the more ironic was that as a younger teen, she'd been way off the rails. The fact that she could laugh about it showed how far she'd come.

"Don't expect me to get you out of an arrest."

"Why are you even here? Aren't you supposed to be smiling at the cameras like a dork somewhere?"

"Since when were you guys cat people?"

"We're human people. We just happen to own a cat now. Huh, Boots? You gonna stay with us now?"

"Since when?"

"Since he wandered into the house. We put up signs to find his owner but no one's called, and it's very sad. He clearly misses his old owner."

The rest of the conversation was drowned out with the sound of my hairdryer. I'd heard enough of their bickering to get the general gist.

By the time I got my hair dry and my makeup on, Jason was gathering his things to leave. We managed a quick kiss before he had to hurry out the door.

2
DISTRESS CALL

OPENING SCENE from the season premiere of *Blood Ritual*:
The strobe of patrol car lights cut into the pitch black night as a siren screamed its way towards a suburban home. The house door stood open, the lights off. One of the front windows was shattered.

The police cruiser skidded to a stop in the driveway and the two officers got out, flashlights in hand, sweeping the beams over the front yard to illuminate a smiling and cheery yard gnome and a wild rabbit that hopped away from the noise to get lost in the bushes.

"Hello?" one of the officers shouted. "Anyone here?"

When there was no answer, he and his partner exchanged a knowing look. "Hello!" he yelled again. Into his radio he said, "We're at the property, the door's open and there's no sign of anyone."

"Mack!" shouted his partner. He shone his flashlight into the front door onto a lifeless hand in a pool of blood. The arm and the rest of the body were hidden from view.

"That's probable cause. Let's go."

The two cops stormed into the house, testing the light switch to find no electricity. Their flashlights animated the shadows of knickknacks on the mantle, shoes set out against the wall, and a frightened housecat that yowled and ran out of frame.

Mackenzie dropped to his knees next to the lifeless hand and checked *for a pulse. "It's faint," he said, "but it's there."*

His partner just shook his head, pulled out his radio, and barked, "We need an ambulance."

CUT TO:

An office, with a woman in a suit, her feet up, her badge lying on top of a pile of papers. The phone rang and she answered, "Drew Clayborn." Her expression changed from casual to serious as she took her feet down and leaned in closer to the phone base, as if this might improve her ability to hear what the caller said. "Understood. Yes, I'm on my way."

She grabbed her badge, pulled on a trenchcoat, and marched out of the office. A secretary behind a desk looked up to follow her with his gaze as she swept past, checking her gun and slipping it back into her shoulder holster.

BEGIN OPENING CREDITS.

THE FIRST thing I heard when I walked into the lab was the police dispatcher's voice coming from a police scanner set up on the counter.

"Okay... We've had a call in to 911 that someone heard popping noises at a house. Hernandez? Wolfson? Can you guys get over to a house in Volcano Cliffs?"

"Popping noises?"

"That might have been gunshots. It's all I've got. Can you go check?"

"Not right now. We've got someone stalled out in the middle of Coors and then pretty sure we got a DWI. And two people just ran a stoplight."

"Well, when you get a chance, here's the address."

"Yeah, okay."

The lab was in a basement and had enough fluorescent light banks in the ceiling to make anyone look like a walking corpse. The place was still empty; I was the second person to arrive today.

The first to arrive, a man, straightened up when he saw me. He'd been leaning against a worktable at the back of the room and had his dark hair buzzed short. His gray green eyes looked me over and his mouth turned down at the corners. "Chloe Vanderholt?"

"Yeah, hi." I debated holding out my hand for a handshake, but since he didn't, I didn't.

"Right... so..." He looked me up and down, in an appraising rather than lecherous way, and said, "Come back to my desk. We should probably talk. I'm the new supervisor here."

"Miguel Gonzolas?"

"Yeah, that's me." He turned to lead the way. The lab was one large room with desks at the back, shelves of books in the corner, and equipment arrayed on counters and worktables throughout.

From his aloof manner, I got the distinct impression that this wasn't a friendly, welcome-to-the-team kind of chat. Once at his desk, he hooked a chair from a nearby desk for me and sank down into his seat. "I've never met you before, which is kind of strange since I've been interviewing new applicants since before I got promoted to supervisor."

"I was interviewed by the previous supervisor and the Police Chief-"

"I know. That's not normal."

Because this lab was under the jurisdiction of the police department, the Chief of Police was its director, so her conducting an interview was something she had the power to do, even if it wasn't the sort of thing she ever, actually did. I wondered now if this new supervisor was going to terminate me on the spot just to get back at her. That idea did have a certain appeal.

"You went to a good school and got good references and all that," he said. "I'm sure you can be a good crim." "Crim" was short for criminalist, and was what most forensic scientists called themselves. "But, we haven't had any job openings lately. Our budget is real tight. I mean, how did you even apply?"

It was all I could do not to squirm on the rock hard cushion of the office chair. "I was just offered an interview a few months ago." Not my usual style at all. Jason and I had discussed it at length, since it was obviously a courtesy extended to the Vanderholt name. In the end I'd chosen to believe that it was just the APD's way of keeping the whole thing under wraps. No one else in the lab would find out unless the Chief decided to hire me.

"So you're saying you didn't even apply?"

"No. The pay they offered was extremely low. They told me about the tight budget." I also liked to think this meant the whole deal wasn't corrupt.

He looked me over again.

"The pay's kind of a non-issue for me," I said.

His mouth quirked up at the corners.

"This is the field I want to work in. This is a city I know. Two years ago I was just another undergrad at UNM working my way towards a job like this. Now I've got a famous last name, but I'm the same person."

No one ever believed me when I said that, other than the Vanderholts, at least.

"Listen," I said, "if this is a problem, I can leave. I won't ever breathe a word to anyone about it–"

"No. If Madame Chief says you have a job, you have a job. Let's get you set up in your desk, get your phone line, stuff like that. The other guys, when they come in, they're all going to know something's fishy, though."

And he made no offer to smooth ruffled feathers. He was polite enough when he showed me my desk and my little personal safe. The evidence was stored on site, and Miguel took me into the other rooms, which included a walk in freezer (which had, besides the evidence, a small stash of frozen Evol Burritos), walk in refrigerator, and a room with rack after rack of shelves. There was a simple procedure to log what piece of evidence I was working on and I could then store it in my personal safe until I was done with it.

By the time we got back from the tour of the evidence storage, the lab had filled up with a dozen or so other people. Now that I saw them, I could see what Miguel meant when he called them "the other guys."

Every single one of them was male.

"Okay, we've got a second call in regarding a house in Volcano Cliffs." I only half listened as the dispatcher confirmed that this was the same house in Volcano Cliffs that two cops had checked on just a little while ago, over an hour after the first phone call. The cops had knocked on the door, gotten no answer, and that was that. An unanswered door was not grounds for a search warrant.

"Tell the caller to go over and check. We can't just break the door down."

"Yeah, the operator gave that same advice."

"Okay, so what do you want us to do about it?"

"Just make a note of the second call. I'll let you know if anything else comes of it."

As they spoke, I took heated superglue in a metal tray and put it and a baseball bat that had been used in an assault and battery, into a large glass terrarium, which I sealed up tight. This was one way to reveal latent fingerprints. Some crime labs had fancy cyanoacrylate fuming tanks, but this was not a fancy lab.

After a painful round of introductions, in which I had gone to each person by myself and said hello, I'd decided to keep to myself and just do my job for the rest of the day. I hadn't given out my last name, but I heard it in whispers throughout the lab. More than once, I felt an irritated gaze. But I would make this work. Eventually they'd see I just wanted to do the job and get over their reservations about me. There was no shortcut through this process.

I did wish, though, when lunchtime rolled around, that someone would offer me an Evol Burrito. Several guys grabbed them, so I wasn't sure whose stash it was. Once they were microwaved, the scent of green chile and lime hung in the air for the rest of the afternoon.

On the way home, I could tell I was being tailed by one car, perhaps two. The sun was just low enough in the sky that I couldn't block it with the fold-down visor. It cast a rich rose light over the city, so that even the glints in the silver chrome of cars nearby looked deep gold. I drove with one hand outstretched to shade my eyes. One of the cars was so close to my tail that I fought the urge to slam on the brakes and mash its grille, but I knew that even the legitimate press would run wild with that one. My friend, the white sedan, pulled into the passing lane two cars behind me. Great.

Three cars followed me down the exit ramp, but I didn't want to believe they were all tailing me. The farther into the Sandia Foothills I drove, though, the more obvious it became. *Three* paparazzi? I did not want to know what kind of headline had given me this kind of fame, but I was sure I'd find out. I felt a certain lightness as I turned down the private road to Jen's house and saw my unwanted entourage pull over.

When I reached the house, Jason's Prius was out front. I got out and ran inside with a mix of excitement and worry.

I found him in the living room, talking to Jen, who looked at him with her usual sisterly condescension. To her, he would always be her ridiculous, irresponsible little brother, even though he was only three minutes younger. He'd once thought that it was because he was the last of the siblings to get married, but our wedding hadn't changed a thing.

My suspicion was that because Jason had moved away from the rest of the family when he was fifteen, he'd always be fifteen to Jen. He and their mother had gone to Hollywood, where he'd soon gotten work and become a star. Hence Jen had seen the rest of his adolescence in brief visits, on television, and projected large on the movie screen and it was as if all of it had become fiction in her mind. Even their little brother, Steve, was more of an adult in her eyes than Jason.

Right now my husband wasn't going to give her any hassle over it. She was seven months pregnant with twins, which was why I didn't see a whole lot of her even though I lived in her house. The doctor had ordered her to keep her activity to a minimum. At the sight of me, her face lit up. "Chloe!" She had the same deep blue eyes as Jason and the same color hair, though hers had curls. Once people found out Jen was Jason's twin, they wondered how they hadn't noticed it before. The family resemblance was strong.

I took a deep breath. There was definitely a lingering scent of garlic in the air. "That better not be your cooking I smell."

"Don't you get after me, too." She was a professional chef who liked to cook to relieve stress, boredom, anger… pretty much any emotion. At times it was endearing, but right now it was bad for her health and that of her babies. "That's Kyle's cooking you smell. He made a bunch of meals this afternoon and put them in the freezer."

I'd learned during this visit that he was a master chef in his own right. Kyra had explained to me that this was how they met; he'd been foreman of a building site next to her old restaurant and had plied her with homemade New Mexican food and offers to teach her some family recipes. Only, when he found out he was flirting with Jason Vanderholt's sister, that had been a shock. Jen didn't see him for a week, until she started go to past his building site with deliveries of fresh baked bread and cookies. According to her, it'd taken until the end of the construction project to talk him around.

Jason got to his feet and came over to hug me. "Hey," he said softly, right into my ear. "My last interview for today got pushed into tomorrow."

Jen grinned at the sight of us with our arms around each other. I'd been Jason's friend for months before anything romantic happened, and I gather all during that time the family had been in agreement that Jason should try to become more than a friend, if he knew what was good for him. I'm still not entirely sure why they all voted for a girl who grew up in a trailer park in the South Valley and had bullet scars on her person.

"Okay," I said, "so there isn't a news story out that we're on the brink of divorce again?"

I expected the usual chuckles, but Jen and Jason exchanged a look. "There's always some kind of story like that." He sounded defensive. "I just wanted to come see you."

"Ignore the tabloids," said Jen. "Pure fiction." She'd once banned Jason from visiting when his bad press got to be too much. Like their parents, she had a rigid idea about how people should live and was especially protective of Kyra, who hadn't had a lot of structure in her early childhood. If she thought the tabloids were printing pure fiction, then she was likely right. She'd been dealing with this for much longer than I had.

"What is the story?" I asked. "Just out of curiosity?"

"There are a few, and they're all stupid," said Jason. "Forget about it." This time, he turned away from his sister. I saw his expression blank for a split second, like a shadow passing, and then he looked at me as if he had nothing to hide.

My phone rang before I could think of what to say next. The number that popped up wasn't one I knew. "Hello?"

"Vanderholt. It's Miguel."

"Oh, hi."

"We've got a crime scene on the West Side. Wilson's the other crim on call tonight, but he grew up a block away from there. It's too likely he's got a personal connection. Neither of the ballistics guys can make it, so I'm calling you. Can you come work the scene?"

"This the one that we heard the calls about all day?"

"Yep."

"So it's a homicide?"

"Miraculously, no. Not yet. The victim's in bad shape and lost a lot of blood, but dang if she isn't still alive. Listen, can you come? I need an answer pronto."

"What is it?" Jen asked.

"Crime scene on the West Side."

"Go," said Jason. "If they need you, definitely go."

"That a yes?" asked Miguel.

"Sure. Yes. Meet you at the lab?"

"Yeah, we'll take the van – the CSI van. We'll drive it from there."

"All right, I'm on my way."

"Was that your husband?"

"Yeah, why? Want his autograph?"

"Ah… no. See you soon."

Jason had already escorted me to the door by the time I ended the call. We had a quick kiss and then I was on my way back to work.

I'D LIKE to think I'm an intelligent person, but that doesn't mean I always do intelligent things. As soon as I got in my car, I dialed my mother and put the phone on speakerphone.

"Chloe?" she answered.

"What's up, Mom?" I pulled away from the curb and had to shield my eyes once again from the sun. The light was still honey rich, the kind that made adobe homes appear to glow from the inside. It'd still be a while until sunset, so I rested my arm on the steering wheel so that I could keep my hand in position to block the sun. As luck would have it, I was driving west.

"Honey, how are things?"

"Fine. Why do you ask?"

"Well, I assume you've seen the news."

"Nope. Do I want to?"

"Oh, honey…"

This paperback interior was designed and formatted by

www.emtippettsbookdesigns.com

Artisan interiors for discerning authors and publishers.

Made in the USA
Charleston, SC
25 January 2017